Even witches can't escape destiny.

HIDING till DAWN

the Cross Chronicles

E.M. RINALDI

Copyright © 2017 E. M. Rinaldi
All Rights Reserved
Cover by Mae I Design
Edited by Melanie Williams
Formatted by EK Formatting

Published by Anchor Group Publishing
PO Box 551
Flushing, MI. 48433
http://www.ancorgrouppublishing.com/

All rights reserved. Published by Anchor Group Publishing. No part of this book may be reproduced or transmitted in any form or by any means, electronic or mechanical, including photocopying, recording, or by any information storage and retrieval system, without written permission from the publisher.

Hiding Till Dawn

The Cross Chronicles

Book 2

E.M. Rinaldi

To my very own fairy godmother,

thank you for fighting to help make my dreams come true

Chapter 1

They say you can see your life flash before you when you die. That explained a lot.

I found myself reliving every pivotal moment of my life like a cassette tape on fast forward. Every so often it would freeze and I would watch as my mom was murdered. I'd once again feel how terrified I was on my first night at the Academy, and I even saw the moment Eli told me magic was real. Just as I would get a grasp on the memory, it would be ripped away and replaced by another; like Cedric telling me he liked me and leaning in for a kiss. I wish I could have continued that one, but yet again, it was gone too soon. I wasn't trying to fool myself; I knew I was dead. Why else would I be reliving my past? I just had to wait for the slideshow to be over and then I could continue on. On to where, I wasn't sure. Our world didn't put much stock in religion, so I had never thought about it. Witches were highly in tune with nature, much like the Fae, and we were taught that the Earth took us back after we've passed.

I hoped She would still take me. I didn't have your average elemental power, but hopefully Healing counted for some points. To be honest, it wasn't such a bad thing to be dead. It happened at an ideal time—if such a thing exists. My family, friends, and all that I loved were dead too. I wouldn't want to be alive without them, and they weren't about to suffer the pain of going on without me. It was a win/win. I allowed the memories to engulf me and waited for the stream of images to stop.

I didn't get that far, however. Midway through a particularly cheerful memory of Cedric and me, the sidereal froze. Where I had once been seated in a theater chair enjoying the show, I now found myself in a meadow. Everything around me was lush with green, from the tickling grass beneath my bare feet to the swaying tops of the trees giving me shade. A soft breeze blew by and I watched as the grass ruffled and bent in a joyous wave across the hills. The air was fresh with a hint of apple,

1

though I saw no orchards nearby. If this was how the Earth took us back, I was so down. I smiled and fell back with my arms stretched out to either side as the grass cushioned me better than any cloud-filled pillow-top.

This was peace.

"No honey, *this* is just pathetic." I opened my eyes and looked toward where the voice originated.

Standing at the bottom of my feet was a woman, her age hard to distinguish. She was petite, with a few life lines around her face, and she had hair the color of spun fire. She looked no more than mid-twenties, but it was her eyes that spoke of age and hard earned wisdom.

"You give a girl some power and what does she do? She lets herself get killed. Then, I come to save the day and find you enjoying your demise. Pa-the-*tic*."

I sat up. "Excuse me?" Who did this bitch think she was?

"The name's Gwendolyn. Call me Gwen, ever, and I will set your entrails on fire while they hang from your neck." And then she smiled, a fake, monstrous contortion of her lips. "And I'm the bitch who gave you those badass powers."

I couldn't have heard her right. Some tiny, adolescent-looking, evil pixie with threats straight out of the renaissance couldn't have given me my powers.

"I thought it was a mutated Witch gene or something."

Gwendolyn snorted. "Hardly. You've got some mutated genes all right, but don't put that on me."

I shrugged. What did it matter anyway? I was dead.

Her eyes narrowed into thin slits, and the sky above went from picturesque sunny to Category Three tornado in the blink of an eye.

"A little more gratitude and a little less attitude would be nice," she said with a pout and the sun came back out fast enough to give me visual whiplash.

I scooted away from her with as much speed as I could muster. "What the hell are you?"

"I'm a Fae," she rolled her eyes, as if it were obvious.

This chick was really starting to get on my nerves.

I glared at her, "If I'm dead then how did you get here? If I have to spend the rest of eternity with you, I wanted a refund."

"*I* am the one who brought you here, you ungrateful little brat!" She said it like it was such an achievement. "Do you even know the amount of power it takes to steal someone from out of Mother Nature's line up and bring them to limbo?"

"So I'm in limbo? Cool." My answer only served to annoy her.

She cocked her hip to the side and crossed her arms. "I brought you here so that I could take you back. You have to remember."

"I'm good here." I told her with a smile. "But my whole life was just playing on the big screen. If you want to know something, go take a look."

"You are such a smartass. You're lucky I like that about you." She sighed.

Uncrossing her arms, she slowly brought them up in front of her and began to sing. Her voice became softer, more feminine. And as she sang the trees around me began to sway to and fro along with each phrase. I had no clue what she was saying. It sounded like she was speaking in a different language; her accent was so familiar. Something about that song was tugging at my memory.

"You were the voice! It was *you* who lured me to the woods!" The realization had my mouth hanging open. I couldn't believe this. "So you brought the storm." And this whole time I thought I was going crazy.

She nodded and her voice went back to normal.

"Yes, it was me. I sung the spell that would lure the next chosen Healer." She gestured toward me. "And she came."

"What about the storm and the tree?" I asked.

"In rough translation, the spell I sung was asking for the spirits of Healers past to help me locate the rightful heir to my power. When they found you, the storm was a confirmation, if you will. They needed to know you were strong enough for the responsibility."

And they sent a twister? They couldn't have sent me a questionnaire or something?

"They didn't have to freak me out like that. A bleeding tree is a little overkill, don't you think?"

Gwendolyn began to snicker. Great, the idea of a bleeding tree was crazy even to her.

"The tree was all me. I wanted to have a little fun." She confessed with a shrug. Like it was no big deal that for months I questioned my sanity. This was all one big game to her. The smirk on her face told me so.

She didn't care that I almost lost my mind or that these stupid powers were the cause of all of this. Because she gave me these powers, the Dean thought I was the star in his prophecy. That led to him torturing me, threatening those I loved, and eventually forcing us to try and escape.

A shiver slivered down my spine once, twice; when it happened a third time I finally took notice of what was causing it. The meadow looked the same—still a green wonderland—but the dancing sun couldn't stop the frost and ice that spread across the grass like a blanket, trapping each blade in a crystalized fortress. The frost already covered me from my feet up to my knees. I shivered again.

"Good. You're beginning to remember. Think harder, Casey. What happened when you tried to escape?"

I tried to fight it. I didn't want to go back, but the visions plowed on like a runaway freight train through my mind. I saw flashes of the four of us crawling through a dark tunnel toward an unknown destination, the storm arriving out of nowhere to smother us with its fury, and more visions of us separating and falling victim to the cold.

I didn't want to see anymore.

"Come on, Casey. You're almost there." Gwendolyn had kept silent through it all. But she wasn't going to let me end here.

I shook my head in denial. The frost had spread from my knees to my chest. The ice around me was becoming so thick I could no longer shiver, though I felt my lips turning blue.

"Stop fighting it! Remember what comes next," she demanded.

But I already did, and I was ashamed.

"I gave up!" I screamed the statement so loud that a frightened flock of birds flew from the nearest tree.

"You must remember." Gwendolyn spoke softly.

And I did. I remembered it all. I could feel my heart, heavy with sadness and guilt, weigh me down. I felt the poker hot stab of rage at what the Dean had caused. And I was utterly ashamed as I watched myself give in and no longer fight. It was one of my lowest moments. The frost continued to spread up my neck toward my face.

"It is done. We only have a few seconds left, so listen closely." Gwendolyn crouched in front of me and once again her eyes took on an aged aura. "There *is* a prophecy and you are at the heart of it. Keep fighting, Casey. Trust in your instincts, and when you're ready, come find me."

The frost engulfed my head just as pain unlike anything I've ever felt punctured my heart. The beautiful meadow faded and I was no more.

Chapter 2

I awoke to the sound of voices. They were hushed and soft; indistinguishable murmurs, that quickly settled into the background, forgotten. My sense of touch and smell took over as I tried to figure out where I was. For one thing, I was warm, almost to the point of being uncomfortable.

I wiggled around and tried to move my arms, but they were held down. I had a moment of panic before I realized that they were just under a cover, not actually immobilized. The material I was inside rustled as I moved, a slight *swish swish* sound with the feel of nylon.

The air around me had a woodsy scent carried along by a cool, damp breeze. I fought the urge to open my eyes or make any large movements. Not sure if I was being watched or not, I held still as my survival instincts kicked in. I tried to think of where I could be, but the last thing I remembered was being cold, wet, and sleepy.

The blizzard! We were trying to escape the Academy and put some distance between us and the paranoid, sadistic, son-of-a-bitch Dean. We thought we could beat the incoming storm, but instead we got lost in the middle of it. I remembered thinking we were going to die … no, I did die. Didn't I?

Flashes of a red-headed woman and a green meadow had me questioning if I was delirious. I could see myself talking with the fiery woman and being content in the meadow, but I couldn't remember exactly where I was or what was said. It must have been a fever induced vision or a bad reaction to eating snow.

I didn't think I ate any strange colors, but I was going to take a harder look next time. Note to self, double check for yellow snow. The sound of a soft conversation pulled my attention. I recognized one of those voices, it was Cedric. Sweet relief shot through me. If Cedric was here then I wasn't alone; it was going to be okay.

I opened my eyes and peeked toward where I heard the voice originate. I blinked a few times to clear my blurry vision and was greeted by hundreds of little yellow eyes. Bats. I was in a cave. There was a small fire a few feet away, and I could see Falon's blonde hair poking out of the top of an identical sleeping bag to the one I was in.

Toward the mouth of the cave sat Cedric, next to another fire and among the company of four strangers. Well, three. I could now tell that one of them was the prisoner we had rescued, but I had no idea who the other three were. They weren't Guards, as they weren't wearing the standard black uniform. The three of them actually wore outfits more suitable for the summer: light jeans and a t-shirt.

Nothing that would protect from the arctic weather howling just outside. The group seemed completely absorbed in their conversation, so I strained to hear what they were saying.

"She's not going to like this." That was Cedric. Was he talking about me?

"She has no choice. Whether or not she wants it, the power is hers; she *is* the bringer of the prophecy." I recognized the gravel-edged voice of the prisoner. They *were* talking about me!

But how did the prisoner know about the prophecy? I didn't recall the Dean ever mentioning it any of the times we were in the dungeon. A dark presence slithered around my heart and squeezed as a bitter thought entered my mind. What if the prisoner was never really a prisoner at all?

What if he was somehow working with the Dean all along? This had to be a twisted test or something. The "prisoner" could be reporting our exact location back to the Dean while I just lay here. My breaths came out in erratic puffs as I freaked out. I couldn't go back to that school, I wouldn't.

I refused to ever be a victim to the Dean again. I saw a movement out of the corner of my eye and tilted my head to get a better look. A giant, hulking chunk of a man stood from his position in the corner and walked toward me. His arms were thicker than my head and the rest of him seemed just as proportional.

He had black hair that fell to his shoulders, and like the others, he wore jeans and a t-shirt. Only, he added a leather biker vest to accent the scary-as-shit anacondas this guy had for arms.

"She's awake," he informed the others.

The man looked familiar, but it wasn't until the firelight reflected off his eyes that I gasped. They were red! The precious moments before I passed out in the storm came roaring back.

Eyes, ruby red and narrowed into slits entered my line of sight. The being who they belonged to took a deep sniff and then hissed at me. Two pearly white and pointed fangs glimmered back at me. Vampires—a group of them. More sets of red appeared around the first, and they all hissed in turn after smelling me.

I knew fear was blatantly obvious on my face. This guy had to know that I remembered, that I knew what they all were—Vampires. There was no possible way we would get out of this alive. Cedric was blissfully unaware that he was surrounded by the enemy, Falon was knocked out, and I was wrapped up tighter than Taco Bell's Cheesy Gordita Crunch. We were doomed.

I tried to find the zipper to this stupid sleeping bag but was having no luck. It was the Eskimo kind that zipped around my whole body, head included, and only left my face exposed. I mustered up all the courage and hate I could and sent a glare filled with a promise of vengeance and retribution toward the beast of a Vampire.

He chuckled at me like I was adorable and winked. Winked! What had my life come to? None of this made any sense. My utterly confused expression caused the Vampire to bellow with laughter. The booming vibrations scared the bats roosting above, sending them into a frenzy of screeching and bomb dives.

The rest of the cave's inhabitants finally took notice and came over to join me and the still guffawing but no less evil looking Vampire.

Cedric sat beside me on the cave floor, looking entirely at ease with the company that settled in around us.

"Mahon, leave the girl alone. Can't you see how terrified she is? I would be too if I had to wake up and see you." The one speaking had crouched down on my left side in front of the huge boulder, apparently known as Mahon.

He leaned in close and continued to speak.

"If you want to try again, I can let you gaze upon this work of art," he said, gesturing to his face. "The first time is no charge." And he winked.

What was with these Vampires and winking? Did they think this was normal behavior? I took a hard look at the one propositioning me and couldn't find a single flaw. Seriously. This guy was gorgeous.

His face was perfect, both sides an equal mirror image of the other. Two perfectly spaced oval eyes that held a soft, dark chocolate center straddled over a straight nose and full lips. His tanned skin gave him the look of an ancient Greek god. Someone should definitely make a statue of this guy—if it hadn't already been done.

I was caught starring just a little too long when Cedric cleared his throat. I snapped out of it as the Vampire in front of me gave a cheeky grin. My face radiated heat as I blushed, and I did the only thing I could think of: I stuck my tongue out at him.

He laughed, "Oh, I like her."

Cedric moved closer to me with a warning glare just as the prisoner stepped up and put a hand on the Vamp's shoulder.

"Enough, Leo. Let's give them some privacy. I'm sure she has plenty of questions."

Leo, Mahon, and the other I didn't know the name of, moved away toward the entrance of the cave. The prisoner lingered to give me a small smile and then joined them. I took notice of how the others obeyed and interacted with him, like he was someone to be respected. Almost as if he were in charge. Another clip from our night out in the storm assaulted me.

"His scent is all over her; the girl's over there as well," one of the Vampires said.

I felt the subtle brush of someone sniffing me again. "I don't know what to make of it. She smells like him. I mean, she smells as if she could be him." I had no idea who the "him" they were talking about was, but I didn't think I smelt like a dude.

"Maybe it's because she healed him?" another of the group suggested.

The truth slammed into me. The Vampires had been looking for the prisoner all along. They must have just stumbled upon me and Falon. I looked to Cedric to get some desperately needed answers and locked on to his alluring green eyes.

I watched as the color deepened and as his breathing caught on a hitch. I wasn't doing much better. My stomach fluttered at the mere sight of him, and he was so close that I could feel his warmth even through the sleeping bag.

"I was so scared I lost you," he admitted, a hint of sorrow deepening his voice. "When I looked back and didn't see you, my heart stopped. I retraced my steps, but the wind wouldn't let up and soon I couldn't even see my own tracks."

His lower lip trembled as his gaze roamed my face, trying to memorize every dip and curve. Mine were ensnared on his eyes. I was under his spell and I loved every minute of it. I wanted him to keep talking, anything to keep this connection from breaking.

"What did you do?" I whispered.

"I kept searching. I literally fought the blizzard, throwing all the fire at it that I could, but it was no use." He moved closer to me, snuggling up until he was flush with the side of my body. He propped his head up on one hand and draped the other across my waist. Still wrapped in the sleeping bag, I felt like little more than an oversized body pillow.

"I would still be out wandering if it weren't for those men over there. They were looking for Orin and found him strapped to my back."

"Who's Orin?" I asked.

"The prisoner, that's his name. And those are his men. They led us to this cave and then went out to search for you and Falon."

Where they tracked us by smell because they're Vampires, I mentally added.

"Neither of you were in good shape when they brought you in. For a minute there I thought you were dead."

Me too. "How am I not?"

"That would be thanks to Asa." Cedric nodded toward one of the Vamps by the fire. He was young looking, lean and muscular like the others, but with rich dark hair that fell to his shoulders. "He's a Healer," Cedric continued. "Not like you, he doesn't have the power. He uses more natural routes. You know, plants and herbs and stuff."

I guess I owed Asa my life. I owed them all my life, which only made me more confused. I frowned, trying to make sense of this mess. Vampires killed Jenna, a young witch at the Academy, but Vampires saved us. Orin was obviously a Vampire too if these were his men. Could they have been the ones that killed Jenna? That could be why Orin was in the Dean's dungeon.

Luthos, I healed a murderer! But he hadn't felt like one. When my soul reached for his as I healed him, I felt no malice or evil, only honor and purity — but I had no such connection with his men. Maybe they wanted revenge or they were going to use Jenna as leverage and something went wrong.

"Do you even know who those men are?" I asked Cedric, keeping my voice low. We needed to discuss this. The sooner we both got on the same page, the sooner we could plan our next move.

"I just told you, they're Orin's men," he replied.

"No, I know that. But do you know *what* they are? Orin included?"

The brow between his eyes furrowed as he tried to see where I was going with this. How could he not know? He's been with them for a day so far, and it only took me a few minutes after looking at one to know.

"Cedric, you can't be serious."

"What?" He frowned.

Luthos, he really didn't know. I looked over at the group converged around the fire. Sure, they could probably pass as ordinary humans, but there were subtle differences that stood out. To me, these characteristics were like a flashing sign saying, "Warning. Vampire here." A giant arrow couldn't be more obvious.

Couldn't he see the slight difference in the shading of their skin? It wasn't too far from normal, but it was a shade lighter probably due to the cooler and more sluggish blood that ran through their veins. They obviously weren't affected by the cold, which I didn't know of another being that wasn't. And the biggest giveaway was their eyes. How had he not seen the red by now?

"I can't believe you can't tell," I told Cedric with honest shock.

"Can't tell what? What on Earth are you talking about?" He tossed his hands in the air. "I don't see what I'm missing here!"

A deep chuckle came from behind us. Half hidden in the shadows was Leo. The flames from the nearby fire caused dark shapes to dance across his face, and I shivered.

"Orin thought you might have already figured it out, but I didn't believe him." He broke his gaze from me and looked up at Cedric with a smile, the firelight now glinting off a pair of pointed fangs.

"She's trying to tell you that we're Vampires."

Within seconds, Cedric was moving. He didn't need to be told twice; he was trained to just react. And that's what he did. Jumping between me and Leo, he drew from the nearby, already burning source and shot a beam of pure heat and fire directly at Leo's chest.

Leo simply held up his hands and allowed the flames to make contact. Instead of engulfing him like I hoped they would, the flames that touched his skin fell to the ground beneath him in oozing drops of acid. Oh, shit. Leo had the warped fire element. This wasn't good.

Nothing Cedric threw at him, short of a direct hit to the head or chest, would take Leo down. He would just use Cedric's power as ammo. However, the same couldn't be said the other way around. Cedric wouldn't be able to covert acid into fire. I wriggled and fought to get out of that damned sleeping bag. I even tried to squeeze out of the hole for my face, but my shoulders wouldn't fit.

A boot came straight at my head, and I rolled toward the cave wall at the last second. I heard Cedric growl and watched as he launched another attack. They drew the attention of the other Vampires and I knew I had seconds to act or Cedric would be overpowered. A ball of acid landed on the wall above me and exploded on contact.

I rolled onto my stomach to protect my face and felt drops rain down on my back. The sizzle of burning nylon soon followed. Cool air began to trickle in and I had an idea. Using my fingers, I felt for the new holes in the fabric and ripped. The weakened threads were stubborn, but eventually gave way and the holes were made bigger. When I created an opening wide enough, I slid out and stood for the first time. Around me the cave was in chaos.

Cedric and Leo were still mid-battle, both showing the consequences. Cedric's shirt sported holes with burnt edges where the acid had struck, his skin pink in places from the contact. Leo had taken similar damage. His clothes and skin also showed signs of burns. They were evenly matched. I looked around to see if anyone else had joined in and was surprised at what I saw.

The Vampire Cedric pointed out as Asa was crouched between the fight and Falon's unconscious body. He had her pressed against the wall, and anytime a flame or string of acid came toward them, his whole body would turn to stone as he deflected it. Asa called across the cave for Cedric and Leo to stop, and when I moved to help, an arm as thick as a tree branch blocked my path.

I looked up, way up, into the face of Mahon. He said nothing, but shook his head and at that moment gestured toward the cave entrance. Orin stormed in from outside, his face a mask of fury. He made a beeline for the fighting pair as his hands took on a glow.

He stopped a few feet away and raised his arms in the air. I watched as both Leo and Cedric began to slow down as if they were walking through syrup. When I glanced at their feet, I saw crystals forming only to be broken as a leg kicked to remove them. But it was pointless, the crystals formed too fast and ended up encasing both Cedric and Leo's legs all the way up to their knees.

Leo wouldn't be stopped, though. He tried to throw more acid at Cedric, but found that his arms were encased in ice as well. My mouth dropped open as I watched Orin lower his hands. He was powerful. Really powerful. He had to be extremely old to be able to subdue the opposite element.

"That is enough!" Orin shouted. Whatever bats that had remained through the fight flew out of the cave, obnoxiously voicing their displeasure. "Leo, you know better. I gave you strict orders!"

Leo had the decency to look chagrined, but still mumbled, "He started it."

Orin turned toward Cedric and I felt my muscles stiffen; my first instinct still being to protect him. But Orin just saved us, technically, and the other

Vampire protected Falon. Hell, Mahon even protected me by keeping me out of it. I didn't know what to think. Orin released the ice holding Cedric and looked to me.

"I think it's time we talked."

Chapter 3

The world looked like it had been sprinkled with sugar. Crystalized white powder covered every surface as far as I could see. The blizzard was gone, and in its place it left a changed world. And it wasn't just the scenery around me that had changed, I could feel myself changing inside as well. A lot had happened since the season first arrived. In the course of just a couple months, I had been tortured, attacked by my own people, been forced to let a loved one suffer an unknown fate, almost died, and been kidnapped and saved by Vampires.

What other sixteen-year-old in the world could claim that?

I could feel myself even now adapting to fit this new lifestyle. My reflexes and instincts were sharp and on point. Even my thought process had changed. I had switched into survival mode, and I refused to let anyone or anything take me down. So even though Orin and his men had ultimately saved us, he had a long way to go if he thought he had earned my trust.

I sat across from him now on a frozen log on the opposing side of a small fire. The blizzard had left snow drifts almost as high as my head which provided cover for us. No one would see us or our fire unless they were right upon it. Orin had drastically changed since the last time I was able to get a good look at him. His skin was smooth and flawless, completely healed from his time in the Dean's dungeon.

He no longer looked an inch away from death. His hair was groomed and neat, chocolate brown locks fell to his shoulder in waves. His beard had been shaved, and all that was left was a slight shadow, making his jaw more prominent. Who was this man?

"I can see a lot of questions forming behind those eyes." Orin spoke from across the flames. "What do you want to know?"

Everything seemed too broad an answer, but it was what I wanted. I needed to know who this guy was, everything about him and his men, and why they were here.

"Let's start with, who are you?"

He gave a slight nod and sat up straighter. His body grew as his shoulders pulled back and his chest puffed out until sitting before me was a warrior. I could tell by how he carried himself. There was an air about him as he spoke that seemed to command all living things around him take notice.

"I am Orin Cadmael Vasili, the first and only surviving son of my Father. I am Warrior and Defender of my people and the rightful heir to the throne."

It took a second for his words to sink in, and when they did, I could feel myself begin to shake.

"Heir to the throne? That means ... that makes you ... you're Sebastian's son?"

He gave a grim nod. Sebastian was the original vampire, or so it's said, and he is known as the king of his race. No one knew exactly when the vampire race began, but they had been around for at least a thousand years. It was possible that Sebastian could be a little older than that.

He was a figment of every horror story ever told to the youth of our world. The stories were whispered around fires to scare the new Guards, hauntingly told at sleepovers to thrill the group, and threatened on misbehaving youngsters. The malevolent King of Vampires had become equivalent to the Boogey Man.

Each tale told added more details of his nefarious acts. The most common being his involvement in the Turning War. Sebastian had set his sights on ruling the world, all of it, starting with the Supernatural. He attacked the Shifter communities first with relentless fury, having no mercy, even for the children.

Our world was different then, the races did not get along and were separated, spread far and wide with little to no interaction or contact. This made it exceptionally easy for Sebastian to move in and almost annihilate an entire race before anyone else even knew that something was wrong.

He had too much pride, however, and that was his downfall. He wanted to gloat and strike fear into the heart of the other races. He got off on fear. So he began to leave messages at the scenes of his massacres. The races weren't close, no, but mutilated corpses, random body parts, and oceans of blood couldn't go unnoticed for long.

By the time the Fae came out of their hidden hollows and took notice, it was almost too late. The witches were lined up next for slaughter and were completely unprepared as well. It seemed the Vampire King would be victorious in his enslavement of the magical world. Until a lone Shifter, Luther, took a stand, rallied the races, and sent Sebastian's ass packing.

But still to this day, survivors of the war can't speak of it without trembling. The gruesome stories have been passed down and the grisly photos printed in our textbooks. The man who sat across from me now was of the same flesh and blood as the most horrific monster our world has ever known.

The obsessive lust for death and destruction saturated his genes. It couldn't be a coincidence that Jenna's mangled body had been found after a group of Vampires took up residence in our woods. I just freed their leader from imprisonment!

"What have I done?" I spoke barely above a whisper, but Orin heard me.

He rose from his seat, palm pressed out toward me as if he were calming a frantic animal.

"Casey." He spoke my name slowly, drawing it out over a few seconds. "This is why I wanted to talk. To explain—"

"No!"

I jumped from the log and put more distance between us. My confused thoughts made it impossible to think this through. Orin was the son of Sebastian. The man I saved was evil. But he hadn't felt evil.

I took another step away from him, widening the distance between us. "Don't come any closer! I need to think."

I could still remember the purity of Orin's life force; it was beautiful and unsullied by the deeds of his father. I closed a hand around my locket under my borrowed jacket. I needed to trust myself and my power. What I felt when I healed him combined with the actions I witnessed in the cave gave Orin the right to at least explain, like he was asking to. I looked him in the eye right before he was tackled to the ground.

"Cedric!" I called out in shock as he pinned Orin below him and landed a punch to his face. "What are you doing?"

Leo and Mahon pulled Cedric from Orin and held him between them.

"Let me go!" he growled, still fighting to get to Orin who had already helped himself up out of the snow.

He brushed the remaining powder from his arms and nodded at Leo and Mahon to release Cedric, who immediately put himself between me and the three vampires.

"Cedric, answer me!" I demanded. My thoughts were racing faster than I could process them. The only one that kept reappearing was the thought that something was wrong. "Where's Falon?" I asked frantically. Something must have happened if he felt the need to suddenly pound on Orin.

"She's fine," he spoke over his shoulder. "I felt something was wrong with you and I rushed out here."

15

I was confused. "You *felt* something was wrong?"

He nodded, still refusing to turn his back on the Vamps.

"That's what I said. Now, what happened? What did he do?"

I was not going to continue this conversation speaking to his back. I ducked under his arm and turned to face him with my hands placed firmly on my hips, ignoring his protests and attempts to place me back behind him.

"Casey." He grunted in exasperation as I once again dodged his hand.

"I'm fine, Ced." I glanced over my shoulder at Orin. "Well, sort of."

"That's reassuring."

"Look, I have some things to explain, but first, you. What did you mean you could feel me?"

Knowing this was the quickest way to get me to move, he relented. He blew out a frustrated breath and kept his eyes on the men behind me, ready to grab me and run at the slightest hint of trouble.

"I'm not sure what happened. I was playing cards with that asshat over there—"

"Hey!" Leo grumbled.

"—when I felt a strong force building in my chest. It was like I was kicked in the gut and all the air was forced from my lungs. In my mind I saw your face and knew you were afraid. I couldn't see anything else around you, but I could sense that it was about Orin. So I ran out here and ..." He ended with a nod in the direction of the ploughed snow drifts where he had tackled Orin.

"Since when have you been able to do that?" I asked, and he shrugged.

This was almost too much. For the sake of my sanity, I tucked this incident away in the back of my mind to be worried about later. First things first, we had to deal with the Prince of Vampires.

We were once again inside the cave. Strategically, this wasn't a good idea; a fact Cedric repeatedly cawed about, like an overgrown crow, the entire way in here. But I refused to leave Falon unprotected. I was seated next to her on the cave floor. Here, the fire was almost too hot, I could feel it burn through my jeans.

"Casey, I don't like this," Cedric whispered, glancing around. "They could be trapping us in here. We were safer out there."

"I'm not going to run away and leave Falon," I answered with a harsh murmur of my own.

"I didn't expect you to, *I* don't want to leave her either," he replied. "So let's grab her and run before we all become snacks to this psycho band of wannabe camping Vampires."

I got why he wanted to leave. We were in a cave, an enclosed space with only one exit, and surrounded by Vampires. One of those Vamps we just learned was the son of the most evil being to walk the earth. As scared as I was, and trust me the urge to pee my pants was overwhelming, I needed answers. Orin was the only one who could give them to me.

"We're not leaving until I learn what the hell is going on. My life has essentially been ruined. I have nowhere to go, no safe haven to hide me, and a shitload of unanswered questions. We're staying."

I could tell the moment he conceded. The fire dimmed behind his stare and he settled more into his seat.

"Also, a word of advice: don't talk about your escape plan around beings with supernatural hearing." I tilted my head toward the four beings in question.

Orin seemed unbothered, and Asa was focused on counting Falon's breaths. But the other two openly glared at Cedric. There was no love lost between him and Leo; they had been at each other's throats from the get go.

I was more worried about Mahon. I watched a frown form on the bridge of his eyes as he leaned toward Leo and spoke, "I hate camping."

"Enough." Orin's voice echoed off the walls. "It's time we put this issue to rest. We have a small window and I need you to trust me."

Cedric gave a harsh laugh. "Trust you? Why would we do that? You've lied about who and what you are, you were in the Dean's dungeon, and don't think I haven't noticed you watching Casey. You haven't taken your eyes off her since she woke up."

I placed my hand on his arm to calm him and he settled back onto the floor beside me. His breaths came out in heavy pants and his fists were clenched at his side. I didn't know what was going on with him. He had always been protective over me, but lately his emotions were getting the better of him. He never used to allow an outburst like that to happen.

"Why have you been watching me?" I turned my attention back toward Orin. Things were just getting creepier by the minute.

Orin sighed. "My intent is not to frighten you," he gestured to Cedric, "or to mislead you. My story is a complicated one, and I only ask that you allow me to tell it to you. You can make a fair judgement once you have all the information."

"And the staring?" I asked.

For a split second I saw regret flash across his face, but it was gone as soon as I could register what it was.

"You remind me of someone. She was a dear friend of mine." His lips tilted in one corner in a sad smile. "You're a lot alike."

"What happened to her?" Cedric asked.

"She was murdered about ten years ago by a group of Vampires sent to assassinate me. I know that sounds confusing, but it will make more sense once I explain what I need to."

Dread settled deep in my gut as I listened to Orin. Something about his story seemed eerily familiar. I found myself remembering moments in my life I hadn't thought about in a long time. The flashbacks were persistent and vivid. The last moments of my normal life played on in my mind.

My mom was frantically screaming into her phone that "they were coming" just as I remembered hearing the sounds of our windows shattering. The little me in the flashback was still crouched behind the couch as the sounds of fighting filled our destroyed home.

This time, I was able to identify a sound that I wouldn't have recognized until now. I could clearly hear growling and hissing amidst the slaps of flesh being hit. Vampires; there were vampires in my house that night.

"What was her name?" I shouted, interrupting the conversation the others had taken up.

"Who?" Orin asked.

"Your friend, the one who died ten years ago. What was her name?" My fingers gripped Cedric's arm hard enough to bruise.

"Carina. Her name was Carina."

Chapter 4

My heart had stopped beating. Blood was still flowing through my veins, oxygen was still carried along to the organs who cried out for it, and the signature *thump-thump* could still be heard if one were to put their ear to my chest. And yet, for a split second, I knew it had stopped. A heart could only take so much, and mine had takin punches like Rocky's practice dummy since the moment I became an orphan. This was just the final straw; the last punch to win. Knockout.

I had always wondered who had killed my mother. The small bits and pieces I could remember from that night were never enough to paint a full picture. I used to be thankful for that. It was hard enough to be able to remember my own terror, the destruction of my only home, and the sound of my mother's screams as an innocent child. But now that I'm older, I found myself wishing I could recall more, wishing I knew who did the horrid deed.

And now I did. Vampires killed my mother. Just a few months ago I only knew them as figments of the past, ancient monsters used to motivate us to learn. Now I've been saved by these "monsters" and find that these four might be the only ones of their kind without an insatiable need to kill. Or maybe this was how they worked.

They learn all they can about their victims, get close to them, wait for their walls to go down and then *BAM*—they strike. Maybe they *were* monsters and they took some kind of sick, twisted satisfaction from getting to know their victims before helping them meet their grisly end.

I eyed the four beasts sitting across from me from under hooded lids. I was completely lost. Which did I believe? My breaths must have gone from erratic to hyperventilating because Cedric's face was suddenly in front of mine and he was frantically trying to tell me something. His brow was scrunched with worry.

"Just take deep breaths, Casey. It's going to be okay." He was taking said deep breaths right along with me, trying to get me to match him. "I can feel your panic, but you need to calm down. We'll figure it out, deep breaths."

His little comment about being able to *feel* how I felt didn't help matters, but my mind was still so wrapped up in my mother's death that I didn't want to spend much time dwelling on this new development to our relationship.

We couldn't trust them; they're going to kill us. Cedric prompted me to take another breath, and as the cool air made its way into my lungs, I struggled to bring my mind back under control. I could deal with this; I would.

As my panic attack began to settle and I was able to think more clearly, one single question fought the strongest to be heard. *Why* was my mother slaughtered by Vampires?

The more I thought about it, the less it made sense. She was running from the Dean and had managed to stay hidden from him for at least six years. So how can someone with the power and reach of the Dean not find her, but a band of Vampires could? And how did she know Orin?

I glanced up at him. He remained across the fire and seemed genuinely concerned. I didn't know how he was connected to my mother or if he really was a psycho killer waiting for the perfect moment to attack, but I was going to find out.

"How did you know Carina?" I asked Orin.

Cedric was still in front of me trying to comfort me, but I was done trying to shove everything to the side. It was time to learn the truth. The pain and hysteria was pushed back in their cage and anger came out to play.

"Casey, I know what you're feeling, but—"

I ignored him. The fact that he could yet again feel me was only adding fuel to the fire at this point. I directed my question to Orin again.

"How did you know Carina? What was she to you?"

A sad smile turned his lips, but it was gone not even a second later followed by anguish and then defeat. "She was my best friend. And I failed her."

"Carina was my mother." I could feel my eyes filling with tears but I refused to let them fall.. "I was there the night she was killed, and I think I have the right to know why that happened. You say you failed her, how? And start from the beginning."

If Orin was shocked by my admission he didn't show it. Instead, he only looked at me harder.

"I had a feeling about who you were from the first moment I saw you. You're the spitting image of her, you know that?"

20

I refused to answer. I knew how much I looked like my mother; Eli told me enough. And I didn't need to hear it from the likes of him right now. Even so, a lump rose in my throat and I had to fight to speak over it.

"Tell me."

A brief flash of pain swirled in his eyes before he nodded and began to tell his tale.

"I met Carina when she was sixteen. I was freshly escaped from under my father's tyrannical thumb and had found myself lost in the Blue Ridge Mountains. The only good thing about that was if I didn't know where I was, then neither did my father."

His harsh laugh was riddled with pain, and I knew remembering that time still hurt him. I didn't want to sympathize with him, but I knew how it felt to finally be freed from the control of a savage.

"I decided to stay put. There were enough large animals around to sustain me for a time, and I needed to recuperate and come up with a plan." His eyes shifted to the side, and he had begun to rub his hands together in a nervous rhythm.

"When I met your mother, I was ... well, you have to understand that drinking animal blood will keep us alive, but it never really satisfies our hunger. It will drive a Vampire mad. It had driven me mad ..."

Orin shifted where he sat, clearly uncomfortable with what he needed to say next.

"What did you do?" I asked him.

"You need to know," his eyes pleaded with me, "I would never willingly hurt her. I wasn't in my right mind."

"What. Did. You. Do?" I bit out, fearful of the answer I so desperately sought.

"She was running through the forest, away from the Dean and his loyal men—we all know why. She was making such a racket, breathing heavy, snapping twigs, ripping through branches; it was no wonder the Dean's men were hot on her trail. She came upon me, and the smell of blood from her many cuts and abrasions was too much for me in the state I was in."

Frown lines creased between his brows and he lowered his head with shame as he described the thing he had become.

"At this point I had been living for six weeks off animal blood, anything I could find: deer, bear, squirrel, whatever I could get my hands on. The thirst was like a lingering presence in the back of my mind that never let me rest. It was always whispering, a soft continuous hum of angry need."

He was speaking so soft that I almost didn't hear the next part.

"I attacked her."

His head was so low his chin was almost touching his chest. His shoulders were hunched in, as if he could protect himself from his own memories by becoming as small as he could. The proud man I spoke with outside was not here with me right now.

"To this day I am still ashamed. I had never before attacked a human or fellow Supernatural. I have kept myself at a higher level than my father my entire life. So the shame I carry for this act and the one that followed haunts me to this day, but especially because it was her."

I swallowed. "You hurt her."

It didn't come out like an accusation, it was more of a statement. I couldn't see any other outcome from the details he had led up with. So I was surprised when his head jerked up and he vehemently whispered, "No!"

He shook his head, his eyes pleading with me to see that he didn't do whatever appalling act I was ready to accuse him of.

"I never laid a hand on her. I swear."

I urged him to continue. "Then why are you ashamed? What was the event that followed?"

I had to know what he did to my mother. But it turned out, I had nothing to fear. He really never put a hand on her, not for a lack of trying, but my mother could handle herself.

"I didn't even get within two feet of her. I came at her with everything I had. The beast in my mind egging me on, promising me the satisfaction of her sweet, decadent blood if I could only get to her and tear her throat out." He physically shuddered as he relived that moment. "Then with the slightest twitch of her hand the surrounding trees reached down and plucked me from the forest floor. Their branches wound around me until I was in a cocoon of oak suspended high above her." He smiled, it was large and genuine and full of respect. His eyes quickly switched from gloomy to dancing with mirth.

"She was amazing. I think I was halfway in love with her from that act alone."

It felt like a bucket of ice water was dropped on my head. The arctic chill moved through my body and settled into every nook and cranny. He couldn't have just said what I think he did. This self-proclaimed beast could not have been in love with my mother. It was inconceivable.

"In love with her?" I shouted. "You said you were friends, not lovers! Don't lie to me; my mother would never love one of your kind. You're a monster. You said it yourself!"

"Shh. Casey, rein in your rage."

Cedric was trying to get me to sit back down. I had jumped up in my fury to deny Orin's words. I didn't want to think about him being with my mother. He was a Vampire, and if they were in love then all of this was on him. He was the one that put her in danger. This could be all his fault. But Cedric was right, my temper would keep me from the whole truth, and that was what I sought. I sat back down, still fuming.

"Stop *feeling* me, Cedric; it's creepy."

I looked back to Orin and without an apology, bade him continue. The sadness in his eyes hit me hard, but I ignored it. He sighed. The joy from revealing his feelings was quickly sucked back inside and hid behind his wall of anguish.

"I remained suspended in the air, and I could hear the men closing in on her. She could too, I think, because she looked around in a panic as she tried to decide which way to run. I made her a deal. I offered to get rid of those men if she would let me down. Why she would trust me, I don't know. But she was obviously terrified enough to agree."

I could understand how she would make that deal. I personally knew the terror she felt, and she could obviously handle Orin if he came after her again. She chose the best option she could have in that situation.

"The voice was arguing with me the entire time. Encouraging me to sink my teeth into her neck the second she released me. I don't know how I held back, but I did. She let me go, and I completely destroyed the three men following her; they didn't stand a chance. And while I killed them, I drank."

He clenched his fists on his thighs. Whether he was angry at how he let the thirst control him or from remembering how close he came to killing my mother, I wasn't sure.

"The madness eventually faded as the blood made its way through my system and I was hit with so much remorse for what I had done. Not for killing the men since it protected Carina, that in itself was good. But how I felt when I was killing them: satisfaction, entertained, hunger. I enjoyed it! It was in that moment that I realized how much like my father I really was."

His men were silent. I wasn't sure if they already knew the story or were just now hearing it for the first time, but their faces showed their true feelings. They still had immense respect for Orin. He was sitting beside them completely defeated. At this moment he looked nothing like a leader, more like an empty shell of a man. Yet, he had just confessed his greatest regret and it had not deterred their loyalty. It had strengthened it.

"Your mother, she had a kind soul. And was she brave! She approached me, as I was all coated in the Guards' blood, and said thank you. She thanked me for becoming a monster." He gave an amused laugh. "But that wasn't what she saw when she looked at me. She later told me that she could see the real man inside, fighting to get out. After that, I would follow her anywhere, tell her any secret. That is how she learned about who I was, who my father was, and why I'd escaped."

A small tear made its way to the corner of his eye, but he brushed it away before it could fall. I saw more welling up behind the first, but he fought to keep them at bay. "We traveled together for a year, and the whole time she kept telling me to believe in myself like she did, that I could do more and ultimately defeat my father. She was the one who came up with the idea to find others with like minds and create a resistance, much like Luther did, to finally beat Sebastian once and for all. It's known as the training camp; a place to prepare for that final battle."

A wave of pride flew through me.

"So, this camp … it was my mother's idea?"

Orin nodded. "Over the years we met others on our travels who believed in the same cause and it began to grow from there. Meanwhile, Carina and I grew closer. I finally started to see the man in myself that she saw from the very beginning. And I strived to be better, to be all she needed. Life was finally good. We were both free and we were together. But fate had other plans for us."

Asa lifted a hand and firmly grasped Orin's shoulder in a show of support. Orin tried to speak, and I could physically hear the tears in his throat. His voice cracked and his shoulders once again slumped in defeat. Asa picked up the tale.

"We were all there that night." Asa gestured to himself, Leo, and Mahon. "We were men in Sebastian's army, and over the years we had watched Orin stand up to his father, to the other vile creatures under his command as he refused to be molded into the next fiend set to terrorize the world. I speak for all of us when I say he more than earned our loyalty and respect."

Orin showed no reaction to their declaration. He was too lost in his grief, so Asa continued.

"When we heard of the camp and that Orin was running it, we immediately set off to find it. And therein lies the problem. If we had heard about it and were able to find it, it was no major feat for Sebastian to do the same. It wasn't as if the camp was well hidden, we didn't have the resources yet." He took in a heavy breath before moving on. "Deep in the night, they attacked. Sebastian's men, hundreds of them, came out of nowhere and began to slaughter people in their sleep. They were on us before we could even grab our weapons. Those that could, escaped."

Leo looked like he had seen a ghost. His face was drawn tight, and if it could have gotten any paler, he would blend in with the snow outside.

"It was the worst night of my life," Leo said. "I lost many friends, many men I thought of as brothers. Imagine five hundred armed, ruthless soldiers against maybe a hundred unarmed beings from all the races. No one thought to sleep with our weapons back then; we thought we were safe. Too soon, we were surrounded. It was five to one, and we were on the losing end from the get go. We held them off for a time, the few witches we had in residence managed do some damage, but they were slowly picked off. Without their powers, there was nothing we could do."

Leo shook his head, the memories of that night weighing heavy on him. Cedric and I sat across the fire in silence, the gruesome story even rendering us speechless.

"The last Witch lit the closest tree line on fire in hopes of giving us some time to escape. Those caught on the wrong side were murdered within seconds, but it gave the rest of us on the other side enough time to run. We all were separated from there."

The cave fell quiet, the only sound the popping of the firewood. Mahon sat like a silent statue, anger painting a scowl on his face, but his eyes spoke of vengeance. Asa moved to check the materials in his medicine bag, and I think to grieve in private.

Their story hit close to home. It was so similar to my own. It seemed these Vampires had a routine: wait in the darkness for the right moment, then attack and decimate all in their path. It was damn effective—I'd give them that much.

"Carina and I were separated. I don't know how. One minute I held her hand while we ran, and the next, she was gone. I turned back to find her; she was just right there." Orin's voice started off soft, almost too soft to be heard over the sound of our small fire. He was staring at his hand, almost as if by pure willpower he could imagine my mother's back in it.

"She was ripped from me, and I was thrown over a small outcropping. I rolled further and further away from her, and when I finally came to a stop, I was surrounded by my father's most loyal men. They were specifically dispatched to find me and bring me to him, not kill me. I couldn't give a rat's ass what they wanted, I had to get back to Carina."

Asa had returned back to the group, but stayed at the edge of the firelight, careful to not disturb Orin's tale.

"I fought with everything I had in me, but it wasn't enough. I wasn't strong enough."

I found myself defending him. His story had touched my heart, even through all my anger and distrust. "You had been fighting all night and had just fallen off a cliff. There's only so much you could have done."

"I didn't deserve her; I couldn't protect her. My father's loyal followers held me captive for days as they dragged me miles away. I refused any blood thrown my way. I couldn't feed. I wanted to get back to Carina or die. One night, the opportunity presented itself and I took it. I ran back the way we had come, my only thoughts on finding Carina. I finally allowed myself to feed, if only to stay strong and redeem myself by saving her. But my father's men were following me. They weren't trying to hide it, so I kept running. I didn't dare look for your mother again until I knew I was no longer being followed. It wasn't until I learned of her death that I found out what happened to her. She hid among the humans, but they found her anyway."

He couldn't stop the tears that fell down his cheeks this time, and neither could I. This man, for all that he was a Vampire, truly loved my mother. I could feel it in his gaze and in the words that he spoke.

"Thank you for telling me the truth. And I'm sorry for what I said earlier." I swallowed over the lingering ball in my throat. "How did you end up at the Academy? In the Dean's dungeon?"

"That was our fault," Mahon answered; Leo and Asa nodded in agreement. "The five of us left the training camp when we heard rumors of a prophecy that foretold of Sebastian's downfall. New recruits arrive every week and some of them brought these rumors with them. Part of these rumors stated that the bringer of the prophecy was born to the witches. So we set off to learn more and if possible, find this Witch."

Leo smiled. "I'd say that was a success." He winked at me again; the boy must have been going for a record.

"Things started to go wrong from the moment our journey began," Mahon continued, glaring at Leo. "The first Academy we came to had a heavy, lingering scent of Vampire; someone had gotten there before us. We tracked the scent, hoping the owner was still around, and that's when we found the first body."

He was talking about one of the missing students. Eli learned not long before we left campus that the students once thought missing had actually been murdered. So far their story was lining up with what we knew.

"We found three total, each at a different Academy and each of a different race." Mahon looked at me. "The girl killed at your school was the second Witch."

I held his stare. "Her name was Jenna."

He nodded in recognition. "When we came upon her body, she was near a clearing in the woods. There were signs around of a recent fire and litter leftover from a gathering. Her kill was fresh, within ten minutes of us arriving. The scent of Vampires was stronger than any of the previous sites—we were right on top of them. Just a little sooner and we would have been able to prevent her useless death."

There was true regret in his voice and in the faces of the others around him. They felt real remorse for Jenna's death.

"What happened next?" Cedric asked.

"We began to hide the evidence, as we had at the other sites," Leo answered.

"What? Why would you hide evidence?" Cedric shouted. "You nearly brought about the end of the treaties! The other races were blaming the Guardians for losing track of their children."

Mahon's face hardened. "I am sorry for that, but the alternative would have been worse. Allowing bodies of the young to be found murdered on campus without a known cause would have *definitely* broken them."

Cedric scowled, but he knew Mahon was right.

"The group of Vampires that arrived before us were dispatched by Sebastian." Mahon explained. "Their sole purpose was to incite fear and distrust once again between the races. It was the precursor for more to come. We hid their tracks and then the bodies as best we could before moving on."

"So what happened with Jenna?" I wondered aloud.

"We were interrupted." Leo grumbled. "We had just finished erasing the tracks when we heard the guards calling to each other through the trees. They were too close for us to finish, so we split up and ran. Orin was captured."

The rest of the story unraveled in my mind. They caught Orin, assumed he was responsible for Jenna's death, and as a result threw him in the dungeon. Learning that there were Vampires about once again urged the dean to recheck the other campuses, where he then found the other bodies. From there, his fear and paranoia of another war sent him into a downward spiral.

And then he found me.

I looked over at Orin. He sat silent, gazing into the fire, before meeting my eyes. Sebastian and the Dean had been the cause of pain for us both. Neither one of us could change the past, but we could decide the future. We needed to defeat Sebastian and the Dean once and for all.

I knew what had to be done. There was only one place where we would be safe and where we could find the support and backup from likeminded people.

"Take us to the camp."

Chapter 5

The storms had come to a stop and the constant onslaught of howling winds and relentless ice had finally trickled to a halt. We were hit by three different storm systems, one right after the other. The moment we thought it was safe to plan our trip out of these woods, gusts of snow would swirl around outside and *Boom*, another snowstorm.

I hated winter. I hated the cold, I hated the constant gray hue the world took on, but I especially hated the snow. And it was everywhere. Cedric and I took a break from the cave as soon as we noticed the sunlight breaking through the trees. We hadn't seen sunlight in days. It was now shinning down in full glory, almost blinding as it sparkled and danced off the fresh snow.

The revolting white powder was still piled high as far as I could see, but the thought of having to go back in the cave was just a tad worse. It had been three days since our revealing talk with Orin. Three agonizing days with nothing to do but think and wonder and fret over everything. With a new plan and destination in mind, I was itching to start our journey and get to that training camp as soon as possible.

Problem one.

However, we were not only trapped by the last storm, but Falon had yet to wake up.

Problem two.

So far, over the last few days I had done nothing but sit and dwell on the fact that my best friend was still unconscious and only a few snow covered miles separated me from the Dean. Yesterday, Falon gave me a glimmer of hope for recovery, but nothing had happened yet. I sat beside her for a few hours as Asa tried another herbal treatment. My heart broke each time I looked at her; she looked so peaceful and still, almost like death.

"She is no longer in danger," Asa told me as he rummaged through his bag of medicines and herbs. "Her body is ready, but it's her mind that needs more time."

That explained why my power still couldn't heal her. I could only heal physical pains. In a way, I envied Falon. She got to close her eyes and escape from the madness while I was stuck here being the universe's punching bag. If anyone should be in a self-induced mental coma, it was me.

That was such a horrible thing to think, and Asa wasted no time calling me out on it.

"It's not for us to judge what others can handle and what they cannot," he said.

My lingering guilt still brought heat to my face when I thought about it. I had blamed Falon, jealous over the fact that she could escape this crappy hand we had all been dealt. I was jealous that my friend was basically in a coma. What kind of person did that make me?

I had no right to judge her. We were close now, but I still didn't know much about her home life or the hardships she suffered that caused her to volunteer for the Academy. I felt ashamed to have had those bad thoughts toward her, and I kept by her side for hours the day before, fueled by my own guilt.

I refused to move. Instead, I watched as Asa continued to test different herbs in an attempt to rouse Falon from her slumber.

One pouch he opened smelt of fruit. I had an image of an orchard bursting with luscious red apples, succulent and juicy. A feeling of familiarity came along with the scent and flashes of a lush, emerald meadow flickered through my mind.

Even now, thinking back, I could still see the rolling hills and puffy clouds overhead. And there was this voice, she was singing a haunting melody in another language I couldn't identify. I thought a lot about that voice over the past day, but the harder I tried to see who was singing, the more elusive my vision became.

"Casey."

I turned to face Cedric, the glare off the snow behind him nearly blinding me. He took a small step forward and to the right until his body blocked out the sun. He was now so close that the tip of my nose almost touched his chest. I took a deep breath, inhaling the scent that was uniquely Cedric: cinnamon and rain.

His comforting scent moved through me, and I could feel my earlier stress drifting away. I looked up and was quickly ensnared by his eyes. And just like that, my heart started racing. Butterflies took flight in my stomach and I forgot to breathe. He was gorgeous.

The sunlight captured him perfectly: his hair falling across his eyes as he looked down at me, the way his skin practically glowed with warmth, and how the light outlined his broad shoulders. As I continued to stare I began to notice small changes. He had grown, again, over the past months and now the top of my head came just below his shoulder.

His arms had grown too, they weren't thicker, but he no longer had to flex for me to see his muscles, they were more prominent. He had grown into a guardian without my noticing. My eyes left what I'm sure was a six pack hidden beneath his shirt and traveled up, up to his face.

He was smirking. I had just been caught blatantly checking him out. I blushed, embarrassed at being caught. But I wasn't sorry about it. Not one bit. Cedric chuckled and his smirk grew. Dammit, he could feel what I felt. Which meant he now had intimate knowledge of how attractive I found him.

I wanted to go hide in a hole. I started to turn away when those very arms I had just been drooling over wrapped around me and held me close. I could hear Cedric's low chuckles reverberating through his chest. His chin rested on the crown of my head as he squeezed me harder.

"Don't be embarrassed. I already know you like me, remember?"

"Yeah, but you didn't know how much," I mumbled into his shirt, my face still hot.

"I know how much you like my body." He laughed as he blocked my punch to his stomach.

"Where did it come from?" I asked, taking a step away from him. I couldn't think clearly about this new connection we had with him wrapped all around me.

"Where did what come from? My new gift of feeling you?" I nodded and he shrugged.

"That's it, a shrug? How do you *not* know?" I found it hard to believe that he didn't at least have an idea.

"How do you not know where your healing powers come from?" he countered.

Fair point. "Okay, that's fair. But can you think of anything? Has any life changing event happened to you recently? Were you bit by a radioactive spider and didn't tell me?"

He snorted. "Radioactive spider? Try a one-of-a-kind healing Witch."

I smiled. I liked that he saw me as one of a kind. But did he mean that my healing him could have caused our new connection? "My healing did this to you?" The thought that my power could have altered him in some way turned my stomach. Healing was supposed to be helpful, not damaging.

"Hey." Cedric stepped forward and cupped my face in his hands. "You didn't *do* anything to me. Do you understand?"

I nodded, my head still between his hands.

"But what if practicing on you was dangerous? What if my healing is just meant for life threatening situations?"

"Just to be clear, I would do it all over again. I don't care about the consequences. You could have died if you didn't learn control. Any side effect is worth it." He wiggled his eyebrows. "Besides, now I'm privy to all your deep dark fantasies."

My fist landed squarely in his gut this time, and he doubled over as all the air evacuated his lungs.

"You wish, perv."

I wasn't worried. He may be able to pick up on my feelings, but he couldn't read my mind. I wasn't sure if healing him caused this or how far his reading of me would develop, but for right now my thoughts were my own.

A hard tackle on my right side sent me flying into the snow. The soft powder cushioned my landing and lightly settled over me as it slowly fell back to the ground. I was bundled in a jacket and scarf, but now my jeans were wet. That boy was dead.

I popped out of the snow like a shark projecting itself from the sea. Cedric's eyes widened an instant before a wave of snow struck his face. The battle had begun. Taking advantage of my five second head start, I ran as fast as I could, which wasn't much in thigh high snow, and hid behind the nearest tree.

Chest heaving, I peered around the trunk and scanned the clearing. There was nothing but disturbed snow drifts and an untraceable mess of tracks. I turned my body till my chest pressed against the bark and kept an eye out as I bent to create snowballs.

Occasionally, I would glace around before continuing to build my arsenal. I had four projectiles before the lengthy silence registered. Where was Cedric? The shock of bone numbing cold started on my head, slid down my neck, and continued down my back. It took a while for my brain to come out of the deep freeze and realize that Cedric had just dumped snow down the back of my jacket.

I could still feel it dripping down to my waist. My shirt was soaked and so was half of my hair. Whipping around, I came face to face with a snickering Cedric. He was laughing so hard that his tears were literally freezing on his cheeks. I wrapped my arms around myself as my teeth began to chatter.

"Y-you a-assh-hole," I stuttered with a smile.

I took my first stiff steps back toward the cave. I needed to get warm. Cedric came up behind me and slipped his hands beneath my jacket and shirt, resting them on my frozen skin. It wasn't too long before I felt a growing warmth on my lower back.

I yawned and shivered as my body gradually defrosted. The sun was going back down, once again leaving the world in a muted gray. And as much as that sucked, all I wanted to do was get out of these wet clothes and take a nap.

I've always thought the cold took a lot out of you. Cedric's answering yawn only confirmed my theory. Too bad neither one of us was going to get much rest in the near future.

It was the screeching that woke me. The piercing cries sounded like a World War II alarm on helium and I was forced to cover my ears for fear of my head exploding. I peeked out of my sleeping bag at the mayhem surrounding me. Orin and Mahon were in battle against dive-bombing bats swooping from above, Leo was trying to get one little beast untangled from his hair, and I couldn't see Asa.

Cedric crawled over to me from his place in the back. He used one arm to drag himself across the rocky floor and the other to protect his head. A few seconds later and we were face to face.

"What the hell is going on?" I shouted over the clamor. "What spooked them?"

Cedric grimly pointed to the entrance of the cave where a half-dressed Falon stood screaming. Asa was in front of her, crouched down, palms up, as he tried to sooth her. *Falon was awake.* That was the only thought in my mind as I fought my way out of my sleeping bag and over to where she stood.

Falon was awake.

My excitement overshadowed all sane thought and I paid no attention to her almost blue, bare feet or the off-focused look in her eye. It wasn't until I was practically on top of her that I noticed anything was wrong. Her face was frozen in terror and an unceasing wail emitted from her lips.

"What's wrong with her?" I asked Asa. It was slightly easier to hear now. Most of the disturbed bats had dispersed and the only raucous came from Falon.

"I don't know," Asa admitted. He shook his head in confusion. Empathy for my friend clearly written on his face. "I woke up to her like this. How she got here, I'm not sure. She shouldn't have the strength to stand, let alone continue on with this incessant hysteria."

The others in the group made their way over to us and could only watch as Falon unraveled. I tried calling out to her, waving my hand in her face, and even screaming with her a couple times. Nothing worked. Frustrated and out of ideas, I placed my hands on her shoulders and prepared to shake the life back into her, but the moment my hand touched her, the screaming stopped. Falon's head jerked toward me, like my touch was a magnet drawing her attention. Her eyes were clouded over, a milky white fog that dimmed the blue that I knew was hidden beneath. Those eyes remained unfocused as her lips once again began to move.

"They are coming." The voice was hers, but at the same time, not. There was a deeper undertone that made it sound like someone was talking *through* her.

"Who? Who's coming, Falon?"

"You haven't much time; they are coming."

"Who is she talking about?" Cedric asked, a nervous tint to his voice.

"I don't know, but I need Falon to snap out of it." I began shaking her, gently, but enough to hopefully break whatever trance she was in. "Come on, Falon. Wake up."

I began to shake her harder, but she still continued to whisper that same warning.

"They are coming."

I stopped shaking her, but kept my hands on her shoulders. She looked straight ahead, but I knew she couldn't see me. Her mind was somewhere far away, and I wasn't sure how to bring her back.

"Her lips are turning blue." Cedric noted. "Her feet too." Shit. She stood there in only a tank top and underwear; completely exposed to the elements not even feet away.

"This is not good for her. We need to warm her quickly before we reverse all the progress her body has made," came Asa's voice.

Not knowing what else to do, I released my power that had been straining to be let out since I first touched her. Too scared to let it all out at once, it sprung free in short bursts. The first jolt caused her body to jerk, like it had been shocked. I instantly removed my hands, frightened that I had hurt her.

"No, do it again. Look at her face."

Leo was right. Her lips had returned to a normal, healthy pink. Once again grasping her shoulders, I let free more bursts of my power. Falon's body continued to twitch and jump, each jolt stronger than the last until her head whipped back, she gasped, and slumped to the floor.

I went down with her until we were nothing but tangled legs with her head resting on my shoulder. I cradled her protectively as Asa checked her over for injuries.

"She seems fine," he said. "Her extremities are no longer blue and her breathing is steady."

"I don't understand what just happened," I whispered over Falon's head. My hand was running over her hair in a comforting rhythm. "How did she get over here?"

They all shook their heads. My mind was racing; thoughts of what could have happened colliding in a catastrophic mess of possibilities. The lifeless bundle in my arms suddenly began to move. Falon's head lifted from my shoulder and I saw a kaleidoscope of blonde, blues, and greens before her eyes met mine; they were clear and bright.

"Casey?" Falon asked in confusion before looking around at the strangers surrounding her. "What's going on?"

Her body began to shiver so Cedric took off his jacket and placed it over her exposed skin.

"What do you remember?" I asked.

Falon shook her head, as if the action would knock loose that far away and forgotten memory.

"I-I'm not sure. All I can remember is white, everything was white. And being cold."

She peered around at the cave and the ivory glow coming from outside. Leaving me on the floor, she stood on wobbly, weak legs and took a few shaky steps to the cave entrance. The longer she stood starring out into the trees, the more solid her stance became.

Cedric's jacket was still wrapped around her, but it couldn't cover all of her legs. She had to be freezing, but she showed no sign of it. Turning back around, she looked at me, her mouth set in a thin and determined line.

"We've got to go. Now."

She spun around a few times as if she were looking for something, and then took sure and solid steps over to where her clothes were folded by her sleeping bag. As she slid the first foot into her jeans I walked over to help steady her. She may be feeling better and gaining more control over her motor functions, but she was far from fully recovered.

"It's the middle of the night, Fal. Why don't you come sit back down by the fire and we can talk about a plan to leave in the morning."

She ignored me and continued to get dressed, only sitting down to put socks on her feet.

"We don't have time to wait until morning. They're coming now."

We all froze. There were those words again. Had Falon slipped back into a hallucination without us noticing? When she glanced back up at me, I saw that her eyes were still clear, no foggy film to them.

"What did you just say?"

She stopped rolling the sleeping bag and looked me dead in the eye.

"We don't have time for me to convince you that I'm not crazy, okay? I can feel it down to my bones. Danger is coming for us, and it's almost arrived. We need to leave. Now."

Her eyes softened, as if they begged me to believe her, but remained unflinching. Falon has been known to have a strong intuition, even for a Fae. I could count a hundred different times she seemed to have inside knowledge on things that she couldn't possibly know about.

She knew something was wrong when I healed that guard and lay half-dead in the woods. She knew when Tony was kicking the crap out of me in the cafeteria and arrived just in time to save me. She even knew that the Dean was behind my defensive and avoiding behavior, although she didn't know the details about the torture at the time.

Falon had proved time and again that her strong feelings were not something to disregard. I let out the breath I had been holding.

"Okay."

I turned to Cedric and he nodded before packing our things. He must have come to the same conclusion I did; that or he monitored my conflicting emotions until I made a decision. Orin gave the order for his men to quickly dismantle our makeshift camp before coming to stand at my side.

"Are you sure that this is a sound idea? Your friend has only just awoken from her deep slumber."

I nodded. "I understand your concern, but I've learned to listen when Falon has one of these warnings. I don't know what happened before," I paused as I briefly recalled her erratic meltdown, "but she's clear-headed now. I trust her."

Orin's hand clasped my shoulder and gave a gentle squeeze.

"Then we trust her too."

It took a little over an hour for us to pack everything we would need for an impromptu trek through the woods, but we got it done. And soon I was looking around at the skeleton of the place that had been our safe haven for the past week. Hiking my bag and attached sleeping bag over my shoulder, I joined the rest of the group gathered just outside the entrance.

"All right, let's start thi-*hmpf*."

"Shhh," Cedric whispered in my ear as he removed his hand from my mouth. He gestured to Orin who stood out further than the rest of us as he sniffed the air. The other Vampires followed his lead and Leo even let out a small growl.

I squinted and strained to see through the fog dancing around the trees. I thought I might have seen a few shapes, but I wasn't too sure. A faint scratching like the light of a match set to tinder, echoed from the left.

The sound built in volume until a small flicker of light appeared. The light grew larger as it sailed through the trees, directly at Falon. With a war cry, Asa jumped in front of her just in time for the fireball to hit him in the chest.

"Imperials!"

Those blurred shapes I thought I saw solidified until almost forty Imperial guards stepped out of the trees. I heard Falon gasp as Mahon picked her up, bag and all, and began to run. More fireballs were launched, and I stood there as they sizzled out, inches from me on all sides.

Rocks and boulders were also being thrown. A particularly large one exploded on contact above the mouth of the cave and small shards went flying. One sliced my cheek, but I did nothing to stop it. I couldn't. My body was one hundred percent focused on Asa. He was slowly picking himself up from the ground, brushing away Leo's attempts to help.

His wound called out to me. I could feel the heat searing his flesh as if it were my own. The skin around the wound was slowly dying and turning black before my eyes. I took a step toward him, my arm lifting, raw power tingling through my fingers.

"No!" Asa shouted, turning his wound from my gaze. "It's just my shoulder; I'll live. It can wait."

"Casey, come on!" Cedric tugged on my bag as another rock exploded above us.

"I can't," I growled through clenched teeth. I knew now was not the opportune time to heal Asa. We needed to run, and healing would leave me a pile of mush on the floor. But try telling that to my power.

The world spun and I watched the spot we were just standing in explode in flames. Cedric had thrown me over his shoulder and ran toward the tree line with Asa beside us. From upside down the world looked different, but I could still make out Orin's lone figure standing behind a massive cloud of snow and ice.

He spun and mixed it into a raging plume of winter fury. He was buying us time to run. Releasing the storm to do what it willed, Orin turned and sprinted to catch up with us, clearing our tracks as he went.

I wasn't sure how long we ran. Mahon continued to carry Falon, but Cedric had let me down long ago. We were both getting tired. Our night's rest was interrupted and we were running low on energy. It was dark, a kind of thick blackness that only the purest light could penetrate, and none of us were willing to risk the glow of a flashlight.

The snow, while slightly thinner under the cover of dense trees, was still near impossible to run through. These obstacles made for slow moving. We could hear the Imperials gaining ground, and any second I expected to feel the heat of a fireball on my neck.

Suddenly, as if Luther himself heard my prayer, Leo gave the signal to stop. He had found another cave. Well, it wasn't really a cave, more like a small depression in a natural rock formation. Thick bushes grew in front of it and some fallen logs blocked a majority of the entrance. I had no idea how he was able to spot it, but it was exactly what we needed. Orin directed me, Cedric, and Falon inside. There was just enough room to hide us and our packs, but it was tight.

"Asa, you too," Orin ordered.

"Sir, I can help," Asa argued.

But Orin shook his head. "I need someone here with them while the rest of us lead the Imperials away. And with your shoulder, you're the best candidate."

Asa ceded to his order and climbed inside. To make room, I had to scoot over and sit in Cedric's lap. I had absolutely no romantic notions right then, but my cheeks still couldn't help but burn. Asa slid next to Falon and squeezed his pack onto his lap. To say we were uncomfortable would be an understatement.

I was fully on Cedric's lap and all of us were touching in some way to everyone cramped in this hole, but we were hidden and that's what mattered. With a wave of his hand, the snow on top of our hiding place collapsed in front of the entrance, effectively burying us alive. Asa calmly made a few small holes through the barricade to allow air inside.

With nothing else to do, we waited.

Chapter 6

Stress was a word I thought I already knew. Pain was a receptor I thought I was exceptionally familiar with. And sleep was a joy I thought I would never again experience. We had been running so long that I wasn't sure if my legs would remember how to do anything else.

Orin, Mahon, and Leo led the Imperials away from our hidden shelter and then doubled back to retrieve us. By the time Orin removed the snow that provided our coverage, the sun was fighting to shine through the trees. Being trapped in those cramped quarters gave plenty of time for me to catch Falon up on all she had missed while she was unconscious.

It was also plenty of time for all of our limbs to fall into a perpetual deep sleep. When we finally crawled out, I cried out in agony as my muscles seized up in a never ending monster cramp. Unable to support my weight, my knees buckled and I face planted into the top layer of cold slush. The others didn't fare much better.

"I don't mean to come across callous, but we need to move," Orin said as he reached a hand down, grasped my jacket, and yanked me to my feet.

We began to run and hadn't stopped until it was late afternoon. The sun once again started its descent as we settled into a small clearing for a brief break. The urge to keep running was strong, but we needed to refuel or we wouldn't make it much further.

"Can we risk a fire?" Leo asked Cedric as he arranged a few twigs and small branches into a small triangle.

"We have no choice," he replied. "You guys can drink the blood, but we can't eat raw meat."

Mahon was busy plucking a couple grouse he managed to catch. The plan was to make a quick meal, hide all evidence of us having been there, and then continue our mad dash to freedom. This wasn't a time for relaxation and enjoyment, although it was sorely needed.

Every second we had that fire lit was a chance for the Imperials to spot us. There was still enough light out to keep the fire from being a complete homing beacon, but it was an enormous risk. As the sun sank lower on the horizon, more stars became visible through the tangled skeleton arms of the tree tops. Usually, this was a view I would look forward to, watching individual stars flicker to life as the sky changed from pink, to a dark indigo, then finally settle on black.

But tonight the once bewitching view had become a warning sign. A sign that said our time to rest was coming to an end. The easier it was to see the stars, the easier it would be to see our fire. As the glow began to cast dancing shadows across our faces, Orin stood and walked to the center of our circle.

"We're going to have to pick up the pace." Orin's comment rang out through the once comfortable silence. I almost choked on my mouthful of wild bird. Did he just say pick *up* the pace?

"Yeah, cause this trip has been a real stroll through the park already," answered Cedric, dryly.

"Orin, we're exhausted," I told him. "Just the thought of moving my legs right now makes me want to cry, let alone moving them faster than before."

My hand unconsciously moved down my leg and began to massage the quivering muscles that quaked at the knowledge that they would have to run soon. Orin took in the sad sight before him, and I could only imagine what he was thinking.

There was me, sitting on a fallen log with my legs spread out before me like two limp noodles that twitched every few seconds as they tried to hang onto life. Beside me sat Falon, the exact opposite of my commiserable state; her leg was bouncing along to some figmental tune as she dug into her meal with the feral appetite similar to that of a caged tiger.

Cedric tended to the fire, every now and then zapping it with a bit of his gift to make sure it didn't grow further than the bundle of barely fledged embers that it was. Each time he used his power I could tell it took a toll on him.

When a Witch's body was as exhausted as Cedric's was, any use of power, no matter how minuscule, felt like pulling a tooth that wasn't sick. It was like forcing something from you that didn't want to go. With a last pitiful glance at him, I looked further left.

Out of all of us, Asa had it the worst. His wound was hidden beneath half hazard bandages and a light jacket. If I couldn't see it, then I wasn't drawn to it, and therefore didn't heal him. Even so, I could still sense his wound, even from across the clearing; it was that bad.

I could sense the dying skin and how it sickened and spoiled the healthy cells around it; how it spread like a plague of death. In the center of the wound, layers of skin had been seared away, down to the tender muscle below.

No movement, no breath was taken without pain.

His face was drawn tight and beads of sweat formed on his forehead to slowly drip down his face and freeze in small crystals; the only outward sign that something was wrong. We needed to get to where we were going and fast. Asa didn't have much time. Mahon coaxed some of the bird's blood down his throat until Asa motioned for him to stop.

"Don't give it all to me," I heard his voice rasp. "You're close, I can tell."

Mahon grumbled an unintelligible response and tried to get Asa to drink a little more. When he refused again, Mahon stormed off to the opposing side of the fire.

"What's wrong with him?" I asked Leo.

He was slumped on the log next to me, slowly savoring his share of grouse blood and gazing into the fire. When he looked at me, his eyes were strained; red was beginning to pool in the center with smaller streaks violently radiating out into the white.

"It's not just him," he replied, his voice gruff with tension. "It's all of us."

My brow crinkled in confusion. Was it because they were tired? I knew they had to be since they led away the Imperials and then had to run for half a day more, but this didn't seem like it was just fatigue that was bothering them.

With a sigh, Leo tried to relax the taut muscles in his face, but his lips couldn't help but curl back some, revealing the points of his semi-extended fangs.

"The four of us have fed on nothing but animal blood since finding you all in that blizzard. With all the energy we've exerted over the past twenty-four hours, our demons are becoming harder to maintain."

A tremor took hold of my limbs. It was real fear that caused my voice to rattle when I spoke.

"H-how much longer?" I cleared my throat, trying in vain to remove the obvious distress in my tone. "Until—"

"Until we snap?" Leo snarled.

There was so much venom in those three words that I half expected some to come spewing from his mouth to spray me in the face. As it was, I already felt my body jerk and lean away as if it had indeed been struck by a vile poison.

Within seconds, Leo's crazed demeanor dissolved.

"I'm sorry. I'm really not myself. I've never been this long without human blood. Four days was my limit, and here we are at almost two weeks."

My fingers still held a tremble, but I rested a hand lightly on his forearm. No words of comfort were spoken. What helpful words could I have given him? If we did not make it to a food source soon, none of us would come out of these woods the same, if at all.

Leo attempted a wink; a small token to show that he was fighting. A sizzle, accompanied by an abrupt blindness, had my hand tightening on Leo's arm until he hissed. Releasing his now tender flesh from my grip, I looked in the direction of where Orin had stood, slowly allowing my eyes to adjust.

"It's time," was all he said before stepping across the dying coals. Then, with a wave of his hand, a fresh blanket of snow blew across the campsite, hiding all evidence of us ever being here.

Reluctantly, I stood and bit my lip to silence the scream clawing its way up my throat. It felt as if I stood on a bed of hot nails; the sharp points stabbing and blistering as they embedded into my feet. The agony continued through my shins and into my knees before settling down to a tolerable ache in my thighs.

How was I going to keep up?

My fear of lagging behind was, thankfully, unfounded. Orin led our continued trek at a brisk, yet not as grueling, jog. He must have recognized the lifeless way we stumbled through the trees. But still, the pace we kept was not easy to maintain. Any minute now my legs were going to give out, I was sure of it.

Up ahead, Leo let out a whoop of glee before being smacked upside his head by Mahon. Gradually making my way to Cedric, I pulled up alongside him.

"What's he so happy about? Not too long ago he had me convinced he was one step from jumping off the deep end."

Cedric shrugged. "I wasn't paying attention. I was too focused on not allowing my legs to fall off."

I knew how he felt. We all did, well, except maybe Falon. She didn't look half as exhausted as we did. But, she had been asleep for almost a week. Maybe all that rest was catching up to her. I jogged over and bumped my shoulder into hers.

"How come I've been training my entire life for a run like this, and yet I'm the one who's practically out of breath?" I cracked the joke with a smile, but I didn't get one in return. Frowning, I tried a different approach. "Did you hear what Leo was so happy about?"

Falon quickly glanced up at the Vampires running a few feet in front of her and slowly brought her eyes down to focus on the path once more. Her eyes were squinted in concentration, the tip of her tongue peeking out of the front of her teeth.

"Leo spotted a marker they left to help find their way back. He said we were almost there." She delivered that statement in complete monotone, not a single drop of excitement to be found.

I was confused. Hearing that our hellish run was almost at an end was cause for celebration, but Falon didn't look like she cared at all about it.

"Why do you look like reaching our destination is the worst possible thing that could happen right now?"

She sighed and finally gave me a half smile.

"I don't know. Maybe it's my turn to go a little crazy. I just have this nagging feeling that something is wrong. Like we're not safe yet, and we won't be for a long time."

That was a prophetic warning if I've ever heard one. And recently, I've become an expert at recognizing a foreboding hint. A yard ahead, Orin pulled his hand up and made a fist, then signed for us to stay quiet.

Goosebumps broke out across my skin as even beneath my jacket I shivered. Why were we stopping? We had come to a rest on an incline, almost to the peak of a small hill. Peering over the crest, I surveyed the small town.

Through the trees I could make out a couple buildings, what was obviously the main street through the town, and one traffic light. The only thing lying between me and civilization was a few trees on the declining side of this hill and a parked pickup truck.

"That's mine," Mahon declared with pride.

Not wanting to say anything to hurt his feelings, I gave him an honest smile. He lovingly gazed upon his truck like it was a shiny new F150 straight off the lot. This was not the case. The truck was rusted, old, and quite possibly the ugliest vehicle I had ever laid eyes upon. I could barely tell what color it was. It was mostly a rusted brown with a few splotches of a dingy red bleeding through.

The truck was parked on a curb next to a tiny two pump gas station. A single street light was perched on the corner out front, its glow straining to stay lit against the oily spread of the arriving night.

The sun had fully disappeared almost an hour ago and darkness had leaked into this town like spilled oil in the sea: slow and deliberate. The only other light daring to battle the inky twilight was stationed across the street and a few blocks down, in front of the combined general, auto, pharmacy store, and doctor's office. If the signs were to be believed.

This town had to have a whopping population of ten, maybe.

"I believe all the residents are tucked away in their homesteads. On my signal, we move for the truck."

After glancing at each of us in turn, confirming that we were alert and ready, he thrust his hand forward. I crawled the rest of the way up the hill and lifted onto my knees. Just as I pushed with my arms to stand, my right foot was wrenched back. My arms flailed around before I slammed face first into the ground.

The pain had me completely incapacitated as I felt warm liquid stream down my face. The ground in front of me was red with my blood and the stain only continued to spread. Gingerly, fully cognizant of my throbbing head, I scanned the forest around me before inspecting what had caught my foot.

Dread settled deep in my stomach and flared to life with an echoing hysteria. Falon's forewarning rang loud and clear with every frantic stutter of my heart. *"I don't think we're safe yet, and we won't be for a long time."*

And then I screamed.

Pain resonated down to the bone as the branch encircling my ankle tightened even further. Around me, other tree limbs snaked along the ground toward the group. The trees around us had come to life, controlled by the master puppeteers in all black standing behind them.

The Imperials had caught up.

The vicious sliver of bark around my ankle gave another tug and my body slid across the frozen ground leaving a trail of blood in its wake. Frigid slush was forced up the front of my shirt and jacket, freezing my skin on contact. I clawed at the ground, at anything, but it was all either wet, slippery, or buried beneath the snow.

With nothing to anchor myself to, I was pulled deeper into the forest. I looked up one last time and watched as my friends got smaller the further away I was towed. The likelihood of them catching me were slim, they too were fighting their own battles against the very earth herself.

A furious growl echoed behind a small explosion as Cedric disintegrated the branch that was attacking him. He was fighting like hell to get to me. He had small flames in each hand and he scorched anything that came too close. But it wasn't enough, more kept coming.

Leo had the same plan and was melting anything that came into contact with his acid. Unfortunately, short of burning the whole forest down, they couldn't possibly get the upper hand. I heard a yelp from the far right and watched as a rogue branch wound itself around an Imperial and squeezed.

As effective as an anaconda with its prey, the Imperial fell to the ground, dead. Another guard stepped up to take his place and called forth a new branch to do his bidding. He threw his arm forward, sending the branch directly at Falon.

But like the one before it, the limb altered its course just seconds from contact and instead attacked its master. Falon had no power over the elements, but as a Fae, it was against the tree's own nature to attack her.

It would rather maim whoever dared to send it to battle than harm one who is physically of the earth. A Fae and the forest were practically one and the same. Realizing that it was useless to attack her, most of the Imperials ignored Falon and instead focused on the rest of the group. But a select few remained and tried to take her down.

A burn seared my ankle at the same time that I felt a fierce tug in my hip. Crying out in pain, I was lifted straight into the air to dangle above Orin who had been sneaking over from the side. Blood rushed to my head, making my busted nose feel as if the weight of my entire body pushed behind it.

My blood streamed out faster and dripped to the ground below where it splattered at Orin's feet. The trees around me began to spin as the pulsing in my head intensified until I was sure my brains would come spilling out from my ears.

A primitive roar resounded through the grove, literally shaking the ground and uprooting several small trees. From up above, I watched Orin kneel in the snow, thrusting his hands beneath the surface. Throwing his head back, he released another war cry. The other Vampires answered his call with one of their own and morphed into the monsters of legend right before my eyes.

Their faces curled back tight to reveal pointed fangs, resembling those of a venomous snake. Eyes burned a fiery crimson as nails lengthened and curved into weapons as tapered as any well-honed stiletto. They had been pushed over the edge, no longer able to hold onto their sanity or keep their demons at bay.

Attacking with a swiftness I've never seen, Leo, Mahon, and Asa moved as one to surround a worn down Cedric and Falon. Their claws clenched and released with every satisfied sniff of their prey. They moved in closer.

"No!" Orin's command rang clear and the three hunters froze.

Unable to ignore the will of one much older than them, the hunters gave a final snarl before disappearing deep into the trees. Orin briefly glanced in my direction before deliberately lifting his hands from the snow, above his head, and releasing a maelstrom of hail and sleet into the atmosphere.

Within seconds, visibility became nonexistent. I hung there, unable to see my friends or the monsters that lurked about. My hearing, however, was amplified as if every scream, every snap of a broken bone, echoed to the center of the storm. I listened as cries for mercy went ignored, to sounds so gruesome that words had yet to be invented that could adequately describe them.

A shudder went through the branch holding me aloft and I fell to the ground, cushioned by the powder below. Orin stood above me, blood staining his face, around his mouth, and soaking his shirt. His claws dripped with it as he leaned forward and sniffed.

"Go. Now," he gnarled. "You and your friends head for the truck. We won't be far behind."

I couldn't tell if that was a threat or not, but considering what was happening around me, I didn't wait around to ponder. I scrambled to my feet and staggered away. My vision was slightly disoriented from having been upside down for so long and I stumbled into a tree, grabbing the trunk for balance. A few feet away a small glow glimmered through the wintery fury and grew closer until two figures emerged.

"Thank Luthos!" I exclaimed. Cedric reached out to catch me as my knees gave out with relief.

"I've got you," he replied as he used his sleeve to tenderly wipe the blood from my eyes and face. "I don't think it's broken." He lightly pushed on the cartilage of my nose. "Does that hurt?"

"Ouch. Yes!" I swatted his hand away and took a step on shaking knees. "We need to get to that truck."

Without any further mishaps, we made it to the tree line at the bottom of the hill. Still shrouded in the darkness, we surveyed the area for humans. When Falon gave the all clear, we moved to the parked vehicle.

Cedric jumped in on the driver's side and grabbed the keys dangling from the visor. He jammed the key in the ignition and turned it … but the engine only sputtered before dying. He tried two more times till the engine finally sparked to life with a high whine.

Cedric lifted the hood and placed his hands directly on the engine and allowed his power to flow through it. Gradually, the whine faded and Cedric came back behind the wheel, pale and shaking.

"I think I'm out. There's nothing left." Without rest, Cedric had just spent his last connection to fire.

Turning to Falon, I asked her if she would be okay getting into the cab. "I know iron can hurt the Fae. We can find another way if we have to," I told her, even though I knew we had no other way out of here.

But Falon shook her head. "Over time my people have built up a resistance to all but the purest iron. Unless this truck somehow impales me and gets into my bloodstream, I should be fine, if not a little nauseous."

"Then what are you guys waiting for? Come on!" came Cedric's fatigued voice.

Falon hopped into the cab and slid over to make room for me. I had my hands on the frame and one foot hiked up to pull myself in, when Falon shouted.

"Casey, behind you!" I was grabbed by my hair and thrown to the ground. An Imperial stood above me and leered as I let out a pained moan.

"The Dean will reward me greatly for this." He leaned closer to my face. "Returning his little bitch will be a piece of cake."

With a wave of his hand, I felt the air slowly leave my lungs even as I gasped to bring more in. Tears formed in my eyes and rolled into my hair. The cold, my damp clothes, and the unnatural movement of air inside me sent me into a panic. Deep inside, a spirited resistance rose from the sorrow filled memories and stood to fight.

I will not let this happen again. I am not helpless.

Swinging my legs around, I kicked the back of the Imperial's knee causing him to slip over the ice coating the sidewalk. I clambered to all fours and tried to make it back to the truck, but the guard recovered and without warning pounced on me from behind. His hands wrapped around my throat so tight his fingers overlapped.

A banshee scream pierced our struggled silence as Falon repeatedly beat him over the head with her fists. Not trained in combat, they did little damage and the guard threw her off. However, she provided enough of a distraction to allow me to grab his thumb and yank it to the side. Hearing a satisfying *crack*, I flipped to my back and slammed a foot into the guard's gut, sending him flying back.

Cedric yelled for us as he battled with his own guard on the other side of the truck. Cedric dogged a punch meant for his face and instead grabbed the offending arm. With a twist and yank, the guard let out a high-pitched scream as his shoulder was dislocated. With his body now positioned behind the guard, Cedric grabbed him by the hair and slammed his head onto the side of the truck.

The guard fell to the ground in a crumpled heap. Cedric looked up, his eyes widening in fear just as I felt the increasingly familiar sensation of a hand wrapping around the back of my throat.

"You little bitch, you just had to make it difficult." The guard's acrid breath puffed along my ear. A muffled thump to my right showed Falon knocked to the ground, a hand holding her side. That bastard hit her!

Before I could move, the guard's hand was ripped from my neck and my arms waved around me as I tried to catch my balance.

"No! Please … no!" The sound of the guard's begging resonated along the empty street.

A sickening squish, the sound similar to getting one's foot stuck in the mud and then tugging it loose, ended the guard's pleas. A solid thud followed close behind. On the ground lay the guard, a giant hole in his torso. Mahon threw his heart to the side with barely a glance before climbing into the bed of the truck.

The others followed suit as Orin approached us. He looked normal; the fangs and claws had returned to pointy canines and thin fingers. The beast had returned to his cage. With a nod, Orin continued past us and took a seat next to Asa in the back.

The three of us stood on the sidewalk looking at the four of them. We were surrounded by the spreading blood of the dead guard and yards away from countless other mangled bodies. I'm sure if we looked, those other bodies would be drained of blood, whatever was left staining the faces of their killers before us.

Orin and I made eye contact. In mine there was a question: can we still trust you? He gave a subtle nod and held my gaze. I scanned the four of them, searching for any signs that their demons were still in control, and saw nothing but normal faces—albeit, covered in blood. That group of Imperials must have been large enough to sate their appetites.

Not entirely convinced, but with no other option, I muffled my doubts.

"Okay. To the camp we go."

Chapter 7

I was dreaming about the meadow again. The air was succulent with the scent of apples and birds of every color perched on the surrounding trees; their voices melding together in one euphonic tune that rode along the breeze.

My body sank into the tall, downy grass and each muscle gave way, allowing me to melt into the earth until I was practically one with the dirt. It was the first time in days that I wasn't running for my life or fighting to stay one step ahead of the Dean and his relentless stream of Imperials.

Though it wasn't real, this dream allowed me the chance to escape. Because even at this very moment, my body was squeezed into the cab of a rusted, old truck with the hope that it could put hundreds of miles between me and my pursuers before breaking down. I wasn't holding my breath; that truck was one loose bolt away from the junkyard.

"It's about damn time."

My once slackened muscles coiled and flexed within seconds. The choir of birds shrieked their displeasure at being interrupted and took flight. I kept still, crouched low on the ground with my hand clutching a rock, the only weapon within grabbing distance.

In front of me stood a petite redhead. Her beauty almost outshone that of the meadow and her face played canvas to a devious smirk.

"Really, there's no need for that. We're old friends, you and I."

"I highly doubt that." My right hand clutched the rock even tighter until a sharp corner nicked the underside of my knuckle.

The woman huffed, as if my being defensive was somehow annoying to her. The action was familiar, like I'd seen it once before. But that was impossible. I've never met her before; I think I would remember if I had.

"It's unlikely that you'd forget *me*, but you were dead—well, almost dead—so perhaps you would."

Caught up in my thoughts, I hadn't noticed the woman step closer until it was too late. Only a foot away, her beauty could not be denied.

"Who are you?" I asked.

"I really don't have time to answer that question, again. And neither do you." Her hand reached out and she took another step forward. The air in front of her fingers glimmered and danced like a mirage. "You will remember it all this time. And when you're ready, come find me. Your little blonde friend should know how."

With a final step, her hand touched my forehead. I bolted awake with a cry before slamming my head against the back window of the cab. My hand subconsciously tried to rub away the hurt.

"Ow. That *bitch*."

"Who?" asked Falon, her face scrunched up in confusion.

"Gwendolyn."

Cedric mimicked Falon's befuddled expression, but my mind was too busy running like a tape on fast forward. It was like someone opened a door and all the hidden memories behind it came pouring out. I remembered everything: being practically dead, Gwendolyn pulling me to limbo, the fact that she was a psycho bitch.

"Who's Gwendolyn?" Cedric asked.

"She's one of the Fae, very powerful. She brought me to limbo, gave me my powers, and wants me to come find her," I replied.

A large hand gingerly felt the knot on the back of my head.

"Does she live in a castle and need you to come help her slay an evil dragon too?" Leo teased.

The responding chuckles were lost to the wind as I shut the small window on Leo's arm. His teasing grin mocked me until I turned once again to face the front. I could still hear the snickers from Cedric and Falon though.

"Guys, I'm serious. This wasn't a dream and I'm not insane. After all the crap I've brought to you this year, you'd think you would believe me by now."

Still fighting off chuckles, Cedric gave my leg a gentle pat. "It's not that we don't believe you, but come on, limbo?"

"Actually ..." Falon drew the word out. "Limbo is very real, just incredibly hard to get to. There is only one Fae I've ever heard of who can get there, let alone bring someone with her. Coincidentally, her name *is* Gwendolyn."

"Then why do you still sound unconvinced?"

"Gwendolyn is the oldest Fae on record. And she hasn't been seen for generations."

I frowned. "How old are we talking?"

"No one knows for sure," Falon admitted. "But she is older than the current Seelie Queen, and the Queen is thought to be the oldest among those in civilized society."

The miles ticked by in a slow blur of trees and yellow lines on asphalt. We continued our talk about Gwendolyn, eventually including the four in the truck bed in our conversation. By the time Cedric pulled us off the interstate, the sun was on its way down and everyone was on the same page; Gwendolyn was real and so was limbo.

Whether or not I should attempt to find her and whether or not she actually gave me my power was still up for debate. But there was only one way to find out.

We parked the truck behind an ancient grocery store named after a wiggling pig; the seclusion a backup in case we needed to make a quick getaway. Each paired with a list and a handful of bills, we spread out.

We entered the store in twos and a trio not wanting to draw attention to ourselves. But that was hard seeing as we were the only customers here. The building was decrepit and held the faint scent of mold.

The ceiling looked like it had seen better days; there were wires dangling in places like snakes that hissed and sparked. Half the lights flickered and my imagination couldn't help but picture a monster waiting for me at the end of every aisle.

Ever seen the movie *IT*? Yeah, my mind chose *that* monster.

"Let's just get what we came for and go. I don't want to be here longer than we need to," I said. Neither Cedric nor Falon argued, instead, Falon made a beeline for the powdered donuts.

We hoarded junk food and bottled beverages in our cart, enough to last us the entire trip. Hopefully. We passed Asa and Mahon grabbing a few of those Styrofoam coolers as we parked our cart outside the restrooms.

The view of the store didn't leave much hope for the condition of the toilets, but I was desperate. Not lingering with the crusted tiles and drippy sinks, Falon and I did our business and rushed to meet Cedric at the checkout line. I threw a bottle of Purell into the cart for good measure.

We made it through checkout in record time and pushed our cart outside and around to the back lot. I tried to calculate how long I needed to make my Debbie Cakes last.

"Did Orin tell you where we were going?" I asked Cedric, but he shrugged.

"Not specifically. He just mentioned going down south."

That didn't tell me much. "Well, did he tell you how long it would take?"

"I'm going to take an educated guess and say, a long fricken time." Falon said, as she came to a sudden stop.

Catching the direction of her stare, Cedric and I followed her line of sight. Three of our Vamps stood in the middle of the back lot, surrounded by carts of food, shouting at one another. A quick glance around revealed why.

"Where's the truck?" I asked, calmly.

It was Orin who spoke, the other two were too busy glaring at each other. "It appears it has been stolen."

"Did it ever occur to you to *not* leave the keys in the ignition?" Leo roared. His face was inches from Mahon's, his chest puffed up, as they shoved each other. Men.

"I didn't think anyone would take it! I was getting ready to retire her. Who would steal a truck that old?" Mahon shouted back.

"Maybe someone who saw that it still worked!" By now the two were exchanging blows.

Mahon was clearly the better fighter, but Leo had enough frustration to fuel his blocks. Neither had actually landed a hit yet.

"Enough! Both of you, separate corners!" Orin reprimanded as he stepped between them.

I giggled as the two warriors were sent into time out like well-scolded five year olds.

"So what do we do now?" Cedric asked, having already eaten his way through a bag of chips while watching the fight.

"I've sent Asa to acquire another vehicle," Orin sighed. "Now, we wait."

"For the last time, this vehicle in no way resembles a kidnapper's van." Asa's fingers tightened around the steering wheel until they turned white.

Over the past couple hours, I had incessantly teased him about the van he found to replace the stolen truck. He had a very narrow sense of humor. But it wasn't my fault. What else do you call an unmarked, white utility van with no windows?

Exactly.

He might as well be offering candy out the side door.

"Relax, Asa. I'm only kidding. This van is actually perfect."

It wasn't a lie. While ideal for hiding a tied up victim when running from the law, the lack of windows served a dual purpose: hiding me.

His grip on the wheel lessened and I watched as his left hand twitched in a prolonged spasm. The muscles in his arm continued their convulsions all the way up to his shoulder and Asa shifted slightly, the only visible sign of discomfort. The movement pulled at the torn collar of his shirt.

His once festered and oozing wound now looked stale and dead. Quite literally. The inflamed, crimson skin had dulled to a light blush, dotted with small blisters. The guards he fed off of helped to heal most of the burns, but couldn't bring back something already dead.

Completely surrounding the singed shoulder was a ring of charred flesh. Crisp and burnt, the decaying skin only shriveled and peeled. Left alone too long, the wound would become infected.

"How long has this been going on?" I asked him, referring to the spasms and full body shivers I witnessed.

He only shrugged. He was trying to play it off like it was no big deal. But it was.

"Asa, this is serious. You have an infection, and it's only going to get worse." Silence. His eyes never left the road, even as another shiver racked his body.

I glanced over at Orin. He sat behind the driver's seat and had overheard the entire one-sided conversation. Tilting his head in question, his eyes asked if Asa would be fine on his own. When I shook my head in response, Orin sighed. Asa would not recover from this without some help.

"Pull over at the next rest stop." Orin's demand caused Asa to stiffen in his seat, only to shake again with the next round of shivers. "I feel like stretching my legs and taking a turn at driving. Anything is better than sitting on this unforgivable floor."

Asa let out a slow breath and turned on the blinker to signal his exit. Orin basically ordered Asa to stop driving without revealing his weakness to the others. Not that anyone would think less of him for it, but Asa wasn't one to call attention to himself.

The van pulled off the interstate and parked in front of a cluster of picnic tables. A few other cars dotted the lot, but none of them looked suspicious. An assortment of old folks walking their strange poodles or rearranging the trunk seemed to be the only excitement happening.

"All right, listen up." All eyes turned to Orin as he spoke. "We have thirty minutes to use the restrooms, stretch, and eat. It might not look dangerous now, but we don't know how far behind our enemies are. It wouldn't do to have them pull up behind us while we linger about and make sandwiches."

We nodded in understanding and the doors to the van slid open. Mahon and Leo got to work arranging our dinner while Falon, Cedric, and I headed to the restrooms. As I rounded the front of the van, I saw Orin in deep conversation with Asa. After a few more words and a pat on his good shoulder, they both turned to the spread on the picnic table.

With a tentative sniff, Asa held a thin slice of turkey by the corner and pulled a piece between his teeth. I barely stifled a giggle as his eyes grew wide and guttural coughs ripped from his throat in loud barks. Orin pounded on his back with a bemused expression.

I guess Vampires didn't like Boar's Head. I wondered if they could eat human food at all, or were they limited to the liquid diet. Before the table became completely blocked by the van, I saw Mahon pull a clear container of red fluid from a brown paper bag and hand it to Asa. Butcher's blood.

Well, that answered that question.

The restrooms were significantly cleaner than those at the grocery store, but they kept flushing before I was done. A squeal from a nearby stall told me that Falon had experienced the same problem. Some things just shouldn't be combined with technology.

Back at the picnic tables, Cedric was already munching on a sandwich. I'm sure not having water repeatedly sprayed on your ass allowed for the process to go smoother. Cedric offered us a couple premade sandwiches and motioned us over. The group was crowded around Orin as he moved his finger along a map.

"This is where we are." His finger pointed to a spot a little ways past Colombia, SC. "In another hour or so we should reach I-95. We will take that all the way down to the end of Florida. This stretch of the trip will be significantly more dangerous. Florida is home to two major Academies: one in Orlando and the other in Miami."

He used a marker to circle the locations of the other schools. We weren't that close to the one in Orlando, but we would be in the direct route to the one in Miami.

"Be prepared for less bathroom breaks and reduced sleep. From here on out we break at night and don't stop. We drive in shifts; all except you three." He pointed at us with the marker. "Your faces are too well known. We can't risk someone recognizing you." I shrugged, that seemed fair. Besides, I hated driving anyway. "I'll take the first shift. We have another thirteen hours to go, so let's get a move on."

We all piled back in the van; Leo rode shotgun, leaving Mahon and Asa to squeeze in the back with us. After a few miles passed, Asa spoke to me from his spot amongst the sleeping bags. He had stacked them behind his back and head while he tried to recline against them without putting pressure on his injured shoulder.

"Grab my medicine bag over there." He gestured with a lift of his chin. As I pulled it over he began his instructions. "You can't fully heal me with all this dead skin. It needs to be removed. Grab some clean gauze from in there and a few water bottles."

Falon scooched closer and handed me three bottles. "Now what?"

"You need to drench a few pieces and lay them over the blackened skin. Allow them to soak through." His body shook as he spoke, his muscles contracting and releasing in a ceaseless torrent of pain. "You might have to add more water over time. Then remove the wet gauze and replace it with a dry layer. As you continue to alternate, the softened dead skin should come off."

"This seems like a lengthy process," I said.

His teeth chattered as he took a deep breath. "It is."

"Well, then first I'm going to take care of the infection. It will continue to come back until we remove the dead skin, but this way you'll be comfortable."

I pulled back his shirt and gingerly placed my hand over the burn. Almost immediately, his body called out to me, begging me to relieve the pain. His skin sucked at my power like a dehydrated animal withering away in the desert, but what I needed to heal now lay below the surface.

Forcing my power past the blisters and fried skin, I focused on the boiling infection that seeped into the underlying muscle. I watched as my power bathed across the inky black like a gentle wave. It cooled and washed the muscle clean before retreating. I could still see the grimy drip of infection leak down from the wound above.

My power leapt to eradicate it, but I held it back. I would only trap myself in a never-ending cycle if I tried to heal that without first removing the source. My power was stubborn, though. The harder I pulled back, the more vicious it fought to be free.

I labored to maintain control as I brought my other hand up and wrapped it around the wrist attached to the wound. I pulled. Nothing happened. I pulled again, harder. But it felt like super glue held us together. On my last try, Falon added her strength and together we ripped my hand away with enough force to project us across the van.

The body of the vehicle rocked once, twice, and then settled.

"Not that I'm complaining, 'cause I like where you're at, but can you get your elbow out of my kidney?" Cedric hissed.

I looked up and back only to become trapped in Cedric's eyes. The jade orbs danced with mirth and his sensual smile gave a silent promise that caused the butterflies in my stomach to stir in a frenzy. I had landed on his leg, my back to his chest, his arms around my waist as if he caught me, and my elbow was indeed pressed against his lower side.

"Sorry." My voice came out rough and I hoped that no one else noticed.

But the small lift of Cedric's brow told me he had. I braced my body on my right hand as I shifted to remove the pressure on Cedric's body. What I didn't foresee was Cedric having the same idea and him adjusting at the same time.

He no longer had an elbow in his kidney, but my ass was now firmly planted in his lap, atop a hard item that I could feel through my jeans. It could have been a weapon and my heart raced with the knowledge that it might be something completely different.

Cedric's arms tightened around my waist, hands digging into my hips as a soft growl brushed across my ear. I shivered. Nope, definitely not a weapon.

"*Ahem.*" Falon's warning snapped me out of whatever spell I was under and my body stiffened.

Her smug grin practically glowed with approval. I shakenly climbed from Cedric's lap to sit beside him, scooting so an appropriate amount of space lay between us. My cheeks burned with embarrassment and I ducked my head, allowing my hair to create a screen between me and everyone's knowing gaze.

My hands still shook, but as the awkward moment faded I realized it wasn't from getting caught as my boyfriend all but felt me up, it was my body fighting to stay functional as exhaustion took over. The shaking moved from my hands and through to my limbs.

My eyes began to droop as my lids grew heaver and harder to keep open. I felt my body sway when Orin moved the truck into another lane.

"Casey, are you okay?" I could sense the warmth from Cedric's hand spread through my shoulder, and it only served to fuel the fatigue that now had my body ensnared in its grasp.

"The healing caught up to her. She just needs to rest. I'll look after Asa until she wakes up," I heard Falon reassure.

I felt my body being lowered until I rested fully horizontal on the floor of the van. As Cedric bundled a jacket beneath my head, I caught a glimpse of Falon applying the wet gauze to Asa's shoulder, a mixture of concentration and worry morphing her normally delicate features.

A gentle hand brushed the hair from my eyes before cupping my cheek.

"Rest. They will still be there when you wake." He placed a kiss to my temple. "I'll lie with you. I know how much you love using my body."

I didn't have the energy to hit him, but I promised myself that I would as soon as I could lift my arms.

Chapter 8

I t's looking good." I peeled another layer of gauze off, careful to not pull any healthy skin as I did so. "He should be all clear after another day if he continues at this rate."

About ninety-five percent of the dead flesh around Asa's shoulder was clear. I could see pink, baby soft skin just underneath, ready to come through. It had only taken a day to get to this point, and I only had to heal the infection one other time.

"Then why does he look so pale?" Falon asked, her teeth nibbling on her bottom lip in worry.

She had become quite protective over Asa. I wasn't surprised; she had handled a majority of his care. This was actually the first time I had changed the bandages myself, and it was only to give her a small break.

"Look, his brow is moist and the right side of his mouth is turned down. He only makes that face when he's in pain." Falon moved closer to Asa and rested a hand in his, offering whatever comfort she could.

I tried to hide my grin. It seemed to me that Falon felt more toward Asa than a nurse should feel for her patient. When she brushed the hair from his brow, I tacked another tally on my mental "She's Crushing on Asa" list. I mean, I would know, right?

I made a sly glance toward Cedric. He made that gesture often enough for me to catch the feeling behind it. There were other gestures too. I couldn't hold my grin back now. My mind was too overwhelmed with memories from last night.

Being trapped in a van with five other people didn't exactly make it easy to flirt or be romantic. And after the little show we put on yesterday, I was more cautious about how close I let Cedric get to me. He saw that as a challenge, however.

It was his mission to become a master of secret touches. When he moved around the van, his hand would find a way to brush across my arm or shoulder. If he reached across me to grab something, his arm would accidentally graze my chest.

Each time I caught him "accidentally" touching me, I would fake a stern frown, which only caused him to smile back with innocence. My favorite time, though, was at night when we all squeezed in the back to sleep.

The resounding lull of the van's tires created a steady hum that was almost soothing the longer you heard it. With limited space, we had to sleep pretty close together, and it's not hard to guess who slept next to me.

The wall of the van was on one side and Cedric cuddled up on the other. He needed no excuse for how close we were, and he took advantage of the lack of space by moving even closer. The entire front of his body was molded to the back of mine, his arm laid claim to my waist as he burrowed his face into the crook of my neck.

The minutes right before I fell asleep were pure magic. I was surrounded by his warmth, cradled by his touch, and completely taken over by goosebumps as he set little kisses across my neck and behind my ear.

"Hello. Casey!" Leo's waving hand caught my attention and I came out of my daydream. My eyes came back into focus only to see Cedric directly across from me, cheeks creased from grinning.

"What were you thinking about?" Leo asked, pure mischief on his face.

"Nothing," I replied, quickly looking anywhere but at Cedric.

"Are you sure? I could have sworn you were looking at Mr. Fire-Hands over there." Leo kept pushing.

"Nope, I wasn't looking at him. Just glancing out the window—up front—which he just happens to sit in front of …"

"Me thinks she doth protest too much," Leo proclaimed. I moved to punch, him but a hand grabbed mine and interlocked our fingers.

"Me too," Cedric agreed as his thumb rubbed circles across my skin. My heart fluttered at the contact, and he squeezed my hand as if he could feel it. In fact, he probably knew everything I was feeling. He caused some pretty intense emotions to rise.

"Asa!" Falon's shout of panic had the three of us scrambling to get over to her.

"What's wrong?" I asked, already reaching for my power.

Falon was rubbing her hand, the one that had previously been resting in Asa's.

"He just suddenly squeezed so tight that my bones rubbed together. At the same time his lip curled and that's when I saw them. He's in full fang mode."

Before I could speak, Asa's hands clenched and released. Leo cursed and moved to sit on top of him, holding down his arms.

"Go to the other side of the van, as far as you can. Go!"

The three of us moved away as Leo used one of his fangs to make a gash in his arm. Placing it in front of Asa's mouth, he grunted as Asa sank his teeth in.

"Orin, he's close! It must be from all the healing. He needs blood."

Up front, Orin nodded and Mahon stepped on the gas. "There should be a blood donation center close to here if I remember correctly," he said, his voice steady and calm. Glancing back at Leo, whose arm was still under siege, he added, "That should be enough to hold him over."

Placing his other hand against Asa's chin, Leo pressed down until the fangs came out of his arm. He slumped against the wall.

"That was close."

"This town is so quaint I want to puke." I grumbled.

Orin frowned. "I think it looks peaceful, charming."

That it did, but it was too peaceful, too charming. Too *perfect.* Settled just north of Savannah, this town looked like the backdrop for the Hidden Valley commercials. I bet all the kids ate their damned vegetables.

Downtown resembled something out of the Stepford Housewives. The walkways and side streets were all cobblestone and washed clean. The main strip was home to an old barber shop whose red, white, and blue striped pole sat squarely between its owners store and the artful bookseller.

Across the street a small bell chimed as fathers came out of the local diner, arms laden with carryout boxes as they made a final stop at the neighboring pharmacy before continuing home. The light posts were made of iron and equally spaced from each other. Mirroring them were the many flowerboxes that adorned the sides of the picturesque, wooden benches.

I wanted to hurl.

The feeling of wrongness just saturated the place. If we stayed too long, I might find myself baking an apple pie. My stomach churned. As we turned the corner from This-Is-Ridiculous Street and onto You've-Got-To-Be-Kidding-Me Drive, a flash of color screamed its silent protest against the cookie cutter conformity.

The small tag of graffiti was so out of place it brought a defiant smile as I recognized the sign of rebellion. On that alley wall lay the hope that the compliant children of this town would one day rise up, throw down those vegetables, and break free of their monotonous and predictable lives.

But just when I thought this town couldn't get any more stereotypical, we pulled up to a park. Through the trees, on the parallel street stood a brick building sporting a small, blood red cross out front. We were here.

Mahon killed the engine and immediately the sounds of nature hummed through the open windows.

"Mahon and I will retrieve the blood." Orin opened his door but then turned back to look at us. "Leo, stay here with Asa and keep him under control until we return. As for you three," his eyes passed over us before settling back on me, "stay in the van and out of sight. Savannah's Academy is not too far from here. It wouldn't be unheard of for there to be some guardians in town."

I watched the pair sneak off, their silhouettes melting into the shadows around the building. Night had fallen and the crickets all fought for their song to be heard. Through the window I could smell the earthy scent of flowers and moss as it floated through the van on a breeze.

The town might be a nightmare, but this park was a well of untapped beauty. I cracked open the side door and took a step out. I barely had a foot on the ground before Leo tried to be the voice of reason.

"Orin said to stay put." He hadn't moved from Asa's side. Falon sat as close as he would let her, still biting her lip until I could see teeth marks.

"Relax, Leo. I'm not going far. If I see anyone, I'll come right back." Before he could protest again, I hopped out.

"I'll go with her," came Cedric's voice before he landed beside me and slid the door closed.

I could feel my heartrate start to climb. I was alone with Cedric. For the first time since the cave, there were no spying eyes or life threatening situations to intrude upon our time together. Cedric took my hand and led us down the path toward the trickling of a fountain.

Above me the fichus trees stood ancient and proud; their reaching branches stretched to the sky. Out here it was peaceful and serene, but in my head I was losing it. My nerves were really getting to me as we continued our stroll. We'd built up a lot of tension in that van. Like a steaming tea kettle, our feelings were about to boil over.

I wasn't sure how much longer we had, but it remained between us, pulsing with anticipation. By now the van was blocked from our view by a large, foreboding tree. Spanish moss draped across its branches and the town had hung lanterns that let off a gentle glow.

Cedric tugged on my hand until I turned to face him. He took a step forward and instinctively I took one back. The corner of his lips curled as he took another step. He kept coming until I felt the bark of a tree at my shoulders.

Surprised, I tilted my head until our eyes met. He pressed his body against mine and pinned our still joined hands to the tree. With his free hand, he skimmed up my arm, along my neck, until coming to rest on my cheek. My breaths were shallow, and every time I inhaled I could taste him.

"You have a thing about backing me into trees," I taunted, my voice husky and soft.

"Maybe it's a residual habit from having to chase you down in the beginning," came his reply, his voice matching mine.

"Was it worth the wait?" I asked.

He leaned closer, his tongue coming out to wet his lower lip. His eyes finally left mine only to stare in fixation at my own lip pinned between my teeth.

"More than you know."

The hand that cupped my cheek guided my head to just the right angle a second before his lips claimed mine. They were soft and tender as they molded themselves with a confidence that only came from experience.

I caught the barest taste of cinnamon and my body craved more. My free hand came up to rest on his chest then silently moved up to the back of his neck. My fingers played with the soft strands of hair they found there, reveling in the sigh they pulled from him.

I felt a warm, tickling pressure along my bottom lip a moment before Cedric softly bit down. The shock of sensations caused me to gasp, and he quickly took full advantage. His tongue wasted no time as it swept inside and explored every hidden crevice.

When I thought I could no longer stand his teasing explorations, his tongue gently brushed against the tip of mine. A shiver danced down my spine, and when our tongues met once more, he led with a playful guidance. By now, Cedric's hand had found its way to the small of my back, and with every new sweep of his tongue he pulled me closer.

I was caught up in the thrill of the kiss. My arms kept tugging on Cedric as if they could draw him in closer, but there was no space left between us. His hand trailed from my lower back to rest on my stomach. With a gentle glide, it slid beneath my shirt and began to trace unknown shapes on my skin.

My muscles tensed beneath his touch and Cedric broke away. His soft pants tickled my cheek as he rested his forehead against mine. Lost in the afterglow of my first kiss, it took me longer than it should have to react to the snapped twig off to the right.

"What was that?" Cedric asked, leaning to peer around the tree.

My instincts flared to life as we squinted to see through the dark. Almost halfway through the park, toward the fountain, walked a young couple. They strolled arm in arm until the boy stopped to focus his hand over a low bush. Leisurely, a single stem grew and produced a perfect, red rose.

"They're witches!" I hissed.

The boy handed the flower to his companion and they continued along the path.

"We need to get back to the van," Cedric whispered.

"But they're between us. How do we get past them?" Each casual step led them closer to us.

In a perfect world we could just wait until they left, maybe even kiss again to pass the time, but if we didn't move they would see us.

Cedric grabbed my hand again and pulled me toward the path.

"Just follow my lead." He dropped his arm around my shoulders and pulled me forward. "There's no other way around them."

We kept a steady pace and pushed our heads close together like we were whispering sweet nothings. We drew up alongside the couple, but on opposing flanks of the path. I wanted nothing more than to give in to my nerves and allow my legs to carry me far from here, but moving too fast would draw their attention.

They seemed to be taking their time, and we soon outpaced them. I thought we were in the clear until I heard the shutter click of a camera. Turning, the couple stood still, phone pointed at me, as another picture was taken.

"It *is* you!" the girl exclaimed, furiously typing on her cell's keypad.

"Run!" Cedric propelled me ahead of him, his fingers a constant presence on my back.

"Hey!" The boy was chasing after us now as his girlfriend stayed behind on her phone.

We reached the van just as Orin and Mahon came running from the other side. Mahon held a red cooler tightly in his arms.

"I told you to stay in the van!" Orin shouted, fury casting shadows across his face.

We threw ourselves into the van and slammed the doors behind us just in time. The boy pounded on the side, trying to grasp the handle, but Orin peeled the car from the curb with a loud squeal from the tires. It was a race to get back on the interstate.

The fact that it was so large was our saving grace. So many destinations were accessible through I-95 that hopefully, with enough of a head start, we could stay ahead of the oncoming guardians. Orin slowed the van to match the speed limit and let out the breath he had been holding. The stiff silence was roughly punctured by his yell.

"What were you thinking?" His eyes in the rearview mirror were directed at me. "You are at the top of your race's Most Wanted list. That was extremely irresponsible of you, and you put this entire group in jeopardy."

His fingers gripped the steering wheel until I thought it would break off.

"This won't work if you don't *listen*. You're too reckless. One day, you're going to get one of us killed." It was his last statement that felt like a bullet piercing my chest.

With nothing else to add, the van lapsed once more into an uncomfortable silence. Leo glanced over once, but shook his head when I caught his gaze. He had told me to stay put and I ignored him. I watched him feed a bag of blood to Asa and guilt ripped its way through my stomach. They were right; I was selfish.

What would have happened if the other witches had gotten to the van before Orin could drive us away? Or if we were caught now? Asa was in no condition to fight, none of us really were. Not for the overwhelming force that would have descended upon us.

The van rocked down the interstate in a rigid silence, one I had caused. Cedric held onto my hand, but even his support couldn't erase the shame that built in my heart.

Chapter 9

The tension in the van was palpable; so thick that it felt like another physical presence was with us. The only thing worse was the silence, punctuated only by the sound of the van rocking when Orin swiftly changed lanes.

No one would look at me, except Orin, and that was only to glare at me through the rearview mirror as he berated me for my lack of judgement. He gave an indignant snort and continued.

"I can't believe you ignored a direct order. Do you not care for the others in this group?"

His harsh words twisted the thorn that was already needling my heart. The guilt ate at me as I glanced over to where Asa lay. He winced as Falon tenderly pulled dead skin from his shoulder. His wound was healing nicely, and it wouldn't be long before he was well enough for me to fully heal him.

I felt the heated burn of Orin's eyes, and my guilt intensified. What would have happened to Asa if Orin and Mahon hadn't made it back in time? What if it wasn't two students that found us but full-fledged guardians?

I put Asa's life and that of everyone else in danger; I really was selfish. I felt Cedric weave his fingers between mine before giving my hand a sympathetic squeeze. I squeezed back and gave him a half smile. At least one good thing came out of all of this, I finally had my first kiss.

Up front I heard Orin mutter a curse, and this time it wasn't directed at me. I watched, my heart racing, as he covertly glanced out his side window. Whatever he saw caused him to curse again and grip the steering wheel with both hands.

His knuckles were turning white and Leo began to fidget in the passenger seat next to him. Both of their eyes were glued to the road ahead as the van pedaled along at a safe and steady sixty-five miles per hour.

"What's going on?" Cedric asked as he tried to stick his head up front. Mahon stopped him with a firm hand on his shoulder.

"We're being followed," he told us, his expression grave. How had the guardians caught up so fast?

"They're pulling alongside us," Orin called out. "Keep your heads down. They don't know what I look like; they should pass us by."

I held my breath and waited. Seconds passed and Orin's grip on the wheel relaxed, his back muscles following suit until he was once again sitting at ease. I released the death grip I had on Cedric's hand and let out a slow breath. I listened to the van's blinker turn on as Orin signaled our move into the right lane.

"I think we're in the clear." But as the last word flew from Orin's lips, my body was thrown forward until the plastic of the passenger seat stopped my momentum.

The screeching tires mingled with our cries of shock until the van jolted to a stop just inches from the car in front of us. I could hear the squeal of other tires around us as they locked in their desperate attempt to achieve a last minute full stop.

Through the clamor, one other sound could be heard, that of a high powered and accelerating engine. Orin was fervently trying to change gears, but before he could, something collided with the side of the van and sent us into a spiral.

I felt arms grab me around my waist and pull me in tight just before we slammed into the vehicle's wall. Even with Cedric's attempt at cushioning me, the air was knocked from my lungs. The van continued to spin, and with it, we were repeatedly projected from one side of the van to the other.

Cedric tried to take the brunt of it, but I still hit my flailing legs and arms as the others tried in vain to hold on to something. At one point, I viewed the world at a tilt when the van when up on two tires, but Mahon's quick thinking had us back on four wheels after he threw his weight against the propulsion of the van.

We finally came to a stop against the guardrail; the metal of our front bumper crunched inward with an amplified sound similar to nails on a chalkboard. My ears were ringing, but I could faintly hear someone shouting.

I couldn't tell who was speaking or what they were saying. Letting out a pained groan, I pushed up onto my elbow. I hurt all over, my head was throbbing in time with my frantic pulse, and I could feel a trickle of blood stream down the side of my face.

"Casey! Look at me!" Cedric pulled me up until our faces were level.

The quick change in orientation had my head spinning all over again. I felt warm hands cup my cheeks, grounding me, and I looked around until my eyes focused on Cedric.

"Hey. Are you okay?" His eyes instinctively roamed over my body, pausing and making note of each wound he saw. My hearing was returning, albeit slowly. I could make out what he was saying, but it was muffled, as if my ears were stuffed with cotton.

"Is anything broken? You don't *feel* like you're in extreme pain, but all your other emotions are clouding my ability to read you." It took a moment for his question to sink in, and with each second of my silence his eyes grew wider.

I gently shook my head, and he let out a sigh of relief. Glancing around the back of the van, I took stock of the group's condition. Orin and Leo were safe up front having been saved by their seatbelts, Asa was in obvious pain from his shoulder, but showed no other injury as he moved to help Falon.

Falon herself showed no more damage than Cedric or I had sustained and Mahon showed none at all. *Lucky ass Vampires*.

From outside came the repeated slams of car doors and distressed bystanders conversing about the next course of action. Someone shouted to call 911 and that got Orin's attention. We couldn't wait around for the human police, and the longer we stayed put the higher the risk of capture from the guardians who caused this mess.

"Everyone hold on to something." Orin warned as he shifted gears and roughly pulled the van away from the jagged metal of the guardrail.

Our movement provoked outrage from the gawking bystanders and hands rained down on the sides of the van as people tried to get us to stop. I watched out the front windshield as people threw themselves out of the way.

The approaching guardians ran for their own vehicles, but Orin was already stepping on the gas. Being the only moving car gave the illusion that we were flying by at a far greater speed than we actually were. We fought our way through the mass of parked cars and sped further along to merge with the traffic up ahead.

"Dammit!" Orin slammed his hand repeatedly against the steering wheel. "We've got to ditch the van. That's going to cost us precious time."

"How did they know it was us?" I asked. I thought they didn't know what he looked like, but obviously we figured something wrong.

"They must have gotten a description of the van from those teen witches in the park." Our eyes met briefly in the rearview mirror before Orin focused back on the road. Guilt once again surged through me. This was all my fault.

"We've got company," Leo said, looking out his window.

I scrambled to peak out the back and sure enough, a car was weaving its way through the traffic to catch up to us. Orin sped up and jerked the wheel to the right, making a swift exit from the interstate.

We cut off the car next to us and the sound of its horn followed us down the exit ramp. The ramp ended at a three way stop on an old, two lane back road. Turning left, we passed multiple farm houses that dotted the landscape.

Cornfields swayed in the drift we left in our wake, and through the field, glimpses of porch lights and spot lights on barns gave me an idea. Scanning the horizon, I spotted a dilapidated brown structure off to the right and motioned for Orin to make his way to it.

"We can hide the van in that old barn until the guardians give up in this area," I suggested.

Orin turned the van onto a gravel road heading toward a grove of ancient trees. The full moon had no clouds to hide it and its beams reflected off the limestone street below us. A broken sign stood defiantly to the side and announced that we were pulling onto the property of an old plantation.

The further down the road we got, the thicker the trees became. They soon blocked out the light from the moon with their interlocking branches. Ahead of us, the decrepit barn offered its support and protection, but behind us, two beams of light made an obvious turn onto our road.

The guardians were still in pursuit. We would have to take care of them before they brought others. Tires spun as Orin whipped the van behind the barn. Putting it in park, he killed the engine and turned in his chair to face us.

"We're going to have to make a stand. Find as many of the weapons as you can in this mess and suit up."

"I can buy you some time," Falon stated as she moved toward the back doors.

I protested. "Fal, we don't know how many followed us. You could be overpowered in seconds."

But she stood firm in her decision. "I can't fight like you all. Let me help in the only way that I can."

She hopped out and ran around the side of the building. I clambered to follow, there was no way I was going to let her do this alone.

"Casey!" Cedric jumped after me, but Orin grabbed his arm. "Cool it, lover boy. I need you here."

Their voices faded as I found myself in front of the barn. I stood next to Falon just as a car parked and its doors opened.

"Whatever you're going to do, go for it," I whispered and Falon raised her hand, palm out, in the direction of the nearest bunch of trees.

The leaves and branches swayed toward her, but nothing happened. Three guards had fully emerged from their car and I watched them step closer. Falon scrunched her brow and tried again, but still nothing.

"What's wrong?" I asked as she grabbed my hand.

"I think I need to touch the tree," she replied as she pulled me along with her.

Placing her hand on the trunk of the tree, she tried again, but the only movement was the guardians inching steadily closer. One of them stepped out in front and lifted both his hands in a sign of peace.

"We can make this easy," he said. "You're both obviously injured, tired. We can talk it out and get you both some help. You just have to cooperate with us."

I snorted and moved into a defensive stance in front of Falon as she continued to coax her power into submission.

"If you getting back in your shitty car and driving away is cooperation, then I'm all for it." My eyes tracked their every movement as they continued to creep closer.

The closest guardian sneered at me just as he stepped into my strike zone. Wrong move. I spun on my heel, crouched low, and used my other foot to sweep the legs out from the unsuspecting guard. Not giving them a chance to recover, I landed a double kick combination to the stomach and head of the guard on my right.

A strong tug on my arm threw me off balance as I spun to face the third guardian. His fist landed in my gut a moment before his foot hooked behind mine. He threw me to the ground and moved to stomp on my stomach, but I rolled.

The guard I first knocked down was on his way back up, so I jammed my knee into his face as I crawled over him. With one guard knocked out, I only had to worry about the last two. But as I stood, they took positions on either side of me. The element of surprise was gone; they were organized now.

"Any time now, Falon," I yelled over my shoulder as I once again positioned myself between her and the oncoming threat.

I didn't think I could take down two fully trained guards *and* keep one from reaching her at the same time. I was good, but not Xena good. I clenched my right fist and planned to go after the one to the left first, but before I could strike, he screamed.

The roots of the tree burst from the earth like a bunch of vicious snakes chasing their prey. One guard set a ring of fire around them, but the roots just leapt over the flames to wrap around their waists.

Movement to my right drew my attention just in time to see five figures step from the bark of the trees. They were women and extraordinarily beautiful. Their willowy frames seemed to glide as they stepped into the ring of dying flames.

Their hair ranged in color from tawny, golden brown to a deep chestnut, and all had hair reaching down to their waist that was decorated with flowers and bright leaves. They were wood sprites.

They commanded the roots to tighten around their prey like constrictors. The guard's faces turned a blotchy red and then blue as the life was literally squeezed out of them. I couldn't bear to watch.

I turned my back on the dying men and moved to help Falon stand. She was sweating, shaking, and almost too weak to stay on her own feet. The sprites approached us, one stepping out in front of the rest. She was the leader it seemed, although there was no physical marker to note the difference.

As she took in Falon's appearance, she looked confused.

"Why are you ill, sister?" she asked.

Falon remained silent as she regarded the sprite.

"Something is wrong," I blurted out. "Her power is normally troublesome, but it has never *not* worked."

Before I could blink, the sprite reached out to touch Falon's forehead. Falon's hair flashed white, floated into the air like static, and her eyes turned a deeper cobalt. It lasted no more than the length of a breath, and when it was done Falon looked a little better. But the sprite was bent over and panting, her sisters moved to surround her with support. She looked up at Falon, confusion and alarm flashing across her face.

"I've heard of you, *inion banrion.*"

At the foreign term, Falon's eyes hardened and she took a step forward. Her stature changed in an instant from a weak girl to a demanding presence.

"We appreciate the rescue, but if you are seeking conferment, we can offer nothing but our thanks."

The sprite tilted her head, her hair fell across her shoulder and the action sounded like rustling leaves.

"There is one other you can offer as fair trade."

Say what?

Falon stared back a moment longer before nodding in agreement. "It's done. When you wish to collect, you know how to contact me."

What just happened here? Falon pulled on my arm to leave, but the sprite spoke again.

"I did not help you in hope of gaining a boon. It is an act of war for their kind to attack one of ours." She gestured to the dead guards behind her.

She thought the witches were just outright attacking Falon, a Fae, which technically was against the treaties. What she didn't know was that we were considered traitors which made us fair game. I couldn't allow a war to start over this. I stopped Falon from pulling us away and turned back toward the sprite.

"It's more complicated than that. They were actually after me."

The sprite barely glanced my way before looking back to Falon. "Be that as it may, I could not allow them to harm you, *inion banrion.* You are needed back at Court. The Mad Queen—"

"Do not speak to me of her. My place is here now." Falon's expression dared the sprite to argue.

She inclined her head in reply and motioned for the other sprites to depart. "You do not wish to see what we all know to be true. In time you will."

She reached around her neck and removed a thin string of vine. It was a mixture of fresh green and decaying brown, blurred together to create something both living and not. Hung from the middle was a small talisman—an amber stone no bigger than a penny—wrapped in leaves and tied with more vine. She handed it to Falon.

"This should help you the next time you call on your power. It is only a temporary fix; there is more to your … affliction … than you know. When you are ready, return to the land of your birth for the answers you seek."

And with that, she took the final steps back toward her tree and disappeared into the bark. I turned to Falon.

"What the hell was all that?"

Chapter 10

The crimson ichor gradually streamed down my arms and along my fingers, before dribbling from the tips into the water bucket below. There, the blood drops bloomed and began to fan out like a feather being drug through the surface of a puddle, each strand curling at the end before dissolving.

The more of the guard's blood I rinsed off, the darker the bucket became until I could no longer see clear through to the bottom. Some of the blood was mine, but a majority of it was not, and I was thankful to have found this old water pump out behind the barn.

There was nothing I could do to the splotches that already stained my clothes, but I wanted it off of my skin—now. I scrubbed mercilessly with my nails until some of the water splashed on my face. When I went to wipe it away, my hand came back red.

Images of a young guard being squeezed by a tree trunk caused me to flinch as I could almost feel his blood spray across my cheek once again.

I scrubbed harder.

Knowing I had cleaned as much as was possible with a rusted water picket and my own two hands, I dumped the bucket over and watched the contaminated water seep into the grass. I then began to refill the bucket for Falon to use after me.

Following the sprite's departure, Falon refused to answer my questions. Instead, she strolled back here behind the barn and told Orin that someone would have to do something with the bodies. The five men, stuck in the process of pushing the van into the decrepit building, all froze in their awkward stances and turned to stare.

Having just left front row seats to a mini massacre, both Falon and I sported tell-tale splatters that could only come from being in close proximity to a gruesome event. Orin opened his mouth to ask, but I shook my head. There would be time for explanations after we hid this giant hunk of dented evidence.

Inside, the van was parked in the center aisle, stall doors open on either side, and hidden under a dusty tarp. Our packs and supplies were neatly lined against the back wall and I made my way over to mine, nodding to Falon as I did so.

She turned and disappeared out the back door, and sounds of rusted metal soon squeaked through the aged wooden walls. I gathered a fresh pair of jeans, a top, and underthings into my arms and turned a corner to search out a private spot to change.

Pushing against a dingy door that hung loosely on its final hinge, I found myself in what must have been an office. All that remained now were some empty shelves on the wall, a desk, and a small pile of wood that looked like it had been a chair in its former life.

This place would do fine.

I quickly changed out of my torn and bloody clothes, relieved to finally be free of them. It wasn't so much that they had blood on them, or even that the blood wasn't all mine, it was how it got there.

Sprites.

We had been saved by sprites. Although, as more time passed I wondered if saved was the word I should use. I knew we would pay for their deeds one day, long after the memory of them faded to a dull blink in our minds.

I was still trying to make sense out of all that had happened. *Why* did they intervene? They mentioned it was because of Falon, but who was she to them? Movement outside the window brought me over to stare out the soiled and grimy panes.

Leo held one of the bodies under the arms and was dragging it over to join the others in a pile next to their car. The guards looked anything but peaceful in their death, their faces permanently frozen in masks of horror and pain.

Blood oozed to the ground beneath their distorted bodies as the final product of the sprite's ferocity burned itself into my memory. I would not have known these bodies for who they were. Their torsos were deformed and compressed into bits of flattened and twisted flesh.

Under the command of the sprites, the trees had squeezed these men until they popped. Literally. I turned my head, sick to my stomach, as Leo bathed all that remained of the guards in acid.

"Casey?" Orin knocked on the door before peering inside. "There you are. We were wondering where you had wandered off to." He opened the door fully and stepped in.

"Gee, well you found me," I lashed out with barely contained sarcasm.

He frowned and I watched his gaze flick to the window behind me. His eyes then flashed with understanding before settling back on me.

"You know, their deaths weren't your fault. You didn't order those sprites to do anything."

"She told you about them then?" Did Falon tell him *why* they helped?

Orin nodded. "I'm still not sure why they stepped in. The Fair Folk, especially those from the oldest of lore, aren't known for interfering with the other races."

I opened my mouth, but nothing came out. Should I tell him about the boon? About how they addressed Falon?

Sister. Inion banrion. I was missing a piece of the puzzle, and I knew only Falon would know where to find it. Orin had continued on, not noticing my internal dilemma.

"But that's a problem for another time. Right now, I want you to know that this was not your doing." His eyes bore into mine as if he could just imprint how he felt upon me.

But I knew better. This *was* my fault. I was the one they were initially after. I was the one who caught their attention in that park.

"I appreciate the gesture, but you and I both know that this *is* on me. I should have listened to you, back in the park, and stayed in the van. If those witches hadn't spotted me then we would still be cruising along the interstate right now."

Guilt forced the corners of Orin's mouth to turn down. Out of the entire group, he had come down on me the hardest. A rift had grown between us, shattering the fragile relationship we had forged out in those mountains back home.

I had begun to look up to him, to trust him. And his disappointment had lashed into me harder than any man-made weapon. He sighed and pulled me in for a hug. It was unexpected and my arms remained stiff at my sides.

But Orin only held me tighter, until my muscles went limp and my hands found themselves clutching the back of his shirt. I could feel tears soaking the fabric in the front and his chest muffled my sobs.

"I am sorry, Casey. I should not have treated you as I did. You did nothing more that act like the teenager we all forget you are." His hand began to idly stroke my hair. "But no matter what was said before, this is not on you."

He pulled me back from him until he had looked me in the eye once more. "I want to hear you say it."

"This is not my fault," I let out, followed with a few more sniffles.

He smiled at me. "You are a warrior, Casey. But you are also a teenage girl, with the right to make mistakes and mess up. I'll try to remember that from now on if you will."

I gave him a blubbering smile and agreed. The relief I felt from his forgiveness was surprising. I didn't realize how forlorn I was feeling until now. At some point amidst all this madness, Orin had come to mean something to me.

They all had. I wasn't sure where they would all come to fit in my life, but I knew without them I would be lost.

I sat on an antique, wooden crate and watched everyone argue over what our next steps should be. The main debate was between leaving now on foot or risk staying put and finding another vehicle.

"We need a new ride, that's the obvious part. They know what this van looks like now," Leo declared, patting the back door of our tarp covered ride.

"We can find a new one once we leave this area. It's not safe to stay here," Mahon disputed.

Back and forth they went. With no sign of an approaching conclusion, I allowed my eyes to wander and evaluate our temporary hideout. It was old. That was the first thing I noticed; that and that it was untouched. The early morning sun beamed in from the loft windows and struck the cobwebs in such a way that they shimmered like a metallic silk.

Dust particles hung suspended and uninterrupted, dancing anywhere the light touched. It was obvious that the barn hadn't seen much use, or any use, for quite some time. Possibly since the plantation was still active.

The front entrance was the cleanest, if you could call it that, but after a few feet the cobwebs took over. The rich, tawny wood was hidden beneath a layer of dappled soot. Forgotten tools hung on the walls, rusted and lifeless. Mold-riddled hay and manure were still scattered in some of the stalls and only added to the stale, musty scent that clung to this place.

Old saddles, crops, and riding equipment told of the history and purpose. A newer facility closer to the tourists most likely put this old, spider's haven out of business. This barn was probably replaced for something larger and more high tech; a place where the wealthy could board their horses and take a ride through a land lost to time.

I hopped off the crate and walked toward where the rest of the group mingled; I had an idea.

"What if there are cars close by? Can we risk staying here for a few more hours?" I asked.

"That all depends," Orin answered. "Explain."

I took in a deep breath and let it out as I gathered my thoughts.

"According to a sign I saw as we turned in, and from what I can see around us, this property is part of a plantation. This barn is obviously not in use anymore. But there could be another part of the property that is and that might have other vehicles."

It was quiet as the others thought over my suggestion. It was a solid plan, *if* we could find another car and *if* we could afford to stay put long enough to search for one. But those were big if's. A few more minutes of heavy silence passed before Orin spoke.

His first question was addressed to Leo.

"You burned all evidence of those guards that followed us, correct?"

Leo nodded. "Some of the melted framework of their car remains, but it's well hidden."

"Then it goes to reason that we should have some time before anyone looks here. If the enemy hasn't come knocking on the door yet, they won't for a bit more," Orin concluded.

So we were safe for the time being. I could already breathe a little easier.

"Leo, Mahon, and I will search for another vehicle. While we are gone, I want the supplies separated into only what is absolutely needed in case we have to leave on foot. Casey," he turned to face me directly, "I need Asa healed and back at full function. Is he ready?"

Falon had been working real hard on his shoulder, and if I could get a few hours rest after, I could heal him now.

"I can do it," I promised.

"Then we have our plan. It begins now." The three Vamps left out the side door and easily blended with the foliage outside.

I glanced at the others. "Let's get Asa situated somewhere comfortable. Ced, can you clear a place for me to rest after, please?"

Cedric kissed my cheek in reply and set out to do as I asked. Falon settled Asa down in one of the empty stalls. The hay in here was clean, but stale. I knelt beside him and got to work. Gently dousing the wound with some water, I peeled away the gauze that protected his shoulder.

All the black skin had been painstakingly removed and only the red, blistered center was left. It took but seconds for my power to react to the revealed flesh and I rested my hand on his skin. Cold currents left my chest and traveled down my arm to settle in my hand.

My mind's eye could see inside Asa's body, and I was pleased to note that the infection was long gone. Not having to burn away black goo helped the process along exponentially. Having no fear of my power draining me dry with what was left of this wound, my mind began to wander.

"Falon, tell me what happened out there. What the hell was with those sprites?"

It was tough moving my head, but I managed to tilt it enough to catch Falon's ghostly pallor. *So she wasn't oblivious to their threat.* I had wondered. She lifted her shoulder in a shrug.

"They're sprites. Who can know why they do things?" She was trying to brush this off, but I wasn't having it.

"Don't bullshit me," I replied with a soft snarl. "I fought for you. I was out there, by your side, risking my life for you. I deserve to know, dammit." I caught her eye and held it. I refused to let this go.

"She was talking about a Mad Queen? And she seemed to know more about your power glitch than even you. And she called you—"

"I get it!" Falon shouted, but said nothing else.

Her silence seemed to stretch on forever; the only sounds being my soft breaths and the muffled sounds of Cedric at the other end of the barn. But finally, just when I thought I was going to have to ask again, she spoke.

"My family is very high up in the Court and with that status comes responsibility. There are those that think I have sway over the ones in charge and that I can make a difference. They think that just because my mother is of a higher class that I can do something about the *situation* with our ruling queen."

She began to fidget with the talisman that hung from her neck. The amber of the stone shimmered and the sunlight that peeked through the cracks in the wall reflected onto the skin of her hand.

"That's part of the reason why I left and came to the Academy. I was tired of people expecting something from me that I couldn't provide. That, and my power." She released the talisman and stood. She took a few steps away and turned back. "I can't help them, no matter what they think. But I *can* help you, and that's all I'm concerned with.

I grunted in acceptance of her answer. I knew there was more to it, but I wasn't going to push for it right now.

"What about that boon? How much shit are we going to be in for that?"

Asa let out a strangled hiss. "You agreed to a *boon*?" He glared at Falon, and I was surprised to see her blush and avoid his gaze. "That was unwise. Agreeing to a boon is a binding magical contract." His voice softened with a hint of fear. "She could ask you for anything, and you would have to accede."

"I know how a boon works," Falon whispered.

77

Asa's wound accepted a final wave of my power before the chills left my body and I was released. I only felt a little lightheaded, but I decided to wait for Cedric to come back rather than go in search of him.

Asa gracefully stood from the hay and nudged Falon to exit the stall. "You will tell me more of this boon and what was done for you to promise such a thing."

Falon left without argument, and Asa, with a firm dip of his chin, assured that he would get some answers. The hay caused my arms to itch, but I ignored it as I stretched out on my back.

"Okay, I found an area up in—" Cedric swung through the open door and came to a stop. "This spot looks nice."

I laughed. "It comes with a built-in mattress. And bed bugs—real high end this place."

Cedric claimed the space beside me and pulled me close. "Only the fancy places have bugs, you spoiled female."

I listened to our mingled laughter and let it soothe me to sleep.

Chapter 11

The last of the sun's rays fought hard to shine through our new van's tinted windows. I could feel it's warmth on my arm, but the glass acted like a giant pair of aviators. Looking out, everything was shadowed in a golden-brown hue; sharpening the details of the land around us. If one were to try and look in, the silky black material would reflect their image back at them.

This type of tint was illegal, I was sure, but it served our needs. The seven of us were squeezed into an extremely new and ridiculously shiny, seal gray Dodge Caravan. The back window had an absurd family of stick figures being terrorized and eaten by a T-rex and the radio antenna had a decapitated Mickey Mouse as a topper.

What kind of family did this van belong to?

From the inside, it wasn't so bad; the minivan could comfortably seat all of us as well as our supplies. Asa drove with Leo up front to keep him company, Orin and Mahon sat in the rear captain seats, leaving me, Falon, and Cedric in the last row. It wasn't as roomy as our previous vehicle, but it was better than walking.

I gazed out the window at the blurred trees; the speed we were going making it impossible to tell where one ended and another began.

"Won't the owner of this car report it stolen?" I asked Leo.

He turned down the radio and regarded me from the rearview mirror.

"We've got time, maybe another day or so before there could be a problem. And by then we will be well hidden."

I scrunched my face in confusion as I watched the moon's light settle over the interstate ahead of us. Shivering, as my body took notice of the chilly atmosphere, I wrapped my jacket around my shoulders. How could we still have time? The clock on the dash said it was after eight, we had wasted an entire day.

The three Vamps pulled up to our hideaway at mid-morning, before the mist was chased away by the sun. Within minutes we had the supplies packed away and all evidence of our overnight stay eradicated. And then we waited.

And waited. Mahon and Leo spent most of the time under the hood or beneath the belly of the van. While with every rustle of the trees, I thought a horde of law enforcement was about to descend upon us. Until finally, as the sun once again began its descent, we piled into the van and effortlessly drove away.

"I don't understand. We wasted an entire day that we could have spent driving." Wouldn't the police be looking for our car by now?

"It wasn't wasted. There were steps that needed to be taken; well thought out steps," Orin said. "For one thing, the less people that see a gray van leaving the property, the better. It will be as if the vehicle disappeared."

I tilted my head in thought. "So we had to wait until the end of the day because there would be less people on the property and dimmed light?"

Orin nodded in encouragement. "Now you're getting it."

"But wouldn't that give the tourist time to notice that their car was missing? And call the cops?" Cedric asked.

"Well, that's why we didn't take a tourist's car," Leo commented with a sly grin. "We only shopped in the employee lot."

I smiled as it all began to click. "So we waited until it was late in the day when we wouldn't be seen and we picked a car that wouldn't be reported until the property closed, giving us more time to run."

That made sense. Maybe they didn't just wing this.

"What about GPS tracking? Don't all the new cars have that technology?" Falon voiced. That was a solid point. But they were shaking their heads again. Apparently, they had planned for that too.

"That's another reason we couldn't leave right away," Mahon added from behind Leo's seat. "Leo and I spent the day going over this van from nose to tail. We disconnected the GPS transmitter *and* unplugged all the connectors to the OnStar box."

"That transmitter was a bitch to find too." Leo grumbled.

"So we're safe then?" I questioned. But once again, their heads shook.

"Not completely," Orin stated. "If a cop were to pull us over and run our plates, they would find this van reported stolen. Our hope is that we can be out of the state and at our location before the alert has spread."

I couldn't help it, every car that pulled behind us from that moment on made me nervous. In the dark I couldn't tell if it was a cop or civilian whose lights shined through our back window. The human police wouldn't have bothered me in the past.

Due to the Academy's extensive connections, any situation that occurred involving the human police was easily swept under the rug and taken care of. The Council that ran our world had deep connections in all aspects of the human government and in all positions that would be beneficial to maintain our hidden status.

But what was once a benefit was now a major handicap. A stolen vehicle might not be high on the Council's watch list, but I would bet all I had that our descriptions were well known to the human police as well.

Maybe not every officer, but enough for us to get caught if we weren't careful.

"Why don't you relax and get some rest while you can. We have about four hours until we reach Orlando and eight to Miami. Take advantage of this time," Orin advised.

I settled into my seat, wiggling around until I found a comfortable position. Using my jacket as a blanket, I rested my head on Cedric's shoulder and he pulled me closer. Falon curled up under her own jacket against the opposite window.

The van rode steadily along and the sound of the tires pulled at my heavy lids, but I couldn't sleep. I remained wide awake, long after Cedric's measured breathing told me he was slumbering. I watched the mile markers count down and prayed to Luthos that we would get to where we were going with no more incidents.

My chin slipped from its rested position on my hand as my entire body was thrust forward. Pain throbbed at my temple and spread further down the side of my face as my head cracked against the window hard enough to cause lights to flash behind my lids. I began to rub the sore spot on instinct as I glared through the glass at what caused our abrupt halt.

Traffic. The interstate resembled a slow draining parking lot after a concert. The cars were bumper to bumper with horns sounding off repeatedly as the drivers gave in to their frustration. A programmed sign off to the side warned of a closed lane. It bade all drivers to merge left, and it was as if the idiots around us suddenly forgot how to drive.

I didn't know what it was about traffic signals that caused people's minds to go to mush. Weren't these signs supposed to make driving easier?

I watched as an impatient asshole continued to inch forward as he tried to force his way in ahead of us.

Asa slammed on his breaks with a curse. The car behind us honked. Idiots.

To my right, the trees were illuminated by an alternating blue and red light. Shadows of the other cars were projected onto the leaves, adding distorted shapes that only made them look more frightening.

As our line moved forward, a parked cop car was revealed. It was pulled off to the right and completely blocking the right lane. The engine was off, but the lights above were flashing with an intensity that was almost blinding. The further along we traveled, the more cop cars were revealed and the brighter the lights became.

I counted a total of five that I could see parked on either side of the interstate, blocking the right and left lanes until all that remained open was the center. Rows of orange traffic cones were set up along the dashed white lines and spaced equally apart. The reflective bands around the bodies danced in the headlights of the multiple cars passing them.

"Was there an accident?" I asked, the amount of cops making me nervous. This would be just our luck, thinking we were in the clear until fate decided to screw us over for fun.

"I'm not sure what's going on. I can't see anything yet," Leo replied. He had rolled his window down and leaned out to see around the truck in front of us. Others in the cars around us were doing the same.

"I don't like the feel of this," Orin murmured. He turned in his chair to face the three of us in the last row. "Hide yourselves."

It took us a few seconds before we moved. Where did three people hide in a minivan? Falon had hopped over the back seat and began to move our supplies around until she could sit on the floor. Claiming the back right corner, she waved me over to join her.

With a quick glance over the back, I could tell that it wouldn't hide all three of us. But Cedric was already tucking himself onto the floorboards between the back rows. I grabbed our jackets from the seat and covered him. Orin and Mahon passed me their bags from up front to add to his camouflage.

When I was absolutely sure that he was as hidden as I could make him, I climbed over the back seats and tucked myself into the left corner. We pulled our supplies and luggage over us until we were concealed beneath a mountain of junk. From inside my little pocket, small beams of light filtered through the cracks between the sleeping bags and food supplies that hid both me and Falon.

A backpack sat on top of my head and blocked me from the side window. I left a small corner free so that I could peer out, but the window was so deeply tinted that I shouldn't be seen. I could duck further if I had to.

We were moving at a steady pace, maybe five miles an hour. Every now and then we would come to a complete stop and my heart would freeze. I'd hold my breath and pray that this wasn't going to be the moment we were caught.

"What's happening up there?" I hissed. I was beginning to worry that it wasn't an accident after all, but a traffic stop. If this was a roadblock, our chances of making it through undetected were almost zero. If they asked for Asa's license and registration, we would have nothing to show.

"They are searching cars." Leo's message was passed down to me.

My gut churned. We were done; it was over. I just knew it. This was a roadblock that the human police set up to capture us. They were enlisted by the Academy and probably had no idea who we actually were or what we were wanted for.

Undoubtedly, they received a notice for a person or persons of interest that were making their way through the state and all outlets were enlisted to help. How far were we from the front? Was there room for us to make a break for it?

Each fruitless plan that popped into my mind brought a second of hope before I threw it away. We couldn't outrun the cops in a *minivan*. And what were the odds that we could escape and find another vehicle to replace this one?

"They are only stopping white vehicles." Asa's voice was quiet, coming from the front. But he spoke a little louder so we could hear him in the back. "Specifically vans. It's safe to say that our description made it out of Georgia."

It was a good thing we exchanged cars. Our vehicle slowed to a stop again, and I knew we were closer to the front because I could hear voices. I peeked out my corner of the window and saw traces of white lights sweep back and forth.

Falon's hand snuck through the cracks in the bags and grabbed my own. I squeezed, to reassure her or express my own nervousness, I wasn't sure. The officers held their flashlights by their faces as they scanned each vehicle that pulled up. They took extra time to search the white vans that came through.

As if he could feel my eyes on him, a trooper left the car in front of us and made a beeline for our van. I ducked further into my corner and pulled a bag to cover my entire head. Squeezing Falon's hand even tighter, I tried to signal for her to remain completely still.

A harsh ray of light made a sweep through the back window and I knew that the cop had the flashlight pressed directly against the glass as he tried to see through the thick tint. I could almost imagine him squinting and then frowning when he failed.

"Nobody move. He's approaching my window," Mahon all but whispered. The van was so silent I was able to hear him anyway.

The shouts from outside as the cops spoke to one another faded into the background. The only sound I heard was my own harsh breaths and the beating of my panicked heart. Three solid taps on the window made me jump. The sleeping bag over my head slid down the pile and I had no time to replace it before I heard the window roll down.

"Is there a problem officer?" Mahon asked, his voice cool and calm.

Slowly, I turned my head so I could see through the space between the seat and the wall of the van. Mahon's window was halfway down, any lower and Cedric's hair might be noticeable. I prayed to Luthos that the cop wouldn't find it suspicious.

"Evening folks. Sorry about the delay, but we've had a report of a band of criminals moving through the area."

Leo sounded fairly believable as he feigned surprise. "Are we in danger? Should we be on the lookout for anything specific?"

Happy to provide advice, which I was sure was something he wasn't asked for often, the officer puffed his chest and pulled his sagging belt over his jiggling gut.

Pulling himself up real tall, hoping to seem more important, he spoke. "Well the group we know of consists of three delinquent teens, two brunettes and one blonde. But it is thought that they could be in the presence of three to four accomplices. They are all traveling in a white utility van. And it is believed that they could be traveling in this direction, possibly on their way further into Florida."

"Oh my. Well, if we see anyone matching that eloquent description we shall be sure to call the authorities," Asa promised from up front.

I watched the cop puff up once again as he received Asa's well placed compliment. A shout from outside caused the officer to look to his right before waving in reply. Turning back to our open window, he gave a tip of his hat.

"I appreciate your cooperation, folks. Keep an eye out for trouble and have safe travels to your destination."

Mahon rolled his window up with a nod just as our van pulled forward. We let out a collective sigh of relief when the flashing lights could only be seen from the rear window. The three of us kept to our hiding places until Asa could bring the van up to speed with normal traffic and we put some distance between us and the roadblock.

Seated in the back row once again, no one spoke. I watched cars pass alongside us and tried to make my heart stop screaming. Up ahead, a rectangular sign sat high in the air with bright spotlights illuminating its message.

Beautifully engraved words welcomed visitors to the most magical place on earth and a pair of black mouse ears sat on the corner of the billboard.

Orin's voice was gruff, from either relief or anxiety. "Say hello to Orlando everyone. Only four more hours to go."

Chapter 12

I don't understand why we can't stop in for just a *few* hours. It's not like they'd think to look for us there." Falon continued to pout in her seat.

I could hear her mumble under her breath and I laughed. We left Orlando behind long ago. The clock on the dash told me it was past four in the morning; we had been driving all night. Leo had switched to the driver's seat not long after the roadblock, and since then I had been keeping myself entertained by watching Asa sneak glances at Falon through the mirror.

He was doing it now. He had on an amused smile as he listened to Falon complain. She wanted to go to Disney. It didn't matter that we were now four hours away or that we would risk imprisonment if we were caught waiting in line for Space Mountain.

She thought we deserved at least one "magical" experience out of all of this; never mind all the power battles we had already engaged in.

"Let it go, short shit. Mickey isn't ready to handle you anyway."

Falon chucked her water bottle at Mahon's head as he snickered. "Stop calling me that, asshole!"

The rest of us continued to laugh as she growled in frustration. Maybe it was her height or maybe it was the way childlike glee tended to pour off her in waves, but something drew the Vamps to her like elder brothers tormenting their kid sister.

She had that effect on people.

Our laughter faded to silence, and I once again found myself staring out the window. The landscape was drastically different than what I was used to. The steep mountains and rolling valleys gave way to flatlands and strips of asphalt.

I had never seen the world so one dimensional. When I looked out the windshield, my only view was of an endless road with woods on either side. It was the same when I looked out the back. There were no curves, no turns, no dips or inclines to tackle.

I felt exposed out here, even with the forest around us. And what kind of forest was this? I couldn't see the sun yet, but with no mountain peaks to block it, its farthest reaching rays had just begun to light up the sky.

The light allowed me to see past the first line of trees for a couple feet beyond. The trunks were lofty but slender and more tightly packed than I had ever seen. The clumps of trees were occasionally broken up by bits of marsh: murky water with tall grasses and scarecrow branches that provided a perch for a variety of birds.

The land had its own beauty, that was obvious, but it was harsh, with the threat of consumption behind every step. In one direction, the swamp and deep mud pockets promised to swallow you whole and in the other, the trees swore to keep you lost amongst them forever.

"Not again."

It was Leo's tone that pulled my attention to the front. The familiar flashes of red and blue lights caused a feeling of dread to build in my stomach. Headlights shined off the orange cones as we once again joined the traffic at a roadblock. There seemed to be more cop cars present than at the last one.

"So we go hide, Mahon kisses the cop's ass like last time, and we continue on our way. Simple," Falon said. Mahon sent her a glare, and she stuck her tongue out at him in return.

"I don't think that will work this time," Leo replied. "It looks like they are searching every car; no matter the make or color."

As if it was synchronized, all of us took to the windows, pressing our faces against the glass so we could see for ourselves. Sure enough, officers were opening every door, every trunk, and popping every hood.

One officer even had a dog that he walked around each vehicle, directing him to sniff in places that could potentially hide someone. We wouldn't make it through that.

"Shit," Leo cursed.

"I'm afraid our troubles have increased yet again," Asa said. He began to pack his stray items into his bag. "Look to the right, off the shoulder, and behind the K-9 SUV."

Over where Asa directed, an unmarked truck sat parked next to the guardrail. Three figures dressed in all black stood leaning against the truck bed. Even from here I could make out the stars on their collars.

The van pulled forward as another car was allowed to pass through the blockade. My palms began to sweat and the muscles in my legs twitched with their need to run. As I continued to keep an eye on the Imperials behind the roadblock, another car pulled up alongside the truck. Three more Imperials stepped out and joined the others.

"This isn't good." Cedric spoke low. I wasn't sure if anyone else could hear him. I nodded to let him know that I had. "How many more do you think are going to join?"

I shrugged. Who knew? There were already six that we could see. What were we going to do? We couldn't fight our way out, there were too many people around. Exposing magic wasn't going to help anyone.

"Listen up." Orin addressed all of us. "A couple cars ahead of us there is a break in protection, a small opening between the stationary cop cars. I want each of you to pack only the essentials in your bag. We're not that far from our destination."

I checked the clock on the dash again; it was almost five in the morning. The sun was taking its time in waking up, but we needed to be far from here when it finally chose to show itself. We were in the middle of the interstate, between exits, and I wasn't exactly sure how far from the bottom of the state.

The presence of Imperials had to mean we weren't that far from the Miami Academy. Or maybe they came down from Orlando? Either way, this wasn't going to be easy. Orin only confirmed my internal apprehension.

"We go the rest of the way on foot."

Yeah, this was going to suck.

It was déjà vu. Once again I was running through the woods, my bag on my back, and Imperials behind us. The only difference between then and now was the lack of snow. In its place was a humidity so thick I might as well have run through syrup. The sun had yet to peak over the tree tops and already I was sweating. To my right, Cedric and Falon didn't fare much better. Sweat was already running down the sides of their faces and gluing their hair to their foreheads.

"Who the hell lives like this?" I asked aloud.

Orin chuckled as he jogged beside me. He didn't look as afflicted. Of course he would find this funny. "This is nothing, wait until the afternoon."

"Or after it rains!" Leo added.

I groaned. We kept our course through the woods, but still maintained a line of sight to the road. Orin said it would lead us to where we needed to go next. Our pace had slowed to a walk and my feet sunk into the spongy earth.

Around me critters scurried to and fro, paying no attention to the strangers bumbling through their territory. I watched a pair of squirrels chase one another around the ferns and up a tree. They danced around the trunk with agitated chips and chirps.

The longer I watched, the more peculiar the tree became. It appeared to be slanting at an angle ... and moving closer.

"Halt!" Orin's yell registered a moment before he tackled me to the ground. Mud and water stained my clothes, but I ignored it. The tree I had been staring at crashed to the ground in front of me. Birds took flight around us and the trail got quiet, even the bugs seemed to hold their breath.

The others surrounded Orin and I and helped us to our feet. From outside our huddle, branches snapped and leaves crunched as six Imperials approached.

"Now, Harris, didn't I tell you they would come this way?" One of the Imperials stood in front of the rest, his eyes locked on me. "Hello, doll. The Dean is most anxious for *your* return."

Orin growled and drew the guard's eye.

"Ah, yes. Vampire is it? We've been briefed about your lot." He smirked, his whole demeanor screaming confidence. "I'm afraid your ice will be of little use to you here; the morning heat should see to that."

I wanted to punch this guy in the face. His cocky attitude was pissing me off. As he spoke, the Vamps had covertly shifted until they were between me and the Imperials. I was sure the guards noticed, but they still made no move toward us.

"Why don't you make it easier on yourselves." This dickwad was still talking. "Surrender the students and we promise to let the rest of you go."

"You can't really believe that will work?" Orin asked as he grabbed my arm. "You know very well how this will end. Cedric, now!"

I was pulled sideways as Cedric released a stream of flames at the feet of the Imperials. The fire was snuffed out by a guard in the back, but it gave us a few seconds head start. We ran; Cedric, Falon, and I in the front, while the Vamps brought up the rear.

Leo sprayed acid at any guard who drew too close, but there was nothing we could do about the wind. It tore through the trees, bending smaller ones in half and ripping at the backpack on my shoulder.

My hair whipped across my face and into my eyes. The current pushed against us and I ran at an odd angle to the ground as I fought to keep moving forward.

Soon, the Imperials behind us began to lag; their sprint reduced to a trot before they slowed to a walk. Actually, it was more like a stroll. The distance grew between us and them until I couldn't see them anymore. But they hadn't seemed worried that we were getting away.

That's because we weren't.

The wind still raged around us, gradually creating a suction that pulled me ahead. Where the wind had only a moment before been a force to push against, now it was almost corralling us forward.

The intensity of the wind increased until we were forced to the ground. It felt like someone shoved me hard from behind; I could almost feel a hand on my lower back, making sure I stayed down. I landed on my hands and knees, using every muscle I had to keep from face planting in the mud. Several yards ahead, six more Imperials stepped into view.

They created a semi-circle in front of us, effectively blocking us in. The only free space was behind us or to the left. But more Imperials would catch up from the rear and a canal blocked our escape to the side.

We were trapped. The option to fight was taken from us as the Imperial controlling the air kept the pressure on us.

"Hold them until Kael catches up."

I tried to look around as much as my position would allow, but I could only see in front of me: the ground, muddy boots, and low resting foliage. But if I tried hard enough, I could see Falon's hands out of the corner of my eye. Her knuckles were white, gripping the ground until her fingers sank in. Her forearms shook and I could make out a swirling mirage around her wrists.

She was working magic, but I wasn't sure what specifically she was aiming for. A few minutes later I got my answer. It started with the squirrels, a mob of them descended from the trees and leapt onto the faces of the nearest guards.

Their screams became harder to hear as they ran further away from our group; the squirrels on their heads disorienting their sense of direction. Before the other Imperials could make a move to help, birds of all kinds screeched an attack and dive bombed to peck at their eyes.

Too busy trying to protect their faces, the remaining guards fell to their knees as their feet were dragged from under them. The guard lost his connection with air when he lost his concentration; the air pressure was lifted and we were once again able to stand.

Movement in the forest bed started as rustles in the fallen leaves and twigs, but grew into tendrils of water that engulfed the lower halves of the guard's bodies with snake-like tubes of liquid that connected all the way back to the canal.

The guards screamed as the liquid moved from their feet, up their legs, and squeezed around their wastes. My jaw dropped when I saw who the water vines led to.

"Another cousin?" I asked Falon, gesturing to the green creature who came to our rescue.

She gasped when she saw it. "A water sprite. I didn't think *they* would answer my call."

"Who did you call?" Asa asked as he stepped up to protect Falon's right side.

"No one in particular. I just screamed for help." She shrugged.

Like the others, the body of this sprite very obviously resembled the female form with curves and breasts. Her skin was a deep, pea green with reflective flakes that looked suspiciously like scales. Her ears and hands were webbed like fins and I was sure her feet were as well. She had slits for eyes with a dull film layer on the outside, and her mouth held several rows of serrated teeth. My instincts recoiled against her grotesque yet alluring form, even as she waved her fin and signaled us to join her in the water.

"What do we do?" I asked. The Imperials around us were subdued for the moment, but I didn't know how much longer we had before the group with Kael arrived.

"They will hide us," Falon assured, moving toward the river spirit.

Orin stepped in front of her and gave her a hard look. "Are you sure? The Fae are not known for their honesty or for helping without a price. No offense to yourself."

Falon squared her shoulders and lifted her chin.

"They won't lie to *me*."

Her confidence was genuine and I trusted her word. There was just something about the way she stood, the determined look on her face, and the way she spoke that compelled me to believe her. Orin had come to the same conclusion and nodded. Falon stepped around him and walked toward the sprite, the rest of us following close behind.

Chapter 13

It was a peculiar feeling, being watched. I could feel hundreds of eyes following my every step and the hair on the back of my neck reacted, trying to warn me of something I was already aware of. This sixth sense had flared to life the second our group disappeared behind the layers of sawgrass.

My instincts were in a permanent state of alert; a pulsing hum that buzzed in the back of my mind, never ceasing. A splash in the channel to my right caused this instinct to flutter, and I caught sight of two lucent orbs observing me from beneath the brackish water.

No sooner had I noticed the sprite before she submerged completely, only to reappear further up the channel to wave at Falon. Falon nodded back and gestured to the rustling cattails and rippling water. The sprite tilted her head, the fins on the side flicking back and forth as if she were listening.

She let loose a series of clicks and whistles. Much like a dolphin and with a large splash from the larger fins on her back feet, she dove underwater and didn't resurface. More splashes further upstream told me the other sprites had followed suit.

I jogged to the front of our group until I walked shoulder to shoulder with Falon. With a gentle nudge, I got her attention.

"So, what was that about?"

"Just securing a marriage between you and a warrior of the tribe in return for safe passage through their lands."

"You did *what*?" She tried to fight it, but her lips twitched. I was going to strangle her. "That wasn't funny!"

Her laugh echoed across the now placid water, disturbing a flock of roosting vultures on a far tree.

"Relax," she giggled. "As if Cedric would let one of them swim off with you. Besides, there are no male sprites. I told her that her tribe was making you all nervous, so she sent them ahead to wait for our arrival at the village."

"Oh." Glancing around, I noticed that the water's surface was smooth and calm, and the feeling of being watched had almost entirely disappeared.

"How can you talk with them?" I asked her. "They don't speak."

"Actually, that's not true," she corrected me. "They can communicate just as well as we are right now."

"So, then why don't they say anything?"

Were these sprites like their cousins in the trees? Were they so prejudiced against others not of their kind that they deemed us too lowly to speak with? Back on the plantation, I had spoken directly to the tree sprites, and they looked right through me, refusing to even acknowledge my presence. Maybe the water sprites were the same way.

"They're saying plenty, trust me. You just can't hear them."

Now I was confused. "I can hear them just fine, Fal. But I don't speak aquatic mammal."

She shook her head and stepped over a fallen branch across the path. "That's only how they speak to one another, or to other animals of the water. If you were to completely submerge yourself, it would feel to you as if the water was vibrating with the hum of their communication. It echoes."

I could understand something like that. Echolocation was how many other mammals spoke to one another beneath the waves. Everyone knew that. But how did *she* speak with them? I hadn't heard any squeaks come out of her mouth.

"You haven't been speaking Dory for the past hour, so how are you all talking?"

She frowned at me, confused. "Who's Dory?"

My jaw dropped. "You don't know who Dory is?" She shook her head. "You've never seen Finding Nemo, the story of an adorable clown fish searching the ocean for his son?"

"Why would a clown fish leave the safety of its anemone for the open ocean? That seems far from its natural behavior." Asa approached from the rear. "Was this fish spelled perhaps?"

I could only stare in appalled horror at the perplexed faces around me. They didn't know about Finding Nemo. I was traveling with barbarians. I turned pleading eyes to Cedric, and he wrapped his arms around me, forcing my head into his shoulder.

"It's okay. We can introduce them to Disney another time." He then spoke over my head to the rest of the group. "At the risk of her catching you up on every Disney movie ever made, let's just answer her question. Falon, how can you speak with the sprites?"

"Because I'm Fae." Her tone suggested there should be a *Duh* at the end and she was being polite in not saying it. "And because this one is young. The older the sprite, the stronger their mental communication with others. Their young have a weaker telepathic connection and communicated best with their own kind or in their mortal form."

We resumed our walk and I once again felt the weight of eyes on me. I guess the sprites couldn't keep themselves away for long. Curious creatures.

"But you're not a sprite and you can still communicate with her?" I asked.

"It must be easier with close relatives like other Fae," Orin said and Falon nodded. "There have been stories of some humans being able to communicate with their minds, but they are rare," he concluded.

"Yeah, and they tend to go missing. Much like humans with the Sight," Mahon added.

Falon turned on him, hands made into tiny fists on her hips. "That hasn't happened in generations! It's forbidden for the Fae to harm humans who can see us. Stop spreading rumors."

Mahon smirked. Clearly, he enjoyed taunting her. "That's funny. Wasn't there a village in Ireland not long ago that reported a large number of their men missing?" Falon was fuming. "I recall hearing that guardians had to be dispatched to deal with that problem."

"The law prevents us from hunting humans, Vampire. But we can do what we want when they wander to us willingly." The silky voice interrupted their argument.

I couldn't hear the voice as one normally does on the receiving end of words. It was more like a silky echo in my mind that ebbed and rose like the tide. The voice was female and cold, like the darkest depths of the deepest ocean.

At the edge of the water now, a sprite approached from the center of the canal. Half of her body was exposed with the water leveled below her navel. She was a cerulean, blue with spots of teal green overtaking sections of her body.

The afternoon sun reflected off her scales, enhancing her unearthly presence. *She* was the one who spoke? She must be older than the smaller green sprite beside her if I could hear her voice in my head.

"My mother awaits your arrival. *I* shall escort you for the rest of your journey to my home." Her mouth didn't move, but the words were clearly imprinted on my mind.

Her glossy eyes locked on Falon and widened. If her facial expressions mirrored that of a human, I would have said she was shocked to see her.

"I did not know it was *you* who called." Her head dipped once in respect before she looked at the rest of us; her eyes lingered longer than I would have liked on Cedric and I took a half step forward. "Come. I will guide your safe passage through our lands."

Falon was the first to follow, Cedric and I behind her, and the Vamps brought up the rear. I kept an eye on Falon as we walked. Her shoulders were pinched with stress and her hands continued to twist and pull at the edge of her t-shirt.

However, each time the sprite peeked above the water to gage our progress, her posture would do a one-eighty; she held her head high and marched along like she had a purpose. Something was nagging at me about her behavior, a sensation that I had pushed to the back of my mind before.

It had been there since we met those forest sprites on the plantation. I tried to ignore what my senses kept telling me, giving Falon the benefit of the doubt. But here it was again, the feeling that my best friend was hiding something.

Where was the shy, yet mouthy midget who rambled on about everything she saw? Standing before me was a quiet, brooding, and less enthusiastic version of my friend. I didn't know what caused her to change, but I was going to find out.

The sprite kept to the water, guiding us with brief directions in our minds.

Cedric pulled up alongside me and grabbed my hand, his thumb rubbing circles on my palm. "I think they're creepy as hell, the sprites. Have you seen their teeth? And those eyes?" He shuddered.

Falon frowned. "That's actually kind of odd for you to say. The water sprites are renowned for their great beauty as well as lethal natures in most cultures. Their glamour is hard to see through."

Cedric snorted. "Have you seen them? They have *fins*."

I elbowed him in warning and jerked my head to the spot of blue in the water. She was watching us. I gave a soft growl. I didn't like the way she was looking at Cedric. I knew the lore about her kind. Water sprites used their glamour to mesmerize human men and basically brainwash them into willingly following them.

Whether it's to be their slaves, their newest mate, or just for sadistic fun in drowning them, the sprites *always* had an eye out for potential victims.

"She is allowing you to see through her glamour, otherwise you would follow her to the bottom of even the deepest oceans. They are quite alluring to males of all species." Falon continued, "There are countless myths of undines luring men to the water and pulling them under to dwell in their realms. Mahon was right about that part." She seemed reluctant to admit that there had been some truth to Mahon's teasing.

Cedric paled and put more distance between himself and the canal. I gripped his hand, for both his comfort and mine. Falon confirming my knowledge on the danger of the water sprite did nothing to ease my mind.

"Are you sure it's a good idea to be following them?" I asked for about the fiftieth time.

Falon rolled her eyes. "Don't worry, the Summer Queen outlawed the killing of men centuries ago. They can only take those who enter the water of their own will."

"That sure as hell won't be me," Cedric exclaimed.

He looked across the water and his gaze clashed with the shiny orbs of the sprite's. She had been listening to our conversation. The blue figure treaded water only a couple feet from the water's edge. How had she gotten so close?

The corner of her mouth tilted in what I knew to be a smirk, and she stared. Her eyes never left Cedric and that smirk never left her face. In fact, it seemed to grow. Her mouth was now wide open in a fangy-toothed grin as Cedric's hand squeezed mine.

I squeezed back just in time to feel him tug against me as his body slowly took one step toward the water. I pulled back on his hand, but he only gripped me harder, until I could feel the bones in my hand rubbing together.

"Ouch! Cedric, what are—"

Small sounds of distress stemmed from his mouth as beads of sweat broke out across his forehead. His foot lifted from the ground and moved forward and then back, as if undecided on where it wanted to go, before leaping out and tugging us closer to the canal.

Back in the water, the sprite had moved closer yet again. Her gaze was fixed on Cedric as her body softly swayed from side to side. I watched helplessly as Cedric swayed as well, his body in sync with hers.

There was nothing I could do as Cedric released my hand from his death grip. I tried to hold onto him, but with one forceful push against my shoulder, he knocked me to the floor with a hard *thud.* Two more steps were taken toward the sprite as I watched.

"Enough," I called to the water.

The sprite ignored me. Just feet away, she blew bubbles on the surface of the water and her eyes shined with mirth. That little bitch. Cedric was an arm's length away from her now. Lunging forward, I gripped his shoulders and anchored myself as I swung my leg around.

I landed a kick to the side of the sprite's head before my momentum took both Cedric and I to the ground. I landed on top of his chest, perpendicular to his body.

"Are you okay?" he asked as he helped me to sit up.

"Am *I* okay? You're the one who almost went for a swim with that thing." My eyes flicked back and forth between his face and the rest of him as I checked him out for injury or lasting mental damage.

Without warning, the sprite sprung for the bank, water spraying from between her pointed teeth to hit me directly in the face.

My hands rose on instinct to block the attack as I screamed to Falon. "Make her stop!"

The water was unrelenting as it battered my arms and head. Underneath the shouts of my friends, I heard a steady hum coming from the water. Shrills and whistles called back and forth as an entire world below our feet continued on without a care for what was happening to us above.

Sharp words punctured the aquatic melody, but I couldn't make them all out. I recognized: Insolent. Female. Challenge. The sprite was shouting at me through her water attack.

"*Scoirfidh!*"

The assault ceased and the sprite gave me a sassy flick of her fin before diving beneath the surface once more. I pushed my sopping hair from my face and turned to look at Falon. She stood knee deep in the canal and seemed to be having a very heated conversation with the sprite.

"Casey, are you harmed?" Orin questioned as he helped me to stand.

I shook my head. "I'm not hurt, just soaked."

He gave me a once over, just to be thorough before patting my shoulder. A tap on my other one brought me face to face with an extremely pissed off Falon. Her eyes practically sparked with concealed magic.

"I am so sorry, Casey. I swear the sprite was only teasing; she wouldn't have hurt Cedric. Not that she should have mesmerized him in the first place. We had a long conversation about *that,* I promise you. And she won't be trying it again."

She gave a withering look over her shoulder, but the sprite couldn't be seen. There were only bubbles on the surface to mark her place in the water.

"Hey, what about me?" Cedric asked with a good natured grin.

It looked as if he had already moved past this questionable matter, like almost being drug to the bottom of the canal was an everyday occurrence. Me, not so much.

"The hell, Falon? Why are we following them in the first place? You said that we would be fine, that we could trust them."

Before, she had so much confidence in the fact that these sprites wouldn't betray her, like it would be a crime if they did. And yet here we are.

"I swear to you the sprite knows her place now. She won't try something like this again."

The sparks still crackled behind her gaze and the ends of her hair lifted with residual static. I knew that she meant every word of her promise. The sprite wouldn't attack us again. I actually feared for her if she tried. I let out the breath I was holding and gestured for Falon to lead the way.

I trusted her, even if she was still hiding something. But the sooner we moved on, the sooner we could leave the sprites behind, so on we walked.

You'd think having wet clothes would offer a sweet relief from the Florida heat, but you'd be wrong; it only felt good for the first two minutes. Now, my damp jeans chafed and the humidity caused my hair and shirt to stick to my skin.

Mosquitos flocked to me and I could hear their obnoxious buzzing right before the slight sting of a bite. I smacked at yet another one and glared at the trees where they hid their massive population.

The closer we got to larger bodies of water, the more there seemed to be. And there was a huge amount of water ahead, I was sure of it. The landscape was becoming harder to navigate. The land we traveled on had gradually increased in saturation until I could hear the *squish* under each step.

Water rapidly filled the shallow depression left behind by my footprints. We were running out of solid ground. The Cyprus trees around us were more green and lively than those further out from the water. Algae grew along the base of their trunks and discolored rings showed the different water levels this location could flood to in the rainy season.

I stopped walking when the trail ended. The tree line opened up to reveal grassy water punctured with fields of lily pads. An elegant, white egret walked among the giant, green petals; its eyes on the schools of fish below.

The sprite poked her head above the surface exactly halfway between us and the next patch of solid land. I eyed the wide channel in front of me, but couldn't see deeper than a few inches. I didn't like thinking about what waited for us out there.

"She expects us to swim? What about alligators?" I wondered, unnerved.

We would be defenseless out there. Our powers would be useless and so would all of my hard earned training. I wasn't taught how to protect myself from a damn prehistoric reptile. Falon tested the soil's structure with a foot and only paused for a brief moment before wading deeper.

"She promises that the wildlife will leave us alone. They have sway over creatures of the water, so we should be safe."

The *should be* was the part that bothered me. I didn't exactly trust her with my life, not after what happened earlier. Especially because of that. But as I've said before, I trusted Falon, so I followed her into the water. It was way warmer than I thought it would be and not so unpleasant as it re-soaked my damp jeans.

"Be careful, the embankment drops off after a couple feet," came a warning from Leo who had already caught up to Falon.

Not wanting to be at the back as we traveled across, I immersed myself up to my neck and began to swim. Leo wasn't lying about that drop off. The current beneath me turned chilly only a jumps distance from shore.

Halfway across, having drawn even with Falon and the sprite, something gripped my leg around my calf. In a natural panic, I began to thrash, which only tightened the grip of whatever held onto me until it started to drag me under.

My imagination plagued me with visions of jagged toothed monsters of the deep, dragging me down to be their next meal. The relentless grip on my leg suddenly disappeared just as the sprite's head broke the water in front of me.

This close I could see each individual scale shimmer and reflect either the blue or green skin it covered. I could also see two thin slits above her mouth that must have been her nose. I could virtually feel her in my head as she gave an obnoxious eye roll.

"It was only a weed, young Witch. Calm yourself." As she spoke to me, the gleeful humor was evident in her tone.

Bitch, I thought for the hundredth time. She dove beneath the surface with a parting tug on my foot. That was enough for me. I dragged myself onto land, my water-logged jeans weighing me down and making it difficult to pull to my feet. Mud squelched under my finger nails as I literally clawed the last few inches onto solid land.

The rest of the group was not far behind. The sprite kept to the water and patiently waited for us to organize ourselves.

When she deemed us fit to continue, she spoke, "The path to your right leads to a natural pool in the center of the island. My people and I will meet you there. Welcome to *Uisge Oileán.*"

Chapter 14

"How are there sprites living in the Everglades?" I kicked a small rock and the scuff from my shoe sent a cloud of dust and sand to poof around my ankles.

On my next step, the stone crunched beneath my heel. Not a rock then. The limestone-pale path we walked along was made of shells, both crushed and whole. We were at least an hour from the ocean. How had shells made it to the heart of this river of grass?

"The question is, why *wouldn't* there be sprites here? It's literally a land of water," Cedric replied.

I gave his shoulder a playful shove. "I *know* that. I just thought they kept to deep, ancient lakes and waterways that they could hide in. You know, somewhere close enough to humans for their needs but secluded enough to keep out of sight."

"And you don't think this fits the bill?" he teased, and I shook my head.

"I've never heard a tale of the fearsome sprites of the Everglades. The old lore circulates around rivers and lochs."

Our winding path became shaded, and I looked up to the overhanging umbrella of the Cyprus dome. The leaves of the swamp bay trees were large and elliptical, intermingling with the sun-fire blooms of the red maples.

Orchids and mossy air plants clung to the barks of the Cyprus trees and together it created a lively cover from the midday sun. Falon slowed to walk beside me, and I pulled my attention from the tree tops to once again focus on the path ahead.

"Sprites live in anything containing water: at the bottom of waterfalls, rivers, marshes, and fens. From mountain lakes to ocean waves. You can find their homes in colorful coral caves or beneath a murky sea of lily pads. Though, this tribe must be very large to have to push their territory this far out."

A sting at my temple prompted my hand to smack the hurt on a reflex, by now knowing a mosquito was responsible. I was going to look like I had the chicken pox by the time I made it out of here. Sweat tickled down my back in a cool stream until it was absorbed by the waistband of my jeans.

Falon's insight on the sprites hadn't given any relief to my jumbled nerves. How large of a tribe were we walking toward? We had no idea why they saved us and what they really wanted. Whatever it was, if we refused, could we even make it back out of here alive?

A rustle in the ferns lining the path revealed the rushed flight of an osprey to a barely visible nest on a low branch of a red maple. Other birds were chirping nearby. Small, green parrots flocked from tree to tree, cheerfully conversing with one another.

As I watched them, I noticed the tree line had begun to thin. As it did, the closer it got to water. But before I could voice my thoughts to the others, the path suddenly opened to reveal a decent sized clearing with a teardrop pool right in the center.

Still surrounded by trees and vibrant bursts of greens, the sandy path led straight to the water's edge. I stopped about five feet back and the group fanned out behind me. The water below was a clear, crystal blue; the sky above reflected off the sandstone bottom instead of the mud and substrate that lined the rest of the marsh's waterways.

On the opposing side of the pool, directly across from us, stood a lone tree. Its massive trunk would take four of me, hand to hand, to wrap around it. It stood so tall that the sun blurred out the top until I could no longer bear to look up.

Its gnarled branches reached across the pool on both sides and stopped halfway across in either direction. Sweet smelling orchids in greens, whites, reds, and purples held fast to the lower branches and hid in the shade they provided.

I counted almost a hundred women lounging in and around the pool. Their bodies laid out and posed in alluring positions as they eyed us strangers. I felt as though I had stepped through a portal to some sirenic land. These women were all eerily gorgeous, like their cousins of the forest, but with a more seductive edge.

Their skin was as white as the sandstone beneath the water and random splotches shimmered with color where the sun touched them, as if their true form was resisting its imprisonment beneath the mortal cage they held it in.

They wore sheer dresses that resembled the moss that hung from the trees around them. The garments were completely see-through and I had a deep, feminine urge to cover Cedric's eyes. But even I couldn't look away from their beauty.

No wonder men drowned themselves to get to them. They were utterly captivating.

One of the closer women tilted her head with a playful smile. Her azure hair danced in the sun as it slid over her shoulder to curl around her breast. She held out a hand, and it was like pulling on a string deep inside me.

Out of nowhere a deep, fervent compulsion took root in the very center of my being. I *needed* to be with that woman. Her beauty had no match, I wanted to throw myself at her feet and beg for even a sliver of her attention.

I no longer cared about the Dean, my friends, or why we had come here in the first place; none of that mattered anymore. All I cared about was her. How I could please her, what I could do to make her happy. She smiled at me, and I almost fell to my knees.

That smile enticed me forward, my shoes scraped across the sand. My only desire: to get to that water and to her … until I stopped. Falon had swung her arm out in front of me like an iron blockade across my stomach.

"Casey, snap out of it," Falon demanded. Her voice echoed in my ear, but nothing she said could deter me from reaching that angel. I fought against the force that dared to hold me back. I kicked and scratched, screeching with an unholy fury at being held away from that source of perfection.

Through it all, Falon held on. She settled herself behind me, and with strength I didn't know she had, restrained me.

"*Throid sé. Throid sé. Resist.*"

Slowly, her words slithered through the cracks in the cloud that muffled my mind. Like a giant wave washing shells from the shore, her words engulfed the foreign desires that had burrowed deep in my psyche. Within seconds, the spell had cleared and I blinked to see Falon lift her hand from my temple, tendrils of her magic bridged from me back to her fingers.

Whatever she did had worked. I blinked as my vision blurred in front of me. When I next turned to look upon the sprite whose beauty had consumed my every thought, I saw beneath her glamour to her true form. Like how the ripple of water distorts the true details of an image, her glamour distorted her beauty.

I looked upon the other sprites in the pool and watched as their mortal forms flickered to show the scales that lie beneath. Cedric's arm brushed my shoulder as he stepped past me and toward the sprite who still held her hand out.

That *bitch*. Was this going to happen every time?

I lurched forward and grabbed Cedric's arm, tugging him back and interlocking my fingers with his. That stopped him for a moment, like he recognized who I was, but seconds later he continued to struggle and made every attempt to move toward the water.

I ducked under his fist and brought my arm up to block another punch.

"Cedric, it's a spell. Fight it! You have to see through it."

He growled and swung again. The fury in his eyes was all too familiar—I, myself, had felt it not minutes before. He was lost in the compulsion of that scaly whore with the blue hair. Sweeping a leg out from under him, I knocked Cedric to the ground and threw my body weight on top of him.

This wasn't going to hold him for long. I called over my shoulder for the Vamps to help. Surely they were immune to the sprite's glamour, but even the three of them fought their own internal battle of control against the sprites closest to them.

Their movements were jerky as they walked toward the water, like they knew what was happening but were powerless to stop it. Orin and Mahon stood stiff, like an unbending trunk of an ancient tree. Every muscle in their bodies were taunt and tight as they fought against the siren's call.

Orin's left foot jerked back and forth in a hypnotic twitch as the appeal of the siren pulled at him, while his own internal strength fought against it.

Asa and Leo took small rigid steps toward the pool. Like Orin, they obviously fought against the lure, but couldn't keep their own feet from moving inches at a time. Asa's hand clutched Leo's shoulder so tightly I was sure there would be bruises.

He grunted as he pulled Leo's shoulder with a strength that he dug deep to find. As he pulled Leo back, he simultaneously inched forward himself. In turn, Leo reached out to grasp the back of Asa's shirt and drew him back, before his own foot slammed down.

To an unknowing eye they looked to be fighting one another to get to the sprites that tempted them from the clear water. But I knew they were trying to save one another. Each one was trying to pull the other back, but that loss of focus allowed the sprite to slip deeper into their minds and draw them closer.

It only took a second. The Vamps fared better than Cedric, but how long could they hold out? They were mere steps from the water's edge now. The air ruptured from my chest as Cedric threw me off him.

I lay on my back, wheezing as my lungs contracted and tried to bring in more oxygen at the same time. My head fell to the side and I could only watch as Cedric knelt on all fours, his muscles shaking with exhaustion as he fought the sprite's call.

The azure-haired beauty kept her greedy eyes on him the entire time. She taunted him with a flirty smile, the flash of a breast, and when those didn't work, she opened her mouth and sang. Like the siren tales of old, her melodic voice drew the attention of every mortal being in the immediate area.

I felt my own resolve weakening as I swayed to and fro along with the dips and swells of her song. The other sprites stalked closer, their eyes hungry. This was it. This was how it was going to end. I wouldn't die shackled to a grungy wall, glaring into the eyes of the twins while my loved ones screamed for mercy.

No. Instead, I was going to drown. Or live in a zombified, barely conscious state, tending to the needs of my new masters as they took whatever they wanted from me, and then drowning. There were probably worse ways to go.

Falon's movement barely registered as I lost my final hold on resistance. Behind me, Falon growled and the air cracked as she gathered magic in her clenched fists. The amulet around her neck pulsed with the ferocity of the power it helped to focus.

"Release my friends. *Now*."

I had never heard that tone from her before. She wasn't asking the sprites; she was commanding them. The sprite who sang stopped mid word and actually looked afraid as Falon stared her down. Cedric's struggles ceased and the other she-devils stopped staring at us just as the center of the pool began to boil.

Instantly, the fog that danced densely around my mind lifted and blew away. Planting an elbow on the ground beneath me, I half lifted in time to see the women, as one, turn and bow low toward the frothing bubbles.

Three sprites, in their true forms, broke the surface. I recognized the blue-green sprite that led us to this island, the one that taunted Cedric and tried to establish dominance over me.

I also saw the younger sprite who had come to our rescue and saved us from the Imperials. Both now sported a single white shell in the middle of their foreheads. Between them, the water lifting her higher than the others, stood who I knew to be the Queen.

Her skin was the deepest shade of sapphire I had ever seen. The sun didn't just reflect off her scales, her entire body glowed with it. A string of alligator teeth adorned her head in a barbarous crown. She looked down upon us, and I fought to pull my aching body from the ground.

I stood on shaking knees, my hand gently pressed against my sore side, and took my place beside Cedric. He stood with the Vamps, the lot of them also freed from the siren's spell, and watched as the royal family arrived.

"That was close," Leo whispered. His normally tan complexion was pale and insipid; he resembled how I originally thought a blood-consuming being would look.

"Too close," Orin agreed, looking better than the others, but even he couldn't hide the slight sway in his stance.

Personally, I was beyond pissed. "When I get my hands on those scaly, dead fish smelling, bout to be stuffed and hung on my wall, motherfu—"

"Welcome, *Banphrionsa* and friends to *Uisge Oileán*. I am Keela, Queen of the *Riasc* Tribe. My daughters you have already met, Aednat," the queen nodded to her right at our guide, "and my youngest, Einin." She gestured to the smaller sprite on her left. "My daughters have both saved you and brought you to our sacred grove."

Her words slowed and trailed off into silence and a tense stillness settled uncomfortably over our group. Her eyes continued to flick back and forth between us as she waited. Did she expect us to bow? Because I had a thing or two to tell her highness and it was not going to be as pleasant as bowing.

Wary, Falon took a small step forward, cleared her throat, and reluctantly dipped her head in a small sign of respect. "We thank you, *do soilse,* for your aid. We are most humbly grateful."

I let out a most unladylike snort. It echoed across the silent clearing and the queen's mouth tilted down as her eyes flashed. Meanwhile, Falon kept her head bent until the queen once again looked upon her and gave the barest of nods in her direction. When Falon finally straightened, the queen opened her mouth to speak again.

But I didn't let her get that far. "You conniving, twisted, immoral, little aquatic *bitch*."

The sharp gasps from around the pool told me I definitely had their attention. I knew I did when the queen slowly turned to face me head on. Beside her, her eldest daughter, and fellow shrewd cow, stood with an excited smirk plastered across her face. The youngest sister ducked under the water until only her eyes were visible.

"*What* did you just call me?" The queen's voice slithered across my already tender mind like a greasy serpent.

"You heard what I said and I don't feel like repeating myself—my ribs kind of hurt at the moment. However, if you give me a minute I'm sure I could gather up enough strength to come up with even more descriptive words."

The water around her swirled in a growing vortex before it suddenly dissipated and left choppy waves in its wake.

"The only reason you live, insolent Witch, is because of your blonde friend beside you. If not for her, I would have you fed yourself to a gator one body part at a time, so you could watch as you are slowly consumed into nothing."

Whoa. The imagination on this one. But Falon was my only saving grace? Maybe it was because her mother was influential in the court. At my puzzled expression, the queen laughed.

The shrill cackle grated inside my head like nails on a chalk board. It took everything in me to keep my hands from gripping my head in pain, but I didn't want this sadistic twat to see that she affected me.

"You haven't told them." The queen focused her gaze on Falon and continued to crow. "This is precious. Your friends have no idea who you truly are. *Tsk, tsk, Banphrionsa.* That's no way to treat your friends."

She actually waggled a fin back and forth as if she were scolding a young toddler who had just stolen a cookie.

"Should I tell them?" She looked back at the rest of our group and her mouth split to reveal her jagged teeth in a mocking smile. "Would you all like to know what your *friend* has been hiding?"

"Enough of your games, Keela!" Falon's voice cut through the queen's haughty jeers. Her eyes were the palest I had ever seen them, but were lit up from behind with some internal glow.

Her hair smoldered a silvery white as the strands lifted to float in the air. A static charge danced from the tips, across her shoulders, and down to her hands at her sides. Small sparks jumped from her hand to sting my arm closest to her, but I dared not move.

"Seeing as you know who I am, it is your sworn duty to offer me and mine safe passage through your lands. To threaten and magic my friends was an offense in and of itself, but I shall let it pass. This time."

The queen's eldest daughter, Aednat, shrank back to hide behind her mother, who didn't look as confident anymore herself. Still, she wasn't going to back down easy.

"This little parlor trick with the lightning is cute, really. But what makes you think I'd obey a single one of your commands. You are not your mother. I may not be able to kill you, but your little friends are fair game."

At her threat, bolts of electricity shot from the bottom of Falon's fists, exploding in the dirt below us. The wind picked up and cleaved around us in a whirlwind of rage as Falon gradually floated into the air.

She stopped only feet above my head, but the display of power was enough to silence the overconfident queen before us.

"I may not be my mother, Keela, but if you or your people raise a single fin against us, I will end your pathetic life, as is my right as princess of the Summer Court."

My world dropped out from beneath my feet and my arms floundered around until they could clutch something solid and true. I gripped Cedric's arm as I tried to keep my world from spinning.

Did Falon say princess?

Chapter 15

I sat beneath a Southern live oak and leaned against the massive base of its trunk. A bed of leaves layered over powder-soft sand made a pliable cushion for me to recline on. Out of the corner of my eye, I could see the tree's branches; lanky and majestic, they dipped to touch the ground before continuing to reach outward.

Cedric lounged in one of these low dips, using the branch as a natural hammock. I took a moment to study him while he was relaxed and unknowing. His skin was darker from all the sun here, the complexion a smooth, tawny gold that made me jealous.

I've never had the ability to tan. I just burn and soon after peel back to what I called "base white." I was sure that by now, the Florida sun had me resembling a boiled lobster and the fact that that boy could come out looking like an Egyptian god was just wrong.

I couldn't help the smile, though, that took over my lips and forced them to curve up at the ends. He was pleasing to look at. His coal dark hair had grown longer and the tips now tickled the middle of his ear. Wilder than I had ever seen it, I was surprised to find that I found it kind of hot.

I wanted to run my fingers through it, to feel it brush against my cheek as he leaned in to kiss me. At that thought I let out a pitiful sigh. Cedric and I had yet to share another kiss; we haven't exactly had the time to, with the Imperials chasing us and all.

I just hoped that things would calm down enough for us to really have a chance to explore our relationship. It felt like we had been on the run the entire time we've been together. Bitterness pooled deep in my gut as I thought of the Dean and his Imperials.

It was their fault that I wasn't home right now, snuggled in my safe, familiar bed, listening to Cedric snore from his mess of stolen blankets. It was their fault that I sat in this mosquito infested swamp near awkwardly attractive females who wished to devour me and my friends.

As long as the Dean hunted me for my power, I could never be a normal sixteen-year-old girl. I groaned. Who was I kidding? I would never be normal. My boyfriend was a Witch, my best friend a Faerie princess, and we traveled with four Vampires. Even without the Dean's help, I was a freak.

"Are you going to join us for dinner or sit here in this dismal heap and keep feeling sorry for yourself?"

My gaze followed the worn boots in front of me, up mud splattered denim, to the friendly smile creasing Orin's cheeks. He held a hand out and I grabbed it as he helped me to stand. I quickly patted the sand from my bottoms and gave him a sheepish smile.

"How did you know? That I was feeling sorry for myself, I mean."

The creases on his face softened and smoothed as he nodded to where Cedric sat.

"I saw you watching him, and I recognized that look. It's the expression one makes when you think about what the world would have been like if only it hadn't been ruined by the monster you're running from."

My mouth dropped. He hit it right on the head; that was exactly what I had been feeling. And thinking back to what I learned of Orin's history, I knew he completely understood. After all, his father took my mother from him. From both of us. Maybe that was why I said what I said next.

"Sometimes I just wish things were different, you know? That there was no magic, no looming prophecies," I swallowed past the lump forming in my throat, "or that my mother was never murdered and I had the chance to grow up with her. Stupid, right?"

I instantly felt foolish for voicing my inner desires. I was the girl given a rare power so that I could save our world from some really cruel people. I was the only Witch in history with no powers, who was suddenly given one not seen for generations.

Yet, I was wishing for magic to not exist, all so I could be normal, so that I could have my mom back. Plenty of guardians lost their families in the battle against evil, and I bet none of them were this selfish.

I was looking down at my feet, fighting to keep the growing tears at bay. Orin's hand squeezed my shoulder until I met his gaze. His face was stern, but filled with understanding.

"*Never* think that your feelings, your wants, are anything less than meaningful. Sometimes, I wish for the exact same thing."

I let out a shaky laugh before I wrapped my arms around his waist and buried my head in his chest. A few tears leaked from my eyes and were absorbed by his shirt, but somehow I didn't think he'd mind.

Orin's arms wrapped tight around me, one hand resting on the back of my head, as he returned my hug. Someone cleared their throat nearby and we pulled apart to reveal Asa standing a respectful distance from our impromptu moment.

"Dinner is now ready if you both are hungry."

My stomach chose that moment to grumble its displeasure at being empty, causing more heat to warm my already rosy cheeks.

"Uh … food would be good."

Orin chuckled at my embarrassed blush and urged me toward our makeshift camp.

"You go ahead; I'll be right behind you."

I nodded, and with a smile to Asa, followed my nose to the campfire. But not even ten steps out, their heated whispers compelled me to look over my shoulder and I caught a quick glimpse of them arguing.

Asa threw his hands in the air, seemingly outraged at Orin's response to his question. Orin's hand shot out, his finger repeatedly pointing at me as he reasoned with him. Asa briefly glanced to where Orin pointed and his gaze quickly widened when he saw that I watched them.

He said something to Orin who turned to face me, slowly retracting his arm. My forehead crinkled at their odd behavior, but my stomach growled again, a biting hunger pain riding on its coattails, and I continued on toward the food I knew was waiting.

There were six of us seated around the fire as the sun finally sank low enough to hide behind the trees. Through the branches I could still make out the clearing with the teardrop pool that housed the local population of water sprites.

Above the water, the sky was absolutely radiant as it ignited in a smoldering swirl of saffron, rose, and fiery orange. I had never seen a sunset like this before. The mountains were known for their luscious sky views, but there was something to be said about sunsets at the ends of the earth.

The silhouette of a man, coming from the clearing, grew larger until I could make out Mahon's features.

"Any sign of her yet?" I asked, worry causing my voice to wobble.

Cedric scooted closer and curled his arm around my waist.

"They are probably still negotiating," he said, trying to reassure me.

Falon had been talking with the sprite queen all afternoon. It hadn't gone smoothly at first, but Falon pulling the princess card had finally gotten the old bat to shut up and listen. It had also completely blindsided the rest of us.

How had I not known who she was? We studied the current royal lines of all the races in school and even though the Fae were extremely protective of their heirs, I feel like I should have known.

I thought all the way back to when I first met Falon in school and tried to pick out any details I might have overlooked. The very first day I met her she had a backfiring spell that she couldn't control, her clothes were far from anything other royals would be caught dead in, and her demeanor was anything but regal.

Within those first few weeks, we'd become close and she had opened up to me many times. She wasn't haughty or self-absorbed, and she gave no inclination of having expected special treatment.

And a princess was supposed to be powerful, right? Falon had power, but enough to be an heir?

Her firework display earlier was the largest show of power I had ever seen her do, and I wasn't one hundred percent convinced that it wasn't due to that amulet she now wore.

Ugh. I could feel a headache coming on. Why didn't she tell us?

Now she was off, bargaining with a spiteful she-fish, *alone.* Asa was just as antsy about it as I was. A scowl permanently marred his usually calm expression the further down the sun sank.

"Why are we allowing her to do this alone?" He jumped to his feet, dropping what remained of his dinner on the ground. "It's time we went after her. She should have our support, our protection. She- she's ... right ... there."

Asa's rant trailed off as he stared over my head in shock. I whipped around, my shoulder knocking into Cedric to see Falon standing behind me. She stood with her shoulders hunched, head dipped low, and just far enough from the firelight to not be considered intrusive.

She wasn't sure if she was welcome.

Well, she did *lie.* My inner bitch had a point. But I had lied to everyone at one time or another, and if I was forgiven, then she had a right to be too. I was still pissed, though. Make no mistake, she had things to answer for.

I was the first of the group to move as I patted the ground next to me. Her shoulders loosened and her gaze was hopeful as she stepped forward and settled in beside me. With her head still down, she let out a soft "Hi."

And I lost it.

"Hi. *Hi?* That's what you start with?" Falon flinched as if I had hit her. "No, hey guys, sorry I didn't tell you that I was a *freaking Faerie princess!*"

Cedric whispered calming words in my ear, but no one stopped me from saying what we all thought. I inhaled deeply through my nose and slowly blew the breath out of my mouth. After a few more times, I felt calm enough to try again.

My voice was low and rough with emotion as I spoke through the hurt caused by my best friend.

"When I was tortured by the twins and didn't tell you about it, you were pissed. And rightfully so. You never came right out and said it, never once told me how hurt you were that I didn't come to you for help. But I'm going to repeat the one thing you did say to me, 'Friends, best friends, don't lie to one another. But, I forgive you.'"

Her head shot up and the firelight glinted off the tear trails on her cheeks. She launched herself at me with a sob.

"I'm sorry." The last of my anger fled as I let Falon cry on my shoulder. "I'm so sorry that I didn't tell you. I wanted to so many times."

"Then why didn't you?" I asked. "You had plenty of opportunity back at the barn."

After the appearance of the forest sprites, I had a lot of questions for Falon. She eventually gave me some half-assed answer about her mom being high up in the court—which you couldn't get higher than the queen—and how others tried to use that against her.

It made a little more sense now, but was that even the truth?

"I was trying to protect you." She sniffled and pulled away to sit up. Looking at me, her tear-stained appearance practically begged for me to believe her. "I swear that's the truth. You were already involved in so much turmoil by the time I trusted you enough to tell you who I was, that I didn't want to add to the weight on your shoulders. You didn't need to be involved in the drama and battle that was going on in my life. None of you did."

Her eyes scanned everyone else in the group, resting slightly longer on Asa. But he was too lost in thought to look at her.

I understood.

I had done the same thing back at the Academy when I kept Falon and Cedric out of the loop to protect them from the dean. It was no different then than it was now.

"I meant what I said," I told Falon. "I forgive you. Just, can we promise no more lies to protect one another?"

She agreed with a weepy smile. Cedric reached around me to pat her on the shoulder while Mahon and Leo immediately got to work on new and improved taunts.

"Don't expect us to start doing your share of the work now that you've outed yourself, *princess*," Leo teased.

Mahon picked it up and added, "And we won't be treating you any different, my *royal* short-shit."

Falon only laughed with them, for once not fighting back but basking in their acceptance. Abruptly, Asa stood and stalked from the group, his shape completely disappearing once the firelight no longer touched him.

Above us, the moon was full and bright, but its glow was no match for the thick shadows between the trees. The moon's light did, however, reflect off two watery orbs as Falon followed Asa's shape while he walked away.

From across the fire, Orin tried to soften the blow. "He's a thinker; it's what he does best. So, let him think. He'll be back."

Falon stared in Asa's direction a bit longer before nodding and turning back to the fire. As I continued to watch her, memories of a conversation we once had emerged from the forgotten depths of my mind.

"Falon, didn't you tell me once that you *chose* to be at the Academy?"

"Yeah," she answered, already knowing where I was headed with my question. "I was in danger and had to hide. What better place than a school protected by guardians?"

It was smart, I had to admit. No race, not even the ruling Fae, could storm an Academy and take a student. Not even one of their own. There was a process.

"What I don't understand is how you got out without detection? Didn't your twin at least know you had gone? And why didn't they come with you?" Orin asked.

"Your *twin*!" Oh Luthos, I couldn't take any more secrets.

But Falon had her hands up, palms out, and waved them frantically as she denied having a twin. "It's not like that, Casey. It's not."

My head was starting to hurt.

"What's the significance of a twin?" I sighed.

"The royal lines of the two Faerie courts are the most powerful, so powerful that we birth in twos or threes at a time, to split the power between siblings," Falon explained. "There is always a more dominant of the siblings, but the multiple births prevent the breed of madness. The power can't overwhelm the individual."

"Okaaay. So what you're telling me is, you're not a twin but a triplet?" I was still confused.

Falon slowly shook her head in denial. She wrung her hands in her lap before sitting on them to stop the nervous tick. "I'm … uh … actually a single birth. I have seven brothers and sisters, all multiple births, of which I am the first born."

Okay, cool. What was wrong with that? Why did Orin look like that was such a revelation?

"Am I missing something?" Cedric asked. "So she's not a twin, question answered."

"But I am left with many more," Orin responded. "If she is a single birth and first in line of power, that means she does not have to share her power with a sibling. She will be a literal force of nature when she matures, more powerful than the current queen."

I gaped at my best friend. She would one day be the most powerful Fae?

"That is so badass!" I cheered.

"Maybe teasing her wasn't the best of ideas, Mahon," Leo muttered from the other side of the flames.

"No, that's not true at all!" Falon had jumped to her feet. Standing above us, her near-white hair caught the light of the moon like a spotlight. "Everyone always thinks that. Everyone back home thinks I will one day be this mystical powerhouse. My mother, my siblings, the court—they all think that."

"Do you not want the power? Is that the problem?" I asked her. Maybe she didn't want to rule. Luthos knows I didn't want the destiny that's been shoved upon me.

"Don't you see? I'm glitchy, my powers don't always work right. Maybe it's a side effect of being a single birth. Maybe I can't control it all on my own. But either way, it's a weakness. One my mother and siblings will use if they think for even one second that I want to rule."

Her own family would use that against her? A flitting memory from our first meeting came to mind. *"I know I'm not exactly welcomed here, but it's not much different than how I'm treated at home with my family."*

I looked into Falon's haunted gaze as she swore, "I am not safe with my family. And because of that, you may not be safe with me."

A piercing whistle split the heavy silence that followed Falon's statement. The sound rose and sharpened in an intricate pattern. It was soon picked up and other tones of the same alarm mixed together to echo across the small clearing to our campsite.

Fervent footsteps thundered closer as a figure took shape, running full speed, directly for us. It was Asa. His face was panic stricken as he ran the last yards to our site.

"We're under attack!"

Chapter 16

The earth shook beneath my feet; the quakes and tremors so violent that it was a constant fight to remain upright. Rocks and other loose stones rattled along the ground, some jumping high enough to sting my shins.

From our makeshift camp in the woods, the pond had looked like a giant pit of boiling water. But from up close, it looked more like a turbulent sea in the prelude of a major storm. Waves leaped high, peaking at a level halfway up the tree before crashing back down on the water's surface.

The wind howled and bit, ripping and pulling at the water, urging it to spin and whirl faster in a feral dance of death.

"Casey!"

Through the barrage of shells, twigs, and other debris accumulating, I thought I heard my name. I listened harder, but only heard the wail of the storm as it besieged itself upon the clearing. Somehow, in all this madness, I'd lost sight of my friends. We sprinted off in different directions and the heavy winds and flying debris came between us, keeping me from finding them. The wind continued to grow in its intensity until I could feel it push against me, trying to force its way behind my clenched eyelids, down my nose and mouth.

This was no normal storm. It sought out the weaker parts of me. It looked for the soft spot in my defenses as it tried to find a way to consume me. I could feel it prodding, like a physical being, and unlike anything I had ever felt before.

The ground shook again with a low rumble as cracks appeared beneath my feet. I watched them grow and spread, the earth splintering wider with each new quake until I was surrounded by a fractured spider web of crevices. There were two near me, one in front and one behind, that were large enough for me to fall into. I wouldn't completely fit, but I would be in for a world of pain if I wasn't careful. I scanned around for anything that could get me out of this mess.

A long reaching tree branch would have been good right about now. But there was nothing. To the left of me was the pond, frothing in the savagery of the storm. And to my right was nothing but blackness and falling trees.

The world was literally coming apart around me.

Squinting through the next volley of debris, I tried to spot the group. Where were they? I could have sworn they were right behind me. But I was alone. Erratically, the wind changed, as if someone had flipped the switch on a fan from high to low.

The surface of the pond had yet to settle, but the trees were less like projectile weapons and more like hunks of swaying wood. No longer overwhelmed by the roar of the windstorm, I could make out the rustle of leaves as the fallen branches blew across the ground like jacked-up tumble weeds.

I heard the sloshing of the waves in the pond as some of the water spilled out to splash across the crippled ground.

And then I heard the laugh.

It was low and depraved; not manic enough to be considered deranged but that made it no less insidious. The hair on my arms stood at attention, fully aware that something was not right about that sound.

My palms began to sweat and the muscles in my legs trembled as I fought the urge to run. The remaining gusts of wind carried the laugh through the clearing. I kept turning my head, looking for the source, but it was coming from everywhere and nowhere at once.

Instinct and self-preservation finally overruled my locked muscles and I took a small step back, right onto the edge of the crevice behind me. More than half my foot stepped onto nothing but air and my arms swung around like a windmill as I tried to regain my balance.

But it was no use; down I went.

Without thinking, I threw my arms out behind me to soften my landing; but that was the worst thing I could have done. My right arm fell directly into the crevice as the rest of my body continued to slide back.

Caught on a root or some sharp rock inside, my arm bent at an unnatural angle for a split second, and that was all it took. I screamed. Lights danced behind my eyes, and I found it hard to take in a breath.

My body was stuck in shock, refusing to move or even breathe until it could process the pain just inflicted upon it. My arm, just below my shoulder, throbbed. I didn't care that I was lying half in a hole, created by some assailant who was probably watching me writhe with amusement.

I didn't care that anyone could come up to me and put a knife through my gut or break my neck. Hell, a sprite could come along and drag me down to the bottom of this swamp and I wouldn't give a damn.

My lungs recovered before any other part of me, and I choked on the breath that my body forced me to take. It was immediately expelled again on a shout of pain when I began to move. I had to get out of this hole.

I rolled toward my right, as far as I could until I couldn't stand it. Putting my good hand on the ground next to me, I pushed up with all the energy I had left. My arm came right out of the hole and I sat upright, panting; my head spinning as I cradled my arm to my chest.

My forearm rested across my belly, but when I tried to move my upper arm, a bolt of complete agony shot to the very tips of my fingers and my stomach rolled with nausea. I looked down, confident that I would find a bone sticking out, but my skin was smooth.

There was no shape distortion and it wasn't dislocated. I must have fractured it then. I released a heavy breath and straightened my back. Okay. A fracture I could deal with.

"Well, would you look at that, boys. Our elusive prey sits before us, alone and injured, like a present. And it's not even my birthday."

From across the clearing, five Imperials emerged. Stepping into the moonlight, the beams landed on the face of the Imperial who spoke. I remembered him from the group off the interstate, he was the cocky one that pissed me off. How had he found us all the way out here?

His eyes gleaned over the ruins of the clearing, from the still aggressive pond to where I sat battered on the ground.

"Hello, doll. Didn't think I'd let you get away so easily, did you?" I glared at him and he grinned. "Those birds by the interstate were a cute trick, but I think you'll find that it won't work this time. There are no vile little creatures around to aid you, and your friends are otherwise occupied at the moment."

My heart started to race as his words sunk in, and I couldn't stop my imagination from coming up with horrid ideas of what had happened to my friends. They could be injured out in the water somewhere, drowning, their bodies floating down the waterways as the wildlife picked them to pieces.

"What did you do, you arrogant bastard!"

"The name is Kael, sweetheart. Remember it. I will be pulling it from your lips every day on our trip back to the Academy."

His grin caused my insides to shrivel and twist. Nausea rose in the back of my throat, like an acrid fire that I couldn't put out. I knew whatever he had planned for me would not be good.

I flipped him off as the wind once again picked up and blew strands of hair across my cheek. It blew at me from across the clearing, from Kael, and carried along with it that nefarious laugh. I could feel the power of air behind it, guiding it into my ear canal until it felt like a sharp needle poking my brain with each calculated chuckle.

I scrunched my good shoulder, pushing my ear against it in an attempt to keep him out. But how did you keep out air? He continued to force his power at me, drilling into my head with a surgeon's precision.

It's like he knew exactly where to poke to make it hurt the worst. I winced with each jab and fought to keep from falling to the floor again with my hands over my ears. As I trembled and moaned, the Imperials laughed.

I heard it echo across the water at the same time that the voice in my head amped up the volume. I shrieked and shook my head, trying to get him out. The jerking only hurt my arm even more, and I cried out again.

"You make this too easy, pet. Harris, if you please."

At Kael's order, the Imperial I assumed to be Harris stepped forward. Pointing both palms to the ground he closed his eyes and let his head fall back. The ground beneath me shuddered. Thinking he meant to open another hole, I stumbled to my knees and made to run. But instead of the ground cracking wide open, a network of tree roots burst from the dirt and wound themselves around me.

The roots tightened around both my legs until they were pressed together. Another set of roots circled my stomach, crossing over my arms and squeezing my injured one that was already held against my side.

I didn't bother fighting, despite the pain. I knew it was no use, and all the jolting would only further damage my arm. I sat there as the Imperials approached and forced my face into an expression of boredom. All the while my heart hammered away in my chest.

"You plan on carrying me the entire way tied up in roots? What happened to good ol' fashioned rope?"

"Why carry around unnecessary items when nature always has something we can use?" Kael swaggered up to me and looked down, so cocky and full of himself.

Luthos, he was such a douche.

"Wow, good for you—going green." I gave him my biggest smile. "It's refreshing to see bad guys care about the environment."

The corner of his eye twitched, the only sign I saw that I had gotten on his nerves. He quickly put on another overconfident smirk and gestured for two of his men to lift me. I risked a quick glance through the trees, in the direction of our little camp.

Real fear built in my chest. If my friends hadn't already come, then something *must* have happened to them. Maybe Kael wasn't just talking out of his ass before. Maybe he actually did do something to my friends.

"They aren't coming, doll. There is no one left to come to your aid."

With a nod from Kael, two of the Imperials lifted me from the ground. One held onto my bound feet and the other gripped me under one arm. Off they went, carrying me between them like a log. Each step upset my fractured arm, but I bit my lip to keep from making a sound.

I wasn't going to give them the satisfaction. As we passed the pond, none of the Imperials paid attention to the bubbles forming in the water. The center had begun to boil. Around the edges, small opaque eyes could be seen moments before tiny ear fins broke the surface.

The sprites had arrived.

One by one, more heads appeared until the pond was filled with them. On land, I saw flashes of pale skin as even more sprites in their mortal form took position in the trees.

"YOU. DARE."

The voice of the queen boomed and the Imperials dropped me as they moved to cover their ears. That wouldn't work. The sprites communicated telepathically, but I guess they didn't know that. As it was, my already sensitive brain took offense to the queen's tone, but I also could do nothing to stop it.

"You dare come into my territory, attack my people, KILL MY DAUGHTER!"

Her roar literally shook the clearing. Vengeful hisses backed the queen's declaration as the other sprites moved in to surround us. The Imperials looked on in fear, all except Kael. His face was frozen in his signature arrogant expression as he gradually backed away from the queen.

And the queen, she was a sight to behold.

Her arms were raised as the water lifted her straight into the air from the very center of the pond. She was level with the top of the Cyprus tree and looked down upon the Imperials like an evil kid about to annihilate an ant mound.

The waves closest to her began to swirl until they cultivated two cyclones that grew in height matching the level of the queen. They silently spun around her and waited for her command. The full moon above was shadowed by dark clouds as the wind stirred once again.

"There will be nothing left of you when we are finished."

The sprites attacked.

The Imperials tried to run, but they had already been surrounded. From the pond, the sprites attacked with water. They shot violent and overpowering streams directly into the Imperial's faces to distract them. As the Imperials tried to protect their eyes, the sprites on land moved in.

Attacking with the fierceness of a feral cat, a sprite in her mortal form leapt onto an Imperial and flayed his neck open with one swipe of her hand. Before her feet touched the ground, Harris sent a volley of roots straight through her, skewering her where she landed.

The queen lost her shit. Pointing her webbed hand at Harris, a cyclone left its rotation around her and thundered to the edge of the pond. Unaware of his impending doom, Harris used the tree roots to suffocate another siren in her mortal form.

The spindly arms wrapped around her throat and squeezed until a sickening crack could be heard even over the bellow of the twisting water. The sprite's head lolled to the side, the bones inside her neck crushed beyond repair.

With the clench of a fist, the cyclone's spin increased, sucking more water from the pond to increase its strength. It traveled to the bank of the pond, mere feet from the still clueless Imperial. And then, with the flick of a fin, small vessels of water grew like arms from the center of the twister.

They caught onto Harris, like snares, and drew him into the heart of the swirling typhoon. He had time to let out a surprise yelp before being drug back to the center of the pond. Having served its purpose, the cyclone slowly dissipated, leaving a half drowned Harris treading water, surrounded by an army of vindictive sprites. As one, they leapt on him, dragging him down, down … until not even bubbles remained on the surface.

Two down, three to go.

On the battle went, the remaining Imperials holding their own. Sprite's were not known for combat—their power lay in ambush, taking their victims unaware. And the further from the pond the Imperials moved, the weaker the sprite's attacks.

The entire time, I watched from the ground. Still tangled in my binds, I could do nothing but wiggle and flop as I tried to inconspicuously move toward the trees. Every thump against my arm ripped the breath from my lungs.

My hoarse barks of pain were concealed by the sounds of battle, and the sprites moved right over me as if I was never even there. But I didn't want to stick around and test their temper after they disposed of their enemy. Their assault pushed the Imperials further from me until I could no longer see them.

I was running out of time.

A small sprite approached me. She was in her mortal form: tiny, dainty, and with ethereal pale skin that glowed like quartz. It was in complete contrast to her hair, which was jet black and curled at her waist. Her cheekbones curved up into a heart shape with plump pink lips in the center.

She knelt beside me and used a sharpened shell to cut at my binds. Her eyes were as blue as the water in the pond, and they were wide under a scrunched brow as she concentrated on freeing me. She was absolutely beautiful.

When the last of my binds fell, she stood and held out her petite hand. This girl couldn't be more than twelve.

"Hurry. Before my mother notices."

She kept stealing glances at the queen, who was too busy trying to murder the Imperials.

"*Einin?*" I asked in complete shock.

She nodded and pulled on my good hand, forcing me into a run. We ducked into the trees, Einin dragging me along with surprising strength. She was astoundingly lithe on her feet, for a creature of the water, and I bet that she spent more time in this form than her mother would have guessed.

I liked her. She was spirited and rebellious, and just a tad too trusting for a princess: a mini Falon. She led me to the edge of the island where I saw two canoes waiting, tied to trees leaning over the shore.

"Casey!"

Cedric bolted from his spot by the canoes and enveloped me in a hug. His arms squeezed me too hard and I let out a strangled cry. He instantly released me, but kept his hands gently on my waist as he stepped back to survey me.

"What happened? Are you hurt? Where were you?"

I shook my head, still riding out the fresh wave of pain. There would be time for questions later.

"My arm," I forced out.

The rest of the group moved in to check me over, concern written on every one of their faces. I smiled despite the pain. Their care comforted me better than any drug.

"You will have time later to take care of her. For now, you must run." Einin spoke, ushering the group away from me. All but Cedric. He refused to let go of me; his hand squeezed mine in a silent signal that he wasn't going anywhere.

"She's right," Orin agreed. "We need to move. Thank you, princess, for all your help."

Einin nodded once in acceptance, then darted back into the trees. What was left of our bags and meager supplies was already in the canoes. Mahon waved me over to the one he had untied. With his help, I settled myself in the center, behind Asa and in front of Falon.

She gave my good shoulder a gentle squeeze, trying to convey all that needed to be said in a second's worth of time. Orin pushed us off from shore and climbed into the rear seat. A few minutes later, Mahon had the other canoe untied and was pushing it away before climbing in.

Cedric sat in the middle, not okay with having to be separated from me. I could feel his gaze on my back as we silently glided down the waterway. The only sounds I heard were the paddles pushing us through the water and the distant splashes of gators going after their evening meals.

Every now and then their yellow eyes reflected off the moonlight. No sounds of battle could be heard and I wondered who won. Would Kael still be around to hunt me? Or did he finally meet his match?

We traveled the last few hours of the night, putting as much distance between us and the sprites as we could, before stopping at another small island. Orin and Mahon hopped out and dragged the canoes close enough to tie to a tree. Without speaking, we moved to make camp.

Asa set up for a fire, Mahon wandered off to find more kindling, and the rest got to work building a temporary place to rest. With only one capable arm, I was no use in any of those tasks. I sat close to Asa, my back against a tree, as I watched him assemble small twigs into a pile.

I tried to stay awake, but I was mentally and physically exhausted. Somewhere between one breath and the next I fell asleep.

Chapter 17

I t's definitely broken."

A twinge of pain shot through my upper arm as Asa finished the final touches on the sling. Using one of Mahon's spare, long-sleeved shirts, my arm was secured tightly against my body. If I was careful, I shouldn't damage it any further. But *you* try moving around in the rural Everglades with knotted sleeves behind your neck and only one useful arm.

This shit sucked.

I leaned back against the tree trunk and let out a tired breath. Around me, the others were busy breaking down our temporary camp. We knew that we couldn't leave a trail or any evidence that we had been here. I wasn't sure how the battle between the sprites and Imperials ended, but you could never be too careful.

With that in mind, I pushed my back against the trunk and used its support to stand. With the extra weight of my right arm awkwardly tied to my body, I was a little off balance. It made the initial act of sitting or standing difficult, but once I was on two feet, I was okay.

From the corner of my eye, I could see Mahon and Orin loading the canoes and knew we were about to leave. I used my foot to kick sand across the dying embers of our campfire. It wasn't enough to just smother it; I needed to completely erase its existence.

Pulling my foot back even farther, I scooped a larger haul, my left arm flailing about as I tried to remain upright. A rock must have been hidden beneath the surface because the next thing I knew I was falling on my ass.

"Dammit!"

That hurt. My tailbone was literally vibrating and a sharp tingle traveled all the way up into my lower back. How was I supposed to be of any help if even a damn rock could take me down? Stifled giggling behind me almost overshadowed the sound of approaching footsteps.

"Whoever is laughing right now is about to take a swim with the alligators." I growled.

"You never did learn how to properly take a fall."

I threw my head back with a groan. Why, of all people, did Cedric have to be the one to see me bust my ass? He was never going to let me hear the end of this.

"Shut up. If I recall, I never learned because *you* would always trip me."

He laughed and I awkwardly maneuvered myself onto my feet. It required a lot of using my knees, my good elbow, and sand making its way into my cutoffs. Waving away his offered hand, I scowled.

Cedric shrugged. "What? We were kids, and I was *supposed* to do that! The point is not knowing the fall is coming."

By habit, I went to punch his shoulder and remembered a second too late that my own arm was bound against me … and broken.

Son of a—

Nausea rolled and my meager lunch found its way into the back of my throat. If I kept this up, this was going to be a very long trip. A very long and very *painful* trip. I had just broken my dominant arm. How long before I got used to using my left side? How long before it wasn't instinct to move something that was broken?

Cedric's arm wrapped around my waist as he took the full weight of my body. "Easy. Just breathe."

I listened to his advice and took in clear, deep breaths. As the nausea and pain began to subside, I could once again stand straight.

"Thanks."

He brushed a strand of hair from my face. "You can always lean on me, Casey."

His face inched closer, blocking the sunlight beaming through the trees. His eyelids lowered as he stared at my lips. I could feel his breath puff across my cheek moments before his lips softly brushed against mine. The kiss was so gentle I could almost convince myself that it wasn't happening. Cedric's tongue flicked against my bottom lip just as Orin shouted for us to load up.

"All right lovebirds, you can canoodle another time. Let's move!"

If I wasn't a role model for one-sided mummies, I would have thrown my arms in the air. Instead, I settled for glaring at Orin as if my eyes could burn a hole through his face. Seriously, the universe hated me.

I could feel Cedric chuckle as he ushered me toward the canoes, his arm still around my waist. "It's okay, Casey. We've got time. I'm not going anywhere."

He kissed the side of my head before helping me settle in the center of the canoe. Falon squeezed in behind me and cleared her throat. When I turned to look at her, her face was red with suppressed laughter. Her lips

125

were pinched together and her cheeks puffed nearly to bursting as she tried to regain her composure.

"What?" I asked.

"*I'm not going anywhere*?" she exclaimed. "Oh honey, he has got it *bad*. And so do you. Yeesh, the way you guys were looking at each other …" She gave me a critical look. "Just don't let me walk behind a tree later and catch you guys doing the nasty, okay?"

"Falon!"

"Cause that would be so, so wrong."

Absolute mortification stained my face, I was sure. Glancing above Falon's head, Orin continued to clear his throat like something was trapped in it. His eyes looked anywhere but at me.

"Can we not have this conversation, please?" I barely sputtered out before turning back around to face the front.

My face was burning. I didn't think Cedric could hear her as far ahead as he was, but Orin and Asa clearly heard every word. Orin continued to make sounds as if he was being strangled and Asa had begun to hum to himself. I wanted to sink to the bottom of the canal. I wasn't anywhere near ready to think about Cedric and me like that. I mean, we only just had our second kiss.

And I was definitely not wanting to talk about it in front of Orin and Asa. An uncomfortable silence settled over our canoe. Well, uncomfortable for all the passengers except a particularly mouthy Fae. While the Vamps and I tried our best to pretend the others didn't exist, Falon sat there, her hand skimming the top of the water, quietly singing to herself.

My shoulder, at that moment, decided that it hadn't had enough attention and began to throb for no apparent reason. The sun shone down on my back and the top of my head, causing sweat to bead and drip into my eyes and mosquitos to flock to me like I had rung the dinner bell.

If we didn't get to where we were going soon, I was going to scream.

"So, why the Everglades?" I asked Orin.

The sun had reached its apex about an hour ago and had begun its journey back down again. We spent the hottest part of the day under whatever sparse shade we could find out here and were only just pushing back out onto the water. Orin said we weren't very far now, but if the camp was around here, I was confused as to why. The Everglades was secluded and rural, with its many channels and waterways making it hard to pinpoint the camp if you didn't already know its location. I understood that.

But looking around, I saw nothing but brown water and grass. The world around us was vast, but flat. The sawgrass was not near enough cover as a tree would be, and the few trees that were out this far were few and far between. And not to mention dead; they were nothing more than thin sticks in the ground.

"All it would take is one Academy plane to fly overhead and we would be seen. How can the camp be kept out here?"

Orin only smiled in reply and pointed to a spot off in the distance behind me. Turning back to look, I saw a large body of dark, murky water between us and what looked like an island. The black water calmly rolled and carried us closer. As the Vamps paddled, I kept my eyes on the skyline.

Suddenly, the sun began to dim as it was blocked out by an explosion of green. The entire day, I had been surrounded by nothing but browns, tans, and grays—the only green being the lily pads. When solid land bleeds away, the Everglades turns into nothing but grass floating on water. It gets dreary after a few hours.

As we floated closer to the island, the trees closest to the water stretched their branches as if welcoming us home. When we pulled into the shade they offered, I gasped. The roots of the trees were climbing and dipping, twisting and weaving between one another to create a network of hardened roots.

The roots were so tightly woven together that they actually created land. We pulled our canoes up alongside them and tied a rope to keep them from drifting off. I cautiously reached out a hand and brushed it along one of the wooden loops.

"What are they?" I asked in wonder.

"These," Orin answered, "are mangroves. They are a special kind of tree that only grows in the tropics, along shores and coastlines, where freshwater meets saltwater."

"Mangroves." I tried the word out. "They're beautiful."

These trees embodied life. Their roots held them together in one giant, lasting embrace. They provided a home for thousands of little lives. I didn't miss the schools of fish and little sharks swimming between the roots as I stepped off the canoe.

I had to climb up a few feet to get onto solid ground, with help of course, and I used the many footholds created by the twisted bark. The wood was wet, even at the top, which told me that these roots spent a majority of the time underwater. It also told me it was currently low tide.

When the rest of the group joined us on solid land, we had moved a ways from the shore and stood on a well-worn path under a thick canopy of greens. Orin led the way and I trailed along, my neck in a permanent crick as I gaped at the view above me.

Flitters of color caught my attention in every direction my eyes settled. The fruit and flowers grew in abundance here, and the birds had feathers in every color of the rainbow. The sun shimmered and danced between the leaves of the canopy, playing peek-a-boo with us down below.

The air was cooler in here, with a light scent of salt and brine mixed with the sweetness of flowers. For the first time since we had arrived in this blasted state, I didn't have a headache and my hair didn't puff out like a cotton ball. A cool ocean breeze flooded our path on its way inland.

I took in a deep breath and let it back out, finally feeling myself start to truly relax for the first time in a week. There was just something about this place.

"It's beautiful, isn't it?" Cedric asked as he pulled alongside me.

I could only nod. I didn't think beautiful was a strong enough word. There were no words, in fact, that I knew to properly describe this place. The symphony of sounds echoing through the trees was better than any recording on one of those soothing machines.

The colors around me were so vibrant that I couldn't help but smile; it was like the island was throwing us a party. The breeze even carried with it a sense of peace. As we continued to walk, the trees thinned out and the birds sang softer. Through the branches I could make out a clearing up ahead.

As we got closer, I noticed it wasn't just one small clearing, but a network of others, broken up by patches of hardy mangroves and Button Wood trees. The clearing we walked into had a decent sized fire in the center with a rather large pot hanging over it.

Other pots, plates, and cooking utensils were lying on a set of homemade shelves off to the side of the fire. People muddled about, not noticing us newcomers, which gave me time to study them. The woman stirring the pot over the fire was just leaving her prime, maybe early fifties, with dirty blonde hair, sprinkled with gray in a long braid down her back.

Her muscles flexed as she stirred, and I noticed a sword strapped to her back. Knives hung from her waist, and I was sure that there were more tucked away out of sight. The weapons didn't surprise me; this was supposed to be a training camp after all. It was the fact that the woman was a Shifter that caught me off guard.

As I continued to scan the clearing, the other men and women were dressed in a similar fashion as the cook: comfortable clothes that would be easy to fight in, with an array of weapons attached to arms, legs, and hips.

There was a couple sitting to my right, eating their evening meal, and something about them caught my attention. The man was a Vampire, I was sure of it. The glint of red in his eyes told me so. But the woman had to be either Fae or Pixie. Her willowy frame was similar to most others of her kind.

I watched as the couple sat next to each other without a care. They were laughing, and the woman swatted the Vamp on his arm like they were friends, which obviously they were. Orin had told me that all the races came together here, but it was one thing to hear it and another to actually see it.

Even at the Academy the races didn't get along this well. People usually kept to their own kind—getting along with others, but not necessarily going out of their way to befriend someone different. It was a rare thing that Falon and I were best friends. Most races were scared of the Fae, so they were avoided.

Shifters had a healthy rivalry with Witches at best, and of course the Vampires were hated. What I was seeing here was as if the boundaries between the races didn't even exist, and it was absolutely amazing.

All around me, the races were mixing. A Vampire was cleaning dishes with a wood sprite, a shifter tossed a ball around with a Witch, and ... was that wood sprite now *making out* with that Vamp?

Orin stepped from the shadows and walked to the center of the clearing, toward the fire. Almost as one, each being in the clearing stopped what they were doing to stare. Excited whispers circled around us, carried along by the afternoon breeze.

"Orin's back."

The same two words tickled against my ear as the Shifter who stirred over the fire walked up to Orin with a big grin. Throwing her arms around his shoulders, she gave him a hug strong enough to snap a tree and then clapped him on the back.

They spoke in hushed whispers and Orin nodded "yes" in answer to the Shifter's question. She looked relieved, if not a little doubtful, until Orin turned with his arm gestured out at me. More people made it to our clearing from the connecting ones, appearing in the bushes and some even dropping out of trees.

I felt the weight of their eyes pressing against me as someone let out a celebratory cheer. The others picked it up, and it grew until even the birds joined in. Orin strolled over to me and grabbed my hand, pulling me along with him to the center.

"Come, they want to meet you. You're who they've been waiting for."

Chapter 18

The voices were what woke me. Mingled laughter and calls for breakfast resounded off the thick bundle of trees that had become my new home. I had kicked my sleeping bag off sometime during the night, and it now resided three feet below me, covered in sand and dirt.

"Great. That's going to be fun."

To my left, Falon still slept—her mouth gaping open as a welcome fly-trap for any wandering bug. I sighed. It was still dark out with the sun behind the trees as it fought to rise. People woke up early here. There was a lot to get done in a day to keep this place running.

As my eyes adjusted to the meager light supply, I blindly felt around for the ladder and silently cursed this island for having such a saturated and spongy outer-layer. To keep from sleeping on the damp ground, we all stayed in small man-made huts on stilts.

An idea borrowed from the native Seminoles, the hut was nothing more than thick Cypress posts and palmetto palm thatch leaves woven together for a roof. We slept on a flat, wooden platform about three feet above the ground and used a small ladder to get up there.

A ladder that was successfully evading me at the moment.

Giving up the search, I slipped on my shoes, swung my legs out over the side, and jumped. I landed with a soft *oompf* and wobbled a bit as I fought to regain my balance. In the neighboring clearing, a large fire was already burning, a diligent Zora tending to its flames.

That woman never slept. In the three days that I had been here, I had never seen her away from that fire. Being the cook for the entire camp was a demanding job, and one that garnered a lot of respect.

Moving slowly through the brush, I stopped on the outer edge of the clearing and waited. A few people were in line for breakfast, but they had yet to see me. And I wanted to keep it that way. Once full daylight arrived, I would once again be sought out by all the curious individuals of this camp.

From day one I had been bombarded by anxious faces, eager to get a look at me—the girl from the prophecy. The older residents smiled from afar and allowed the younger population their time to pester me with excited questions.

By now, the entire camp probably knew my favorite color, favorite food, and my sexual orientation. You'd be surprised how many times I had to answer that last one. There weren't any others here my age, the youngest being in their early twenties, so it felt awkward to be receiving all this attention.

"Stop shuffling, I can't stand that. Now, get over here and grab some breakfast."

Zora's keen gaze was zeroed in on me as she continued to stir the pot held over the fire. Her blonde braid was draped across her shoulder and the lines around her mouth told me there was little room for argument.

Hiding my grimace, I left the safety of the deep shadows and walked to the center of the clearing. A young looking Vamp noticed me and gave a small wave as he headed over. But before he could say a word, Zora was between us.

"I know you have better places to be, Mr. Parker, than bothering this poor girl. Let the child get some breakfast in her belly before the whole camp and their mommas come a swarming. Now go; off with you."

My shoulders slumped in relief and a small tinge went through my right arm at the movement.

"Thanks," I whispered, holding my tin plate out for her to fill. She set a scoop of berries from the garden on one side and a thin, white tube of some kind of animal meat on the other.

"Don't mention it, chickee. I could see on your face that the attention was getting to you. Not to worry. It won't be long before they've had their fill of you and leave you be."

My smile was honest and grateful as I popped a berry in my mouth and watched her drop more meat into the pot.

"It's a tad overwhelming is all. I've never really liked to be the center of attention; it always meant bad things for me."

She nodded as she worked; the weapons on her hip chiming when she moved.

"I could sense that you weren't one to flaunt your talents. Sit, chickee. Eat here by the fire and not a soul will bother you."

And so I did. I kept my head down and allowed myself to lounge in the warmth of the fire and Zora's protection. The sun eventually rose above the treetops and more people stopped by for their breakfast.

If one of them tried to speak to me, Zora would shoo them off. She even used a hot spoon on a few of the younger Shifters that didn't take her order seriously. I gave each person a polite smile, trying to convey that I wasn't being a bitch, but I needed my space.

When my plate was empty, Zora piled it back up without a word. I wasn't sure how long I sat there listening to her hum as she worked, but a familiar voice soon interrupted the soothing sounds and I looked up to greet Orin.

He smiled at Zora as she stepped aside with a nod and moved to help the person in line behind him.

"Morning, Orin," I said with a smile.

I was more relaxed than I had been for days, and Orin's answering grin told me that he noticed.

"Good morning, Casey. Mind if I talk to you for a minute?"

Setting my plate in the dirty dish basket, I wiped my palm on my shorts and stood. Orin led us away from the clearing, smiling and returning waves to those who called out to him. I even returned a few of my own.

"So, what's up?" I asked.

"There's someone I would like you to meet." He pointed to a roughly built Vamp standing at the mouth of a well-worn trail.

As we approached, I took note of his height, which was at least a foot taller than mine. He had blond hair, trimmed short, and a face that looked like it had been chiseled from marble. His nose was crooked from one too many breaks and his muscles could rival Mahon's.

"This is Sacha. He's a childhood friend of mine, and I would like you to train with him if you're okay with that?"

I must not have heard him correctly. Train with him? My arm was broken, not even Eli made me train when that happened.

"How exactly am I supposed to train with one arm?" I asked him.

"It's not training like you're probably thinking. You won't be doing judo, or jump-kicks, and definitely no weapons."

Then what was I going to be doing? At my confused expression, Sacha stepped forward and lightly pushed on my left shoulder. Caught off guard, I would have hit the ground if Orin hadn't grabbed me.

"Hey! What the hell?"

Sacha ignored my shouts. "Your center of gravity is off, your reflexes are childlike at best, and you weren't even properly prepared for that fall you were about to take."

Sacha looked down his nose at me, like I wasn't even worth his time. With a heavy hand on my shoulder, he told me his plans.

"You need to relearn everything you know. From the ground up." He shoved.

And this time, Orin didn't catch me.

Lunch wasn't as peaceful as breakfast had been. This was the hottest part of the day; the sun was blazing at its highest strength, temperatures in the shade were only slightly cooler than not, and even the ocean breeze struggled to puncture the muggy haze that settled over the island.

As a result, the entire camp idled to a halt. Tools were dropped in place, their owners opting to take it easy until the sun relented in its attack on us. Trainings were put on hold in favor for a dip in a nearby pool, and eventually, everyone ended up here, in the main clearing where Zora steadily turned out food.

It was packed, with seating room overflowing into the adjacent clearings. The noise created by this many people was more than I was used to. It took almost three weeks for us to get here. That was three weeks of hiding in a secluded cave and then traveling in a multitude of cars.

The ruckus made by a group of seven wouldn't even dent the cacophony that was generated by this camp. I had gotten too used to the peaceful silence we had traveled in. I could hardly hear the sounds of nature over this rowdy group.

The more I watched, the more I realized that the people here acted much like any other family. There was the older generation, who laughed and mingled but kept a wary eye out for danger and for those they deemed under their charge. And then there was the younger generation, all of them still older than me, but stuck in that that weird between stage where they were no longer kids but acted too stupid to be considered adults.

A small group of young Shifters were locked in a game of dare, each trying to do something more brave and reckless than the one before. Their antics were the main source of entertainment for those on that side of the clearing.

I felt a pang of homesickness as I watched them. They reminded me of the Shifters back at the school and how they were always performing stupid stunts for the delight of the rest of the student body. Walking toward Zora, I grabbed a metal plate from the pile and stepped in line for food. I couldn't tell what was on the menu for today, but it smelled incredible.

"Hey, it's Casey, right?"

A smooth voice spoke to me from my left. Glancing over my shoulder, I recognized the young Vamp that had tried to talk to me earlier this morning. Zora had called him Parker. Right now, he gave me a sheepish grin as his hand lifted to brush the back of his hair. He ducked his head slightly as I nodded.

"Yeah. I knew that was your name, actually. Everyone does. I just didn't know how else to start a conversation with you," he admitted.

I let out a laugh, surprising myself, and he chuckled along with me. He was cute, and I didn't just mean his looks. His entire demeanor came across as sweet and welcoming. It helped that he wasn't looking at me with outright fascination like others had.

I would guess that he was only a few years older than me, definitely one of the youngest members of camp, and I already found him easier to tolerate.

"It's nice to meet you," I told him. "Sorry about earlier. I'm not the most hospitable person when I haven't had my morning chocolate."

He stood speechless for a moment, probably surprised that I answered him. But he quickly recovered with a broad grin.

"I wasn't sure if you would recognize me from this morning. Zora wouldn't let me that close to you."

It was my turn to give a sheepish grin. "My fault again. I think I've been overwhelmed by all the attention here, and she was just being cool, you know, giving me a break from it all."

He nodded like he understood. "I can get that. When more of the other races began to arrive a few years back, they acted like that toward me and the other Vamps. We—"

He stopped mid-sentence as his eyes grew round. His entire body froze, as if he had said something he shouldn't. He slightly cringed as he watched me, like I would freak out at any moment. I frowned and looked around.

Everything was the same as it had been only moments before. We were a little closer to Zora, since the line had moved, but nothing was out of the ordinary.

"Is something wrong?" I finally asked.

If possible, his eyes bugged out even more. "Is something wrong? I just told you I was a Vampire!" His shocked expression quickly turned thoughtful. "I thought you would be freaking out more."

Now I was really confused. "You know I came here with, like, four other Vampires, right? And my current trainer is one too."

"But we were lectured over and over to let you and your friends know when we introduced ourselves, so you wouldn't be caught by surprise." He seemed more upset that he messed that up than the fact that I could still have the potential to freak out.

Was this guy mental? Anyone could see the red tint to his eyes, it was practically blatant in this sunlight. And his skin was a different shade than a human's: lighter and more polished. I understood that these signs weren't as obvious as a pair of fangs, but you'd think that people would notice these small differences the longer they lived around a massive population of Vampires.

"What are you going on about? I wasn't surprised. I knew you were a Vamp from the moment I saw you."

He regarded me, not believing a word I said. "How? Did Zora tell you?"

Maybe this guy *was* mental. I opened my mouth to tell him that it was his creepy ass eyes that had given him away, but I was interrupted by a short, older woman wielding a spoon.

"This food's going cold, chickee. Either put out your plate or get out of line."

I swiftly turned to face Zora who held out a hunk of meat she pulled from the fire. Thrusting out my plate, I practically salivated as I watched the steaming fish settle next to some home grown veggies she put beside them.

"Sorry, Zora."

"Mmhmm," she replied before waving me away as she got back to work.

I strolled from the line, in search of a spot to stop where I could dig into my lunch and had almost forgotten about Parker. He ran up beside me, barely managing to keep his food on his plate.

"Wait, wait!"

I paused so he could speak. A little of this morning's frustration returning the longer I was kept from my meal.

"How can you tell that I'm a Vampire? You never answered me."

I'm sure *duh* was plastered across my face. Was this guy playing me for stupid? I studied him, but his expression remained sincere and my brain hurt as I tried to figure out if he was setting me up for something or if he was honestly that clueless.

"Is there a problem here?" Orin cautiously approached from the side and stopped when he was only a foot away. Close enough to not be overheard if he needed to resolve something quietly.

"I'm not sure. I can't tell if this guy is just being an asshole and teasing the new girl, or if he just isn't all there." Orin's eyebrows shot up at my tone.

I was getting kind of cranky, not gonna lie. I was hungry, hot, bruised from training, and this kid was pushing all my buttons right now.

"Hey! I'm not sure what pissed her off, sir." Parker spoke to Orin, his tone way more respectful than mine. "I was asking who told her I was a Vampire."

"No one told me! Stop acting like I'm an idiot. Like I said, I knew what you were the moment I saw you."

If I wasn't so afraid of dropping my food, or embarrassing myself, I would have swung on him. But since I didn't want to go back through the lunch line, and a punch with my left side would have had half a chance at landing, I refrained.

Orin stood there, completely at a loss for words. He kept swinging his head back and forth between us as he tried to figure out what was going on. Clearing his throat, he put his arm around Parker's shoulder and steered him away from me.

Glancing back, he fixed me with what I called his authoritative glare. "Don't move."

With a huff, I leaned against the nearest tree and longingly stared at my cooling food. Not for the first time I wished my arm wasn't broken. If I had both hands, I could be eating right now.

"What was that all about?" Orin demanded when he returned. Behind him, Parker sat with a group of others his age and continued to send me confused glances. "Why are you lying and picking fights? Did he say something to upset you?"

Orin seemed genuinely concerned, but I couldn't get over the fact that he thought *I* was the one lying.

"Why don't you guys believe me? I don't get why this is such a big deal. And I wasn't picking fights. It's not like I made fun of his jacked up red eyes or his disturbingly smooth skin." I mumbled the last part, like a sullen child. But Orin still heard me.

"What did you just say?" Oh, no. Maybe that was a little too far.

"I didn't mean—"

Orin shook his head. "Do you mean to tell me that you can see these traits?"

Maybe it was something in the water. Orin was acting pretty slow right now too. I literally just told him that. I nodded yes.

"Seriously, what is the big deal?" I was beyond exasperated at this point.

Orin grabbed my good arm and gently walked me to the other side of the tree. He looked around, seeing if anyone was close enough to hear our conversation. Across the clearing, he locked eyes with Asa but shook his head when he made to come over.

"Casey, not many people can see these traits in us. It's part of what makes us such ideal hunters. You can't see the monsters we are until it's too late."

I gaped at him. But those traits were so obvious to me. They had been since the first time I noticed them in the cave. The only reason I hadn't known Orin for who he was earlier was because he was emaciated and covered in crap.

"I don't understand." I finally managed to say.

"Neither do I. But I think it best that we don't discuss it with anyone until I do more research. Fair?"

I nodded. That seemed like the right choice. Peeking back over to where Parker sat, I felt guilty for how I had yelled at him. I guess it really was me who was being the asshole. Orin gave my arm a reassuring squeeze before walking away across the clearing, to where Asa stood.

I sat on the soft ground, setting my plate beside me. My appetite had waned, taking a back seat to this new discovery. Others couldn't recognize what I could; they couldn't tell Vampires from humans.

Analyzing all the encounters I had had with Orin and the gang, a light clicked on in my mind. When I had first woke-up in the cave, I was petrified, because I could tell what race Orin and his men belonged to. But Cedric, he was absolutely clueless. At the time, I couldn't understand how he could have sat there with them and not noticed. But now it all made sense; he couldn't see what I could. He literally had no idea.

How could I tell the difference? It was possible that my healing powers allowed me to differentiate between the races. Maybe the distinction was needed to make the healing work. Although, I hadn't noticed a difference between healing Cedric, Falon, or Asa.

I closed my eyes and leaned my head back. Tension had begun to build in my neck, stemming from the pounding in my temples. I was exhausted. Between my morning training, the heat, and now this mental riddle, I needed a nap.

My hut wasn't that far away, and afternoon break lasted a few hours, until the heat lessened. Knowing that I could probably get in a good hour's rest, I left the clearing and the confusing people it held for the safety and solitude of my bed.

Chapter 19

Let me tell you, training with only one arm sucked worse than the fact that there were no chocolate chips on this island, or waffles. I had to take it back to the basics. All the way back. Like, six-year-old training, back.

My reflexes were nonexistent on my left side, I could hardly punch with any kind of control, and every defensive move I had ever learned felt alien to me without my right arm to guide the maneuver. My trainer told me that this was actually a blessing.

He thought that having to solely rely on my left hand for everything would make learning to fight with this side a quicker process. After slamming onto my back for the fifth time that day, *I* thought he was an asshole.

"Again."

My trainer stood several steps away as he waited for me to stand. This was also part of my training—falling down and learning how to get back on my feet with only one side to aid me. I had to say, I was getting quicker at it. It only took a handful of tries before my body made it work.

Sacha had been my trainer for almost two weeks now. In all that time he had never cracked a joke, and I noticed that he's utterly single minded when it comes to teaching me. Aside from his obvious aversion to happiness, I couldn't argue with why Orin had recommended him. He knew his stuff. I just wished he would smile a little more.

"Are you just going to lay there, or can we continue?"

I rolled to my left and pushed off the ground with my forearm before using my knees. Turning to face Sacha, I adjusted my sling and moved within striking range.

"That was better, but you're still too slow. You leave yourself exposed when you get up like that," Sacha said as he lifted his hands into the guard position.

I nodded and readied myself for his attack: right foot back, and left hand up to protect my face. He gave almost no warning; he was that good. Most people have a tell—a small signal that hinted when they were about to strike.

Me, I tended to scrunch my brow, which was something I was working on. With Sacha, the corner of his eye gave a single tick and that was the only heads up I got. He struck, faster than a cobra's bite, and his palm passed right through my defenses to hit me square in the chest.

This time, I dug my foot in and remained upright, if not a little winded. A frustrated growl escaped my lips. I was supposed to block him, but each time I was too slow.

"Well, at least we know you can take a hit. But that wasn't the point of the—"

"I know!" I interrupted with a shout. "I was supposed to block you. I'm trying, okay?" He watched me pace around as I tried to work out my agitation. "You told me my blocks were good now. So what am I doing wrong?"

I stopped directly in front of him with my hand on my hip.

"Nothing,." he replied. "Your blocks *are* good; perfect form and they're solid. You just haven't developed the speed yet. Your body's first instinct is still to call on your right hand, before it remembers it can't. That split second causes you to get hit."

"But how do I fix that?"

He grinned. It was the first time I had seen him do that and it was scary as hell. His lips didn't pull to the corners in a graceful slide, no, they fully receded from his gums like a dog baring his teeth.

"Practice," he answered.

The corner of his eye twitched and I was far from ready when he struck again. I wasn't able to block his attack. Shocker. However, by pure luck I sidestepped his hand and watched as it flew past me.

Smirking like a badass, I looked up, daring him not to acknowledge that move. But he shook his head, his expression telling me I still had a lot to learn. With a movement too quick to catch, he hooked his foot behind mine and pulled.

The ground disappeared from beneath me as I once again landed on my back. Self-preservation had me rolling to the left so I wouldn't jar my arm. But the shock of the fall still reverberated through my body and caused my teeth to clench to prevent the scream from escaping.

I was never going to heal at this rate.

"That looked like it hurt."

I slowly pushed to my feet with a groan. "How are you always around to see me fall on my ass?"

Cedric only laughed as he walked over. He looked at Sacha and gave him that nod that seemed to be universal to all guys. Sacha lifted his chin in return before setting his gaze back on me. What I saw in that look filled me with dread for tomorrow's training.

"You can go," he told me, waving us away. "It's heat break anyway. But we will pick back up right here tomorrow," he promised.

Cedric held his arm out and I gladly stepped into it. He then steered me away with an arm around my waist. I leaned into him as he guided us over roots and rocks to the smooth main clearing where Zora was serving lunch. As we got closer to the crowd, we were recognized by many.

The older residents smiled at our youth as we wandered by, fitting snug together like perfect pieces of a puzzle. The younger residents had no hang ups about approaching us, however. It didn't bother me as much as it used to.

Our newness was finally starting to wear off, and I was now being approached by people with whom I had begun tentative friendships with, rather than those just curious to get a look at me. With my mind on new friendships, it wasn't too much of a leap to think about my failed attempt with Parker.

Especially since he was sitting just feet away from us.

He glanced our way as we strolled by and I met his stare with a cautious smile and a small wave. Some time had passed since I blew up on him for not believing that I could see the true traits of a Vampire and I was hoping that he had gotten over it so we could move on.

But Parker answered my wave with a frown before turning away. Guilt wound through my chest as Zora piled our plates with food, and it stayed even after Falon caught up with us. The three of us left the clogged arteries of the main clearing and its neighboring meadows for our favorite spot out behind the sleeping huts.

A large group of fichus trees made the focal point of this section of the island. They were the thickest and tallest around, with ropes of dead vines that tangled through their twisted branches before hanging down to the ground like curtains of hair.

One tree had enough indents and footholds along its trunk to make one hell of a climb. I couldn't wait for my arm to heal so that I could give it a shot.

"That douche boat still not talking to you?" Falon asked as she sat down beside me.

We leaned against the large tree, enjoying the shade it offered.

"He's not a douche boat, Fal. He has every reason to be pissed at me."

I was the one who caught an attitude with him and basically made him out to be a scheming asshole in front of Orin. Granted, Parker hadn't known that I was telling the truth; I'm not even sure Orin truly believed me.

"It's been long enough now that he can get over it," Cedric said, adding his input. "Besides, why would you lie about something like that?"

I rolled my eyes. "He doesn't know me like you guys do." I finished the last bite of meat and stood. "None of this will matter if I can't get further in my training with Sacha. No one in this camp will want to talk to me if they think I'm a loser who can't even block a push."

"I actually have some ideas about that," Cedric replied.

And that's how I spent the rest of heat break *not* breaking. When I should have been relaxing and cooling off, Cedric had me doing squats and running an obstacle course. The squats helped me in centering my balance as I came up from the ground and again when I crouched back down. When I mastered the balance required for these I began to add to it.

I would squat down, roll to my back, then use my legs and abs to propel me from the ground and back to a squat, before standing again. Confident that I could now rebound from Sacha's pushes with speed, I moved on to the next training exercise.

A nearby fallen tree provided the ultimate test when Cedric told me to run across it. Walking was doable, but I couldn't run it yet. The faster I tried to go, the more my body wobbled. Without an arm on either side to balance me, I fell. I fell *a lot*.

This one was going to take more than one afternoon to tackle. Frustrated, I asked for something else. The third obstacle was actually Falon's idea. She recommended that I wove through the grounded vines that hung from the fichus trees.

And I had to say, it was a genius idea. As I twisted and moved between them, the goal was to turn my body so the vines didn't touch me. There was enough room between each one for me to fit, but it was a matter of getting my body to work with me and to learn how to trust my less dominant side.

I made it to the other side and was about to turn around to go back when a flash of color caught my eye. Hanging on a vine like a child would hang on a rope swing, a Fae no taller than a number two pencil bared his teeth in a smile.

I opened my mouth to scream, but he leapt from his vine to land on my face and hold my lips shut with his hands.

"No, no. Don't scream. I won't hurt you."

My eyes crossed as I tried to get a look at him. I could only see the half of him that reached over the end of my nose, and even that was blurry. He looked like a tiny human, but with pointed ears and skin the color of decaying leaves. The longer I tried to look, the more my eyes hurt.

Sensing that my urge to scream had passed, he released my lips and jumped back onto a vine. Springy little fellow. From this view, I saw that he wore a pair of frayed pants made from an unknown material—leaves maybe?—and a small cap sat upon his head.

"What *are* you?" I blurted out, and then winced.

Not the most polite way to ask, but he didn't seem to mind.

"I'm a gnome," he answered, his voice high pitched but loud enough that I could hear him clearly.

"A gnome? I thought you guys wore pointy hats and loved haunting gardens?"

His eyes narrowed. What? It's not like I had ever seen a real gnome before. They didn't stray much from Fae lands, and none had ever enrolled at the school. How was I supposed to know that they didn't actually have rosy cheeks or carry around small gardening equipment?

"She told me you were a smartass," he said, sliding down the vine until he was at eye level.

"Hey, I wasn't trying to—" Did he say *she*?

I took a closer look at him as he hung there with a smirk. Who told him I was a smartass? I could only think of one person who would call me that and then send a gnome to talk to me.

"Gwendolyn."

The gnome rewarded my answer with a grin. "She also said you weren't dumb."

I was too shocked and confused to have a comeback. It was one thing to dream about her and another to strongly think that she was real. But to have a flesh and bone being confirm it all ... it took a moment to process.

"She wants you to come to her. It's time to master your power," he said.

"Come to her? I don't even know where she is. And I-I can't leave now." I argued with the small Fae. My mind was spinning, not having enough to time to catch up to what he said. "M-my arm is broken. And there is more here for me to learn."

I thought about what it would be like to be out there, traveling to wherever she was while dodging Imperials and other threats. I couldn't even run across a fallen tree right now to save my life. I wouldn't last five minutes out there. I shook my head.

"I can't. Not yet."

The gnome sighed, obviously displeased with my answer. "I'll tell her, but you better be ready next time. She won't wait forever." He leapt from vine to vine, slowly gaining altitude as he went.

"Wait! What's your name?" I called after him.

Just before he was out of sight, he turned to me. "Leif."

That was all he said, then disappeared in a blink.

Water lapped against the side of the canoe as the gentle waves rocked me back and forth. Not far from where the Everglades met the ocean, the water here rolled with small waves rather than remaining flat like the channels further inland.

We paddled along the canal's winding length, the ore making soft splashes as it moved through the lily pads. I sat in the front, making it easier to see everything Orin pointed out.

"See that clump of trees over there?"

I nodded. The clump of trees he pointed to were short in comparison to those around it. Their narrow trunks had a gray hue to them with broad, oval leaves ranging in shades of green.

"*That* is the sweetest treasure trove out here. When those fruit ripen, they turn green, some even go yellow. It's best to get to them before the critters and bees do or you're going to miss out."

As we floated closer I noted that the fruit was still a muted brown—not ripe then.

"What's it called?" I asked.

"It has many names," he replied. "The most popular being the Alligator Apple."

A half hour later, we pulled to shore and tied our boat to a low hanging branch. A wall of grass bordered my end of the boat, and I didn't think much of it until I felt sharp stings along my bare arms and legs.

The faster I tried to push the grass away, the more it cut me.

"Motherfu— *Ouch!*"

When I finally made it out, Orin sat on a fallen log with a small knife in his hand. His face was stern, but his eyes held amusement. I fought the urge to stick my tongue out at him; he could have helped me.

"And that's why I brought you here." He gestured toward the evil strands of grass that swayed behind me. "That is called sawgrass, and it can save your life."

Knowing a lesson was about to begin, I tried my best to ignore the small cuts up and down my body and pay attention. Orin was a great teacher, and I enjoyed our afternoons together. Afternoons with him were a refreshing mental break, like my mornings with Zora. Orin had countless stories about times before the war, and even though he acted like it was a hassle, I knew he secretly enjoyed having someone to listen.

My afternoons were spent with him, traveling the island as he taught me about the land and what could be used for survival. I loved our time out here, away from everyone. It was peaceful and wild, the only sounds being nature itself ... and Orin, of course.

He took his knife and cut off a stalk of sawgrass. I noticed how he didn't grip the plant with his hand, but rather pinched the flat sides between his fingers as he cut. He brought the piece before me and began his lesson.

"If you look closely on the one side, you will see serrated little teeth. These are what cut you as you climbed from the boat. The other side is smooth, allowing for handling. Never walk through a clump of sawgrass again. The stalks grow in different directions so you can never tell which side is the sharp one until it's too late."

Whoever named this plant had named it well. No more than two inches wide, it resembled a thin blade, and I now knew from experience that it was wicked sharp.

"Its main uses are obvious," Orin continued. "It can be used as a weapon or as a tool when traveling the waterways. But what many don't know is ... this."

Using his real blade, Orin pushed the tip carefully into the smooth side of the sawgrass, until the strand cracked open. He pulled the top half away, and nestled in the bottom sat a pool of clear water.

"The grass pulls the water in from below, filters it, and then stores it; leaving a refreshing and lifesaving drink for those that know where to look."

He handed the half to me and I slowly brought it to my lips. Tilting it, I allowed the cool water to flow into my mouth, clenching my thirst and soothing my parched throat. There wasn't more than a few swallows, but it was enough for now.

Orin rewarded me with a rare smile before walking me over to another stalk of sawgrass. He handed me his knife and motioned for me to get to work.

"Your turn."

Chapter 20

Ismiled as I brought my left arm up to once again block Sacha's push. When he swung his other arm around, I weaved around it. I moved so quick it was like seeing his arm in slow motion. The extra practices I had been squeezing in during heat break were really starting to pay off.

After only two weeks, I had noticed an improvement. I was finally able to run across that damn log and weaving through the vines had become child's play. At first, I could only block a few of Sacha's attacks, specifically the one's that I knew were coming.

But eventually, I could block even the one's he tried to sneak in. So far today I had blocked them all. Sacha crouched low and spun, throwing his leg out to sweep across my ankles. Not expecting the move, I was too slow to jump, and his leg hit my right foot, taking me down.

Rolling onto my upper back and ignoring the brief pain in my arm, I tightened the muscles in my core and threw my legs forward. As I sprang to my feet, I didn't miss the surprised look on Sacha's face before I slammed a sidekick into his stomach.

It didn't knock him down, but it was a solid hit. I hadn't even broken a sweat. The sound of applause drew our attention to the slow approach of a Fae warrior. She was lean yet toned; every inch of her body screamed power.

She walked with the grace and elegance of a feral cat and her eyes blazed with a latent intensity barely kept in check. Her hair was a rich gold with flecks of light reflecting off the many weapons at her side to gleam on the treasure-colored strands.

"That was quite impressive, young one. And with one arm no less." She gestured at the side that still rested in the sling. "You have done well with her, my friend."

Sacha inclined his head in acceptance of her compliment. "I told you she was ready."

Ready for what?

The Fae gave me an appraising look. "So you did. From what I saw, she is well prepared for the next step."

The rest of their conversation was in mild whispers and I could only make out a few words. They stood just feet from me, talking about what they thought *I* was ready for, and acted like I wasn't even here. I refused to stand there and not be included.

"Um, hello?" The Fae and Sacha both turned to me. "I'm ready for what?"

The woman smirked at my tone as she gave me a once over. Her eyes took in everything, from my bare feet, my scratched and bruised legs, to the firm set of my jaw as I waited for her to finish. Giving no criticism for what she saw, she introduced herself.

"My apologies, young healer. My name is Alora, and I am to take over your training from here."

I raised a brow. "Why?"

Confused, Alora shook her head with a frown. "I'm not sure I understand."

"Well, that makes two of us." I was quick to retort.

Sacha released an overdramatic sigh. "Alora is to take your training to the next level. You will still work with me, but less frequently as more trainers are added to your schedule."

His answer only left me more confused than before. My expression must have matched my thoughts because he elaborated.

"My objective was to get you used to working with only one arm; you have achieved that. Now, you are to work with others to learn the particular skills they have to offer."

That made more sense. Sacha was an old friend, so he was the only one Orin trusted to work with me while I was vulnerable. Now that I was competent at fighting once again, it was time for specialty training. We had a similar program back at the Academy. By senior year we were taking lessons from teachers visiting from the other races.

It was meant to be part of a well-rounded training plan. I turned back to Alora who had remained silent through Sacha's explanations.

"So what will you be teaching me?"

The corner of her mouth twitched. She gave a brief nod to Sacha before turning on her heel and disappearing into the trees.

"*Okay.* Where's she going? Am I supposed to follow her?" My eyes remained locked on the last place I saw her, but she didn't reveal herself. "What kind of training is this?"

From his back pocket, Sacha pulled out a blindfold.

"You'll understand soon enough," he told me as he had me turn around.

He put the thin slip of material over my eyes and tied it in a briskly efficient manner. No longer feeling his presence behind me, I swiveled my head from side to side as I tried to hear him. The snap of a branch caused me to jerk my head to the right.

Another sound, the rustle of leaves, pulled my head back in the other direction. Remaining perfectly still, I tried to catch any faint sounds or signs of Sacha. But I heard nothing. At least until the next branch broke. That one I knew came from directly behind me.

The wind picked up, drawing my hair across the back of my neck. Goosebumps broke out across my skin. I slowly tilted my head to the left again, thinking I heard a sound. Suddenly, a puff of breath ghosted across my cheek, at the same time something pushed my shoulder.

I jumped, whirling round in circles as my mind tried in vain to convince me that everything was okay. My breaths came rapid and heavy. The anticipation of something else touching me was overwhelming.

"Settle yourself," came Alora's voice, but I couldn't tell from which direction. "Calm your breathing and use your senses. Listen to the world around you, hear the natural sounds and point out what does not belong."

"How the hell do I do that?" I growled.

With a swift knock to the back of my knees, I fell forward. The only thing keeping me from kissing the ground was the quick reflex of my left hand.

"No more talking. *Listen*."

Biting my lip, it was an effort to keep from sharing what I thought about her training exercise. The words I wished to call her lined up in a row behind my teeth, ready to be thrown from my mouth like symbolic knives. I knew before I was back on my feet that this was going to get a lot worse before it got better. This was definitely going to suck.

Having to do even the most remedial of tasks with my left side, surprisingly built my strength up rather quickly. Things were a little easier when I wasn't falling on my ass from the slightest misstep or trying to figure out how to feed myself without getting food everywhere.

Life in the camp was good. I had finally settled into a routine, one that I enjoyed. I would wake each morning and spend an hour or so sitting with

Zora. Sometimes she would talk, but mostly she just hummed a tune and stuffed me with food.

I enjoyed the silence though. I've never been much of a morning person, and sitting next to her kept me from having to interact with people. I sat in relaxed comfort by the fire until it was time to train with Sacha.

I'd spend the rest of the morning working out and enhancing my reflexes until it was time for heat break. Cedric added extra training in that time and I suffered through it until the air took on a cooler feel. Then my afternoons were pretty random. I either hung out with Cedric and Falon, or I went off with Orin for a wilderness lesson.

But, of course, as soon as I got comfortable, the universe laughed and decided to throw me something harder. Enter Alora. Training with her was kicking my ass. Today's lesson was so brutal that I think I might have re-fractured my arm when I walked into a tree.

Long story.

I was just grateful to be alive.

I allowed my muscles to gradually relax. Starting at my feet, I worked my way up my legs and focused on making my body loosen until I resembled a pile of mush. And that was how Cedric found me: lying on my back and staring at the thatched roof of the hut I shared with Falon.

With the base of the hut lifted off the ground, Cedric's stomach came level to the platform I rested on. He perched his arms on the wood and leaned against it. I could feel his eyes on me, and I only lasted a minute or so before a smile broke across my face.

"You're pretty when you smile," he said.

"*Only* when I smile?" I sat up and swung my legs over the side until I faced him.

Stepping between them, Cedric placed his hands on my thighs and shook his head. He knew I was teasing.

"I have a surprise for you. Come on."

With a quick kiss on my lips, he pulled me from the platform. I landed with a soft *thud* and held onto his hand as I followed him through the ferns and bushes. He led us out behind the huts, but in a different direction than we normally took to get to our usual hang out.

We stepped on a small, well-worn path that I hadn't noticed before. Only a thin track, no more than a foot wide, it was easily overlooked. The sun was beginning its decent, and with the heavy canopy above us, the darkness approached quickly.

Using his power, Cedric called a ball of flame to his free hand and held it in front of us. I took the opportunity to admire him while he was focused on navigation. The firelight danced across his face, his lower lip trapped between his teeth as he concentrated.

I wanted to run my hand through his hair, which had grown in our time here. The tips now covered his ears.

"Here we are."

We stopped at the edge of another clearing; this one was far different than the others we more commonly frequented. A soft vibration enveloped the area and caressed my skin as well as the surrounding foliage.

Few people were around; it made sense that most would be wrapping up their daily tasks in preparation for the night. It was hard to make out who specifically was here. The few beams of moonlight reflected off the flawless skin of the people who walked under them, easily identifying them as Vampires.

But it wasn't until one of them approached, allowing Cedric's flame to highlight their face, that I realized I knew some of them.

"What are you two doing over here?" Mahon asked.

There was no anger in his tone, just surprise. Peeking around him, I counted eight rather large rectangular objects arranged in a large semicircle in the center of the clearing. At a closer inspection, I realized that they were the source of the humming.

"What is this place?" I asked Mahon as I stepped further in.

Cedric followed and his light allowed me to get a better look. The eight objects were actually professional grade refrigerators. Two ancient propane generators sat behind the semicircle and were connected to the out-of-place coolers by heavy, black power cords that snaked along the ground in thick coils.

"It's called the blood bank," Mahon answered. "It's where we store the camp's blood supply for the Vampire population."

I had wondered about that. I knew it only took a few weeks without blood—sometimes longer for the older ones—before the inner monsters inside the Vampires became harder to control. We had witnessed firsthand what that looked like, and it would spell disaster if it happened here in the camp.

Turning to face Cedric, I was a little confused when I asked, "Was this your surprise?"

With a teasing smirk he left me and walked toward one of the refrigerators. With a firm tug, he pulled open the door, allowing the light from inside to spill out for about two feet. Wisps of fog curled around him as the coolness of the fridge met the muggy heat of our island. Looking past him, I saw levels of empty shelves, only a few bags of blood on each.

Did each fridge look like that on the inside? That was not near enough of a supply to cover the population we had here. I hoped more was in route, because I didn't want to think about more than half the camp turning into sadistic murderers.

That thought led to a quick visual of Parker—his face twisted into a snarl as he hunted me through the trees. I shuddered.

"What are you doing here?" Orin's voice caught me by surprise and I jumped.

He stood next to Mahon, having quietly approached. He wore a frown as he watched Cedric rummage through the fridge. Cedric had moved onto a different one, obviously not finding what he was looking for in the first.

"Is there something I can help you find?" Orin offered.

But Cedric was already walking back over, hands behind his back and a broad grin on his face. He stopped in front of me, his eyes shining with an eager glow.

"I put it here because I knew none of the Vampires would eat it. I couldn't say the same about the rest of the camp."

Pulling his arms back to the front, in his left he held a small, blue box. My mouth started to water as I stared at the tiny picture on the front.

"I don't understand. What is that?" Mahon asked, wrinkling his nose.

"It's Pop-Tarts!" I practically squealed.

I had gone months without chocolate. While I was painfully craving a homemade waffle taco, chocolate Pop-Tarts would more than hold me over until I could get my hands on some. Cedric smiled as I held the little box to my chest. It was still cold from being stored in the fridge, and it felt good in the sticky humidity.

Orin coughed in a not so subtle way of getting our attention.

"I'd appreciate it if you wouldn't ask my runners to risk themselves on something as nonessential as *Pop-Tarts*. They are in enough danger on a usual run. Asking them to deviate and expose themselves longer just for a little snack, it's selfish."

Cedric shrugged. "He owed me one."

That statement led Orin to further his lecture on foregoing his runner's safety to fulfill trivial debts. Mahon and I awkwardly stood to the side, not wanting to interrupt but having nothing to distract us while they spoke.

In the end, Cedric nodded, promising to not use the couriers as his own personal shoppers again. And from what I gathered from their conversation, Orin was extremely protective of his runners. They were his trusted agents that went out into civilization to grab blood from various donation centers in order to stock the fridges.

But from what I had seen, they either couldn't get enough stock or there were not enough runners to bring back the amount needed to sustain the Vampires here. I was curious as to how Orin would fix the problem.

"Are the other Vampires tending to the fridges there, your runners?" I asked Orin, interrupting whatever new conversation he had begun with Mahon. "No wonder the stock is so low; they can hardly carry back what's needed."

"He told me that you could tell Vampires apart from other races, but I didn't believe him," Mahon told me.

His expression held wonder, confusion, and a bit of determination. Under his gaze I felt like a new puzzle that he was eager to solve.

"Yeah." I drew the word out as I tried to figure out what the big deal was.

Orin seemed just as shocked when he first found out, but he had yet to speak to me about what the true meaning behind this realization was.

"I understand that it's rare for another being to have the ability to differentiate you all, but I assumed it was just part of my healing powers. Being able to tell the races apart could come in handy, I guess."

Mahon seemed less than convinced.

His finger rubbed over his chin in a repeated motion as he thought over my answer. "You might be on to something there. A healer hasn't been around for hundreds of years, so knowledge of this ability could have been lost to time. How can you tell us apart, if you don't mind my asking?"

"There is a hint of red in the eye. In stronger light almost the entire pupil is red. That's how I knew you guys were Vampires when I first woke in the cave. And also your skin; it's almost too perfect, like living marble."

Mahon's eyes widened in excitement, like I had given him a missing piece to the puzzle. "That can't be just your healing power."

My heart rate slowly increased, matching the rising excitement in Mahon's tone. Did he know something I didn't? Until my argument with Parker and Orin's subsequent reaction, I didn't think what I did was anything special. Maybe I was wrong.

"Well, what does it—"

Orin cut me off. "That's enough questions for now. Mahon, we have work to do."

"But only—" Another glare from Orin cut him off as well.

Glancing between them, I tried to see what the big deal was. They both obviously knew something and weren't telling. Well, Mahon wanted to, but for some reason Orin wouldn't let him.

"What's the big deal?" I asked, annoyed that I was being kept in the dark.

Orin sighed. He knew that I wouldn't let this go. And honestly, why should I? If he knew something about me, I had the right to know.

"It's just a rare ability. That's all." His eyes pleaded with me to settle for that answer. "Please. It's getting late and you have a full morning of training to look forward to."

Leaving it at that, he nodded for Cedric to walk me back. I felt his arm around my waist, but wasn't ready to give up on this conversation. However, Cedric knew I wouldn't get anything out of Orin tonight. So with a strong nudge, I stumbled forward and was pulled along, back to the trail.

Cedric's flame once again kept the persistent shadows at bay. The low ferns and spider-hanging trees cast expressive shadows on the ground ahead. Unable to resist, I peered back over my shoulder. Orin stood with Mahon, their heads close together in an obvious argument.

This was not the first time I had seen him in such a situation. He frequently argued with Asa, also in whispers after I had been led away. Orin was hiding something; something about me. And somehow I was going to find out what it was.

Chapter 21

The sky above me swayed to the left and a heartbeat later swayed to the right. The sun peeked through the branches and leaves, but even it couldn't touch me. I was lying on my back in the bottom of the boat, hoping that no one would find me here.

I needed a minute alone; just one minute without Sacha kicking me into the dirt or Orin introducing me to a new trainer. I needed some time where I wasn't learning a new technique or defense strategy, time where I could just be me.

My once peaceful afternoons had been stuffed full of training sessions with seasoned warriors from each of the races. On top of my sessions with Sacha and Alora, I now worked with a Witch who was teaching me the knife training I would have had if I had stayed at the Academy and a Shifter who worked on conditioning.

That was my last session each day. We met when the sun was at its lowest and the air was cooler. The temperature was crucial because evenings with him consisted of running sprints around the island, swimming the channels, and he said he would add climbing once my sling was gone. It was all to build my endurance.

I would completely hate it if Cedric and Falon weren't required to participate. I still laugh when I picture Falon's face when Orin told her her attendance was nonnegotiable. Our mad dash down to this camp was stunted and slow, mainly because our endurance was not up to par with that of a Vampire. A problem Orin intended to fix.

I made myself more comfortable on the bottom of the narrow boat. I awoke this morning with a heavy weight pressing on me. Maybe I was tired. Who wouldn't be after running all over the damn island?

Or maybe it was a reaction to the sword that had perpetually hung over my neck as of late. Whatever the reason, getting repeatedly knocked around a clearing wasn't my idea of a good morning. So here I was.

"Casey."

Oh, no. Crunched leaves sounded under the steps of whoever approached. I flattened further against the bottom of the canoe, wishing that I'd had the foresight to bring some ferns down with me to hide under.

"Casey, it's me. Where are you hiding?" It was Cedric. His voice dropped down a level, and I swear I heard laughter in his tone as he stepped closer to my hiding place. "I know you're over here, somewhere. I can feel a lot of frustration stemming from this area."

He could *find* me by feeling me now?

"What kind of shit is that?" I exclaimed as I shot up in the canoe. "Am I a satellite now? Can you just tune in to the Casey channel whenever you fricken please?"

He was crouching a few feet above me at the edge of the tangled roots. The sunlight and the afternoon breeze made him look like one of those romantic heroes that were always posing on the cover of my books.

The breeze softly blew strands of his dark hair across his eyes. His time here in Florida only deepened that rich olive complexion with which he was gifted, and he looked more like some kind of demigod with each passing day.

Luthos, that boy was gorgeous.

A sensual smile slowly curled the corners of his mouth as he gazed down upon me with a knowing attitude.

"Ugh, stop that!" My cheeks burned.

I still hadn't gotten used to this new connection we had. He was my boyfriend. He already knew how I felt about him, but it didn't make this any less embarrassing.

"I can't help it, I like when you blush. It's sweet." He smirked as he climbed down the roots to sit beside me in the canoe.

We leaned toward shore almost too much before the small boat righted itself, leaving Cedric and me sitting face to face at the bottom.

"Rough day?" he asked, and I shrugged. He already knew that it was.

"It's just overwhelming sometimes, you know? Everyone is pushing really hard. I know they all want me to be prepared for whatever comes, but …"

He reached out and grabbed my hand, then busied himself with drawing indecipherable shapes on my palm.

"But sometimes it's too much," he finished for me.

"Exactly."

We didn't know if or when the next attack would happen, but they were trying their hardest to have me primed and ready for it. They wanted me prepared because when I was deemed fully trained, I was expected to lead these people. Or at least direct them in some way against Sebastian and his army.

I wasn't sure; the prophecy wasn't very clear on that part.

This camp may seem crowded, but in the scheme of things our population wasn't even large enough to be considered a town. Sebastian had an entire race under his control. How were we supposed to defeat anyone with this kind of manpower?

"Did Orin ever talk to you about what the plan was when it came time to leave this place? Or did you ever overhear the Vamps talking about it?" I asked Cedric.

His finger paused its drawing on my skin and I instantly felt the loss. His brow furrowed as he contemplated my question, but he eventually shook his head.

"No. I can't recall hearing anything about what came next. I would think finding more people to join our side? We can't possibly win with only those that are here—a quarter of them are old enough to be great grandparents. What would *they* do in a fight?"

I threw my good arm in the air. "Thank you! That's exactly what I was thinking."

Cedric chuckled at my over dramatic gestures and gently brought my hand back down so he could continue drawing on it.

"We need to expose more people to what we are doing here. Show them that the races *can* work together, *truly* work together, and that we can use that strength to take down our enemies. But we can't do that hiding out at the bottom of the country."

As I spoke my thoughts aloud I knew them to be true. We wouldn't get much done hiding out here on some secret island. Likeminded people couldn't find us here, and each time we brought someone back, the risk to our safe haven grew.

"How long do you think Orin intends to stay?" Cedric wondered.

I had no definitive answer to give him. "Until I'm fully trained, at the very least."

Cedric eventually convinced me to walk back to camp with him. We approached the main clearing where lunch was just beginning. No one paid any mind as we crept through, aiming for the path on the opposing side. A slim, lithe figure stepped into our line of sight, arms crossed in front of her with a scowl to match.

One look at Alora's face told me all I needed to know about how she felt. I could practically hear her teeth grinding from across the clearing. I didn't know what her problem was; it wasn't like I skipped out on *her* training.

I glanced over to where Sacha stood, grouped with some other Vamps and laughing at something one of them said; he didn't seem too put out. We reached Alora within minutes, but her attitude hadn't changed in the time it took us to get to her. I could feel her irritation, so potent it smothered this corner of the meadow. There could have been another body standing with us her emotions were so concentrated.

"What?" I snapped with some irritation of my own.

She narrowed her eyes, but that was all before she turned down the path, not pausing to see if I followed. She knew I would. With an irked sigh, a sound all females mastered at some point, I set off after her.

Cedric stuck close to my heels until Alora growled. "Leave the boy."

He huffed at being called a boy, but knew an order when he heard it. With a quick kiss to the side of my head, he left. I traveled behind Alora along the worn trail in silence until it dumped us out at our usual training field. Positioning me in the center, I took the blindfold Alora offered without being told.

I was used to the feel of it by now. I held it tight as she tied it around my head, knowing she would take the time to inspect it when she was done, and waited for her instructions. It wasn't Alora's voice that I heard next, however.

"Whatever pulled your attention from our training session must have been important."

Oh, shit. My head jerked to the right, where his voice originated. I could picture him standing there, a sick kind of glee reflecting in his eyes.

Sacha continued, "So, Alora graciously allowed me to sit in on some of her time."

I mentally followed his voice, the sound of his boots over the smooth dirt, and each measured breath as he stopped directly in front of me.

"It is irresponsible of you to skip training, especially when the fate of each soul here rests upon your shoulders. We'll just have to try and make up for lost time. Guard position," he demanded.

My heartrate kicked into overdrive, and my palms were damp with sweat as I clenched them and brought them up between us. My back foot had barely hit the ground to settle into the stance when he swung.

The fact that my hands were already up was the only thing that saved me from a black eye. Sacha's punch did manage to graze my cheek, though, before my back peddling had me landing on my ass.

"Are you insane?" I shrieked, ripping the blindfold down to let it hang around my neck.

My cheek throbbed, the dull ache sinking lower into my jaw. I resisted the urge to rub it.

"I didn't take you as one who went for the cheap shot." I glared up at Sacha, remaining on the ground where I landed.

The stern set of his jaw gave no quarter. "Again."

Biting back a string of curses, I stood to once again face Sacha, mere feet separating us. I blew strands of hair off my face, allowing him to see the red mark I knew had already formed. But he gave no reaction.

"Put the blindfold back on."

My instincts rebelled against the order. My body knew it would be defenseless if I couldn't see him. I stood there, my fingers playing with the blindfold while I dug for the courage it would take to put it back on. My mind balked.

No, not courage, stupidity. Because I would be utterly stupid if I allowed Sacha to take another shot at me.

"Do it, Casey. And remember all I have taught you these last weeks." Alora appeared behind Sacha.

Her attitude had vanished, replaced with an obvious need for me to succeed. This was a test, I realized. Sacha probably used it as a form of punishment, but it was ultimately a test of all I had learned from Alora.

I gave her a confident nod; I could do this. Though the thought of being blind to Sacha's attack made my knees weak, I pulled the blindfold over my eyes and settled into my stance. Maybe there was a hint of guilt in Sacha's heart because he gave me a moment to gather myself.

A moment I didn't waste.

I took a deep breath and let it out slowly, spreading my awareness down my arms and legs. I focused in on the energy around me, just like Alora taught, and pushed until I felt the steady hum of all the living things within my limited range.

The earth itself let off a muted, continuous whine that I had learned to push aside. It was nothing but background noise. What I was looking for was the vibrant purr of life. Trees and plants were dull in comparison to larger creatures, like Sacha and Alora.

Their life energy spread out from their core, like soundwaves traveling away from a strummed guitar. It was these waves that told me Sacha had moved. I knew he now stood off to my side, the echo of his steps told me so.

When he shifted his weight and kicked out, the steady pulse from the earth warned me it was coming. I dodged. Feeling an outside force interact with my own energy, I knew his next strike would be close, a punch, which I blocked.

Grinning now, we continued our dance around the clearing. My eyes were covered, and yet I could see as clear as if they weren't. I laughed aloud with the sheer joy of it. How could I ever lose, how could anyone, when they used this sixth sense? No wonder Shifters and the Fae were fierce fighters.

"Focus, Casey!"

But Alora's warning was too late. I had let my concentration wander, and Sacha had crept closer than he should have been able to. I could tell the precise moment he pulled his strike, but the impact of his punch still hurt. When I ripped my blindfold off this time, it wasn't to scream at him. In fact, I was smiling.

"Let's do that again."

I was permitted to skip conditioning that night to instead visit Asa and have my arm checked over. His hut was easy to find, larger than the rest because it doubled as the medical center. Built in the same style as the others, the medical hut had two platforms, the highest one being where Asa slept and the lower reserved for patients.

It was the lower platform that he sat on now, and I watched him as I approached. He puttered around on a crude, handmade table, organizing his herbs and supplies. I didn't bother announcing myself, he knew I was coming and had probably recognized my footsteps. He greeted me with a smile, taking the time from his task to say a proper hello.

"It's been a couple weeks, I think, since you last came to see me."

I nodded my head as I took a seat next to him. He knew exactly how long it had been since I was last here. I was instructed to come to him every two weeks for follow ups. At our first meeting, he discovered that while I couldn't use my own power to outright heal myself, I seemed to have a faster than normal healing rate.

I would have rather got it all over and done with, but I would take accelerated healing over nothing. Two weeks ago he told me I wouldn't be in this sling for much longer, and since then I had been itching to get it off.

"How have you been? Any pain?" he asked, motioning for me to scoot closer.

I shook my head. "Nope. Haven't even felt a twinge."

Asa murmured as he worked. He gently untied the knot behind my neck that held the sling together and pulled the cloth away from my body. Just as he had two weeks ago, he asked me to slowly extend my elbow. That was the extent of what I could do last time, but with the severity of my break, even that little motion should have been impossible.

Now came the true test, turning my arm.

"If there is any part of the fracture not yet healed, turning the humerus should prove ... uncomfortable."

Basically, if it was still broken, this would hurt like a bitch.

Steeling myself against pain I hoped wouldn't come, I lifted my arm. When nothing happened, I rotated my elbow until the underside of my forearm pointed up to the thatched roof of the hut.

"Nothing. I feel nothing," I told Asa. Excitement rushed through me in a euphoric wave.

True to his questioning nature, Asa had me perform a multitude of tasks to confirm that my arm was indeed healed. He asked me to lift a wide variety of objects, their sizes and weights gradually increasing.

I started by lifting a small bowl of chopped herbs and graduated to a thick textbook on local plants. Asa had me drag a chair behind me for a full two yards and then push myself up from the ground using both arms. But he stopped me from testing my full weight on my right arm.

"Let's not push it," he advised. "Light duty for the next week, okay? Take the time to build your strength back before plunging full speed ahead."

I nodded along at his instructions, knowing full well that I wouldn't adhere to them. He smiled, his eyes revealing his true thoughts. He knew me, and he knew I wasn't going to hold back, not after finally regaining my freedom.

"I want you to spend your mornings with me over the next week." He held up his hand to stop my complaints. "I will speak with Sacha and confirm. You can spend your mornings learning more natural ways to heal. Then, when I know you are completely recovered, you will be free to train."

I had no choice but to comply. I dipped my chin in agreement, although I scowled while doing so. Hearing Zora give the call for dinner, I waved goodbye with my right hand, reveling in the knowledge that I wouldn't make a mess with my food tonight. Tomorrow was looking brighter and my steps felt lighter than the heavy weights they resembled this morning.

I walked to dinner feeling more like myself than I had in months.

Chapter 22

I climbed higher, the branch beneath my palms sticky with sap. The fichus tree we were in was the tallest of its bunch. It took a little hiking to get to, but the air was cooler up here, less muggy. I shot a playful grin at Cedric.

"Come on, guys. Don't you think we're high enough already?" Falon whined as she squeezed the life out of a tree limb below.

I laughed. There was a kind of freedom in climbing a tree. From up here, it felt like no one could reach me; nothing could hurt me. I was here every chance I got lately. From the moment Asa cleared me to train, I had been testing the limits of my once injured arm.

The first thing I did was hike out here and climb this tree, and I had been climbing it every day since. Today, Falon wanted to know what all the fuss was about and decided to tag along. But she realized too late that heights weren't her thing.

I looked down, squinting through the swaying leaves as another breeze tossed my branch to and fro. Falon's light blonde hair stood out among the dark browns and greens, so she was easy to spot. Her high pitched squeal made it even easier.

"You're almost there, Fal. If you'd let go of the branch and open your eyes, you could see that," I told her and laughed again. The sound was carried away as soon as it left my mouth, whisked away on the next gust that blew through.

"Well, if the tree would stop trying to *kill* me, I would!" she shouted.

"Maybe I should go back down and get her," Cedric offered. He stared down at Falon with worry.

"She's fine, Ced. She's literally on like the second branch."

Falon would figure it out for herself; either she would stay there or climb higher, the choice was hers. I swung a leg over the branch I sat on until I was straddling it. Cedric leaned against a split branch, making himself comfortable in the small niche it offered.

I looked out over the island, a large portion of it viewable from where I sat. This camp had begun to feel like home these last couple months. I couldn't see any people from here, too many other trees and shrubs were in the way, but I knew they were all down there.

I could see clearly in my mind's eye Zora steadily working at the communal fire to prepare our next meal.

Sacha I knew was off with Orin, reviewing our escape routes and double checking our security. They worked day and night to assure that the camp remained hidden and that our safety continued on. The runners, scouts, guards on duty—everyone really—answered to them.

My Witch trainer, was undoubtedly off with the other witches, practicing their elements a safe distance from the rest of camp. Cedric was supposed to be with them, learning new attacks for his fire, but I couldn't keep him away from me today.

Now that I thought about it, I couldn't keep either of them away, Cedric or Falon. Both had refused to leave me alone, even though I knew both of them had their own trainers expecting them. I turned on my branch, enough to see Cedric, but not enough to fall off.

"You and Falon have been sticking to me a lot lately, like a pair of shadows. Is something going on?" I asked him.

I knew he was going to lie the minute he opened his mouth. I didn't need supernatural access to his feelings to know that he was keeping something from me. He paused before answering, long enough to come up with something other than the truth.

I wasn't facing him fully, but I could see enough of him to watch his eyes flick back and forth from me down to Falon. So whatever he was trying to hide included her. I figured that.

Glancing down at his hands, I could make out small singe marks where his fingertips touched the bark of the branch. His power was reacting to his emotions and that was enough to make me worry. His control was usually solid, unless I was involved, or my safety.

I cleared my throat, causing his eyes to meet mine and reminding him that he had yet to answer my question.

"I got nothing," he finally answered.

A small head, covered with reflective blonde strands, poked up from the branch below.

"You're hopeless." Falon told him as she pulled herself up to our level.

Her hands shook, so much that I thought her grip would slip. Her lips made a firm line over her chin, but her gaze was steady. Determined. Out of breath when she finally got situated, she sat right next to me on a parallel branch, wrapping her arms around it once again to hold it in a death grip.

"I don't know why I tell him anything; that boy can't keep a secret to save his life. I'd hoped that we wouldn't have to worry you," she said.

"It involves her. I wasn't sure I *should* be keeping it a secret," he replied, not at all bothered by her words.

I studied Falon. Her entire body trembled, from the tips of her fingers to her ankles locked around the tree. The whites of her eyes were abnormally visible, frantic in their need to keep a solid branch in their sights. She was terrified. Truly.

And yet, she still climbed all the way up here. She forced herself to climb to the top of a rather gigantic tree, gritting her teeth against the taunting wind, and planted herself as close as she could get to me.

Something was wrong.

"Didn't we promise honesty to one another, to always trust before judging and to share even the most terrifying secrets?" My question was meant for both of them.

We swore, that night by the sprite's pool, that we would never again lie to one another, even as a form of protection. We promised to talk things out and listen before we made any plans, because we were in this together.

It felt like so long ago, but that night was the turning point in our journey. By that time, we had seen the true monsters we would face, the true demons that potentially hid inside each Vampire. We tasted death, just a pinch away from it, for the third time since leaving the Academy when those sprites attempted to lure us into their waters.

It was this promise that I called on now. It was a gentle reminder that even if it was for my own benefit, the truth was my right to know. Another gust of wind blew through our tree. A storm was moving in; I could see it in the dark clouds that inched closer each minute. It was almost time to climb back down, but not before I got an answer.

"What's going on?" I asked.

Falon worried her bottom lip between her teeth. "It's just a feeling, like back at the school when I knew something wasn't right. Every time I look at you lately, my stomach turns in knots and that sensation returns."

"Well there have been a few attempts on our lives lately. I mean, we're still hiding from the Dean and his Imperials. Maybe you're just picking up on that?" I suggested.

But Falon shook her head. The wind picked up and her trembling increased each time her branch swayed, but she kept her gaze on me the entire time. With the storm rolling ever closer, the gust that blew through was stronger than the previous.

"Can you tell yet where it's coming from?" I asked, referring to her intuition.

She answered with a frustrated groan. "No. It takes over randomly, but the reason for the gut feeling isn't usually far behind and it's almost always followed by trouble."

Cedric shifted closer to me, as if his presence could protect me from the words. I thought them over. I was in the safest place I knew, protected by a camp of warriors and hidden in a swamp that no one would think to look. Except ... except Kael.

If he survived his battle with the sprites, Kael knew that we were out here. It only took us two days to travel to this camp from the sprite's island. But he's had two months to find us; that was plenty of time.

Thunder rumbled off in the distance, but close enough for me to sense the electricity that saturated the approaching clouds. The gray fluffs of moisture lit up from the inside as lightning fought to reach the ground.

It wasn't some light rain moving in. This was a full blown summer storm, and it would soon be upon us. We needed to go. Orin needed to hear of Falon's latest warning, and we all needed to be prepared in case Kael arrived. Who knew how much time we had left?

A single note, piercing and sharp lifted above the trees, above the growing wind and punctured the oncoming gloom. An alarm. The Shifter's call was followed by three quick bursts of light: flames being shot into the sky.

Proof that this was the real deal and not a drill. Someone had found the island.

The storm had arrived by the time we made it to the clearing. Zora stood by her smothered fire, the pots nearby now filled with water. She appeared frantic, looking for a specific face in the mass of those surrounding her. Lightning emphasized the relief in her gaze as she saw me emerge from the trees.

"She's over here!" she called out as she ran toward me.

I was soon wrapped in her arms, the breath nearly squeezed out of me, as she thanked Luthos over and over for bringing me to her. Over her shoulder I saw Orin burst into the clearing, soaked head to toe from the rain, and not giving a damn about it.

He pulled me from Zora's embrace and enveloped me in one of his own. I hugged him back, glad to see that he was okay. From the look of things, they all were. People were being directed to their huts and told to stay there for the remainder of the storm.

I didn't see any injuries or swarming Imperials, only looks of confusion. Was it a false alarm? I looked up at Orin, squinting against the rain, and saw genuine relief that I was here. *Something* had to have happened for everyone to be worried over me.

"Where were you?" Orin asked, his fingers digging into my shoulders.

"The three of us were just hanging out over behind the huts. Why? What was the alarm for?"

Orin shook his head and glanced around. There were others standing nearby, also waiting to hear what the alarm was about. But Orin bade us to follow him, away from the questioning crowd and further into the trees.

The canopy was thicker here and kept most of the rain at bay. The ground beneath my feet was soft and damp, but had yet to turn into the sucking mud pile I knew it would become. I hoped to be warm and dry in my hut before the storm got that bad.

Orin led us through the ferns and low hanging vines. We walked along unmarked paths, the shrubs below split in a multitude of ways, letting me know that whoever came out here took different routes each time to prevent a path from forming.

We walked for another handful of minutes until we reached the edge of the island and stopped beneath a mangrove tree. Its roots looped and climbed high in the water until most of them were level with the ground we stood on.

Under the tree, a few people were already gathered, and I instantly recognized Sacha and Mahon; the other two I was not familiar with. My gaze zeroed in on what they held between them. Enclosed within a single shackle from a medieval chain, Leif stood atop a root, his face twisted in obvious pain.

I ran to him, only to be held away by Sacha.

"What is wrong with you people? Look at him, he's not a danger to anyone!" I looked to Mahon, pleading with him to release the shackle. "Is that *iron*?"

I fought Sacha's hold, but he held strong. The last time I saw Leif, he was leaving to report back to Gwendolyn. Had he reached her already? Had she sent him back to fetch me? And how was he caught?

I didn't realize I was asking these questions aloud until Orin was in front of me, petitioning for me to slow down.

"How do you know this creature, Casey? And, did you say its name was Leif?" he asked when I had finally stopped struggling.

"How can you do that to him? You of all people know what it's like to be in chains. And you used iron? He's *Fae*. You're hurting him!"

My struggles renewed with little to show for it. Sacha still held strong, and I was no closer to reaching Leif. I slumped in defeat. Leif just stood there, the pain of the iron had to be excruciating, but he made no sound.

My heart broke for him.

"Casey," Orin softly spoke to me, trying to get me to look at him. "Tell me how you know him."

He wiped at a tear on my cheek. I didn't even know I was crying. Orin gave a nod to Sacha over my shoulder and my arms were released. I stepped away from the both of them and into the warmth offered at Cedric's side.

"He came to me a week or so after we first arrived with a message from Gwendolyn that I needed to learn more about my power." I sniffled.

Cedric rubbed circles along my back but said nothing. I had forgotten to tell him and Falon about the gnome's visit, and that guilt made me feel even worse.

"He said that Gwendolyn wanted me to come to her, for training. But my arm was still broken at the time, and I knew that it would have been too dangerous to be anywhere else until it healed."

"*Only* because of your broken arm? Casey, how do you know Gwendolyn is even real? He could have been luring you away, delivering you right to Sebastian without anyone ever knowing." Orin's tone was fueled by outrage and disbelief.

He looked down at me, anger causing the muscles in his jaw to tick, for his hands to clench and then release at his sides. He very much looked the part of a frustrated parent, and I knew I filled the role of misguided teen.

"He's not working with Sebastian. I told you he's a friend. And harmless. Look at him; he's barely a foot tall!"

Mahon scoffed at that last comment and looked to make sure the shackle was still secure around Leif. Orin stood silent for a moment, seeming to rein in his anger before he spoke.

"You can't be that naive. Sebastian has plenty of spies hidden within the other races. You have no possible way of knowing whether or not the gnome was telling the truth. Taking you to Gwendolyn! Honestly, Casey. I expected you to know a lie when you heard one."

The disappointment in his tone only served to piss me off. Who was he to talk to me like that? I wasn't stupid.

"Gwendolyn has been trying to get me to come to her since we were in North Carolina. It's not unlikely that she would send someone to emphasize her message," I told him, refusing to back down.

But my explanation only infuriated him. "Enough! I don't want to hear any more about this Gwendolyn character. Your focus needs to be here on your training and not on an ancient Fae that may or may not be real."

We stood toe to toe, his height over me forcing him to look down. My neck throbbed from the angle I strained to keep, but I wouldn't be the first to look away. I had never seen Orin like this. He was all worked up over a being who wasn't even a threat to me.

And no matter what I said I knew I wouldn't convince him of that. For some reason, he was stuck on thinking the worse of Leif, without even listening to reason for an opposing argument. I knew it was all to protect me; his anger, his hurtful words, they all stemmed from his need to keep me safe.

But that didn't make it right. I decided to let the matter go, for now. If I kept pushing, we would get nowhere. Orin needed to calm down, to let the feeling of danger pass, and to think and listen with an open mind. He wouldn't be doing that tonight.

Instead, I moved onto another topic that Cedric and I had discussed lately.

"If you're so set on me needing to be here, then how about you actually follow through on your promise. I've been here for almost three months. I'm healed and I'm trained; when do we go after the Dean?"

Orin frowned at my quick change in topic, but at least he didn't seem angry at this question.

"When I feel you're ready to face him, I will personally escort you back to campus."

That wasn't a good enough answer. His idea of me being ready could be years from now, and I refused to wait that long.

"I think I've trained enough. I'm ready now."

Orin disagreed. "You've only just healed from your injury. You need more time. Besides, with an army after you, you wouldn't be safe even if I thought you were fully trained."

"What does that mean? How long do you expect me to sit here? There are people I love back at that campus, Orin. Who knows what the Dean is doing to them?"

I fought to maintain my composure, but the sudden thought of Eli caught me off guard. I hadn't thought about him in months and to suddenly have him pop into my mind was a little overwhelming. I was the worst possible kind of person. Who forgot about their family like that?

I hadn't spared one thought about Eli since we left that cave. I'd been too busy cozying up to Cedric and getting to know Orin and his men. Granted, there were many attempts on my life since I had been on the run. But still, to not even think of him; that was horrible.

Orin wiped a hand over his face, the gesture reminded me so much of Eli that my heart lurched again.

"Fine. Let's make a deal. I will give you tasks to prove that you're ready. Pass them, and I promise we will go after the Dean. Fair?"

"What's the first task?" I asked.

He smirked, and in that movement I learned all I needed to. Orin was going to give me impossible tasks, or at least near impossible. He didn't want me to go, so he would assign me things he didn't think I could conquer.

"Your first task will be to defeat Mahon in a hand-to-hand match."

He smirked at me again, but his eyes were filled with pity. He knew he set an impossible task in front of me; Mahon was a beast. There was no way I was going to defeat him without a weapon. My shoulders slumped in defeat, but I nodded my acceptance.

Orin gave my shoulder a squeeze before giving orders to the men around him. He left without another word to me. I looked back over to Leif, and then to Mahon who guarded him.

"Can you at least remove the iron?" I asked.

I was going to need time to help Leif escape. Keeping him in iron would leave him too weak to move, and I needed him to show me a way off this island. Orin didn't know it, but giving me an impossible task was just what I needed.

It would be the perfect distraction. He would think I spent my time trying to follow his rules and gain his support in leaving. When really, I planned to run away. I was going to find Gwendolyn and then take down the Dean, with or without his help. And Leif was crucial to my plans.

Mahon gave me a weak smile. "He has to stay in the shackle for questioning, but I will make sure he is secured by other means afterwards."

"Thank you," I replied. And I meant it.

I turned away from the writhing gnome, wanting to be as far as possible from this area when the questioning began. I gestured for Cedric and Falon to follow me. I had a lot to catch them up on. This storm was exactly what I needed and thankfully, it had yet to hit its peak. The sound of thunder and lightning should mask any plans we hatched tonight for escape.

Tomorrow we would put it into motion. I planned on being out of here before month's end.

Chapter 23

Life went back to normal for the camp once the storm cleared. And for all everyone knew, life went back to normal for me as well. For the first couple days, Orin kept a close eye on me. Each time I attempted to speak to Leif, I was redirected or escorted away.

I never got close enough to talk, but I was able to see that Mahon had kept his promise. Leif was no longer shackled in iron. His little body was tied to the tree with thick vines, tight enough that I knew even he couldn't squeeze out. That couldn't have been comfortable, but at least the vines didn't burn his skin off.

We were going to have to try another way to get to Leif. I had every intention of leaving this camp, but I didn't know how yet. I knew the only way off was by boat; it was where we were headed after that I was unsure of. I didn't know the area. But Leif did. If he was sent by Gwendolyn to find me, then I would bet everything I had that he could take us back to her.

"Any luck?" Falon asked as I climbed the short ladder to sit on the platform of our hut.

I slumped in defeat next to her and Cedric and shook my head. "No. Orin has the security on him too tight. There is no way I can get to him without being seen."

Orin's overprotective crap was getting old. I knew he only acted this way because he cared, but I wished that he would trust me enough to at least listen to what I had to say. If I was supposed to be some prophesized bringer-of-peace, how was I expected to do anything without the support from people like him?

I'll tell you how. I was expected to be a fully trained centerpiece. I would be put on display to rally the forces and unite our people, but after that I would be "sheltered" back in my box for protection and then left there.

I knew Orin's game now. I knew it the moment he stated what my first task would be. In that moment, he proved that he had no intention of letting me anywhere near battle, or near anything that mattered. All his arguments with Asa, whispering behind my back about things that were obviously connected to me; I wasn't stupid.

But he obviously thought I was and that hurt. There was a pain in my chest when I thought of him now. It felt like a hand, gently caged around my heart for protection. But instead of defending it and shielding it from heartache, it squeezed and said it was for its own good.

"Casey, are you listening?" Falon's hand waved in front of my face, almost brushing my nose it was so close.

I turned to look at them, expecting irritation, but only found concern on their faces.

"Sorry, guys. I've been a bit distracted lately. What were you saying?"

"It's almost time for your task," Falon replied, obviously not wanting to be the one to bring it up.

But she was right. The sun was sinking below the tree line and the night fires were being lit within the clearings.

"Let's get this over with." I sighed and slid off the platform.

Cedric came up alongside me and wrapped his arm around my shoulder. He could sense the anxiety building in me. Hell, I was sure the entire camp could sense it. The beat down I was about to get was no less embarrassing each time.

This was the fourth night I'd attempted the task Orin set. The last three nights left me uninjured, but humiliated. Beating me was child's play to Mahon. My strikes hurt, sure, but they weren't enough to take him down.

"You're doing great, Casey. Honestly. There are very few people here who can actually beat Mahon, and you hold your own better than most. We're all proud of you for it."

Cedric was trying to cheer me up. He spoke the truth, but it didn't make it any less painful. The entire camp has watched me have my ass handed to me for three nights now. It was hard to live something like that down.

The closer we got to the task ring, the more faces appeared to offer me support. There were pats on the back and waves of encouragement as the other members of the camp wished me luck. They were all cheering for me to succeed. They *needed* me to. Beating a beast like Mahon meant there was hope for me against Sebastian's army.

So it made me feel even worse each time I lost.

We stopped at the edge of the main clearing. The task ring sat in the center—a large circle drawn in the dirt a few yards in diameter. The fire burned high behind the crowd of spectators and combined with the moon; it cast just enough light for everyone to see.

Mahon stood with Orin on the opposite side of the ring. His shirt was off, leaving his muscles on full display. It was meant to intimidate me, and it was working. I already knew how strong he was; I'd experienced it each time he threw me from the ring. The anticipation of it happening again caused my hands to shake.

Cedric stepped in my line of sight, blocking out the imposing figure across from me. His warm hands settled on my bare shoulders, and his thumbs rubbed along the straps of my tank top.

"You remember what we talked about? You *can* do this, Casey. You're smaller and faster than him. All it takes is one trip, one strong, well placed strike, and he can easily topple out of the ring, that's all you need. Hey, look at me." His fingers gripped my chin until I looked him in the eye. "No one else matters. Focus."

He kissed the side of my head and squeezed me tight. Before letting me go, his breath tickled the hairs by my ear.

"I believe in you" was the last phrase I heard before stepping into the ring.

The silence that settled over the clearing was smothering. The minute Mahon and I crossed those lines in the dirt, all sound ceased to exist. I blocked out all the chants and cries, I ignored my frantic heart racing, and I focused everything on the Vampire that stood before me.

"It's not too late to back out," Mahon offered, like he did each night before we began.

I flipped him off. He lifted a shoulder, the gesture showing that he'd given me a chance, and then charged. The first night he'd done this, the sight of him barreling down upon me had me back peddling until I pushed myself out of the ring.

But I knew better now. I leapt to the side and rolled to my feet. I stood behind him, foot striking to the back of his knee as he slowed at the edge of the ring. If I could just get him to topple over, I would win.

I should have known that wouldn't work. Mahon might be huge, but that didn't mean he was slow. He spun around, just a body's length from the line, and grabbed my foot. He lightly tugged, a sly grin thrown my way, as he taunted me with defeat.

It would only take one strong pull, and he could easily throw me over the line. Knowing he was drawing the moment out, I had a split second to act. I dropped my body to the ground, going dead weight in his grasp. He couldn't risk pulling me like this without injuring me, and as much as he wanted to win, I knew he didn't want to hurt me to do it.

With a sly smile of my own, I kicked at the side of his knee with my free foot. I didn't hit hard enough to cause any permanent damage, but I'd be lying if I said I wasn't hoping for him to limp tomorrow.

His bark of pain was accompanied by my freedom as his hands moved to clutch his afflicted knee. Not wasting a head start when it's given, I swung my legs back and threw them forward. Pushing off with my hands, I popped up and landed on my feet with only seconds left to execute my attack.

Knowing better than to strike his well-muscled abdomen, I aimed instead for the face. No matter how strong he made his body, there would always be natural weak spots. And this was one of them. A strong, spinning-hook kick knocked his head to the side and a punch to his exposed throat had him gasping for air.

His hands struck out, trying to grab me, but I was already dropping to the ground and sliding between his legs. I swiftly clamored back to my feet behind him and landed a full powered round kick to his unprotected side. On anyone else, that strike would have broken ribs. But on Mahon, the only obvious damage would be a bruise.

My aim wasn't to hurt him, though, it was to knock him over. Which I managed to do for a few precious seconds before he rebounded and lunged for me again. That was how our match continued—for how long, I wasn't sure.

Mahon was unrelenting with his reaches and strikes, trying to land just one. That was all he needed. One of his strikes had enough force to push me out of the ring. But I was holding my own, better than before. I danced around, evading his grabs and landing my own strikes in his unguarded soft spots.

Slowly but surely, I was corralling him to one side of the ring. Just a little longer and he would be over the line. Suddenly, with a speed I didn't know him capable of, Mahon's hand struck out and grabbed my arm.

His fist fit around my entire bicep and had a grip too strong for me to break out of. With growing panic, I turned and struck out with a kick. But Mahon had all the power. All it took was one jerk on my arm and I was off balance enough for my kick to miss. The same with any strike I tried. I felt like a puppet, jolted and yanked from one side to the other, made to dance as Mahon laughed at my frustration.

"All right, you've had your fun. Time for this match to end," Mahon whispered, low enough for my ears alone.

What did he mean by, 'I'd had my fun'? I turned my head to look over my shoulder and saw Orin give the nod to Mahon, as if this was all planned. At Orin's subtle command, Mahon reached down and scooped me up. His hand kept a strong hold on me while my legs were trapped in the relentless pin of his other arm.

No, this couldn't be how it ended. Not after all that. I'd worked so hard and actually thought I was winning for once. It couldn't have all been an act. Mahon began his walk to the line, prepared to drop me over like a sack of flour.

Over his shoulder, Orin stood with his arms crossed, pity in his eyes, and a clenched jaw. They had planned this. Mahon *let* me think that I was winning to spare my feelings, but the end game had stayed the same. The sympathy in the eyes of my friends and the others around us told me they all knew what happened.

Every soul here knew that Mahon had only been toying with me, like a mountain cat does with its fresh kill. Rage and desperation clawed from a dark hole within me; one I kept covered and under control at all times.

But right now, in this moment, there was no stopping it. I was tired of fighting it, tired of being helpless and at the whim of those around me. I had held back for fear of hurting my friend, a person I thought was on my side, but no more.

I saw it in the eyes of each face I looked into. These people didn't think I had it in me; they felt *sorry* for me. The humiliation burned. It burned past my heart, past the point of caring that Mahon was supposed to be a friend. Deep down it seared a path until it settled into the very center of me. The small ball of ice I had hardened and learned to control, the root of my power, hissed and spit as the heat of my rage invaded even that part of me.

I wiggled and fought in Mahon's arms, yelling and cussing as I struggled to get free. But Mahon's steps never faltered. My mind was frantic; it would not accept defeat, not again.

No, no, no, no, no, no, no, no.

I chanted the word over in my mind, not even realizing when I began to recite it aloud. I pushed my hands against Mahon's bare chest, scratching and clawing in my desperation to make him stop.

No, no, no, no, stop, no, no, stop. Stop, stop, stop.

I hammered my clenched fists against his chest, screaming with each hit. When that didn't work, I tried again with my palms, alternating between hitting him and pushing against him. My frustration was reaching desperate levels and my power surged with each thump against him.

No, no, no. Not like this. I will not lose like this. No. Stop.

Mahon was only two steps from the line now. I fought harder, giving everything I had and more. From deep within me, my power rose to answer my frenzied plea for help. An overwhelming wave of ice started from my toes, flowed over my calves and thighs, flooded through my chest and arms, to erupt from my hands against Mahon's chest.

With a jolt strong enough to stop his heart, Mahon's body ceased all movement and all control. His muscles spasmed, releasing their hold on me only moments before his knees gave out. Pushing from his body, I landed safely on the ground an instant before Mahon fell over the line.

He didn't move.

I knelt beside him, hand shaking as I tentatively reached out. I shook him.

"Mahon?" I whispered.

When he didn't move, I shook harder. Still nothing. I closed my eyes and pushed with my power, but there was none left. That jolt I gave him had drained me for the moment, to the point where I couldn't get a sense of him.

"Out of the way! Move out of the way!" Asa's voice pierced the growing cacophony around us.

He knelt by my side, and I scrambled to move so he could help. With a strong heave, Mahon was rolled over and Asa put his fingers to his neck, feeling for a pulse. Laying his head against Mahon's chest, Asa closed his eyes and listened.

When he opened them again, his gaze found mine.

"He's dead," Asa whispered, right before Mahon moved.

Mahon gasped, his chest expanding so far I thought it would burst. His eyes darted wildly as he took in the crowd of faces hovering over him while his chest resumed its normal rise and fall, albeit a bit faster than usual.

Leo and Cedric worked to push the gathering crowd back, giving Asa and Orin room to check over their friend. Asa was already assessing Mahon's pulse and asking him to perform the basic checkup routine: follow the finger with your eyes, does it hurt to take a deep breath? The list went on.

Meanwhile, I made myself small and squeezed through the onlookers until I was safe on the other side of them. No one really noticed me leave, they were all too busy watching the freak show I left in front of them.

The only people keeping an eye out for me were my friends, and both of them were at my side within record time.

"That was the best damn thing I ever saw! Did you see him go down? He was all like 'Muahaha, I win. *Stomp. Stomp.*' and then you were all, '*ZAP!*' and there he went!"

Falon's excitement was almost too much for me to bear, but even Cedric seemed to be feeding off it. He wrapped me in a giant hug, pride pulling at each corner of his broad smile.

"I told you you could do it!" He spun me around once before setting my feet back on the ground.

When he saw that I wasn't returning their smiles though, he was immediately concerned. His first thought was that I was injured. He held onto me while his eyes checked over my face and neck, lingering on the bruise forming around my bicep where I had fought Mahon's hold. It took him a few minutes to tune in to me, in the special way that only he could.

"Please don't feel that way about yourself. It's okay. *He's* okay."

He enveloped me in another hug, and I returned it this time. I buried my face in his chest, fighting the tears and shakes that my body wanted to give in to. I thought I had killed Mahon, my friend. I had dug deep inside myself to find the strength to win, and what did I pull out?

A monster.

I shook harder, my breaths coming in sharp gasps as I tried to calm myself. Falon rubbed her hand on my back in soothing circles as I fought the hysteria that threatened to take over. What had I done back there? All I remember feeling is rage and resentment, had that wicked person been in me all along?

"*Shh*, Casey. You didn't mean for this to happen; we know you didn't." Cedric tried to calm me down, denying what he knew I was feeling inside.

But even if he could pick up on what I felt, he couldn't *stop* me from feeling it. And I felt like a monster. I would completely understand if Mahon and everyone else on this island hated me for what I had done, for what I had shown I was capable of.

I could only apologize to Mahon, beg his forgiveness, and swear to work hard every day to make sure I never let that side of myself loose again. When the tears finally stopped threatening to take over, and my shaking had settled to tremors, I released my hold on Cedric.

"Do you want to talk about what happened back there?" he asked, his tone gentle.

"I'd like to know the same thing," came Orin's voice from behind me.

Spinning around, I watched as he approached, a concerned Asa on his heels. I studied Orin, looking for signs of anger or disgust. So far, if he felt either, he managed to keep it concealed. I couldn't say the same for myself.

"What happened here is what you caused," I told him. My voice was level, tame. But underneath there was a hint of steel.

Both Asa and Orin looked confused at my accusation. But I felt the truth to my words in every fiber of my being.

"*You* were the one who assigned me this asinine task; a task you were sure I wouldn't win." I pointed at Orin, fury darkening my pitch. "You knew how humiliated I was each time he threw me over that line and how desperate I was to find a way to win. So what do you do? You tell him to let me think I'm winning and then to shut it down before I actually do. Were you hoping for a good show? Because you sure as hell got one!"

Orin blanched at my words, guilt causing him to wince as I used each one like a bullet. Asa slightly cringed behind him, an indirect victim of my verbal assault.

"Casey, just let me explain. It wasn't like that," he tried to reason with me.

"Bullshit! I saw you give him the order to end it. You were the damn puppet master. Did you enjoy humiliating me? Were you hoping it would make me quit? Because all you succeeded in doing was forcing me to cross a line and unleash a part of my power that I didn't even know was there. A part that almost killed my friend."

I put my hands down to my side and clenched them to keep from physically striking him. Cedric forced one of his hands in mine in a sign of comfort, or maybe he was reigning me in. Either way, it helped.

I watched Orin as he stood there. He knew what he had done was wrong, his guilt obvious. And it would be a while before I could forgive him, even longer before I forgave myself.

I turned to go, pulling Cedric along with me. "I played a part in this too; there's no denying that. But you were the one that ultimately brought us here."

I had nothing else to say, the fight and anger had left me as suddenly as they'd come. All I wanted to do now was sleep. Hopefully I was strong enough to deal with the backlash of my actions in the morning.

Chapter 24

 It had been so long that I'd almost forgotten what it felt like to be the resident outcast. My entire life was spent living on the outskirts, hiding from mocking stares and malicious taunts. I never knew a time where I fit in, until I came to this camp.

For the first time, I was wanted by others that I didn't see as family. Finally, I was on the receiving end of kind smiles and offers of friendship. Until the night I turned into a monster and once again became the neighborhood freak.

"Stop being so overdramatic. You know the others don't see you like that."

Cedric's steady footsteps made soft thuds as he closed the distance between us. If he had wanted to, he could have completely hidden his approach from me. He was the best out of our trio at moving through the foliage undetected—a fact he liked to point out every chance he got.

He stopped, kicked a rock out of the way, and crouched next to me. "This pity party of yours has to end. It's been two days, Casey. Why don't you *try* coming back to training?"

I shook my head. "I couldn't take the stares."

"They're staring because you're such a badass," he replied, and I glared.

"I almost killed a friend! Some badass."

Cedric stood, forcing me to look up and squint at the few rays of sunlight that made it through the canopy. His face held a scowl, the same one that he directed at me each time our conversation headed in this direction.

"For the last time, no one is blaming you for what happened. You didn't even know you could do something like that, so it's not as if you did it on purpose. Right?"

"Of course not!"

Cedric nodded and moved on. "All the more reason for you to return to training. The faster you learn to control it, the better you will feel about it."

I knew he was right. *Of course* he was right. But I was wracked with latent fears of losing the acceptance I had found here. Mahon was a leader at camp. If he held this against me, others would follow suit.

I hadn't spoken to Mahon since our fight. At first, he was secluded in Asa's hut. Most of his recuperation remained private and under careful observation from our favorite Vampire medic. He had since been released, having made a full recovery, and I had become a coward.

I hid out here, not straying too far from my own hut, and avoiding people when I could. I was afraid that when I confronted Mahon, I would see disgust in his eyes. Or anger. I deserved both. Cedric sighed and stepped away. If he couldn't convince me to come with him today, he would only come back and try again tomorrow.

But he wasn't leaving quite yet.

"It's better if you get this over with now, so we can all move on."

He waved to a figure that leaned against a thick mangrove. There was only one person on this island with that height and build. Mahon. Taller than even Cedric at six feet, Mahon's shoulder width was wider than most of the trees out here. He really was a beast.

With a nod to him and a wink at me, Cedric left us. I swallowed past the lump in my throat and waited for Mahon to speak. He didn't berate me right away, instead he found a tree wider than him and leaned against it.

We sat in silence as the birds and other wildlife continued on around us. Tropical breezes blew through the leaves and canopy, echoed laughter and shouts reached us from the camp, and random splashes from fish in the canal to my right were the only sounds I heard.

I sat frozen, waiting for Mahon to make a move. But the anticipation had become too much.

"What are you waiting for?" I finally asked.

He didn't move at first, like he hadn't heard me, and I almost asked the question again. But then he tilted his head, just enough to look at me, and spoke.

"I'm waiting on you. You're the only one here who seems to have a problem. So, I'm patiently waiting for you to fix it."

I was dumbstruck, and I'm sure my face showed it. He hadn't spoken in a malicious tone, just matter of fact. He didn't have a problem, I did. Was he referring to my wayward strand of power? Was my problem that I had no control over it?

Or maybe he meant my attitude. Did he think my self-imposed isolation was selfish? His chuckle only added to my confusion.

"Cedric told me you were tore up about it, but it wasn't until now that I understood just how much." He exhaled on a laugh and smiled. "Kid, I'm not mad at you for what happened during our fight. Quite the opposite; I'm proud."

"You're *proud* that I almost killed you?" I couldn't blink. If I did, I was afraid I'd realize that this was all a fantasy made up in my head from lack of sleep.

"Hell yeah I'm proud." He was grinning at me, good natured and honest. "You beat me. There aren't many that can claim that."

He really was okay with this. He attempted to sit on the log beside me, but when the wood groaned beneath his weight, he stood again. Finding the ground an acceptable replacement, he instead sat in front of me.

He bent one knee to the side and lounged back on his palms, the perfect picture of peace. Even with him sitting, he was still a few inches taller than me and we were close enough to eye level that I couldn't avoid his gaze.

That was it. We sat opposite one another, in complete silence, with that calm grin still plastered across Mahon's face. A grin that was slowly beginning to infuriate me. What else did he want from me?

"What now?" I huffed with exasperation.

Mahon raised a brow. "I'm still waiting."

"For what?" I was digging my fingers into the log now. Soft, rotted bark, came away under my nails.

"For you to forgive yourself."

I released my grip on the decaying wood and slumped my shoulders. What he was asking for was more difficult than it seemed. He may not hold what happened in our fight against me, but he wasn't inside my head.

He hadn't heard my thoughts, felt my rage, and didn't know what kind of monster peeked out from some dark depth I didn't know I had. He thinks I was provoked into using this aspect of my power, and to a degree I was.

But I had to *allow* for it to be used. He just didn't understand.

"Listen, kid. We all do things at some point in our life that are difficult to come to terms with. But the way I look at it, how you feel about it after the fact is just as important as how you felt when it happened."

He shifted on the ground, sitting at his full height with that grin nowhere in sight. It was replaced with a stern frown, like he was fighting to not shake his own feelings into me.

"Look, that night, did you decide to zap me just because you could and because you hated me? Or were you pushed into it, pushed to a point that your power overtook your control?"

"I didn't even know I could ..." I swallowed and cleared my dry throat. "I would never have ..."

Mahon nodded, like he knew what I was trying to say. Maybe he did.

"Not having control over a power as strong as yours will have consequences. That, in and of itself is a bad thing. But how do you feel right now? For the past couple days?"

Did he even have to ask? I mean, look at me. I had secluded myself from everyone and everything I had come to love about this place.

"Mortified. Guilty. Completely undeserving of forgiveness."

Mahon stood and took the two steps it took to reach me. Holding out his hand, he didn't say another word, didn't move, until I grabbed it. He pulled me from the deteriorating log and held fast to my hand even after I was settled on my feet.

"Those emotions tell me that you are still the girl who fought by my side all the way from North Carolina. You are still the kind-hearted Witch that denied the Dean and saved a complete stranger at great cost to yourself. Fight. Work hard to control your power so something like this doesn't happen again. But don't identify as anything else than who we all know you to be: our champion."

The walk to the main clearing was nerve wracking to say the least. Both Mahon and Cedric kept me company, one flanking either side of me, but their presence was not enough to keep the anxiety fueled thoughts from my head.

Will they still like me?

That same question played on repeat in my mind. I couldn't escape it. Our picturesque walk through the wild island was tranquil and quiet. The perfect setting for my already frantic thoughts to run rampant and center around that one maddening thought, like a scratched disk that skipped.

The closer we walked to the center of camp, the louder it became. They hadn't mentioned it was lunch when the boys convinced me to come back with them. They conveniently left that part out. The only upside to the noise was that my train of thought was finally interrupted. I was now too nervous to think past making sure one foot was planted in front of the other.

I spotted movement through the trees ahead and knew my time of peace had come and gone. We had arrived at the outer clearings. News of my arrival would spread faster than it took me to walk, and too soon, the entire camp would be waiting to catch a glimpse of me in the main clearing.

"Everything is going to be fine. They still love you." Cedric interlaced his fingers with mine as we walked.

His hand was comforting and familiar, an anchor in the madness that was about to unfold. I held on tight. A group of Shifters were the first to spot us as we cleared the trees. I cringed in anticipation of rejection, fully prepared for the looks of disdain that I thought I deserved.

They only raised their hands in greeting as we passed, full blown smiles of admiration on their faces. I let out a breath, the tightness in my chest instantly loosening. More people appeared the deeper into camp we went, and they all had similar reactions.

Admiration. Respect. Joy at seeing me.

By the time I saw Zora's fire ahead, I was returning waves and greetings, smiling for the first time in days. As if she sensed my approach, Zora's head lifted and her gaze met mine. She smiled, her eyes shining with pride, as she opened her arms and welcomed me.

I ran to her, almost crushing her in a long overdue embrace. Tears built up behind my lids, but they were happy ones. Zora's opinion meant a great deal to me, and if she held no hatred for what I had done that night, then there was hope for me yet.

"It's about time you stopped moping, chickee. We do what we must in this war, you hear? There's not a single breathing body here that isn't proud to call you our champion. Walk with pride."

She released me with a firm squeeze to my shoulders and handed me a plate of whatever was cooking over her fire. Falon and Cedric had seats under a shaded part of the clearing, so I made my way over to them.

I scanned the camp as I walked, a smile firmly plastered across my face. Relief was rushing through me so fast I feared I would be swept away. I wasn't an outcast. I was still accepted. Luthos, even Parker was smiling at me.

I almost did a double take when I saw the young Vamp shoot me a shy grin. I responded with one of my own before looking ahead to my destination. Another person had joined the duo already waiting for me in the shade.

Leo laughed at something Cedric said and winked at me as I closed the distance between us. He still hadn't broken that habit. I swear, he would wink at Sebastian if given the chance.

"Hey Leo, what's up?"

"Glad to see you out of hiding." His tone was genuine; he really was happy to see me.

The feeling was mutual. I hadn't seen much of him lately since Orin always had him out on one task or another.

"So I just stopped by to give you a heads up. Orin needed Sacha for an assignment off the island. You won't be training with him for a couple weeks."

I shrugged. Sacha was all right, but I wasn't going to complain about a canceled training session. Especially the one that gave me the most bruises.

"Sweet. I can sleep in."

Leo shook his head, and I could tell by his smirk that he really enjoyed what he had to say next. "I've been appointed your new trainer until Sacha returns."

And then he winked at me. Again.

Chapter 25

It was nearing the end of the cool season, if Florida had such a thing. I figured the date to be somewhere in April, when the rainstorms were more frequent, but the temperature wasn't the sweltering torture it had been when we first arrived.

I had been at this camp for months; time spent unwasted as I morphed my body into a weapon. The strict routine Orin had applied to me combined with the unique terrain of the swamp and nearby ocean had put training on a higher level than I ever could have gotten at the Academy.

I'd learned all styles of fighting from Judo, to Taekwondo, to Krav Maga. The different races had their own way of fighting, and I was able to learn from each of them here. By the time the weather went from slightly less hot to I-think-it's-getting-humid-again, I felt like a whole new person.

For almost four months I had ate, slept, and breathed training. Every aspect of it. I could now track in the swamp as well as I could in the forest back home. My endurance was at an all-time high, and my reflexes were insane. I'd never felt stronger.

I felt I was finally ready to confront the Dean. I was ready to make him pay. There was only one problem: Orin. After his first attempt at giving me what he saw as an unachievable task, he has avoided assigning me another.

Maybe it was the guilt I laid on him about Mahon, or maybe he was just thinking of something even harder. I didn't know what it was, but he still refused to let me leave the island. He wouldn't even include me in any important decisions.

I had no idea why he held Leif captive; he wouldn't let me anywhere near him. I heard nothing about why he sent my combat trainer, Sacha, away on an assignment. I was literally clueless about anything and everything important.

It wasn't for a lack of trying. Cedric and Falon had been eavesdropping whenever they could, and I continued to make daily attempts to reach Leif. So far, nothing had worked.

A burning wave of agony brushed across my forearm. I could feel my skin begin to blister underneath the bright red splotch that now spread across it.

"Shit!" Leo ran up to me, guilt and worry blatantly morphing his features. "Why weren't you paying attention? We're working with *acid*, Casey. If I had known that you wouldn't take this seriously, I never would have agreed to it."

"I *am* taking this seriously. I just got distracted is all," I grumbled.

But he was right. I was the one that convinced him to use his power today. I told him that I wouldn't know how to properly defend against it if we couldn't even practice with it. He'd relented, barely. And then I'd allowed my mind to wander when it should have been focused.

The wound wasn't too serious, thank Luthos, but it was going to require a trip to Asa's hut. And since he was obligated to report any injury I sustained, Orin would know about this incident before Zora called for lunch.

I winced when I thought of what Orin would do to Leo for allowing this to happen.

"I'm sorry, Leo."

He brushed off the apology, carefully pouring cool water over my burn. He flicked his blond hair out of his eyes with a shake of his head.

"What has you so distracted that you don't watch a ball of acid when it's thrown at you?" he asked with obvious concern.

I wondered at what I could tell him. He was one of Orin's right hand men, and he wasn't going to give away any of his secrets. But maybe he could help me understand where Orin's thoughts were coming from.

"Sometimes, I feel like Orin doesn't see me as anything more than a kid, as someone who needs constant protection. I feel like he is never going to let me leave this island, and that I'm going to be here forever while those I love are out fighting in my stead."

I winced again as Leo bound a cloth around the burn to protect it until I got to Asa. At my involuntary jerk, he shot me an apologetic glance and loosened the wrapping.

"You've got to understand where Orin is coming from. He is a natural leader, one who cares about all that are under his command. And on this island that includes you and your friends." He finished tying a small knot in the cloth to hold it in place and gave me a pat on the shoulder. "He won't keep you here forever. But I think he feels that after all that has happened to you, you have been robbed of your childhood. You have the opportunity to grow here, in a safe environment where you can truly be ready to fight when the time comes."

I jerked out from under Leo's hand. "That's not his decision to make."

Something flashed in Leo's eyes before he averted them from my gaze. He wasn't being completely honest with me.

"What? You know why Orin wants to keep me here, why he doesn't want me fighting. Tell me! None of the decisions concerning my life are under his control. He has no claim to me other than saving my life."

But Leo wouldn't speak on the topic anymore. He refused to answer any direct question I fired at him, and barely spoke a word to me when I tried a more oblique approach. His frustration was growing, I could tell. He all but threw me at Asa when we finally reached his hut.

Before he left though, Leo pulled me close. His whispers were low, but they were harsh enough that some of the words might carry on the breeze.

"Listen to me. Everything Orin does is to protect the people in this camp. But above all of them, Orin does what he does to protect *you*. While you might not understand his reasoning now, trust him. I'd think he's earned it."

With a final nod to cement his statement, Leo turned and disappeared into the trees. A persistent throbbing began at my temples, the rhythm punctured by sharp jabs that radiated behind my eyes. All this stress was giving me a headache.

Combined with my raw and tender arm, today officially sucked. I understood where Leo was coming from, I really did. I knew Orin was a good guy. I wouldn't have trusted him or followed him out here if I didn't believe that, but lately he had been going too far. I had agreed to come out here because I thought we had a common goal, one that I was willing to help him with. I didn't realize that my being here was at the sacrifice of my freedom.

"He's right, you know." Asa's smooth voice aggravated my pulsing head. "About trusting Orin. He knows what he's doing."

"That may be," I muttered. "But that doesn't give him exclusive rights over my future."

As I followed Asa back to his hut, the smell of herbs and dried grasses grew stronger, more pleasing. No matter what he was working on, I could always make out the scent of lavender under all the other aromas.

I settled on a thin woven cushion made from the ferns that grew in the area. It wasn't very squishy, but it was better than sitting on the rough wood of the platform. Asa puttered around with his supplies, giving me time to cool off.

When he turned to me again, he offered a small cup filled with brackish water. It looked disgusting, but it smelled of citrus.

"For your head," Asa told me when I looked like I was about to tip the contents over the side of the hut.

Not even bothering to ask how he knew my head hurt, I downed the contents of the cup. I only cringed once. As I drank his no doubt genius concoction, he had gotten to work on my arm. Thanks to Leo's quick thinking with the cool water, it wasn't as bad as it could have been. No more than a second degree burn at the worst places.

"I'm going to give you this jar of aloe when I'm finished. Reapply generously for the next couple days and then rewrap it," he advised. "With your rate of healing this should be gone by the end of the week."

I sighed as the aloe he applied went to work, soothing my terrorized skin with a cool touch.

"Thanks."

He smiled as he handed me the jar. "Just think about what you've heard today. Trust Orin. He has his reasons."

I left before he could say anything else. I know it was rude, but I couldn't listen to any more of that 'trust Orin' preach they all seemed to have in their back pocket. Did I trust him with my life and those of my friends? One hundred percent.

But did I trust him to know what was right for me, to trust *me* in return and allow me to do what was necessary? Absolutely not.

I found Cedric and Falon exactly where I knew they'd be: at our tree. Word must have already gone around camp about what happened at training today with Leo. I could tell by the way Cedric zeroed in on my bandaged arm.

"It doesn't feel like you're still in pain. At least, nothing like what I felt before when it happened."

"I'm going to skip over how creepy that *still* is and just confirm that I'm okay." I told him as I held up the jar of aloe that was responsible for my current pain free existence.

Cedric gave me a playful frown before hugging me. True to his nature, he used that moment to check me over for further injury. He also took advantage of the opportunity to cop a feel, until I punched him in the stomach.

I wasn't much for PDA and Falon was still sitting over by the tree, watching us. Cedric laughed through his wheezing, knowing that I didn't intend him any real harm.

"So, does that mean you had to see Asa?" Falon asked, aiming for nonchalant, but I could hear the pain underneath.

Ever since Asa had found out Falon was a princess, he had distanced himself. He no longer hung around. He didn't joke with her when they ran into one another. He didn't acknowledge her at all. It was like the bond they had formed while we were on the run no longer existed.

I wasn't sure if it was because Falon had lied about who she was or if he couldn't take her royal station. Either way, she was hurting because of it, and I knew he was too. I hadn't missed the pain in his eyes any time I caught him looking at her.

Although, she hadn't noticed; he was better at hiding it than she was.

"Try not to think about him, Fal. It will get better." I failed to keep the pity from my eyes, but it was hard not to feel bad for her.

A roll of thunder rumbled in the distance, carried along by a southern wind smelling of salt and brine. A storm was moving in. The trees around us swayed, the leaves rustling so hard I thought they would fall off. When a storm came off the coast like that, it meant business.

Like the flashes of lightning that lit up the sky overhead, an idea formed in my mind.

"We can leave tonight," I mumbled to myself.

The longer I thought about it, the more right it felt. The storm moving in would provide the perfect cover. We probably had a couple hours before the brunt of the storm arrived, plenty of time to gather supplies. We could be out of here before anyone was the wiser, and by the time they noticed we were gone it would be too late.

The rain would wash away our tracks, giving us a generous head start. It was perfect. Unfortunately, I was the only one who thought that.

"Are you out of your mind?" Cedric all but shouted when I suggested it. "Traveling in a storm like that is dangerous!"

Ever the cynical one, Cedric would be the hardest to convince. Falon, I knew, was already on my side.

"It's the best chance we have. If we can get off this island before the full impact of the storm hits, then we can stay in front of it all the way out of here."

The scowl he wore told me he was listening, but he wasn't completely sold on it yet. I needed him to be on my side. There was a relentless unease that had been building inside me since the night I hurt Mahon.

This anxiety grew each time Orin ignored my plea to leave. It swelled every time I had to hear someone tell me that Orin was doing what was best for me. I knew it was only a matter of time before I lost it.

"I can't stay here much longer, Ced. It's time for us to move on, whether or not those that run this camp agree."

I knew at least that was something we could settle on. Cedric was as ready to get out of here as I was; we both had people back at the Academy we were worried about.

"But are you sure this is the right time? You haven't learned yet how to control this new part of your power. What if something happens?"

"Gwendolyn is the only one who can help me with that." I grabbed both his hands in mine and held them tight. "Please, just trust me on this."

I couldn't force him to go with me; I couldn't force either of them. But I was hoping they understood why this was so urgent.

"When do we leave?" he sighed.

My response was interrupted by another wave of thunder strong enough that I swear I felt the ground shake beneath my feet. We didn't have much time left, but if we could pull it off, it would be the perfect plan.

"First we need to pack as many supplies as we can without suspicion: food, water bottles, fresh clothes, and weapons."

That was step one of the plan. We wouldn't get very far in this terrain without provisions. The second part was more difficult to execute. I needed Leif, his involvement was crucial. Without his directions, I had no way of getting to Gwendolyn and all of this would be for nothing.

"Falon, you and I are going to free Leif and bring him to the edge of the island where they dock the canoes. Ced, I need you to distract Orin somehow. He always seems to know when I'm trying to get over there, and I doubt tonight would be any different."

They nodded along with my ideas and added in suggestions where they thought best. In the end, we actually had a pretty solid plan, as long as everything was timed correctly. If we couldn't make it off the island before the storm, we wouldn't be able to navigate the channels and would be caught the minute the skies cleared.

Knowing what we had to do, we wished each other luck and left to pack. I already had a few knives stashed away in my pack, and I know Falon did too. Water wasn't hard to come by—everyone was thirsty on this damned island.

It was the food that would be the difficult part, but I already had a plan for that too. I would deal with the guilt later, when I was far from the camp and had enough time to dwell on it. I told Zora that I was planning a romantic picnic with Cedric, that I wanted some quality time with him.

She thought the storm was an odd time to have one, but was more than happy to help, piling me with an arm load of food plus a packed basket. My guilt grew with each item she added, but I refused to let it show. This was for the best, even if she didn't understand it at first.

She would eventually. I hoped.

Falon and I filled the bags till they almost burst and hid them in the canoe furthest down the line. That would be the easiest one to get out on when the time came. When we were ready to go to where Leif was held, rain had already begun to fall.

Soft, pitter pats of water drummed around the island as they landed on ferns and trees alike. The ground became softer, less compact, and the mud was already causing me to slip a few times. Most of the camps inhabitants, I knew, were finishing up the afternoon chores and heading to their respective huts.

No one would be around to see us. Thank Luthos for April showers.

The guards watching Leif would be out here all night, regardless of the storm. I could see them clearly, despite the rain that now fell in sheets. They were mildly protected under the canopy of the tree they had tied Leif to, but the frustration at being forced to stand through the storm was obvious on their faces.

I gave the thumbs up to Falon, who crouched behind a large fern toward the side of the tree, and then walked out from my hiding place in the shadows. The guards were instantly at alert, until they saw that it was me.

"Why do you keep trying? You know we can't let you talk to him," said the guard on the right.

He was the chattiest of the two and seemed more approachable than his comrade. He never left his post and refused to disobey his orders to let me by, but he would talk with me until Orin arrived to escort me away.

It was from my previous attempts that I knew I could distract them long enough for Falon to cut away at Leif's restraints. I shrugged at the guards.

"I'm not going to give up until Orin changes his mind." I gave him an innocent smile, but the guard didn't buy it.

In fact, he snorted. "Orin's got his hands full with you."

Falon signaled that she had cut all the way through, and I watched as the vines around the tree fell to the ground. Leif fell with them. The scraping as his body slid couldn't be masked by the rain, and there was no thunder when I needed it most.

The guards caught the movement out of the corner of their eyes and whirled around in shock.

"What the—"

With no time to think of a better option, I made a rash decision and moved. Taking the few lunging steps to reach him, I landed a well-placed punch to the side of the guard's head, right on the temple.

He dropped like a bag of rocks. Turning to my left, I saw that Falon was already clinging to the back of the other guard, her arm wrapped around his neck and pressing against his windpipe. He bucked and fought, but couldn't throw her, and within the span of another volley of thunder, he was out.

"That training has really been paying off for you," I told her with a smirk, but it faded away to a cry of dismay when I looked behind me.

At the bottom of the tree lay Leif, so small and weak that I thought he might have been dead. He was a shade paler than I remember him being, limp and wheezing. There were red scars, only a couple weeks old that spread in a pattern around his body.

They looked like burns.

"It's from the iron. It can burn if it's pure enough," Falon whispered, her expression horrified.

"He looks awful." He barely resembled the lively creature that had visited me before.

"The iron must have gotten into his bloodstream. I don't think he has long," she replied.

Leif took in another breath, and I heard it rattle around his chest before it left his mouth in a *whoosh*. I reached forward, intent on picking him up and healing him. I wanted to take away his pain. But Falon smacked my hand away.

"I'll carry him. You can't touch him, Casey. We can't run with you weak from healing."

She was right, but it almost physically hurt to not heal him. Not because my power was fighting to be released, even though it was. It was because I caused this. He was here, on this island, because he was sent to find *me.*

And I couldn't even save him in time once he got captured. If Orin had just let me see him sooner, I could have kept him from reaching this point.

"Let's go." Falon had already made it back to the path while I stood there and stared at the torn bindings that had held poor Leif's body to the tree.

I packed away my guilt to be felt at another time and ran to catch up. We snuck past the living quarters, the huts now filled with the other residents of this camp. Cedric was waiting for us on the other side, his bag over his shoulder and soaked from the rain.

Lightning flashed, so close that I was momentarily blinded by the brightness of it. If we didn't get off this island soon we were never going to. I could see the edge of the roots off in the distance, the canal right below them. Trees shook and bent as the gust of the storm ripped at them, but we were almost there.

And then, above the shrill call of the wind, penetrating through the deep *crack* of the next wave of thunder, was the piercing howl of the warning call. Picked up by the other Shifters, the call rose to near deafening just as the sounds of battle reached my ears.

We were too late.

Chapter 26

I was disoriented. Elongated shadows appeared and then disappeared as the lightning struck closer with each wasted minute. The brunt of the storm had officially arrived, and we were no closer to getting off this island.

A hefty branch, as long as I was tall, fell from above and almost crushed the unsuspecting Falon below. Fortunately, Cedric saw it at the same time I did and managed to shove her from its path. Rocks and broken shells swirled around us as the wind's fury propelled them like heat seeking missiles.

My arms and cheeks were covered in nicks and scratches; I could feel the blood trickle down my skin to mix with the raindrops that had yet to cease. With the trees bent out of their normal shape and the lightning constantly changing what we could see, the last leg of our trip to the canoes seemed more impossible by the minute.

"Maybe the alarm wasn't for us. It's possible they don't know we're missing yet," came Falon's voice, hopeful.

Almost half of her words were overshadowed by the thunder, but we were squeezed together beneath a steady group of Hammock trees and close enough that I could still hear what she said. With a glance down at Leif, still held in her arms, I noticed that his shivering had increased. The cold rain and harsh wind was only worsening the ailments that he suffered.

"Ced, why don't you take him? You can keep him warm until we figure out our next steps," I suggested.

Falon gently handed her charge over, her hands hovering around him until he was securely settled into Cedric's arms. Pushing my worry for Leif as far from my mind as I could, I focused instead on getting us off this island.

We needed to get to the canoes. The channels between this island and the others were narrow; small enough that the waves wouldn't be impassable. If we stuck to those and hid on one of the outer islands, we could hunker down until the storm passed and would still have enough of a lead from the search parties that would follow.

But which way were the boats?

"Casey!"

My name carried above the rumbling of the thunder, echoing from all around. I couldn't tell where it came from at first, but I recognized the voice. When I heard my name again, my eyes zeroed in on the source. Opposite us, partially hidden by swaying ferns, stood Zora.

The lightning lit across her face, accenting the worry I saw there. Worry that mingled with fear and confusion when she saw our small group, complete with its stolen prisoner. Knowing that it was too late to run, and pointless since she was a Shifter, I hoped that I could reason with her and that I could get her to understand our actions.

I shook where I stood, both from my drenched clothes and the dread of suffering Zora's disappointment. But there was nothing for it now. She stopped in front of me, only half under the protection of the tree.

Her eyes were wide, panicked, as they roamed over our sodden appearance, but her jaw remained firm. I could see her hands shake, and wasn't sure if it was due to the cold or her nerves. Something wasn't right.

"I can't say that I understand what you're doing, chickee, or that I agree with it. But none of that matters now. You all must run."

"Zora, what's happened?" I could barely get the words out.

My mind was distracted, split between listening to what she had to say and trying to convince myself that I couldn't hear the screams of those at camp. The thunder only heightened the menacing atmosphere that seemed to settle over the small island.

Another scream sliced right through the storm's wrath and Falon flinched. Dread started its incapacitating creep through me, causing my heart to race faster than my halted breaths could keep up with.

I hadn't imagined those screams.

"Zora!" Her eyes came back into focus and settled on me.

She came back to herself then, and a steely calm radiated from her determined gaze. "The Imperials have found us. There are too many to hold off for long, you must run."

My head shook of its own accord. Another night eerily similar to this one tugged at the edge of my memory: flashes of running from someone I loved, leaving them to bear the full weight of what I had caused.

I couldn't leave Zora to the same fate, or the others of this camp. I was better trained now, more capable. We all were. Adding us to the fight could turn the tide of battle, we could make a difference. I knew we could.

Zora saw the fight in me, the need to slash and tear at the beings that had made my life a living hell. A proud smile fought to curve her lips, but only managed to tilt the one side.

"My brave, chickee. You are not meant to battle this night. You must go. Run. Be ready to lead our people in the true war that is still yet to come."

"How nauseating."

Reacting faster than I had ever seen her move, Zora whirled around, using her body to shield us from the intruder that approached. Her arm was a band across my waist, both of them spread like wings that yearned to lift us from here and take us to safety. If only.

"I really can't tell how it is you continually succeed in escaping me, my doll, but know that you won't get lucky a third time."

It was Kael. Backed by at least six other men that I could see, they blocked the paths out of here. Sounds of battle rang all around me, originating from the other side of the island, near the main clearings, and spreading in our direction.

Kael and his men, I knew, had skirted along the edge of the island, skipping the dense pockets and remaining fresh for their true mission. They didn't care about the others on this land. It was me they were looking for.

Kael's outline loomed ahead of me, his features hidden in the shadows, but I could see his face clearly as if it were bright as day: the cruel twist to his lips, the evil glint in his eye, the scarred hands that twitched and itched to get a hold of me.

On the inside, I was scared. My intestines seemed to liquefy and turn to mush. The only thing still solid was my heart, and it threatened to run away and leave me behind. My entire body quaked, and I knew that it was not from the cold this time.

The only part of me that remained calm was my mind, as it relentlessly filtered out plans and strategies to get us out of this mess. We were at a standoff, both sides remaining still as we waited to see who would make the first move.

Knowing he loved to hear himself speak, I wasn't surprised when Kael taunted us with his plans.

"I don't think I will take you directly back to the Dean, as I had intended to before. Once we get rid of the vile traitors and beasts that live on this chunk of land, we could take our time getting to know one another, learning what makes you tick and squeal. I'm sure my men would enjoy the company you could offer. It's only fair after you forced us to chase you around this forsaken swamp."

His men chuckled and leered at his promise. I could feel the weight of their eyes on me like sticky hands trying to claim a piece of the prize. Falon's grip on my arm tightened at the same time as Zora spoke.

Her words were directed at us, too low for the Imperials to hear and almost too low for us to understand. "Behind you, on the other side of this tree is a network of roots. Follow the largest one to the end and you will find a hunter's pit. It leads to an escape tunnel to the boats."

Her cheek muscles began to twitch as fur thrust from beneath her skin only to disappear on the next tremor that racked her body.

"Zora, no."

More fur broke out across her arms, rippling as she fought to control the animal within her. "Go. Now. And be brave, my chickee."

She let the animal take over, her body morphing into that of a wolf with a single thought. She landed on soft pads in front of us, her teeth bared in a threatening snarl, and with one flick of her tail she pounced on the Imperial closest to us.

It all happened in the span of a few heartbeats, the Imperial having no idea what was upon him until it was too late. His throat was ripped from his body, blood pulsating out in a waterfall of tangy red that settled on a ground too saturated to soak it up.

The life drained out of him so quickly I hardly felt the stirring of my power. He was gone before the urge to heal him even registered. Things moved even quicker after that. With a shout at his fallen comrade, Kael ordered the remaining men to attack.

I had never seen Zora fight. When she trained, it was with the other Shifters and out of sight. It was hard to picture the strong willed woman who manned the fire as a bloodthirsty wolf with a knack for ripping out throats and stomachs.

But in an odd way, it fit her.

My heel slipped in the mud when Falon tugged on my arm. As my upper body fought to right itself, a meaty fist narrowly avoided my head. With a growl, the Imperial attacked again, and I only managed to block his strike the second time.

Faster than I thought she was capable of, Falon slipped behind the guard, her arm thrusting out in a movement too quick to follow. The Imperial grunted with pain and dropped to the ground, his hands covering a growing red stain on his side.

Falon was left standing with a bloody knife, her chest rapidly rising and falling in pants as her actions sank in. Her eyes flicked back and forth between her hand and the fallen Imperial before a satisfied smirk split across her face.

Holding out her empty hand, she helped me to my feet and pulled me along as she ran. Cedric had set fire to the trees nearest us, creating a flaming maze of branches and vines that kept the other Imperials away.

But with the storm still raining down in full force, the moment he released his power, the flames would sputter out. On the other side, Zora still fought, her ferocity left me in awe. She moved with a fluidity that few could match, weaving between the Imperials as they reached for her.

The ground trembled as an Imperial sank his fingers into the mud and called on the roots that lie beneath. Like torpedoes, they shot from the muck and knotted themselves around the wolf's frame.

Her body fell and was held fast to the earth, no amount of struggles loosened her binds. She let out a whine and pawed at the ground when she saw me standing there. The other Imperials noticed too and eagerly stepped toward me.

It wasn't until that moment that I realized Cedric's flames were no longer between us, they had fizzled out and were now nothing but smoke in the wind. Turning to see where my friends had gone, I couldn't see them.

I vaguely recalled Falon screaming for me to follow them, but I couldn't tell when that happened. I had been too fixated on Zora. As two Imperials moved in on my sides and gripped my arms, I hoped that my friends had made it to the tunnel safely.

My shoulders screamed in protest as my arms were wrenched behind my back and held there by two beefy sets of hands. I was dragged closer to Zora's bound form, her chest laboring as she still fought the roots that held her.

"I told you, you wouldn't be leaving this time." Kael stepped over the wolf and walked up to me.

Running his fingertips down the side of my face, he seemed mesmerized as he watched his skin make contact with mine. I shuddered and jerked my head to the side, but he only smiled and stroked my hair instead.

"We will have time aplenty to become accustomed to one another, pet."

I glared at him, silently swearing that I wouldn't let it get that far. I would drown myself before allowing any of these men to touch me. Zora continued to thrash on the ground, amidst the chuckles from her captors as she made no progress.

The binds were too tight. In a last ditch effort, she ceased her struggles and I watched as her fur receded to reveal pale skin in its place. She shifted back to her human form; a smaller form that wasn't held as tight by the roots.

She was more vulnerable in this position, but perhaps she could escape and go for help. The Imperial, however, had other ideas. Zora barely had time to move to her knees before he tightened the restraints.

The roots wrapped firmly around Zora's naked form; pulling tight until her body was forced to kneel, back straight and arms secured at her sides. Taking a few steps backward, Kael kept his eyes on me as he slowly advanced on Zora.

"You will have a lot to learn in the time to come, as we get to know one another here on this island. There will be many rules that I expect you to obey. But we'll start with rule number one."

He stopped behind Zora, her head coming level with his waist. I could see the whites of her eyes from here as they tried in vain to send me a message. Her lips moved and I could make out the words 'be brave' before the roots squeezed her until she cried out.

I struggled against my captors, thrashing and kicking to try and get to her. But the others only laughed and clamped tighter until another move threatened to break my shoulder. Kael smiled, a warped excuse for what twisted his lips, and placed his hands on either side of Zora's head.

"This is the most important rule you will learn here, my dearest Casey, so listen closely. You have no friends, no family, *nothing,* unless I say you can have it."

And then he snapped her neck.

I screamed, I know I did. But I couldn't tell how long it lasted—a second? Five minutes? Time was lost to me. The moment I saw the light fade from Zora's eyes, I detonated. Something in me broke.

I thought I had protected all the tender parts of me, tucked them deep inside until nothing could touch them. I was wrong. Zora had worked her way in somehow and losing her hurt unlike anything I had ever felt.

My throat was raw from my screams, and I could taste blood in the back of my mouth from the strain. Kael's lips pursed and grew firm, as if he were agitated with my show of grief. Stepping over Zora's now cold body, he moved in close until his face blocked my view of her.

"That's enough." He actually stood there and waited for me to be quiet.

I ignored him. My throat was too hoarse to hear my screams, but my sobs could be heard perfectly. I was slumped as far as my captures allowed, my body completely dead weight against them. My shoulders felt like they were being pulled from their sockets.

A stinging slap knocked my head to the side, silencing my wails of despair. My cheek throbbed and my tongue moved to soothe the hurt on instinct.

"That's your second lesson, doll. You don't make a sound unless I tell you to."

Through my tears I glared at him. He only chuckled and caressed my throbbing cheek, not at all intimidated by the promise of death in my eyes. But he didn't know what he had unleashed. Deep inside, a rage was brewing. Fueled by desperation and anguish, my hatred for him boiled.

My hands longed to wrap around his neck, to strangle him, and forcibly crush his spine like he so thoughtlessly did to Zora. So enthralled in my hatred for him, I didn't notice my fingers twitching along with my thoughts.

I didn't recognize the torrid rage that simmered just below the surface, waiting for an excuse to explode. It was the cold that brought my attention to what was happening. My power had me frozen where I stood, my feet glued to the ground as icy tendrils snaked up through my legs.

I shivered as frost coated my back and stomach, slowly inching up my chest and down my arms. I knew what was coming by now, and I was ready for it. Buried inside me, the dark part of me I thought I had hidden for good cackled with glee.

I swore I would never let that part of me roam free again. But in this moment, I realized that that manic, black spot in my soul could save me. This wouldn't be the same as before; I wasn't in danger of hurting a friend. And these men deserved whatever outcome was to come.

Lowering my eyes, I allowed my shoulders to once again slump against the stronghold of the Imperials at my side. Kael, evidently satisfied with my obedience, turned to direct what remained of his personal faction.

The moment his back was turned, I struck. Kicking at the sensitive knee of the guard on my right, I heard the satisfied pop as the joint bent inward. His screams alerted Kael to my movements, but it wouldn't matter.

With one arm now free, I pressed my hand against the face of the guard on my left. At the skin to skin contact, my power erupted. A rush of frigid ice left my body in one powerful wave to engulf the unsuspecting Imperial.

Still connected, I forced the glacial surge directly to his heart, hardening the frost that grew around it. The Imperial dropped to his knees, and with a strong kick to the stomach, I finished knocking him to the ground.

Taking advantage of their shocked delay, I escaped to the trees in the direction I last remembered seeing my friends. While the rain had slowed to a light drizzle, the ground had absorbed all it could and now overflowed with debris-filled rivulets of murky water.

It was almost impossible to get solid footing, and my running felt more like skating the faster I tried to go. I could only hope that Kael and his men were having as hard a time as I was. The familiar sight of the hammock tree urged my feet to dig deeper into the muck to propel me forward.

An arm reached out from around the trunk to grip my shirt and pull me close. I collided with a firm chest, the smell and feel of it familiar.

"Thank Luthos!" Cedric's arms practically crushed me.

"We were on our way back for you," Falon exclaimed as she stole me from Cedric to give me a hug of her own. "We had to hide Leif in the tunnel first."

She gestured to the hole in the ground about a foot from where we stood. Mud and water dripped in over the sides, and I couldn't see the bottom when I peered down.

"We need to go. Now." I pulled away and draped my legs over the edge of the hole.

"Is everything okay? Did Zora come with you?" Falon anxiously looked around, but I had already jumped, knowing that they would immediately follow.

When we landed, I reached for Cedric's hand. The only sound in this dank hovel was our ragged breaths and my racing pulse. All I wanted to do was curl in a ball and weep, to mourn Zora, and to hide from the world and its endless assaults on my heart.

But there was no time. We needed to escape, and we had only minutes left.

Chapter 27

My hand trailed along the damp surface of the tunnel wall; fingers roaming over lichens and algae that clung to the wood. We had very little light to see by. Cedric used one hand to hold a flame and the other to hold Leif. That meager light combined with what illuminated the end of the tunnel was all we had.

I could tell, mostly from sense of touch, that the tunnel was made entirely of mangrove roots. The wooden limbs were so tightly packed together that they almost bled into one another. The surface of the walls and floor were smooth, like someone had molded this passageway by hand until it seemingly blended with the earth.

The ceiling was just high enough for me to stand upright, but Cedric had to crouch as we moved. Drops of water filtered in from the ground above, and they echoed when they landed in the small pools of water beneath our feet.

Surprisingly, it smelt more of damp wood, like the forest after a rainstorm, rather than a moldy scent that one would expect from such an environment. We traveled at a brisk pace, having no idea how long it took to get to the end. Stopping periodically, we listened to hear if any enemies followed.

So far, the only sounds had been our splashing footsteps and a few irate members of the wildlife who protested us traveling through their home. At our next pause, I drifted closer to Cedric and checked over Leif.

His breathing seemed less labored as Cedric's warmth sunk deeper into his bones, but I longed to feel his skin for fever. I was afraid to touch him. If I made contact, I might not be able to break it until he was entirely healed. And that would leave me too weak to escape.

"What do we do from here, Casey?" Cedric asked as he slumped against the moss ridden wall.

We were feet from the tunnel's exit, and from what we could tell, the opening sat in the side bank of the island's outer left wall. Above us was the cliff's edge and below sat a network of roots that could serve as steps leading down to the canoes.

I saw no movement of sentries or guards by the boats, but that didn't mean that someone wasn't keeping an eye on them. I could see the one we had selected for our getaway, our bags of provisions still tucked at the end.

It was tied by a rope to the base of a mangrove tree; the leaves and branches from the top of the plant provided perfect camouflage to hide the thin strip of curved lumber that floated beneath it. Dark clouds carrying more rain still covered the moon, so the chance of being seen on open water was minimal.

"We still go with our original plan," I told them. "We take the canoe to the outlying islands and put some distance between us and the Imperials. Come day break, we keep to the thinner canals and weave our way out of these wetlands."

We had no other option; it was either that or stay here. If the Imperials won … I shuddered to think about what would happen to the innocent souls on this island—and about what would happen to me when Kael finally got his hands on me.

And even if the Imperials were defeated, Orin would only hold my leash tighter than he had before, keeping me trapped here with no other chance of escape. Neither option was one I could live with.

"But how will you know how to get out of here? This place is a maze of dead ends and ceaseless channels," Cedric questioned.

I threw my head back with a soft groan. He was right. I didn't know the area, and I sure as hell didn't know how to get us back to civilization. What was I thinking? I could have gotten us lost out there until we ran out of food.

"Actually, I think I can help with that," Falon grinned.

She picked up a small rock from the ground near her feet. Walking toward the tunnel's exit, she tossed it over the roots below and watched as it plunked into the water. Cedric and I peered over her shoulder as she waited for … I didn't know what.

Seconds passed. The tension and apprehensive fear of discovery made the moments feel longer until I almost couldn't take it. Just when I thought Falon had lost her marbles, there was a ripple on the surface where she had thrown the rock.

Two shimmering opals gently rose from the briny water until a full face was revealed. The pea green skin with scattered aquamarine scales was a welcome sight. Einin smiled at us from below, her serrated teeth looking even more deadly in the sullen lighting.

She dove back beneath the surface with the flick of a fin, only to reappear under the mangrove trees as she untied the rope that anchored our canoe.

"What's Einin doing here?" I asked in wonder.

I didn't think the sprite queen was going to let her youngest daughter out of her sight after what the Imperials did to her older sister.

"I called for help. And she was close enough to answer," Falon replied.

"She's an audacious little thing, don't you think? You know her mother will lose her shit if she hears of Einin helping us." I couldn't help but smile at the thought.

The young sprite pulled the canoe along the overreaching roots below and waved, her teeth once again bared in what I knew to be a friendly grin.

"She says the coast is clear," Falon informed us.

So we silently began our descent, gripping the slippery roots and choosing each step with thoughtful care. It would only take one misstep, one wayward fall into the water below to alert others of our location.

We moved with caution, and when the roots ended and we stood on the slim strip of shoreline, Einin held the canoe steady as Cedric climbed in, Leif still an unconscious burden in his arms. The waves in the small canal were a little choppy, but didn't pose enough of a threat to tip the canoe over.

Falon pushed us away from shore, trying to keep the splashing to a minimum, and settled in behind me. We couldn't risk the noise that paddling would make, so Einin graciously pulled our little boat along by the rope still attached to it.

It was a quiet ride, and anticlimactic to say the least. I strained to hear anything from the island, hoping that I could gauge who was winning the battle. The chirping of frogs and the synchronized choral of the cicadas was all that reached my ears.

The moon remained hidden as the overbearing thunderstorm lingered with unfinished business. Light showers, not even heavy enough to feel, drizzled with a lazy persistence as I watched the individual raindrops create ripples on the water's surface.

The soothing rock of the boat tricked my body into a false state of peace. I refused to allow my brain to focus on any of the calamities that had befallen me or those I loved these past hours. I was just too tired. My soul couldn't take anymore holes in its foundation; enough damage had been done to it already.

So instead, I drifted off into fitful slumber, vowing to deal with everything later, when it didn't hurt as much.

"I seriously question the judgement of the spirits that chose you as my successor."

I jerked to attention, the familiar voice sending both a sense of dread and relief down my spine. I sat up carefully, afraid that I would capsize the boat if I wasn't careful, but I needn't have worried. I was no longer in the canoe.

In fact, I was on dry land, under a jubilant sun that shone down and wrapped my skin in a comfortable layer of warmth. I couldn't remember the last time I enjoyed the sun without suffocating in humidity. It was a pleasant change, but an obvious sign that I was no longer in Florida.

"By all means, take your time. It's not like you have a sadistic psychopath on your tail or anything."

A shadow moved over the swaying grass next to me. I traced the elongated silhouette back to a pair of ostentatious, studded red heals. The gemstones sparkled below a pair of perfectly tailored skinny jeans and an overly revealing blouse.

"Gwendolyn." Her name released on a sigh.

Her flawlessly manicured foot tapped to an impatient tune as she glared at me. If she crossed her arms any tighter I was sure her chest would squeeze out of that ridiculously tight top. She flung her arms out in a silent question.

"Well?" she asked when her pantomiming didn't get her the answer she was looking for.

"Well what?" I replied.

She growled, the sound similar to that of an upset toddler, and then glared at me as if she could read my thoughts.

"Why the hell are you not here yet?" she all but screeched.

My hands flew up to protect my ears, but her banshee yell made it in anyway.

"I sent Leif to find you months ago, and yet there you are, still in that disgusting swamp." Her nose wrinkled in that cute way that all girls wished theirs would.

Seriously, it was like staring at a supermodel having a tantrum.

"I'm on my way to you right now. Sheesh, you'd think someone immune to time would have some patience."

I sent her a dazzling smile, knowing that she would read between the lines and catch the veiled insult. As she huffed over my audacity, her earlier words had a moment to sink in. Leif. At his name, all the events of our escape came flooding back.

"Oh no, Leif! You have to help him," I demanded. "He was poisoned with iron. Orin's men captured—"

"Yes, yes. I'm well aware of his condition." Gwendolyn waved her hand in an annoyed flutter. *"His people have met up with your friends, and he is on his way to me as we speak."*

I slumped with relief. If he could get to her in time, Leif should make a full recovery, and the guilt of his death would not be laid at my feet as well.

"Now that you are finally leaving that muggy stink hole, you must hurry to me. There is much still to teach you before you are ready. But we're almost out of time."

"Without Leif how am I to find you? Can you send another guide?"

She shook her head. "It's too dangerous now. But ask your little friend, the royal. She knows the way home." She stepped away, her shadow stretching longer as the sun set behind her. *"Move quickly.."*

And then I was drowning.

I sputtered and choked. Even so, some of the water still made its way down my throat. I felt no more soaked than I was before falling asleep, but the fresh droplets that fell down the side of my face confirmed that I had been assaulted by a fresh source.

"What the hell?" I coughed over more water that tickled my throat.

I lay on the ground, a puddle forming around my torso as my friends stood over me. Falon's expression was one of concern; Cedric was all but laughing.

"Sorry, Casey. We had to." Falon's eyes all but pleaded for me not to be mad at her. "You wouldn't wake up."

I sat up slowly, my re-soaked hair plastered to my head with a few twigs mixed in for flare. Annoyed, I started to pick them out as I looked around. We were on another small island; one I didn't recognize which I hoped meant we were far from the camp.

The sky was beginning to clear, but slivers of the moon behind the clouds told me that it was still night. Our canoe was hidden beneath another cluster of mangrove trees and tied so it wouldn't float away.

Standing off to the side, afraid to intrude, was Einin. Her pale skin glowed, even though there was hardly enough light out to cause it to do so. Her ebony locks fell in a sheet of satin, covering a majority of her nude body from view.

Seeing that I was okay, she gave a slight nod and bled into the trees. I shivered as my mind calmed down and finally took notice of its own body. I was freezing and soaked. As another shiver caused my limbs to twitch, Cedric offered me a hand.

"We have a temporary shelter back a ways from the shore. And a fire so you can dry off."

That sounded like heaven. Our makeshift camp was only a few feet from the water, but hidden behind thick ferns. The fire was set low in the ground so it wouldn't be seen, even if someone was looking for it. I was thankful for that. I didn't know if I would make it through the night without its warmth.

A nearby tree limb served as a drying rack as I hung my sodden clothes up to dry; close enough for the flames to speed up the process. After changing into the only extra set of clothes I brought, I leaned against the tree and took in our ragged group.

Einin I assumed had gone back to the water, more comfortable spending the night there than on land. Falon and Cedric sat equally spaced around the fire, both their faces showing the strain from tonight's events.

"Where do we go from here?" Falon whispered, her voice barely audible over the crackling of the burning wood. "Leif was supposed to be the one to guide us but ... his people. They appeared out of nowhere and just took him."

I had a moment's panic before remembering that I already knew about this. Gwendolyn had mentioned something about Leif being brought to her for healing. I didn't take into account how unnerving it probably was for them to suddenly be overrun by a faction of gnomes anxious to get their friend back.

"We need to get to Gwendolyn," I said.

"We know, but how do we find her without Leif?" Cedric interrupted.

I held up a hand to prevent Falon from joining in with her confusion and directed my next statement to her. "She said that you would be able to find her, actually."

That caught the both of them off guard. I could see Falon trying to figure out how she was the one to guide us and Cedric glanced around as if Gwendolyn was somehow nearby and hiding under a rock.

"She specifically said that you would know your way home," I told Falon, hoping she could decipher the meaning behind those words.

She thought about it as she drew vague shapes in the dirt with a stray stick.

"The only thing that comes to mind is Faerie. I mean, that's home." She didn't sound particularly cheerful about that revelation.

Falon is one of the only Fae I know who actually volunteered to leave her lands and enroll at the Academy. From what she's told me and from the things I've learned about her, the school was more of a home to her than Faerie had ever been.

I hated to ask, but if Faerie was where Gwendolyn hid, then Falon *was* the only person who could get me there.

"Do you know where the doorway is?" I asked.

"I *might* know where *a* doorway is," Falon admitted.

The rain returned, falling to an already saturated earth in a steady beat. The fire sizzled and spit as the droplets met the flames, but it remained strong. Cedric and I sat patiently, waiting for Falon to make a decision; one that was obviously difficult for her.

She looked pained, understanding that what we were asking of her was important. I heard her sigh as she threw her drawing stick into the fire.

"We need to go to New Orleans."

Chapter 28

I awoke the next morning pleasantly dry. The storm had moved on, leaving behind calm waters and a blue sky. The atmosphere returned to its humid norm, although it was noticeably less sticky than usual.

My muscles strained as I rose, complaining of the less than pleasant accommodations of sleeping on the ground. My eyes scanned our small camp, taking in details that were hard to make out in the dark. We were closer to the water than I had originally thought, and I could see light reflecting off the canal through the leaves of the surrounding ferns.

When I peered behind the tree, I saw another canal branching off in a different direction than the one that we took to get here. Both sides were lined with sawgrass, higher than a person was tall and dotted with cattails.

Where I stood was nothing more than wet soil accumulated over raised mangrove roots. It was well on its way to becoming a true island, but flood waters could easily submerge it once again. In fact, if it hadn't stopped raining in the night, I wasn't entirely convinced that we wouldn't be underwater right now.

Hearing a splash from behind the ferns, I was reminded of what woke me in the first place. Gentle murmurs were accompanied by a hollow *thunk,* the sound of water hitting the side of a wooden boat.

Cedric and Falon were busy loading the canoe with our supplies when Falon suddenly threw her head back and laughed. She bent at the waist as she tried to control her chortling; the sounds coming out more like snorts as she fought to keep quiet. I smiled. It had been a while since I had seen her laugh like that. The smirking face that hovered just around the end of the canoe seemed to be the cause.

Einin blew bubbles on the surface of the water as she watched Falon break into another fit of giggles. Cedric tried to scold her for the noise, but was having a hard time keeping a smile off his face as he watched her.

Even he had noticed her subdued behavior over the past months. Ever since the truth of who she really was came to light, she had had a hard time trying to fit back into the group's dynamic. Between the three of us, things had returned to normal, but Orin and his men had looked at her differently since.

Especially Asa. And *that* had taken a toll on her. I knew she felt uncomfortable around them now, unsure of what was expected from her. So to see her acting like the Falon I knew before was a welcomed sight.

"Aw hell, we woke her." Cedric looked concerned as he walked over to where I stood watching them. "We were hoping to let you get some more rest before we left," he said.

"I feel fine. A little mentally drained, but there's nothing you can do about that." I gave him a dim smile.

It would be a long time before I would feel normal again. The weight of my thoughts wasn't something that I could easily discard. Just the opposite actually. My guilt and sorrow only continued to grow, and I still had no time to properly deal with it.

Cedric gave me a knowing look and offered his hand. "Might as well head out then. We don't know if it will be friend or foe that hunts us from here."

And so we continued our journey, only this time with a proper destination in mind: New Orleans. Being that we were far enough away from those that sought us, Einin didn't have to pull the canoe this time. We used the paddles, alternating between the three of us so we each had a chance to rest.

It was peaceful out here, a world untouched by the horrors of man. The water was a deep black that rolled and waved without help, almost as if it were alive. Colorful birds with striped beaks and purple wings traveled in pairs across the lily pads, keeping a wary eye out for predators.

For a time, I watched a large white heron regally walk along the shore line. He roamed with confidence and took no notice of our passing. Alligators, of course, were everywhere. They swam in the canal alongside our boat, basked in the sun on muddy banks, and hissed when we passed too close to a nest hidden in the sawgrass.

They were drawn to Einin, able to communicate with her as she swam beside them. Falon said that they wouldn't harm us, Einin had made them promise. But you wouldn't find me anywhere in that water if I could help it.

"Where are we headed?" I asked after we broke for a quick lunch.

As we got closer inland, there were more islands dotted amongst the flat, rolling waterways. We decided to stop at one, seeking the protective shade it offered from the midday sun. We finished the last of our food as we waited for the sun to begin its slow crawl from the center of the sky.

"New Orleans," Falon answered with a puzzled frown. "I thought we'd all agreed on that?"

I rolled my eyes. "Yeah, I know that part. But are we planning on paddling all the way there? We're out of food, I doubt Einin can go that far from home, and it will take weeks to get there by canoe."

I could see that neither one of them had thought that far ahead. And if I was being honest, I hadn't either until this moment. We tried to prepare for our escape, what with food and supplies, but the Imperials and near monsoon either ruined a majority of our stores or outright caused us to lose it. Our packs were still soaked through.

We were overwhelmed by silence as realization sank in; we had no idea what we were doing.

"Well, let's start with what we know." Cedric, ever the rational one, was the first to speak. "We need to get to New Orleans, and we need to get there as fast as we can, right? That means we need a car."

Falon snorted and Einin echoed it with a flurry of bubbles. "Where are we going to get a car out here? From the magical car lot behind this tree?" she countered.

With a quick glare at Falon to silence her, Cedric continued, "We obviously need to reach some kind of civilization first."

As we took the time to think his idea over, specifically how to find said civilization, a low hum resonated across the swaying fields of grass. The birds around us took flight or tucked themselves deeper in the vegetation as they tried to escape the vibrations that rippled along with the swelling waves.

A low wave started small beneath the sawgrass and grew as it traveled across the canal to lap at our feet where we sat on the opposite shore. As waves continued to roll toward us, the unnatural hum grew louder until it resembled more of a buzz.

"It's a motor!" Falon exclaimed at the same time that Einin ducked beneath the water.

The three of us stood, but remained hidden behind the foliage that grew thick along the water's edge. From the end of the canal, we watched as the source of both the waves and strange sound revealed itself. It was a boat, solid metal, and filled with tourists.

They all either held a camera or had one wrapped around their neck on a strap. And as if they purposefully coordinated, they all wore the same style clothes: shorts, polo shirts, and either a visor, fanny pack, or combination of both.

The side of the peculiar boat was painted with scripted letters that read 'Airboat Tours' in an obnoxious green and yellow. One man, who I assumed to be the driver, sat toward the back of the boat, behind his passengers and in front of a giant propeller held in a metal cage. It looked like an oversized fan was attached to the rear of the boat.

Across the water it glided, hopping in places as it tilted from side to side, but never altering from its path. We watched it as it passed, the tourists oblivious to our presence, and continued down the canal. Waves continued to travel the width of the channel even after we could no longer hear the motor.

"What the hell was *that*?" Falon's voice echoed across the unsettled water.

Animals came out of hiding and continued on with their daily foraging. Einin even popped her head back above the water, but didn't fully show herself. She chose instead to tread water in the small shadow of our canoe.

While we all tried to wrangle our thoughts, Cedric was busy packing our supplies back into our little boat.

"Don't just stand there; we need to follow that thing!" he shouted when he saw us still standing.

And so we set off, following the rapidly dispersing trial on the water's surface. We tried to move as fast as we could—all of us paddled while Einin pulled us with the rope. But we were no match for a motor and soon lost the trail. Thankfully, the canal was a straight one, so we only had one direction to travel.

Deciding to conserve our energy, we allowed Einin to pull us along at a steady pace. It felt like the sun was sinking faster as each minute passed. We had maybe a few more hours of light before the darkness set in and we would have to make camp.

Without warning, our canoe stopped moving and Einin appeared alongside it. By her agitated movements and Falon's gestures, I realized they were having a conversation. Before I could ask Falon what it was about, Einin disappeared again. But the canoe remained stagnant.

"What's happening?" I asked, still looking around for Einin.

A sinking feeling developed deep in my gut. It didn't look like Einin would be returning to us. She had abandoned us in the middle of the everglades with no food and no sense of direction. Anger built beneath the dread. How could she do this to us?

"Einin's mother finally noticed her absence. She's been called home." Falon had turned to look at both Cedric and me. "It's an order she can't ignore. Not from her queen."

"Well, can't you demand she stay? I mean, you're a princess." I'd seen the real fear in the sprite queen's eyes the night she met Falon. Surely she would have to listen to Falon's command.

Falon shook her head. "I can bluff with the best of them, but I'm not strong enough to outright challenge her. Not over her kin and not in her territory."

Now what did we do?

"Einin did say another of those strange boats was headed our direction. Maybe we could catch a ride."

She meant for her statement to sound like a joke, but it actually wasn't a bad idea. There wasn't much time to explain, already I could hear the far off hum of the approaching tourist boat. We needed to be ready when they appeared.

I didn't like the idea of making ourselves vulnerable, but it was either that or stay stranded out here. With a deep breath, I turned to my friends and told them my plan.

Alligator meat didn't taste how I expected it to. I dunked another nugget into the ketchup and shoved it in my mouth, ravenous. It tasted like spicy chicken, a little on the rubbery side, but still good. The way Falon and Cedric were inhaling their portions I knew they agreed.

Our fingers and faces were smeared with grease and crumbs. Half empty cans of coke sat in front of us, cool droplets of water dripping down the sides. The wooden picnic table we sat at was occupied by only the three of us and our 'savior.'

The boat captain took one look at us kids floating in the middle of the channel and told us to climb in his boat. The old bats that made up his tour group spent the rest of the trip fussing over us poor things.

So far, everything was going according to plan. When the boat pulled up to the dock, the sign read Everglades National Park Airboat Tours. And there were others pointing to the general store, the camp ground, and the souvenir shop. Things moved pretty quick from the moment we stepped onto dry land, and I had to improvise.

To these people, we were kids that got separated from their parents on a camping trip. We came up with answers for the expected questions. We had been lost for a few days. No, we weren't sure where our parents were, but we knew they must still be here somewhere looking for us.

The adults went to work tracking down the families that were camping in the park to see who was missing their children. In the meantime, we were offered free food. And who were we to turn that down?

"Ya'll act like you haven't eaten in days. How long were you kids out there?" Another plate of alligator nuggets was set on the table in front of us, the breading still steaming from the fryer. "Slow down, there's more where that came from. I promise."

It was awkward sitting there eating while the boat captain stared at us. He didn't take a plate for himself, only nursed a can of coke and watched us devour what he put on the table. Needing for him to give us a little privacy, I tried to distract him with a meaningless errand.

"Do you have some napkins by any chance?" I held up my greasy hands for him to see.

He looked shocked to see me break long enough to speak, but quickly recovered.

"Uh, sure, kid. I'll go grab some from the store over there. How 'bout some candy bars for dessert too, huh?"

He wore the expression of an adult trying to befriend an anxious child: a phony smile, hands always visible, and fake enthusiasm as they offered some kind of treat. I understood that he was just trying to make us feel safe, and I felt kind of bad for deceiving him. But it needed to be done.

"We don't have much time before they realize that no one here is missing any kids. We can't be here when the police get involved." Cedric spoke in-between shoveling the last of the food in his mouth.

"I know. That's why we're leaving. Right now," I ordered, grabbing my coke.

Cedric and Falon scrambled to catch up. Still improvising, I led us past the picnic tables at the end of the parking lot to a line of tour buses. That was our ticket out of here, if we could get on one before our friendly captain returned.

I jumped on the first one that looked ready to pull away. The sign in the window read National Parks Trolley. The three of us squeezed into the last available seat in the back and barely had time to sit before the bus pulled from the curb. My body rocked into Cedric's as the bus traveled over the uneven ground.

Out my window I watched the park steadily disappear behind an overgrown knot of trees that eventually lead to the highway. The driver announced that our first stop would be the city of Homestead. I had no idea where that was, but decided it was as good a place as any to steal a car.

And as it turned out, the parking lot at the bus station was the perfect place. It was large enough for us to separate from the returning crowds and find a secluded section of the lot to hotwire a rusted old mini cooper.

Falon had grabbed some maps from the visitor's shelf at the station, and we used those to navigate our way out of this place. With no money and no supplies, we were in a rush to get to New Orleans. According to the map, we estimated that it would take us roughly thirteen hours to do so.

We drove through the night, obeying every traffic law and hyperaware for areas where there could be a roadblock. The route Falon chose took us straight through Orlando, where we knew there was a large Academy, but we passed through without incident.

We hit a snag when the mini cooper ran out of gas, but there was thankfully an outlet mall only a few miles down the road from where our gas light came on. It was easy enough to steal another car from there and continue on our way.

Not remembering how to deactivate the GPS on newer cars, we stuck to the old ones, and now drove in an ancient Outback. When our wheels pulled onto I-10, we all let out a sigh of relief. We could take this interstate the rest of the way. The tank was full, the interstate was wide open, and we were scheduled to reach our destination by early afternoon.

I settled into the front seat, leaning it back as far as it would go. Falon was sprawled across the back seat, already snoring, and Cedric was driving. I knew he could handle a few more hours before needing to switch. So I closed my eyes and allowed my body to be lulled to sleep by the sound of our tires on the interstate.

Chapter 29

I thought my sacrificial months deep in the Florida Everglades taught me all I needed to know about what heat could do to a body, and it was enough of an experience to last me a lifetime. But I was wrong. So, so wrong.

Louisiana gave a whole new meaning to the word humidity. While Florida heat felt like a warm blanket at the best of times, the air in New Orleans seemed to weigh you down and smother you each day of the year.

We were in the middle of April, the atmosphere should be cooler, right? Wrong. I felt like I was going to pass out. Almost every building in the French Quarter had an iron-worked balcony with potted ferns and overgrown vines that cast shade along the sidewalks wandering beneath them. But even with these frequent respites from the sun, I could feel my skin sizzle.

Falon dragged us around for hours, setting us on a mission to find the hidden doorway to Faerie from the moment we ditched our car. My heart pounded each time we turned a new corner, worried that we would run into a guardian on patrol or someone from the Supernatural community that would recognize us.

Thankfully, this city was so jam packed with tourists that we were often lost in the crowd. Sometime after mid-morning, Falon brought us to a seemingly popular store, Boutique du Vampyre. A fancy sign was the only thing that marked the entrance.

Entering through a nondescript door in the side of the building, I quickly realized that this place was a far cry from a voodoo shop. But Falon said she had felt some kind of pull toward it, so here we were. Inside could be called nothing more than a homage to all that is Vampire.

There was fake blood to be tested by the daring tourist, mystic boxes said to trap the very essence of a Vampire—I snickered at that one—and all kinds of dolls and memorabilia celebrating that which was the predator of the night.

"Is this what I think it is?" Cedric asked, his face wrinkled with disgust like he had a foul taste in his mouth.

He was standing in front of a large rectangular case, similar in look to a storage trunk, but more sturdy and filled with wooden stakes. There were mini bottles of holy water lining the top, under the lid there were two wooden crosses with the longest ends also sharpened into stakes, and a mallet. More weapons filled the bottom segments, but none were truly useful against a Vampire.

I giggled as I watched Cedric pick a small stake from the selection.

"I would love to see the look on Leo's face if you came after him with one of those." He laughed along with me at the mental image. "What are these people thinking? I swear I saw *garlic* hanging in the back."

A frowning clerk at the checkout desk whispered to her coworker as she glared at us from behind the register. She had on fake fangs, the expensive kind, and her makeup resembled a goth experimenting with eyeliner for the first time.

I covered my mouth with my hand and laughed again.

"I got nothing." Falon's face blocked my view of the irritated shop clerk. "I don't know what pulled me in here to begin with, probably a strong protection spell that the owner bought to put on the shop. But now that I'm here, I can see that whatever it is, it isn't strong enough to be a doorway."

The disappointment on her face was enough to kill my laughter. If this wasn't the place, then we needed to move on. We still had no money, nowhere to stay tonight, and were hoping to find the doorway before sundown.

With reluctant steps, I left the chilled air of the misinformed shop to greet the blistering heat that was all too happy to smother me again. The anxiety of being grabbed the moment I stepped on the street overwhelmed me for a second.

There was a jazz band on the street corner, the clarinet blaring a colorful tune with the help of a trombone and a snare. Tourists and even some locals had gathered around to listen, the band's talent blatantly obvious. It was this overbearing ruckus that caught me off guard after the peaceful quiet of the shop we were just in.

We were jostled and pushed as we forced our way through the dancing crowd and each touch on my arm or grab to the back of my shirt had me fearing the worst. When we finally broke free of the crowd that had swelled for two blocks in an impromptu party, the tightness in my chest remained for a different reason.

There, on the corner of St. Peter and Royal, stood a guardian. He was easily identifiable, wearing the plain all black that was required. His outfit would appear normal to those around him, but I knew from experience that there were at least ten different weapons hidden within arm's reach on his person.

He leaned against the lamp post, seeming at ease amongst the expanding crowd. His eyes scanned every face, looking for threats or fugitives, I wasn't sure. But we weren't going to sit around and find out.

Ducking into the first place we could, the three of us found ourselves in yet another tourist trap. The sign said it was a voodoo shop owned by some kind of Reverend Zombie. The store front was a mess of chipped and peeling paint with a neon sign that promised readings in the back.

Inside was no less extreme. Tokens and souvenirs hung overlapping on the walls while life sized statues stood distorted in awkward positions that were meant to be sexual. The store was packed with tourists, all clamoring to see what hid behind the glass case up front or to try and spy on the readings happening in the rear of the shop.

"Is he gone? Do you see him?" Falon pestered Cedric who peered out the door for any sign of the guard.

He held up a hand to quiet her, his head still pushed outside. After another moment he gently waved for us to follow him. Back on the road, the guardian was gone. I scanned the street, but saw no sign of him and my pulse calmed.

"Let's find a place to rest and regroup," I suggested. "We can't just keep wandering like this. We're going to make a wrong turn somewhere, and next time, there might not be a crowd or store we can hide in."

With murmurs of agreement from my friends, we turned and headed back to the only place we had seen benches and the promise of a reprieve from the sun. Fifteen minutes later found the three of us huddled under a sparse strip of shade that ran along the gate of Jackson Square. Sitting on its solid foundation of concrete, we watched as the natives and tourists intermingled as life went on around us.

This was an interesting place, New Orleans; I'd give it that. Here was a world where old mixed with new, eccentric overshined the ordinary, and normal was a word that had a different meaning. It was a city known for the outrageous and the strange; a place where free spirts thrived alongside supernatural ones. It was a beautiful example of a misfit's paradise.

And it stank. Bad.

That was a key fact that no one ever mentioned. The city was dirty, crumbling, and downright disgusting in places. The smell of heated day old garbage and litter on the street is somehow overlooked and hidden behind the striking architecture and Creole cooking.

One minute I'm gazing in awe at buildings rich with history, imagining the people that must have stood where I stood and walked the very path I did in a time long forgotten. Then the next, I'm hit with a rotting stench from a nearby trash can that had been baking too long in the afternoon sun.

Roots from overhanging trees were ripping up the stone walkways. Multiple spots had holes where brick had crumbled or tile had been lifted and misaligned, tilted and cracked. I'd nearly fallen flat on my face multiple times from catching my foot on an upturned brick.

Then, around another corner was a building so pristine, renovated to almost mint condition that it took my breath away. This place was full of contradictions.

And here, in the heart of the French Quarter, I could get a taste of what life would have been like back when this place was new. On Jackson Square is an ancient church, rooted on an enormous plot of bright green grass that is separated from the rest of the city by towering wrought iron gates.

Around this overly popular tourist attraction is where the real magic happens. A well cared for stone promenade surrounds the gate, providing a sanctuary for local artists and the wandering lost. Sheltered beneath the shady ancient oaks that hung over the gate, Cedric, Falon, and I were immersed in the truth of New Orleans.

Here, the tourists wandered with their weighted purses and clutched at their fraying straps while gazing upon the local art. And it was a sight to behold. This was where the truth was told, these paintings and murals of the native culture and sights. These desperate artists captured the spirit of musicians as they paraded down Bourbon Street and the haunting reality of the ghosts and magic that soaked every inch of this bewitching city.

"Sweet. Someone left us a five."

Falon's annoyingly chipper tone pulled my attention from the couple haggling over the price of a rather large painting of a dog. My body was slumped against the gate and the metal bars were digging into my shoulders and spine. I leaned forward for some relief, only to feel a river of sweat trickle down my back.

This heat was sucking the life out of me. How could she have enough energy to be excited?

"We have enough here for lunch and dinner. As long as both meals are plates of beignets; can't afford much more than that." Falon said, as she counted our money.

Our once empty hat that sat welcoming on the ground before us was now filled with several one's and that special five that had Falon so animated. I took a look at our group and cringed. The tourists must have thought we were a gang of homeless kids. We certainly looked the part.

After a day of trekking through the city, we were covered in sweat, grime, and dirt. My hair hadn't been brushed in two days and Cedric had stubble covering half his face. Even stained with dust and street muck, Falon had a glow about her that drew more tourists in to drop a dollar in the hat.

It wasn't uncommon to see homeless people lying about the city or sitting on street corners. In fact, New Orleans had the highest percentage of homeless citizens than even some of the bigger cities across the country.

While it might be paying for our next meal, I didn't like being labeled a street urchin.

"Great. I'm starving," Cedric answered. "Why don't we grab some lunch and then continue our search before the sun goes down?"

He somehow found the strength to stand and pulled me up with him. More sweat slid down the back of my legs where they had been pressed together. I would have loved nothing more than a cold shower and a soft bed, but we were broke and relying on charity from the tourists wasn't enough to spring for a hotel in this place.

My stomach rumbled, reminding me that I hadn't eaten since the alligator nuggets back in Florida. Begrudgingly, I trailed along after my friends. Where we were headed wasn't far. Café du Monde sold the best beignets in the city, and it was conveniently located on the corner of St. Ann's, a street that ran alongside the square.

The old building had no A/C, but there were fans throughout that I hoped to catch a breeze from. We stole a recently vacated table under the iconic green and white striped awning, and I wiped powdered sugar from the table before dropping into my seat.

The ground beneath my feet looked like it stood host to a crack addict's birthday party. Powdered sugar covered everything, and I'm sure that my ass would be covered with it when I stood. How did this place not have an ant problem? They must have the Orkin man on speed dial.

Our server took our order, three plates of beignets and three cups of water, then disappeared into the crowded indoors. Falon pulled out a map of the city, the kind you could get for free from the many stores that offered the wide variety of scheduled tours.

"We already tried everything from Toulouse Street to Canal … Let's just take St. Ann's and cover the two streets we missed. I don't think we have much time left today for more."

Cedric and I nodded along, agreeing with whatever she came up with. We had no idea what to look for—Falon was the only one who could feel the doorway. She said that last she'd heard it was kept hidden in the back of a voodoo shop.

We didn't realize how many such shops were spread across the Quarter, each one swearing to be genuine and to have a real psychic in the back who offered readings for a great price. We walked inside each and every one; they were all mirror copies of one another.

Tourist gifts and offerings were stored in baskets for people to rifle through. Candles, stones, and talismans were laid upon a decorated shrine to some powerful voodoo god and books promising to reveal the secrets of the ancients sold for big bucks on the shelves.

Each one turned out to be a dud. The old ladies with colored hair who claimed to see your future were fakes—the real ones would know what we were the moment we crossed the threshold. Falon turned her thumb down at each shop, the signal that there was no hidden doorway stuck in the back of any of those.

Our planning was interrupted when our server laid plates piled high with fried dough before us. My mouth watered as I took in the rich scent of freshly made beignets. Falon already had half of one shoved in her mouth, powdered sugar coating her face from her cheeks to the tip of her nose.

Cedric and I were a little more delicate with our meal. I moaned as I had my first taste; it was like funnel cake on crack. Or maybe it actually had crack in it. It's possible; they were that good. All too soon our plates were empty, even the leftover sugar was scooped up by our fingers and licked clean.

I could have eaten more; my stomach was far from full. But we needed to make what money we had last through another meal tonight. With a sigh, we pushed out our chairs and left. The scattered sugar that now stained our clothes only added to the destitute look we were rocking. Falon led the way to another shop she said had a pull to it. Cedric grabbed my hand as we walked, pretending for all he was worth that we were just a normal couple on vacation to see the sights.

I smiled. It was nice to feel normal for a while, and in this crowd we could get away with it. No one noticed us here, even our appearance was passed off for typical. This anonymity brought a renewed pep to my step.

For the first time, I allowed myself to relax and enjoy the city. I kept an eye out for guardians, but otherwise enjoyed the music and the eccentric people that shouted hellos from alleys lined with art.

"Dammit!" Falon kicked an already dented trashcan. "Where the hell is it?"

Cedric and I lounged on a double-sided bench in the middle of the promenade around Jackson Square and watched Falon lose her shit. The moon shone bright against the stones, creating light on what would have otherwise been a dim road.

The locals that set up shop here kept a wide berth from Falon and her mini rampage. These people were anything but normal, and yet they were frightened by her. They sat at pop-up tables, stringed lights and random talismans decorating the surface as they offered tarot readings to the tourists passing on their way to Bourbon.

One guy had on all black with a feather hanging from one ear. Heavy with eyeliner and sporting multiple bracelets, his chin hair was separated into two braids, and he wore a top hat with zebra print and more feathers. People easily mingled with him, yet they veered strongly from the blonde midget with anger issues.

We hadn't found the doorway. We covered half the Quarter in an entire day, walking into every store that gave Falon any kind of tingle and even some that were plainly dead ends. Nothing. If there was a doorway to Faerie here, it was well hidden.

My feet were throbbing and my stomach clenched with hunger, even though it had been fed more beignets not even an hour ago. When Falon's anger ran its course, she came to sit beside us. Her body slumped with disappointment as reality sank in for her.

We were stuck here for another day with nowhere to sleep and once again out of money.

"What do we do from here?" She sounded so pitiful.

I knew she thought that this was her fault, being that she was the only one who could sense what we were looking for. I put an arm around her shoulders and gave them a squeeze.

"We're going to be okay. The doorway must be on the other half of the Quarter. We'll find it," I promised.

"That doesn't help us tonight, though. Where are we gonna sleep?" she asked in a small voice, looking around.

Some tarot readers were packing their things as the light got dimmer. The doorways and sidewalks that lined the square were already overtaken by the homeless that had bedded down for the night around their meager possessions.

Rowdy teenagers tricked with their boards on the far end of the square where the lights from Café du Monde were still brightly lit. The area was active enough for this time of night, and while it might die down at some point, it was as safe a place as any to bed down.

In the end, Cedric made the decision for us.

"Falon, lay here on the bench attached to the back of this one. Casey will stay on this side with me and I'll keep watch. When I start to doze, I'll wake one of you to take the next shift. Okay?"

She nodded and curled onto her side on the metal bench. Her arm cushioned her head and hung off the side, under the armrest. I reached mine out and held her hand, letting her know that we were in this together. At least it was dry and it was warm. We had slept in worse conditions for a longer time. We would make it through this. We would be okay. And tomorrow would dawn on an unveiled doorway to our future. She squeezed my hand until she fell asleep.

I rested my head in Cedric's lap, gently dozing as he played with my hair. The random shouts from the overactive teens made it hard to settle in, but eventually my eyelids became too heavy to keep open.

Cedric's hand continued its steady, gentle brush. Everything would be okay. It had to be.

Chapter 30

The sun shone down with an unforgiving glare on all the people who roamed Chartres Street, including us. We took to walking the crowded sidewalks, choosing to fight for elbow room rather than be victim to the sun's pain-fueled kiss.

Beneath the iron glided balconies, the square was busier than ever, filled with gawking tourists and local entrepreneurs alike. You couldn't see from one end to the other it was so packed. The palm readers were back, out in full force to take advantage of the weekend crowd. Their umbrellas ranged in colors and designs, and all swayed in the afternoon breeze as they sheltered those willing to gamble for a glimpse into their future.

The stoic fence standing guard around the cultured and groomed grounds of Jackson Square was overwhelmed with portraits and tile works, caricatures, and eccentric artists looking for appreciation. All around were people sporting dyed hair and tattered clothes; tough looking, but with kindness in their eyes.

They smiled at you when they caught you looking at their artwork, an encouraging offer to come talk and learn what they could tell you about the city. It felt almost like a festival with all the people and colors that were on display, very different from the atmosphere we had left this morning.

We had set out with the rising of the sun and spent the entire day looking for the gateway. My feet were blistered and aching from the countless blocks they strolled in vain, and we found ourselves, yet again, wandering aimlessly around the four most popular blocks in the Quarter.

"Maybe it moved?" I suggested with a grunt as a passing tourist's hefty shopping bags took a chunk out of my side.

We moved off the flooded walkways and onto the more spacious street. The live oaks that dotted the square grounds offered enough shade here to combat the merciless assault of the sun.

"Where could it have moved to?" Falon almost cried with frustration. "The doorway has always been hidden in the Quarter and guarded by a human with the Sight. The problem is, every damn shop here claims to have a door in the back with a woman who can read your thread lines."

We all shared her frustration. I hadn't thought that finding the doorway would be easy—if it were, every odd soul would wander into Faerie—but I hadn't thought that it would be this difficult either. We were running out of time. Each day spent pathetically drifting along was more of an opportunity to be captured.

New Orleans was a Supernatural hot spot, and only the sheer overly populated streets kept us anonymous. But that wouldn't last forever. Already we had seen and avoided four more guardians. It must be the weekend crowds that called for more on duty, but I half expected to see one on every corner.

"Maybe it's been moved further out." Cedric proposed as he pulled me out of the path of an oblivious biker. "Think about it. All these shops are nothing but tourist traps, you said it yourself; a real psychic would know what we are. So, the real ones are probably on the outskirts of the Quarter, where locals can get to them without having to fight these ridiculous crowds."

It made sense. Why would those who called the city home and practiced the art of voodoo in their everyday lives want to travel all the way here, only to be bombarded by non-believers who congested their stores and sought after ingredients for a gag Christmas gift?

"So we go where then?" I asked.

Falon pulled out her map, and we tucked our backs against an empty spot on the fence, not wanting to be trampled as we decided our next step. Falon and Cedric debated over which direction we should go. To outsiders looking in, we probably looked like a bunch of kids arguing about what to see next. If only it were that simple.

Cedric suggested we head toward the Warehouse District, but Falon argued that that would be nothing but city businesses and privately owned storage.

"Let's just follow Decatur along the Mississippi. It's the lifeblood of this city; everything it touches has a natural power to it. I'm sure we'll find the real shops or at least *something* if we follow it."

With no better argument, and trusting that Falon's sense of magic would lead us true, we left Jackson Square. My stomach grumbled as we passed an open doorway to Muriel's. The smell of spiced meat and that special New Orleans seasoning had me salivating. Through wide arches where the double French doors were propped open, I watched as families and friends sat clustered in a formal dining area, plates piled high with food.

I forced my feet to keep moving, one foot in front of the other. I ignored the sound of silverware tapping plates, blocking out the relaxed laughter that came with the satisfaction of a full belly. A group from one of those haunted tours blocked the sidewalk, but moved when they saw us approaching.

On my left, as I passed the end of Muriel's, I caught a glimpse of a lonely room with a single table. Two chairs were arranged beneath a pristine white table cloth, a candle sat lit in the middle, and a full meal laid unwatched on fine china.

I thought about just walking in and grabbing the plate; no one seemed to be actually sitting there. But then I overheard the tour guide tell his group about how the staff set up a table for some long dead ghost that haunted this place. And how if he wasn't given a table each night, accidents would plague the establishment.

My shoulders drooped with my sigh. It figured. Even dead people could get food in this city, but we couldn't catch a break. I focused on my steps, trying to distract my mind from feeling the gnawing pain of hunger.

Beneath my feet, the paved sidewalks became dirtier and more neglected the further out of the Quarter we traveled. Bricks and overturned stones littered the path, and I felt pity for the crumbling city around me. There was water running through the cracks in the stones and pooling in dips along the side of the street as if the swamp was fighting to reclaim what was once taken from it.

It hadn't even rained, yet the sides of my shoes were splattered with mud and sludge. Above ground, the architecture wasn't fairing much better. Away from the judging eyes of the Quarter, the homes and buildings left standing here were in a lot worse shape. Some were under construction for restoration, most likely a rich owner looking to buy a piece of The Crescent City, but most of the homes were in dire need of some TLC. The architecture ranged from the original Spanish style of brick and iron and alternated with the French influence of the Cyprus cabins. All were surrounded by iron fencing and overgrown yards. The porches were open and wide, styled after the southern pastime of neighbors sitting outside and calling on one another.

Overhanging porches and second floor balconies were upheld by Cyprus pillars that were equally spaced along the front of the houses. Potted plants hung in front of shuttered windows whose frames were painted every color of the rainbow.

It was quite beautiful in its dilapidation.

My arm was pulled roughly until I came to stop. Cedric kept his tight hold on my arm, just above my elbow, and drew me to his side. He and

Falon pretended to look over their map, trying to appear as lost tourists, but neither of them were paying attention to the plotted streets in front of them, their eyes were fixed on something else.

Two blocks behind us, on the opposite side of the street, were three guardians. Dressed in everyday clothes, I could tell that they weren't Imperials and were most likely off duty from the local Academy. Their proximity made me nervous. What if they had already seen us? Would they recognize us?

"We need to get off the street," Cedric whispered, voice hoarse with alarm. His eyes darted around as he tried to remain inconspicuous but still find a clear path to safety.

"Where exactly are we going to go? You want to just walk up to a home and knock on the door?" Falon was fighting fear of her own. Her hands pinched the map until her knuckles turned white. The flimsy paper was all but crumpled now.

"The sarcasm isn't helping, Fal. And you both need to calm down. You're drawing more attention to yourselves," I hissed.

There weren't many people about, only a few strolling couples and individuals on bikes. And the longer we stood here to argue, the more distance was closed between us and the guards.

"We need to keep moving. Pretend you found what you were looking for and start walking. If the guards get too close … it's over," I instructed.

We had minutes left. The guards were already on our side of the street now. We picked up our pace and fell in line with a group of young teens loitering on a corner. The guards were keeping a slow pace, in no obvious hurry to go anywhere. It was possible that we were still in the clear.

They would have to pass us if we stopped moving, and the risk of letting them that close was one we couldn't take. About a block ahead, the noise of a larger crowd spilled over onto our street and the echoes of a saxophone could be heard.

Pushing on, we rounded the corner onto Frenchmen Street. Multi-colored buildings lined both sides where people mingled and congregated around open doors. The crowd wasn't as large as those back in the Quarter, but we should be able to lose ourselves in what was available.

Our steps slowed as we tried to merge with the flow of traffic. The guards had reached the corner we stood at just a minute before. The hair on the back of my neck stood on end. Were they moving faster now, or was that just paranoia?

When I glanced back over my shoulder to double check, my heart stopped. I grabbed Cedric's arm like he had done to me and kept him from going further. He and Falon circled around and the three of us huddled in the center of the busy street.

"They're gone."

It was an unnerving feeling, and one I had felt before, of being watched. Only, instead of it being isolated sprites curious to get a look at us, this time we were being watched by everyday shoppers and loitering teenagers.

We remained grouped in the middle of the street, too afraid to move in either direction until we knew where the guards had disappeared to. The crowd that had just moments before been so boisterous and lively were now muted and reserved. A wide berth was given to our little group as the street was slowly emptied.

The nosey locals watched us with a quizzical interest, some wondering who we were while others, I think, already knew. The onlookers stood alongside the multicolored buildings, their appearances ranging from comfortable norm to outfits and hairstyles that almost blended with the unconventional murals on the side of the buildings.

Somehow we stuck out like a sore thumb, like everyone could tell that we weren't from around here. After staring just a little longer, the crowd began to disperse. I watched the teenagers jump on their bikes and boards and disappear around the corner without a single glance back. The adults moved more subtly until they all resided inside a shop or café, the bells over the doors ringing like a sickening call bell.

Before we even knew what happened, we were all alone. I could see faces peering out the windows, through the drawn shutters and pulled curtains. Some defective part of my brain had me giggling as it compared our situation to that of a Wild West tale, where the town barricaded themselves indoors right as the rowdy gang of wanted criminals rolled through.

My giggling stopped when I realized that *we* were those wanted criminals. Fear pulsed through my veins, encouraging a spout of endurance that had me running to the nearest closed door. I yanked on the handle, but it was locked. I turned to banging on the windows, my panic ever-growing.

I watched as the people inside backed away from my desperate knocks. There wasn't an ounce of pity on their faces, most actually ignored my calls for help and turned their backs on the storefront where I stood. I ignored the dark voice in the deep recesses of my mind that warned of the anomaly of this behavior.

I had no time to ponder on it. Some innate sense within me knew that something was coming. It roared for me to get inside and to get off the street. We were sitting ducks out here.

"Help! Come on, let us in!" Falon's pleas could be heard down the street. She hammered on a large window of what looked like a club. The glass had no shutters or curtains to conceal the unwavering faces that looked out from behind it.

"I know you can see me, dammit!" Falon's next hit shook the glass, but it held firm.

No one was going to help us. We were alone in whatever battle was about to come. We must have come to this realization at the same time because we unconsciously found ourselves drawn back to one another.

"Just run," Cedric called, as he grabbed my hand.

We took off in the opposite direction from where we had last seen the guards, which lead us further down Frenchmen Street. The buildings on either side of me blurred into indistinct streaks of color that flashed out of the corners of my eyes.

We were approaching a turn in the road. I had no idea where it led, but I knew we had to take it. I could feel that something was behind us. It was the same feeling one gets when walking alone down a dark alley, the sense that someone is right behind you and no matter how hard you run you will never outreach them.

The pounding of Cedric's footsteps came to a scuffled halt as he tried to stop a full sprint on a dime. Falon ran into my back and almost took us all down, but I managed to keep hold of my balance. Our turn was blocked.

Guardians, in full uniform, stood in a row across the street. Equal distance apart, they appeared relaxed, like they already knew that we didn't pose a threat. Not waiting for them to make the first move, Cedric hauled us back. We made to run, but came up short when the three guards we ran from before took a stance, blocking the other end of the street.

We were surrounded.

"Fun Fact that most are unaware of: a majority of the businesses in the French Quarter—mainly on this street, actually—are owned and operated by Witches."

No!

As my mind screamed in denial, my heart fell to my feet. How had he caught up with us? Kael stepped out from behind the unmarked guardians. Seeing the stars on his collar, the other guards saluted him and took position at his rear and flanks.

The usual team he traveled with was nowhere in sight, and I could only hope that they were defeated back at camp. I prayed that Orin and his men had survived, that the camp had survived. Because I knew now that they were the only ones who could save us.

"Now, you may also find a Shifter here or there, as most of the businesses are run and sanctioned by the Council," Kael continued. "They decided to capitalize on the tourist industry long ago. Got a good internship program for the Academy right here in our own backyard! Isn't that something?"

Cedric moved to stand in front of me, and Falon stood fearlessly by his side. Their gestures both calmed me and sent my heart into overdrive at the same time. The love I felt from each of them, the love that it must have took to put themselves between Kael and me, was something that I would never forget. But I also couldn't forget what Kael had done back at the camp, what he was capable of doing to those that I loved.

I couldn't let that happen again. Moving from the safety of their shadows, I allowed myself to be seen. My knees began to shake, so I locked them. My palms began to sweat and my fingertips shook, so I tucked them in my pockets. I refused to show him fear, no matter how deep it ran inside me.

"You sound like a brochure, Kael." I managed to sound bored, even though inside I felt like I could sprint a mile. "Maybe the Council should hire you for their travel office, you know, so you could tell the leading families where all the hot spots are to vacation."

Like a demented hunter who had cornered his prey, Kael's lips twisted into a cruel smile. His eyes roamed my body, lingering in places that had Cedric tightening his hold on my hand.

"Casey." The way he said my name was like man greeting his lover. I couldn't fight the revolting shudder that slithered down my spine. "How I've missed our time together. Our last meeting was one for remembering, don't you agree?"

I felt the thick wall of ice around my heart, the one I surrounded it with to hold it together, splinter into pieces. The triumphant look in his eye confirmed that he knew his words had gotten to me. The small whimper that escaped my lips didn't help.

"What's he talking about?" Cedric whispered in my ear, but Kael heard him.

"Oh, she didn't tell you?" Kale tsked. "Casey, I don't want you keeping secrets about what goes on between us. Rule number three, doll."

Cedric shook me, trying to snap me out of the trance that I found myself trapped in. Around me, I only heard muffled words, like listening to a conversation while being underwater. I was too focused on not falling apart. Inner me was consumed with picking up the pieces of my shattered defenses. I vaguely recalled Kale informing my friends of what happened that night back at camp, of him describing how he bested me and then killed Zora. Cedric's growl of rage was the first thing to truly penetrate the wounded cocoon I had wrapped myself in, but it was Falon's cry of pain that jerked me out of it.

I watched in muted shock as she fell to the ground, Cedric's arms cushioning her landing. The power that she held swarming in her fists fizzled and went out. In her shoulder, tipped with a blood red feather, was a dart.

"We can't have your little friend hurting your fellow Witches now, can we?" Kael moved forward, the group of unmarked guardians following close behind.

I unconsciously moved to stand in front of Cedric, vowing to do everything in my power to protect him. My limbs quaked as Kael walked ever closer. Cedric tried to pull me behind him instead, but I wasn't moving. I would keep this bastard from my friends or die trying.

In the end, our sacrifices didn't matter. Cedric only had time to clutch at his shoulder before he too went down, victim to another dart. With both my protectors incapacitated, the guards that were behind us moved in. In a brisk and all too quick manner, they had me and both my friends bound with rope.

I watched them carry Cedric and Falon to an unmarked van on the corner. Knocked out, and with both their hands and feet bound, they offered no resistance when they were thrown in the back. My hands were tightly secured behind my back, but my legs were left free. I half-heartedly tried to kick at the guards who attempted to walk me to the van, but there was really no point in fighting back.

What good would it do? They already had my friends. So I conceded and glared at each shuttered storefront as I walked to the open doors of the van. I sat on the rear bumper and allowed the guards to bind my feet before scooting to sit next to Falon.

I vowed to cooperate until my friends woke. There was no point in all of us being unconscious, someone needed to plan. I fully intended to stick to that vow, until Kael pulled himself into the back of the van with us.

"Sir, don't you want to sit up front?" the driver asked, honestly confused at where the Imperial was choosing to ride.

Kael kept his gaze on me as he answered. "I think I'd like to spend some quality time with my sweet Casey. It's been too long since we've last been together, and I'd very much like to hold her."

My eyes rounded in horror as he pointed the dart gun and fired. A sting lit up my arm before a wave of numbness flowed down to my fingers. I struggled to move away, twisting my limbs in a feeble attempt to free them, but I could feel my head getting heavy and my breaths were coming in deep and labored. My body relaxed against the wall, betraying every order to fight that my brain fired off.

I could form no resistance as Kael gathered me into his arms and pulled me onto his lap. Arranging me so that my head rested against his shoulder, he stroked me. From the top of my head, down my side to my hip, against my bare thigh, and back again.

I wished the drug could have made me numb to sensations because each touch was burned into my memory. My stomach rolled with nausea, but my body made no move to answer its call. I sat there defenseless, as Kael became more liberal with his touches.

Trapped inside my own body, I fought. I screamed, I cried, I tried to keep my sanity. In the end, I could do nothing but withdraw. I pulled every piece of myself that I could gather and locked it away behind a wall of ice. Next to my tattered heart, my demolished pieces and I waited.

In the lap of a monster, my body sat violated, but whole. The sound of his chuckle was the last thing I heard before the drug finally blessed my mind with an unfeeling silence.

Chapter 31

The sound of a sputtering engine coupled with a repeated hollow clanging roughly woke me from my grim slumber. I peeled my eyes open and fought to hold back my nausea as the world rocked around me in an unremitting sway. I was in a boat.

The open strip of sky above me showed a blazing sunset that fought to be seen from behind the pointed treetops. A small bird took off from an exposed branch to swoop down like a kamikaze pilot, disappearing from view after dipping lower than the side of the boat. Seconds later I watched it struggle to rise, fervently beating its wings in an attempt to hold on to the fresh meal clutched in its talons.

It was the pain in my own shoulders that made me realize I was trying to fly away with it. But a coarse rope coiled around my torso, wrists, and ankles, rubbing my skin raw in places while I struggled.

The damp metal that lined the bottom of the boat was frigid against my skin, and I could feel the cold sink into the very center of my being, clashing with the ever growing numbness that was leaking from the hole in my defenses. I didn't move as I listened to the sounds around me. Gruff voices, muffled by the time their words reached my ears, quarreled at a distance before growing louder as they drew near.

Thick, rubber boots thudded against the wooden dock before they entered my line of sight, one nearly missing my head as it landed on the floor beside me. Scarred arms with the sleeves half rolled strained to lift the still lifeless body of Falon. With a deep huff, he tossed her up and I held my breath until I heard the echoing grunt from the guard who caught her.

My tongue was thick and dry, it stuck to the roof of my mouth and wouldn't cooperate no matter how hard I tried to make it. Unable to scream or shout, to make any viable sound, I lay there, utterly powerless as the guard turned to lift me next.

"Not that one, Jaco. I'll see to her myself."

An uncontrollable panic erupted inside me, stemming from muddled memories that had yet to clear from the drug's hold. I squirmed under his gaze, knowing I needed to stay away from him, but not fully understanding my body's reaction.

With nowhere to run, capturing me was as easy as trying to catch a fish in a bucket. The minute Kael's hands touched me, my mouth found the will to free itself and I screamed. My skin crawled and my stomach threatened to empty its meager contents. Like a brisk wind blowing away a heavy fog, Kael's touch sparked every memory that my mind fought so hard to conceal.

I screamed louder and tears gushed over my cheeks as a cracked whine squeezed from my throat.

"Don't touch me!" I wriggled and fought, trying with everything I had to get out of his arms. The boat dangerously rocked beneath us, but I would have welcomed the prolonged death of drowning if it got me away from him.

"Cedric. Falon. *Please!*" My cries for help were interrupted by my stuttering sobs, and Kael only smiled at the guards whose heads turned at my screams. "Get him off of me!"

"Jaco, if you wouldn't mind?" Not bothering to look up, Kael's breath blew across my cheek as he watched me. "Try not to hold a grudge, pet. Jaco is only doing as he's told."

The said guard appeared next to me, a dirty rag held in his hand. Knowing his intentions, I vigorously kicked my legs to try and get Kael to drop me, but he only held me tighter. I clenched my teeth and shook my head, refusing to open my mouth again. I would not allow them to gag me.

Kael pinched my bare leg, hard enough that his nail broke the skin, and I felt blood trickle across my thigh. Unable to prevent the gasp that followed, Jaco took advantage and shoved the grimy gag as far between my lips as he could reach. Only when I started to choke did he pull back.

"Much better. It wouldn't do to have you disrupting the other students with this absurd tantrum."

With a spring in his step, Kael carried me down the dock, following the guards ahead who held my friends. Cedric was dragged along by two men, and he fought their grip with everything he had. He was bound more extensively than I was, only the guards on either side of him keeping him off the ground.

He kept struggling to look over his shoulder, his eyes near crazed when they landed on me in Kael's arms.

"Control him!" Kael ordered, and one of the guards landed a blow to Cedric's head that had him slumping forward.

I fought back my tears. With the gag firmly stuffed in my mouth and my nose half congested from my crying, I was close to suffocating. The fact that I knew Kael wouldn't allow me such an easy escape was not a comforting thought.

I couldn't stop from shaking, though. My entire body was repulsed by the pervert that held me. I thought I already knew what helpless felt like, but I truly had no idea. Unable to run, unable to scream, or to fight, or escape; I felt myself sinking deeper into the emotionless chill that grew in my heart.

The only thing that kept me from fully giving in to the unfeeling power inside me, was my friends. I couldn't allow myself to disappear, not yet. They needed me.

Kael's footsteps softened as we left the plank wood of the dock to travel across spongy grass. If I could gasp without choking, I would have. Ahead of us spread an expansive lawn that led to the front steps of a decaying plantation home, rooted on the only solid ground to be found. Made entirely of stone, the mansion had a gothic look to it.

Slender gallery posts, as round as the ancient live oaks that surrounded them, bore a double-layered front balcony with shutter-framed windows spaced equally along. The thick orange of oil lights lit the paned glass from within and small flames danced behind the iron lanterns that held them captive.

The house had a dark beauty and was probably once a classic sight. But now it stood stoic, silently resisting the swamp's attempts to reclaim it. The results left the mansion encased between eternal sentries whose branches grew wildly around the structure, as well as through it.

Branches dripping with Spanish moss crept their way through aired hallways and open balconies. Vines wound themselves around the many pillars and squeezed themselves into whatever cracks were revealed in the stone.

Moss and algae clung to all surfaces exposed to the elements, giving the mansion an eerie green hue that was hauntingly ghoulish when touched by the light of the oil lamps. As we bypassed the front of the house, Kael's friend Jaco lead us around the side.

Here, a small compound was made of old shacks on stilts that held them above the water. Other boats and canoes rested beneath them with wooden rope bridges connecting all the buildings. The smell of decaying bark was near overwhelming as Kael stepped onto the first swaying rope bridge.

Frogs croaked and the katydids sang an ominous farewell cadence that could be heard long before the darkness smothered my senses. The air in here felt dank and humid, the putrid smell similar to that of the Dean's dungeon.

The inside of the shack was bare except for four cells, one in each corner. Rusted iron bars, slimy with mildew and other unmentionable liquids stood unmoving, and I whimpered when another sweep of the room revealed Falon already locked inside one.

Her binds were cut and lay limp around her prone form and her once vibrant blonde hair now soaked up the sludge that pooled beneath her. Still dazed from the hit to his head, Cedric was easily thrown in the cell across from her.

His moan of pain shot straight to my heart as he gripped the bars and pulled himself to a sitting position. His hands slid down the crusted metal, but he managed.

"I can see by your expression that this room doesn't meet to your standards. Don't worry, my spirited pet, you won't be staying here."

The guards looked shocked at his declaration, and I hoped the clear revulsion on my face would be enough for them to finally step in.

"But s-sir," one stammered, afraid to argue. "Prisoners are to stay in the holding cells. It's Academy policy. We could be punished if we let—"

"Fine." He waved a hand for the guard to shut up. "I'll leave her here … for now." Impatience sharpened his tone and one of the guards winced.

Kael had no choice, even he couldn't go against three guards who obviously didn't want to get in trouble just so he could live out his sick fetishes. Stepping inside Falon's cell, Kael's grip on me tightened as he realized he would have to put me down. As unhappy as a toddler being told to let go of his plaything, he abruptly dropped me. I landed on my back, my groan of pain stifled by the rag still trapped in my mouth. With a brisk yank, Kale pulled the cloth from between my teeth and knelt in front of me.

Slipping a hand under my head, he gripped a fistful of my hair and pulled my head back. When my face was level with his, he leaned forward and mashed his lips against mine. I scrunched my face and tried to pull away despite the strands of hair that were ripping as I moved. But Kael held fast.

He seized my lower lip between his teeth in a mockery of a lover's nip and when I gave no reaction, he bit hard enough to draw blood. My wail of pain was enough to satisfy his sick need and he let me go.

Petting my hair before he left, he leaned down one more time to whisper in my ear. Quiet sobs racked my body as I stared off into the empty cell behind him.

"*Shh*, don't despair. I'll be back for you. I've been forced to hold back twice now, love. But I will not be denied. You *will* be mine."

The metal bars clanged with a hollow anguish as he shut and locked my cell door. The light left with them, leaving us in an inky dark so deep it was smothering. Still bound by rope, I could only curl into a ball. Tears leaked from the corners of my eyes, but I hardly noticed them.

The rank sludge and grime that soaked through my clothes were nothing compared to his touch. The nick on my leg and blood dripping down my chin were child's play compared to the pain I knew was coming. Everything I felt right now was just a precursor for later.

I could endure this, because I knew that whatever Kael had planned for me would be far, far worse.

"Casey!" Cedric's harsh whisper was like a bomb blast in this deathly silence.

My eyes had gotten used to the darkness, and I could easily make out his shape in the cell across from me. He had been calling to me for almost a half hour now, but I'd refused to answer.

"Come on, don't do this. You can talk to us." His pleas fell on deaf ears.

I hadn't moved from where Kael dropped me, even though Falon had long since removed the ropes that he left on my body. My right side was completely soaked in muck and whatever else grew in this sodden prison.

My hair was matted with it, sticking to the side of my head like Elmer's glue. At first, I couldn't stop shivering and my teeth chattered so hard I thought they'd go right through my already bleeding lip. But when I welcomed the cold, once I accepted that I couldn't fight this, the shivering stopped.

My limbs were overcome by the ever growing frost that was spreading through my body. The patches I hastily put over my heart for protection were shredding at the seams. With each remembered forced touch, I lost more of myself to the emerging storm.

My only chance at surviving this, I knew, was to bury myself so deep inside the welcoming ice that even *he* couldn't reach me. It was a slow decent, especially when my friends continued to intervene.

"Is she breathing?" I heard Cedric ask, his voice cracking at the end of that last word.

I felt more than saw Falon move. Small vibrations carried across the slick floor to slosh whatever filth I lay in until eventually I felt warmth radiating off of her body in front of me. I could sense something in front of my face, and when my cheeks were bathed in a subtle moist heat, I knew it was her hand checking for my breaths.

"Yeah, she's breathing fine. But ... she's just lying here."

Falon's hand gently brushed along my shoulder, and I flinched. Her hand jerked back at the sudden movement, but returned to rub along my arm, my side, my face. She was checking me for injuries. Her thumb was feather light across my swollen lip, but I knew she could feel the dried blood on it.

Her touch was different from Kael's; it was kind, gentle, and not at all defiling. It was the touch of a worried friend. And even so, it was almost too much to bear. My skin no longer felt like my own. I felt like I was trapped in a stranger's body, tied behind someone weaker and unable to protect themselves from a depraved predator.

"What did he do to you?" Falon whispered.

Wood creaked as the door to our shack swung open and a bright light briefly exposed the face of my nightmares, before the lantern was adjusted and dimmed.

"Good news, pet. You're going to come stay with me."

Kael's voice was chip with enthusiasm while my rapid heartbeats continued on with a growing dread. This was it. I rolled to a sitting position and stared at the man who planned to destroy me. His grin was feral and smug, still every bit as cocky as when I first met him. He lifted the lantern to get a better look and wrinkled his nose when he saw me.

"First thing on the list is a bath, love. We can't have you bringing this filth into our bed."

"Over my dead body!" Cedric's growl only caused Kael to grin harder as he unlocked my cell door.

I needed to hurry this along. I didn't want my friends to have to witness anymore of this than necessary. But when I went to stand, my muscles refused to listen.

I didn't want to go with him and somewhere deep inside me, *something* was still fighting. Kael stood with his hand on the cell door, his face quickly creasing with his growing anger.

"Don't forget my rules, Casey." His eyes briefly flicked over to where Falon kneeled behind me.

That was all it took to get me moving. His eyes never left Falon as I pushed myself to stand on quivering knees. It was a natural instinct for me to step back when his eyes roamed down my body. The knowledge that he planned to touch me everywhere his eyes lingered had me faint and trembling.

Falon took a step forward and gripped my hand. Standing shoulder to shoulder with me, she refused to back down from Kael's glare. When she spoke, her voice was low but strong and filled with reckless determination.

"You don't have to do this, Casey. *Fight him.* Don't let him take this from you."

I wanted to tell her that I was, that I was fighting with every fiber of my being to protect her and Cedric. To keep them alive. She hadn't seen the horrors that I had; she wasn't there each time Kael took a chunk out of my defenses.

There was nothing more important to me than my friends. I would die for them, would give up my very self to see them safe. But how did you explain that in words? How did you put reasoning behind a love like that? You couldn't. So my sacrifice would have to be explanation enough.

I tried to smile, to let her know that everything was going to be okay. But my lower lip only cracked where it was split, once again allowing my blood to flow freely.

"It's okay, Fal," I managed to whisper, my voice tight with unshed tears.

I turned to face my destroyer, refusing to feel anything when I looked at him. I focused on sinking within myself to the safe place that I had created. I took one step toward his outstretched hand and was knocked to the ground.

"If you won't fight for yourself, then I will," Falon cried, and then launched herself at Kael.

In her hand was a tiny knife, barely longer than her thumb. A weapon she had managed to smuggle in here even despite the searches the guards undoubtedly performed. Her face was set in a ferocious glare, the very one that dared the queen of sprites to defy her.

I could tell by the positioning of her strike that she would fail. Her arm was too high, the attack going too wide. Before I could shout a warning, Kael easily blocked her arm. Pushing it aside as if she were no more than a child. His other hand moved forward … and buried a knife directly into her gut.

"Falon!" I roared, as I watched her collapse upon herself and sink to the ground.

Blood pooled beneath her, faster than I had ever seen it flow. The color of her life's blood was so dark that I couldn't distinguish it from the liquid already puddled on the ground. My power awoke, and I crawled over to her, reaching out a hand to save her life.

But my head was wrenched back by a clenched fist in my hair.

"I told you what my first rule was, Casey. Pity you didn't pass on the message to your little friend."

He dragged me by my hair through the grime and Falon's spreading blood. The warm liquid coated my hands and arms as I tried to drag myself back to her. In the cell across from us, Cedric was throwing himself against the metal bars, trying in vain to dislodge them.

"Enough of this!" Kael ordered, as he swooped down and slammed me face first into the floor.

My nose broke with a sickening *crunch* and warm blood filled the back of my throat. My head swam and the room spun. Dazed with the pain, I didn't resist when Kael threw me over his shoulder and shut the cell door behind him.

From upside down, I watched Falon. She had both hands pressed to her stomach to try and staunch the flow of blood, but more kept squeezing out from around her fingers. I could see red tinting her teeth and lips as she fought to speak.

"Fight ... him," she called.

And deep inside me, the anchored beast awoke.

Chapter 32

One hundred and thirty-seven steps. That's how long it took for Kael to carry me out of the holding cells, past the slowly rising swamp water, and to this somber excuse of a bedroom. It was situated as far from the main house as possible, while keeping just out of the flood zones that surrounded this tiny speck of a floating land. The concrete barracks that he brought me to had multiple rooms that appeared to house the other guards on campus.

I wondered if they would be able to hear my screams tonight and, more morbidly, if they would do anything to stop them. I shivered at the dark thoughts as goosebumps rose across my flesh. No rescue would come for me this time. Nothing was done to stop Kael from touching me earlier, or that kept him from stabbing Falon.

My lip trembled, and I bit it in an attempt to keep in my cries. Falon was dead by now. I saw the wound, *felt* how deep it had perforated; there was no surviving that. I could have saved her, I know I could, if Kael hadn't dragged me away. Now one of my best friends was gone and the other was forced to remain in that miserable cell, staring at her body.

The door slammed shut and I jumped in place. Brought back to the new reality I now faced, I took in my surroundings. Standing as far inside the room as space would allow, I was entrapped between a narrow bed on a rusted metal frame, a stout dresser, and a barren nightstand. That was all. There were no windows, no television, nothing to provide a semblance of warmth in this forgotten chamber.

A layer of dust had accumulated over nearly everything and the off-white, almost beige walls, were chipped to reveal the matching gray of the concrete beneath.

"Not given the VIP suite, I see. Guess you're not as special as you thought." The taunt was out of my mouth before I could register the words.

The room stood still as I focused on keeping my breaths even. Kael chuckled.

"I chose this room because it's part of the old barracks, no one uses them much anymore. I wanted us to have all the privacy we needed to enjoy our special evening together."

Terror-stricken, my eyes darted around the room and were continuously drawn to the door, the only exit. The bed and Kael stood between us, a fact I'm sure my captor had intended when he placed me here.

Kael moved at a slow pace, as if he had all the time in the world. Leisurely, he removed each weapon stashed on his person and placed them on top of the dresser. The disturbed dust swam in an angry cloud just in front of his face, but he paid it no mind. His eyes remained focused on me through the reflection in the small mirror mounted on the wall.

"Through that door behind you is a small sink. You have five minutes to clean yourself up."

The door in question was so small that I had missed it entirely in my inspection of the room. The bottom was chipped and warped, but it swung open easily when I turned the handle. Wanting to place anything between me and Kael, I shut the door and looked for something I could use to hold it in place.

Unfortunately, the bathroom was as barren as the room outside. There was no chair to prop the door, no lock to twist or push, and no window to quietly sneak out of. I was well and truly trapped. Leaning against the brittle wood, I caught my reflection in the aged mirror above the sink.

I had a feeling that my nose was broken and my appearance only confirmed my suspicions. Dried blood had crusted a trail from my nostrils to my upper lip before veering around the side of my mouth and down to my chin. Bruises had already formed beneath my eyes, but my nose was thankfully straight, if only smashed and swollen.

"Three minutes."

Kael's voice sounded closer than before, as if he were right on the other side of the door. I instinctively took a step closer to the sink, which was as far from him as I could get. I turned the tap and waited as the water that came out went from a thick mud to what could almost be considered clear.

With no towel or even toilet paper available, I used my hands to tenderly scrub the blood from my face and arms. I winced the closer I got to my nose but managed to get almost all of it. As I cleaned the evidence of my abuse, as I watched my blood spiral around the white ceramic, a gaping pit opened inside me. A beast as feral as a starved Vampire paced back and forth.

"Your time is up, pet."

At the expectant call, the beast inside me roared. Anger brewed as I stared at my reflection, and I sniffed to swallow the blood that continued to leak from my nose, my mind lost in a sea of pain. I thought of Falon and her helpless body lying at the bottom of a cell. I pictured Cedric, battered and injured as he tried to break through hardened metal to get to me.

Memories of Zora's final moments only caused the beast within to claw at the walls that entombed it. However, it was the pale creature that stared back at me through the glass that really got to me. It was the bruises on her face, the empty look in her eyes, the cloud of utter hopelessness that floated around her.

Kael made her into this. He *owned* her. But that was about to change.

"You don't want me to come in there after you, Casey. I promise you won't enjoy it as much as I will."

Controlling the tremors in my hand, I turned the doorknob and pushed open the last barrier between me and the monster. Kael stood at the end of the bed, clad in only his pants. His naked chest held pits and scars from past battles, and I silently cursed the foes who had failed to put him down.

He walked toward me, a smirk pulling at his lips.

"Still so defiant," he crooned, stopping just in front of me.

My eyes darted to the exit, but Kael stepped even closer, blocking it from view. He gripped my chin with his fingers and rubbed his thumb along the seam of my lips. As he leaned down, I took a final step back and just barely kept out of reach of his kiss. His fingers remained on my chin and their grip squeezed tighter as his anger came to the surface.

"There is nowhere for you to go, better to just give in."

The nightstand dug into my lower back as I tried in vain to keep away from his touch. Like a spider watching a helpless victim in its web, Kael enjoyed my struggles. He pressed the front of his body fully against mine and pinned me to the nightstand.

Running a hand up my bare leg, he paused at my hip before moving higher to rest against my lower ribs. His thumb rubbed back and forth along the underside of my breast. There was no hiding my fear now.

My breaths were ragged and uneven, like my own lungs were trying to suffocate me and put me out of my misery. I turned my head away, the only movement of defiance I had left. I could feel the grumbles of pleasure through Kael's chest. His pants came in deeper as he continued to rub his hands along my sides and chest.

"Take of your shirt," he growled before putting some space between our bodies.

I stared at him in shock. It shouldn't have come as a surprise; I knew what he expected of this night. But to think horrible thoughts and to

243

actually live them out were two separate things. It wasn't something I could have prepared for.

"Either you take off your shirt or I do it for you." He threatened while his hands reached for me.

Refusing to give him even more power over me, my hands gripped the bottom of my t-shirt. My arms shook as I drew the material over my head and chucked it at his face. He caught it just before impact and stared at me with unabashed greed. Everywhere his eyes touched, I felt my skin try to peel off my body to run and hide.

It took everything in me to stand before him with my chin held high. I refused to let him have my pride as well. Faster than I was prepared for, Kael once again stepped in close. I could feel the heat radiating off his body as our skin touched, my bra the only barrier between his chest and mine.

He wrapped his arms around me and squeezed me to him, trapping my arms between us. His head leaned in and I turned mine away. But he wasn't aiming for my lips this time. His mouth trailed licks and bites from my shoulder to my neck. When I tried to scrunch my shoulders, he only bit me harder.

The pressure against my arms increased as he leaned my upper body partially over the nightstand. With my hands even more tightly pinned, his were free to roam. I felt his palms against my hips and stood helpless as his fingertips found their way beneath the waistband of my shorts.

Bile rose in the back of my throat as he played with the band of my underwear before sliding his hands beneath them as well. His palms rubbed along the bare skin of my hips and I twisted to try and get them off. But they only continued their slow journey, taking their time to move around and grab my ass.

He pulled the lower half of me against him, and I knew what was going to come next. The only part of my body free from his grasp was my head and the moment he pulled back to look at me, I slammed it against his face.

The shock of my strike was enough for him to release me, and I followed my head-butt with a knee to his groin. Not wasting a single second, I pushed past his hunched body and crawled over the top of the bed toward the door.

Before I could even get a foot off, Kael had a hold of my ankle and dragged me back. I flipped to my back and kicked out at his face. When a lucky hit pushed him back, I tried instead to run around the bed. But in these close quarters, he was never more than an arm's reach away.

He grabbed me from behind, his arms squeezing around me so tight I thought he might break a rib. He pulled back and lifted my feet from the ground as he walked us toward the wall. I twisted and fought, strained my arms with all the strength I had in me, but still couldn't break his hold. With every passing second of my struggles, the beast within me escaped more from its cage.

When I felt Kael lick along the side of my neck, that was all it took to break the last bit of chain that kept the beast in check. I gripped his forearms with my hands and pushed. The icy cold that always accompanied the beast burst from me in a torrent of wintery fury.

Kael screamed as I listened to his skin sizzle and crack beneath my hands. Unable to keep his hold on me, I fell to the floor and watched as he struck his arms against himself as if he were trying to put out a fire. When he stopped thrashing I noticed two black handprints burned into his flesh.

Upon closer inspection, though, I could see that it was frostbite and not a burn that adorned his arms. Tiny crystals were still visible when he moved.

"What are you?" he murmured.

Still confused and focused on his arms, he was not prepared when I rushed at him to slam my hands against his chest. His eyes met mine as I forced the ice down my arms. Fueled by every ounce of my fear and hate for him, for every memory of him hurting me, for each time he made my skin crawl and for the anger at how he made me feel about myself, I encased him in ice.

Frost grew across his skin and he screamed in pain as it spread. He lost control of his arms first. The frost completely covered them keeping them stiff at his sides. His hips and legs were next, until each part of his body succumbed to my power.

Unable to control his muscles, his body fell to the floor and landed with me crouched over him. I stopped when every inch of his body stood immobilized except his head. His eyes darted around in panic, as mine had when he brought me to this room. His breaths were shallow and harsh, as Falon's were after he stabbed her.

Pain was blatantly obvious across his face, as I'm sure it was for each of his victims before me. Slowly standing from my crouch, I reached for the knife he left on the top of the dresser. There was still a bit of Falon's blood on it, and I thought it fitting that he would meet his end this way.

Standing over his body, I refused to break eye contact as I slammed the knife home, straight through his heart.

I wasn't sure how long I sat there, staring at the pool of blood. My shirt was twisted in my hands, but I couldn't bring myself to put it on yet. It would mean taking my eyes off his body for a split second, and that was more than I could allow.

I couldn't quite convince myself that he was dead. Factually it had to be true, after all, I was the one that stabbed him, but I couldn't shake the nagging voice in the back of my head that said it wasn't over.

"Oh goody, you already killed him. I do hate when I have to get messy."

Standing in the doorway, finding herself at the pointy end of my stolen knife, was Gwendolyn. She had not a hair out of place and wore a pair of heels that I knew had to sink in the mud when she walked, but they looked spotless.

"Seriously? That thing might work against him, honey, but not me."

She looked bored as she leaned against the doorframe. I stood there, half naked, covered in blood, holding a weapon at her throat, and she started counting like she was trying to calm down a toddler.

"Why the hell are you here?" I growled.

I couldn't deal with her shit right now. I was too busy trying not to go insane. She rolled her eyes as if the answer should have been obvious.

"I'm here to save you of course."

I clenched my jaw until it hurt. It was a good thing she was immortal because I was about to stab the hell out of her.

"Release me so I can wake up. I have other things to take care of." My arm shook with the strength it took to hold back from trying to kill her.

She pulled me into one of her dream talks at the worst possible time. Cedric was still trapped in the cell, we needed to do something with Falon's body, and I wasn't comfortable being this vulnerable around Kael—even if he was no longer breathing.

"You're not asleep, Casey." The voice came from behind Gwendolyn, and I took a step back, not trusting what I saw.

"Falon?" I cried.

The knife fell from my hand as I dropped to my knees. There she was, alive and whole, right in front of me. Blood still stained her clothes, but the skin beneath the jagged hole in her shirt was unblemished. I watched in disbelief as she knelt in front of me and gripped me in the tightest hug I'd ever had.

"How?" I asked, knowing it was going to take some serious therapy to get me to trust my senses after this.

"Gwendolyn appeared just seconds after Kael dragged you out. She healed me, which took some time, and then got us out. We searched all over for you, but it wasn't until we heard Kael's screams that we knew where to look."

I tried to laugh, but it came out a half-sob. They were okay. We were all okay. How had we turned this around?

"That's enough hugging for now," Gwendolyn barked. "We need to get you guys out of here, and I'm sure you don't want to let your other friend out there see you like this."

At the thought of Cedric seeing the marks Kael left on my body, I nearly threw up. With Falon's help, I managed to clean myself off in the small bathroom, my eyes glancing to Kael's body on the floor each time we passed it.

When I was presentable enough, Gwendolyn approached me cautiously, as if I were a wild animal backed into a corner. Her fingertips gently brushed across my battered nose and the pain of her touch was quickly replaced by a warm tingle that spread outward across my cheeks.

My breaths came unhindered as my nose returned to its previous unbroken state. Blood no longer dripped down the back of my throat, and my eyes felt less puffy and clearer.

As if what she had done was no more special than sneezing, Gwendolyn ushered us out the door and across the lawn to where it ended in a line of trees. With each step I took away from that room, I felt more like myself. The internal wounds would take more time to heal than those on my skin, and I knew that I had an uphill battle ahead of me.

Hopefully, the support of my friends would be enough to keep me from sliding down into an even darker place than where my mind currently resided.

Chapter 33

The grove of trees that bordered the edge of the island was thin, but dense. The trunks stood so tightly packed together that the leaves blocked most of the moonlight from reaching the ground. Even so, ferns and bushes covered the spaces between the trunks and grew until they reached as high as my waist. I stumbled over the network of roots that crisscrossed the ground and continuously fought against the pull of the ankle-deep water and mud that seemed to get deeper the further out we went.

Gwendolyn led the way, weaving between the gaps in the trees as fluently as a park ranger familiar with her territory. Despite her appearance, she was comfortable with this rugged environment. Her stiletto heels never sank more than an inch into the ground and somehow remained clean when they came back out.

Her designer clothes had not a single speck of dirt on them and her hair remained free of debris. As I watched her, I swore it was almost like the small branches with low hanging moss moved out of the way when she passed by. They were stubbornly indifferent to me. I was already picking twigs out of my hair as we continued on.

A tall figure stepped out from behind a tree, and under the thick cover I could only make out that they were male with broad shoulders and an overpowering height. My hands shook as I slowly reached for the mid-sized knife I had stolen from Kael. His blood still remained, camouflaging the first layer beneath that had come from Falon. The blood of two different bodies stained this knife. Was I going to have to add a third?

Gwendolyn continued on, either oblivious to the silent individual ahead or overconfident. I wasn't going to take any chances. My steps slowed, and I changed my gate in preparation for an attack. My knees were slightly bent as I balanced on the balls of my feet. We moved closer and I kept the knife loose but secure in my hand.

I didn't want to kill another person. No matter what I had suffered at his hands, killing Kael had blackened a part of my soul. I could still feel the knife reverberating off bone as I pushed it into his chest. I didn't know if I could do it again, but I was prepared to find out. I would darken the rest of my soul if it meant never being captured again.

I squeezed the cool hilt in my palm and adjusted my stance, ready to pounce the moment I got close enough.

"Stop," came a command from behind the tree.

The tenor and lilt of the voice was familiar. My hand loosened its grip on the knife just as the figure fully emerged from the shadows. Dried blood still painted Cedric's face just above his eyebrow, but the wound was healed beneath. His eyes ignored the movement of Gwendolyn and Falon to focus in on me.

The emerald orbs darkened as they took in my appearance, and his jaw hardened the longer he stared. I looked down and tried to find what caused his reaction, but I had cleaned off all the blood from my skin and covered whatever bruises I had found. Could he still see them—the places Kael had touched? I felt like those parts of my body were highlighted, that they were screaming their revulsion loud enough for anyone to see. Maybe he was sickened by what he saw, a once strong girl now broken and abused. Luthos knew I was sickened with myself.

Cedric stalked up to me, closing the distance between us in mere heartbeats. One second a few yards separated us and the next he was in my space. His hand gripped tight around my wrist, but the knife held strong in my hand as his forearm strained to keep both under his control.

His eyes searched mine, his heavy silence and close proximity causing my heart to race. Inside, I shook with apprehension. Did he want to see the broken pieces of me up close? And why wouldn't he let go of my weapon? Did he think I was so far gone that I would stab him?

"Let it go," he commanded.

I loosened my hand until the knife fell to the ground with a muted thud. Cedric still held my wrist and his nostrils flared as he continued to stare me down.

"Let. It. Go," he growled, his eyes flashing with contained fury.

I shook with a growing anger of my own. I had released the freakin' weapon, what more did he want from me? We glared at one another, neither one willing to back down. My hand went numb as he clenched tighter around my wrist. He stepped closer until our chests almost touched, but purposefully maintained some space between us.

"I can see it inside you, moving around, looking out from behind your eyes. I can *feel* its anger, its thirst. Let the beast go; you don't need it anymore."

My eyes widened as I understood his meaning. The beast was still roaming free within me. I was so numb from what happened that I hadn't even noticed the power flowing unchecked. How had I not noticed the crystals beaded across my skin, like a fine layer of sparkling dust that shimmered in the stray rays of moonlight.

Where Cedric's hand touched me, the frost melted and regrew in an endless battle between our powers. Looking inside myself, I could feel the beast moving. It was strong even though it kept out of reach. The deep pit at the bottom of my soul where I usually trapped it was damaged, but still intact.

I knew that to reclaim full control of myself I needed to close that door, but it was no simple task. The beast did not want to return to the dark hole I kept it in. It enjoyed its freedom. I could feel its pleasure in our earlier actions and knew it wanted more. It wanted me to pick up the knife and use it on everyone back at that school, to feel blood once again coating our fingers.

"You can do it, Casey. I'll help you," Cedric spoke, his voice calm. "Focus on me, on Falon, on the lighter parts of your life. Think of our laughter and our jokes. Use the light to push the beast back."

Cedric's eyes were closed now as he focused on the battle unfolding within me. I could almost feel his presence in my mind, a blanket of warmth melting the frigid environment it had become. I did what he advised and concentrated on what I knew to be the good things in my life. I pushed back against the hopeless memories from the past couple days and fought to keep the good ones within my grasp. I thought of my love for my friends and our loyalty for one another. I remembered sleepless nights filled with laughter and teasing. Of a time when affection and safety was all that I knew.

From around me, Cedric and Falon offered their own memories to fuel my fight. Whispered moments of happiness helped me to slowly force the beast back in its cage and slam the door shut. My mind shook with the force of its fury, but it gradually faded until I was left alone with my own thoughts.

I opened my eyes to see the shining, bright green of Cedric's staring back at me. His grip on me lessened until my wrist rested loosely in his hand, his thumb rubbing back and forth across my skin.

"Interesting," Gwendolyn murmured, her keen gaze narrowed on me and Cedric.

Withdrawing my arm, I drew back until Cedric and I no longer touched. Confusion caused a throb to build behind my temples. I didn't know what to feel in that moment. With my mind no longer clouded from the influence of the beast, my body reacted of its own accord, finally free once again to do so.

While Cedric's touch wasn't completely unwanted, it felt different than I had come to know. Unsure of myself, I stepped away until I stood beside Falon, making sure I didn't come into contact with her either. The swirling anger that fueled my every step was gone, leaving a desolate vacancy in its wake.

When the anger left, the frost went with it, and I immediately took notice of the humid temperature that surrounded me. When that feral beast was free, I was filled with strength and confident in my ability to take down my enemies. Nothing could touch me when it was in control.

But now I felt small and alone, even though I was in the company of friends. I suddenly wished that I could have the beast back, if only so that I didn't notice how wrong I felt. So I didn't have to feel like an empty shell of what I used to be.

Cedric's eyes softened as he watched me, and in that moment I hated that he could read me so well. I hated that he could see the dark revulsion that I had for myself, that he could probably feel every ounce of self-loathing. I knew that in that gaze he was searching for the girl he used to know, hoping to catch a glimmer of her hiding somewhere inside. He wouldn't find her.

"We should go," I whispered as I fell into step behind an already moving Gwendolyn.

Not much farther ahead I could make out a faint glow. The near full moon glimmered across the water's calm surface and exposed the two boats that bobbed against the shore. Similar to a canoe, but shallower and wider, the boats had a flat bottom rather than the rounded one I was more familiar with.

"They're called pirogues," Gwendolyn explained. "It's one thing the humans in these parts invented that I don't find to be a complete waste of ingenuity."

Seating herself in the middle of one, like a queen mounting her throne, Gwendolyn gestured for us to board the other. Situating myself at the front, with a solemn Cedric and silent Falon behind me, I looked around for the paddles.

"How do we move these things? I'm not using my hands," I told her.

With a cheeky grin, Gwendolyn brought her fingers to her lips and whistled. The shrill sound carried across the water, and I feared the nearby guards would be alerted. I scanned the trees for hiding bodies and listened hard for warning shouts. Only the crickets and fireflies could be heard or seen.

Across the channel, shallow splashes drew my attention. The water rippled out from a spot on the opposing shore, and I watched the rings grow outward until they hit our boat. In the mud along the water's edge, two massive smudges spread down the bank.

With faint memories haunting me from my science classes, I now examined the water with a growing anxiety. Two sets of small, yellow spheres caught my attention. Whenever I tried to get a better look, they disappeared, only to then reappear even closer.

"Gwendolyn," I whispered with unease. "What did you call?"

But I didn't need to her to tell me. Now completely visible to our small party, two massive alligators carelessly swam up to our pitiful boats. I was resting so close to the surface of the water that either one of the reptiles could have taken my head with one little jump. I gaped as the huge predators pulled themselves to the front of our boats.

Vanishing beneath the water, they returned seconds later with thick rope encircling their necks. With another whistle from Gwendolyn, they swam away. I watched the rope at the end of our boat grow taut before we were pulled along to the center of the channel and beyond.

"You have pet alligators?" Falon exclaimed from behind me. "You're my new hero."

I snorted at Falon's enthusiasm. She *would* want a giant scaly killer as a pet. The novelty of our transportation wore off as we put more distance between us and the school. For some time, the chimneys could still be seen over the tops of the trees, and I couldn't shake the sense that the house was watching me.

But once we turned through a bend, the house was completely hidden from view and I let out a sigh of relief. The alligators pulled us deeper into the bayou, the moon lighting the way like a beacon of hope. Reflective yellow eyes could be seen along the channel we traveled, but they stayed well away from our boats and the much larger creatures that pulled them.

The trees grew in thickness the deeper in we went. Branches swopped low, nearly kissing the water, as moss hung and swayed with the breeze.

Fireflies glowed everywhere I looked, and I entertained myself with watching them dance.

After what felt like hours of traveling, my aches and bruises began to catch up with me. The muscles in my back screamed in protest as I stretched them out. As I lifted my arms, my hands grazed the soft hanging moss that rested just above me. The branches here were expansive, allowed to grow and develop far from civilization.

Some stretched nearly the entire width of the channel. As they grew and reached toward the opposing bank, the channel began to narrow until it ended at a mound of land holding the largest tree I had ever seen. Enormous and foreboding, its branches were as thick around as Falon was tall, with a reach that was longer than the twenty foot gators that pulled our boats.

The closer we got, the larger it seemed. I craned my neck as far back as I could and I still couldn't see the top of it. When our boats hit land, Gwendolyn dismounted and waved away our drivers. A low rumbling vibrated the water, and it took a moment for me to realize that it was coming from the gators. They hissed, jaws opening, as they swam along the side of our boat, sending small splashes over me with the irritated swipes of their tails.

"Don't make me tell you again. I'll turn you into my next pair of boots, you ungrateful brute. Don't think I won't," Gwendolyn scolded.

It would have been comical if the subject of her reprimand wasn't looking at me as its next meal. Fortunately, they heeded her warning and disappeared back down the channel. Once I was sure they had left, I scampered onto dry land and moved as far from the water as I could. Cedric and Falon did the same.

"Where are we?" Falon asked in awe. "There is so much power here, it's like … nothing I've ever felt before."

She walked around, arms outstretched in front of her, as she followed some hidden signal that she felt. It led her straight to the center of the tree. Standing beside it, Falon looked like an ant in comparison.

"What you feel, young Fae, is a doorway to Faerie." Gwendolyn tilted her head in acknowledgment of Falon's status, but said no more.

Falon's apprehension was obvious and her throat bobbed with a thick swallow. "Where does this doorway open? Please don't say the Summer Court," she whined.

Gwendolyn laughed at Falon's blatant aversion at being so close to her childhood home. "This specific door does not open to any one court. It is a portal directly to my personal lands, gifted to me by both rulers a long time ago."

Falon's expression told me that she wasn't entirely sold on going through that door, but it was either that or go back to the Academy behind us. I had no intention of ever being captured again, so forward was my only option.

I stood between my friends, the three of us in a spread line as we watched Gwendolyn call upon the door. It started with a low buzz and the atmosphere around us became so charged, I felt strands of my hair stand on end. Gwendolyn's hair was, of course, untouched.

The tree trunk before us glowed, the light pulsing as its radiance grew stronger until the entire body of the tree was a bright, crisp white. Gwendolyn turned to us with a smirk, fully expecting us to be in awe of what was on display behind her. Conceited much?

"Through this doorway lies my home, and while it may seem beautiful and serene, be warned. Not all is as it seems. I govern my lands as best I can, but evil nasties still sneak through from time to time." She shrugged as though the trespassing didn't really bother her. "It's Faerie, the land has a magic of its own that calls to many a creature. So heed my warning and do not stray far."

Turning her back to us, she walked toward the blinding light and disappeared into the tree.

"I'm not so sure that this is a good idea. Faerie isn't safe for us, Casey," Cedric warned, obviously distressed.

I knew it wasn't, there were reasons why songs and warning tales had been passed around about what happened to mortals who wandered in there. It was a world meant only for those that were born of it. Visitors have always been welcome, but who's to say they wouldn't become dinner for some nasty creature that lurked in the shadows? Or become trapped in an endless dance for the amusement of their company.

The Fae were fickle creatures and not all of them were cognizant like Falon's kind. They had their own creatures and monsters that made ours look like something from a kid's picture book. But I was confident that Gwendolyn wouldn't allow anything to happen to us, so long as we didn't stray.

I had no other options. I had questions that needed answers and a power I couldn't control. That wasn't including this new power that seemed to come leashed to a murderous beast.

"We need to do this, Ced. I need to know how to control my healing, and *you* need to know why you can feel my emotions. I don't know if she has the answers to everything, like why I'm suddenly able to control frost, but I'm sure she can at least point us to someone who does."

I turned to Falon, who with every passing second became a shade paler. Something through that doorway scared her, but her jaw was clenched with pure determination.

"I swore that I would never return home," she said before looking at me. "But I will go with you, if only to keep you from doing something stupid. Mortals and Faerie don't mix."

She gave me a half smile, trying to make a joke out of the nervous shaking in her voice.

"So it's settled then? We follow?" I asked, and they nodded.

I offered my hand to Cedric, steeling myself for the uneasy feeling of being touched. When his hand gripped mine, I only felt warmth and comfort, a feeling that felt foreign to me—as if the girl Kael made me into couldn't recognize something so innocent.

I pushed away my peculiar thoughts and focused on what laid ahead. Falon gripped Cedric's other hand and together we walked through the doorway to whatever awaited us.

Chapter 34

The first thing I noticed was the sunlight. Beams of radiant gold punctured the canopy above and saturated the meadow below with warmth. The doorway opened directly behind a small cluster of bushes, and we took advantage of the cover to take in our surroundings.

Birds were singing. I couldn't see them, but their voices blended with the afternoon breeze. Small animals nosed around and romped through the undergrowth and a pair of squirrels chased one another from branch to branch.

"Is this place for real?" Cedric asked in awe, and I had to wonder the same.

The grass beneath my knees was as downy as a breeze-dried blanket and as vibrant a green I had ever seen. You could smell the earth here: a heady aroma similar to the scent of rain before it hits the ground. Flowers in full bloom threw pollen in the air like summertime confetti, allowing the honeyed dust to gently settle over everything within its windswept reach.

"The sights, the sounds, Luthos, even the smell of this place is intoxicating," I exclaimed. "No wonder mortals are so enchanted."

"You should taste the food," Falon teased, knowing full well that mortals couldn't eat the food from Faerie.

I stole a sidelong glance at her and fought to cover my smile. Falon's eyes were closed, her hands sunk deep into the dirt, and the most peaceful smile she'd ever worn was serenely displayed across her face. Her hair had a glow to it, one I hadn't seen since the night she first arrived in my dorm. She was home.

Most Fae chose to live here in Faerie. They had a deep connection with their lands, and no one knew if the magic of this place came from them or from the earth itself. Many found it hard to be away for any length of time, and the fact that Falon had been gone nearly a year had to have taken a toll on her.

"Did either of you see which way Gwen went?" Cedric asked while searching the meadow in front of us.

A nagging feeling prickled at the back of my mind as I peered over the bushes. I strained hard to see past the first row of trees, thinking that Gwendolyn must have passed through quicker than we thought. But I saw no designer jeans or marks of a heel print in the soil.

"Aw crap," Falon mumbled, but our close quarters made for easy hearing. "I was afraid this might happen."

My uneasy feeling grew with her words.

"Please tell me we're not trapped in Faerie without a guide," I groaned.

That would be just my luck. Of *course* I would escape from the most abhorrent experience I had ever been in, killing a man in the process, to only find myself lost in a land known to drive people insane.

"Portals can be very finicky." Falon worried her lip as she looked around. "We must have taken too long to pass through after Gwendolyn. The portal probably changed destinations while we were deciding whether or not to follow."

Great. Now what did we do?

"You're from here, could you guide us through to wherever she is?" Cedric asked.

Falon rolled her eyes. "I've never been to this part of Faerie. I'd be just as lost as you guys."

Frustrated and tired, we slumped beneath the shade of the bushes and tried to decide our next move. Sitting here for much longer was out of the question. It wasn't smart to be out in the open once it got dark.

"We could just wander around a bit, try and find a trail," Cedric offered.

I didn't think that was a very wise idea. "As long as we don't wander too far from the meadow during this search. That band of trees to the right there are perfect for climbing."

"So?" Cedric looked at me like I'd lost my mind.

"So we could climb them if we're stuck here after the sun goes down? You know, for safety?"

It was better than being caught on the ground. At least from up there we could see whatever came for us before it actually arrived. Cedric and I argued over whose suggestion was a better choice, and I grew more frustrated the longer the dispute ran. Falon told us to quiet down multiple times, but we ignored her.

It wasn't until she slapped her hands over both our mouths that she had our full attention.

"I said *shut up*. Are you both really so dense that you can't follow a simple direction?" She whispered, harshly. "If either of you had paid attention to your surroundings rather than fight over who had the better idea, you'd know that we're about to be in some deep shit."

Her anger caught me off guard, and it took longer than it should have for her words to sink in. She was right. The world around us had drowned in complete silence, like someone had grabbed the remote and pressed mute. The animals no longer frolicked in the meadow, which now looked cold and barren. The sunlight was gone, sucked away until the only lighting that remained resembled twilight.

It had been the middle of the day just minutes before, I was sure of it. It was like all the goodness had been sucked out of the area, leaving behind only the rotten and ugly parts that daylight tried to mask.

"And I think that's our cue to go," Cedric said, as he moved to stand.

Falon knocked him back to the ground, her tiny body using all its weight to hold him in place. "You had your chance to run, but you both decided that arguing with one another was a better plan."

A faint moaning and clanking of metal came from behind the trees to our left. Falon grabbed my shirt and pulled me down beside her and Cedric.

"Don't make a sound. Don't even breathe if you can help it."

She pointed through the leaves of the bush to a hunched figure moving on the outskirts of the tree line. The creature's skin was so pale that it was near translucent. It had shaggy gray hair and dark pools for eyes that took up half its face. Its arms were twice as long as its legs, and it had a chain wrapped around its neck, with the tail of it dragging along after.

It passed through the center of the meadow; its moans causing me to shiver. Never before had I heard something so heart wrenching and filled with sorrow. Darkness clung to its hollowed frame like a parasite. The shadows suffocated everything they touched, leaving a withered trail of death in its wake. I couldn't begin to imagine what would happen to a human unlucky enough to stumble upon this thing. My skin prickled with fear as my breath swelled up behind my tongue, afraid that even the slightest sound would draw its attention.

When the creature finally disappeared and its moans could no longer be heard, I allowed myself to gulp in fresh air. The sun slowly returned, casting a light on the dismal scene that remained. The trees that once stood powerful and proud, now cracked with decay—their trunks overwhelmed with a growing mold that leeched the color from the bark. The flowers and grass withered and drooped, crumbling into dust at the slightest breeze. The once vibrant meadow was now a field of death.

"What the hell was that?" My skin was still covered in goosebumps as I glanced around, making sure the creature hadn't returned.

"It's called a Bocan," Falon answered. "An entity known to kill travelers. Stories say that it was once a traveler itself before it suffered at the cruel hands of fate, and now it wanders alone, dispensing death to those as clueless and unwary as it had been."

My body was wracked with shivers as I surveyed the damage it caused. I wanted to get out of here before the Boca-whatever the hell it was came back. If that was the first taste of what lurked in the dark here, I didn't want to wait for round two.

"It was indeed a Bocan, my lady. Very astute of you to recognize such a rare creature."

I whirled around with a scream, ready to pummel whoever had just snuck up on me. I lowered my fist when I recognized the small being before us.

"Leif!" I cried, wanting to hug him but afraid I would only crush his small body in my arms.

He nodded in recognition before frowning at me, exasperation clearly visible across his small face. "She told you not to stray, and what's the first thing you do?" Before I could argue that it wasn't our fault, he turned and began walking away. "Come, we haven't much time before dusk. I, for one, don't want to be a chew toy for the big nasties that come out then."

I stared after his retreating form in shock before scrambling to catch up, Falon and Cedric close on my heels.

I almost didn't notice we had arrived until I heard Cedric gasp. Following his stare, my eyes caught on a chunk of rock peeking out from behind a wall of honeysuckle. I followed the large mass to another partially viewable piece below it, seeing more bits of rock the harder and longer I looked. Gwendolyn's home was arched stone walls and pillars, reminiscent of a fallen medieval church. It was covered in vines and nearly hidden behind the foliage and trees.

The stone had become one with nature, and they fused together to create a whole new masterpiece. Leif led us through an arched doorway obscured by hanging ivy with bloomed flowers so blue they glowed.

Pushing the soft buds aside, we entered into a grand greeting hall. Columns were spaced out equally on either side. Hallways and doorways were hidden in the shadows between them, tunneling further into the home. What took command of our attention though was the entire wall made of stained glass across from the entryway.

Sunlight filtered through the multitude of colors to create a mirrored work of art on the stone floor. Our footsteps echoed in the deep chamber and the shuffles from the staircase in the corner could barely be heard over them.

Gliding down the stone steps in a comfortable, but no less extravagant ensemble of jeans and a sweater, came Gwendolyn. Behind her strolled a man both handsome and young. He had a chiseled jaw coming to point at a cleft chin. His brown hair was buzzed close to his head and his muscles looked to carry on for days.

"I told you not to stray." Her voice resounded off the high ceiling and stone outcroppings. "Why do you insist on ignoring what I say?"

She stopped at the end of the stairs, the gentleman coming to rest directly at her side. He kept his gaze level, refusing to give away any secrets as he watched us with uncommonly warm eyes. Something about the way he carried himself, about how his body moved in reaction to Gwendolyn's was familiar.

"Who's the dude?" I asked, choosing to ignore her question.

Of all the times she had appeared to me, I have never seen nor heard mention of this man. To say I was curious would be an understatement. Gwendolyn's eyes softened, becoming almost tender when she looked at him.

"This is Warin, and he is as much to me as Cedric is to you. He is my Protector."

"So he's your boyfriend," I deadpanned.

Gwendolyn glared at me, her expression somewhere between annoyed and confused. "I don't know what gave you that idea. Warin cannot be my companion; he's my Protector."

Now *I* was the one confused. Was there a difference? Cedric protected me as much as I did him, that's just how caring for someone worked, but Gwendolyn was talking like Protector meant something much different in this case.

"He's her bodyguard," Cedric assumed.

Gwendolyn dipped her head in acceptance of his answer. "Very similar to a bodyguard, yes. But we are connected on a much deeper level. We *feel* one another differently than a normal partnership."

At that explanation Cedric seemed to catch on, a light of understanding brightening his eyes. I could sense the excitement coursing through him even before he turned to me with his wide grin.

"Don't you get it, Casey?" I obviously didn't because he continued on. "Warin can *feel* her. He can sense her emotions and uses that connection to better protect her. Right?"

He directed the last question to Warin himself, who nodded. A spark of excitement awoke within me as well. Finally, I was going to get answers. They would be able to help us understand what was happening between us.

"I have so many questions," Cedric rambled.

Gwendolyn held up her hand to silence him and smirked.

"I'm sure you do." Brushing him off like nothing more than an excited child, she turned her attention back to me. "We have much to discuss and not much time left to do it. Due to the ... delay in your arrival, our timetable has significantly decreased since I last spoke with you."

Her tone suggested that she blamed this all on me, seeing as I didn't come when originally called. But I had no choice in the matter. A lot had taken place since the last time she sent for me.

"Maybe next time you should send a formal invitation."

She frowned. "I'm trying to remember what made me like your sass in the first place. It's starting to grate on my nerves now."

I smiled back at her innocently. "It's all in the delivery."

With a soft touch to her elbow, Warin pulled Gwendolyn back from whatever retort she was about to deliver. Sharing an incomprehensible look, she gave him a rewarding smile and moved on.

"How silly of me. You three must be tired from your journey. Leif here will show you to your rooms where you can rest and change before dinner. There, we will discuss what comes next. Follow the bells when they toll."

With those obscure instructions delivered, she and Warin ascended back up the spiraled steps and out of sight.

"Come along," Leif commanded when he caught me staring after their departed forms.

He took us through the closest door on our right. The hallway it led to was dark and cool, but soon brightened with the warm glow of a torchlight on the wall. The other torches simultaneously lit as well the further along we went.

The halls were a maze of turns and dead ends, each one as indifferent as the last. The tapestries that hung on the walls were impressive, but too similar for me to tell apart. Randomly placed tables, statues, and potted plants also dotted our path. How were we supposed to find our way back?

Abruptly, Leif stopped in front of an aged wooden door. Arched like many of the others in this place, it had a large cast iron knocker in the middle and a rusted doorknob.

"This room is for the ladies," Leif spoke. "The one just to the left here is for the boy."

Thinking that was all the explanation needed, he disappeared, not bothering to stick around in case we had any other questions. Pushing the worry of our future navigation aside, I shrugged my shoulders and pushed open the heavy door.

The room was nothing special. There were no fancy curtains made of expensive fabrics or overly embellished furniture. I fully expected Gwendolyn's home to look like a designer catalogue had thrown up, but was pleasantly surprised with what it actually was.

It was comfortable. Although the material of the curtains and bedsheets weren't fancy, they looked worn and soft. The carpet beneath my feet was plush and clean. And the solid oak furniture was beautiful in its timeless style.

"This isn't so bad," Falon called from where she stood at the bathroom door. "Looks like she has updated plumbing at least."

I laughed. I didn't care how modernized the accommodations were. I didn't plan on being here longer than it took to get my answers. Opening a random drawer in the massive wardrobe against the wall, I found an assortment of clothes for the taking. After changing into a fresh pair of shorts and top—that fit surprisingly well—I turned toward the four poster bed centered in the room.

I burrowed under covers that smelt of fresh cut grass and tried to settle in for a nap. I couldn't remember the last time I slept, and the past few days were finally catching up with me. Yawning so hard I heard my jaw pop, I rolled onto my side with my back to the door.

"Wake me if you hear those damn bells she was talking about," I told Falon a moment before sleep claimed me.

Chapter 35

A recurring chime shook the room. The alarm tolled, filling the chamber with an overpowering peal of church bells. The hollow knells resonated in overlapping waves, creating what would have probably been a beautiful hymn had it not been loud enough to vibrate the walls. These had to be those blasted bells Gwendolyn had mentioned.

Knowing we were being called, Falon and I covered our ears and quickly shuffled to the door. Out in the hall the bells were worse, in a smaller enclosure the echoing tolls were harsh and painful. Cedric was already waiting for us, hunched in a similar position with his hands over his ears, trying in vain to keep the reverberations at bay.

"Where … supposed to … ?" he shouted. I saw his lips move, but only made out a few of the words.

"What?" I called back.

Another round of clanging caused pressure to build behind my eyes, and I knew that any attempt at conversation was futile. Gwendolyn had said to follow the bells, so that's where I decided to start. Turning around, I guided us back in the direction we had come from earlier that afternoon. We passed a large tapestry, one that only stood out to me because the woman on the threads looked suspiciously like Gwendolyn.

I knew we were going in the right direction until the hall branched off into two corridors, one left and the other to the right. In a split second decision, I chose the one on the left, but when the sounds of our scuffled footsteps overpowered those unremitting bells we knew we'd made a wrong turn.

"I think we have to go back down the other corridor," Falon suggested, her voice a whisper against our pounding heads.

Annoyed that I had to purposefully walk back into that clamor, I agreed with her. "She freakin' *would* get pleasure out of this. Did you see her smirk when she told me to follow the bells? That bitch."

Back down the corridor we went, continuing until we once again heard the chimes and had to cover our ears from the pain. When we noticed a faded light glowing faintly from the end of the hall, the bells ceased. Just like that. I let out a breath of relief and brought my arms down from around my head.

"Thank Luthos. I was about to say 'screw it' and go back the other way," said Cedric with a dry grin.

We followed the hall to where it ended in a spacious room lit with varying candles around an archaic candelabrum. It was hung above an expansive mahogany table with enough seats to sit nearly twenty people. Only five of its settings were arranged tonight. Gwendolyn was already seated at the head of the table with her ever present bodyguard to her right.

"Didn't I tell you, Warin? They would find their way eventually." Looking at me, she winked. "I'm sure you noticed the bells can be quite persuasive."

I held back the growl that crawled up the back of my throat and pulled out a chair. Gwendolyn was getting on my last nerve. She was trying to play house when all I wanted to do was get some answers. Was this dinner really necessary? It's not like Cedric or I could eat food made in Faerie.

"You seem agitated, Casey. Penny for your thoughts?" Gwendolyn twittered.

"I was just trying to figure you out. You say you can help me, and yet all I've learned is that your house is weird and you have sheets that smell delicious." The sarcasm in my tone was obvious, but she didn't seem affronted. "When are you going to answer my questions?"

Gwendolyn tsked me, her finger wagging back and forth like she was scolding a child. "Patience, Casey. I'm trying to be a good host for my guests."

"By inviting us to a dinner we can't eat? Real hospitable." I growled.

She took a sip from the pewter goblet in front of her, taking her time before answering.

"I'll have you know, I took the liberty of ordering food from *outside* Faerie and having it delivered. Do you like chicken? Leif says the mortals have some Colonel with a secret recipe that you might enjoy."

Cedric nearly sprayed his drink across the table. He looked to me to confirm what he thought he'd heard, but I was just as surprised as he was. Gwendolyn couldn't be serious. Just to prove me wrong, in walked Leif with a giant bucket from KFC that he set in the middle of the table. Beside it he placed a tray with all the fixings and began to serve them out on the fine china before us.

We sat in silence as Leif finished, glancing at one another as we waited for the punchline. The fried chicken and mashed potatoes looked out of place in this room. A roasted pig with an apple stuffed in its mouth would fit the venue better.

"Now that we have that little problem out of the way, we can talk about your schedule," Gwendolyn chirped.

She was poking a drumstick with her fork, obviously displeased with her meal for the night. Warin on the other hand, didn't seem to care. He was shoving food in his mouth faster than Cedric, and that was saying something.

"We don't plan on staying that long. I just need to learn whatever it is that will allow me to control my power and then we're gone. Maybe have a few questions answered while we're at it."

A laugh escaped from Gwendolyn's lips, and she quickly covered her mouth with the back of her hand.

"What confidence you have. How long do you expect this task of yours to take?" she asked, clearly amused.

"I figured a few hours would suffice," I replied with a scowl.

My answer pulled another laugh from her, and even Warin had a chuckle or two at my expense.

"Honey, it will take more than a couple hours for you to learn what you must to gain control." She held up her hand to keep me from countering. "I will work with you until I deem you fit enough to leave. In the meantime, Cedric can work with Warin and the young princess can do as she wishes."

Cedric seemed willing enough to follow that plan. I knew he'd been dying to get answers from Warin since he'd learned of the Protector's connection with his charge. He would have no problem agreeing with her plan.

Falon only shrugged when I looked at her. "As long as I don't have to go near my mother's court while I'm here, I don't care."

I huffed. Neither one of them were much help. I needed to get back to the Academy. There were people there suffering under the hands of the Dean; people I cared deeply for. Distant memories of Eli rose to the surface of my mind. I'd forced myself to keep them at bay, but there was little I could to in that moment.

I wanted to go home. I *needed* to go home. But I also needed to learn what I could from Gwendolyn. My uncontrolled power could easily be a weakness the Dean could exploit, and I refused to become a weapon used against my friends.

"Very well," I replied. "I'll work with you, *if* you also answer any questions I have while I'm here."

Gwendolyn nodded her agreement. "You have a deal. Although, you might not like the answers you so desperately seek."

"Do hurry up. You're moving slower than a herd of turtles through peanut butter."

I bit back my retort and instead focused on trying to put one foot in front of the other, anger at Gwendolyn's words fueling my forward movement. Ahead of me, lying in an ever-growing pool of effervescent blood, was an Imp. Her pointed ears drooped with fatigue as more blood left her small body. Her once agile tail lay limp beside her, the tiny tuff of hair at the end lying flat in the grass.

This morning, after deliberately avoiding my questions at breakfast, Gwendolyn had Warin escort me here to the "training grounds." In the midst of hundreds of long hallways and endless rooms, the center of Gwendolyn's home opened to a wild field of swaying grass boarded and protected by high walls of aged stone. Trees and boulders dotted the strip of land the size of a football field and created a terrain unique and perfect for all types of drills and exercises.

Some would call it a courtyard, but I called it the torture arena. Currently, Gwendolyn lounged in a plush chair underneath the shade of an overgrown tree and appeared, to the world and anyone who looked, as bored out of her mind. But I could feel her eyes tracking my sluggish movements.

"I've seen severed limbs crawl faster than you. Move your ass!" she shouted as she came to her feet. She watched me struggle a little longer before stomping over to the dying Imp.

"She'd be dead if this were a real accident," she criticized and put her hands over the slashes in the Imp's wrists.

I could sense life returning to the frail body. Each second that passed brought strength to the once flickering force. Bouncing to her feet like she wasn't just seconds away from death, the Imp stuck her tongue out at me and vanished with a blink. With her wounds gone, there was nothing left to call on my power and the ice running through my veins dissolved.

My body pitched forward like it was on the end of a tugged string. I spit dirt out of my mouth and glared at the Fae bitch before me.

"I would have gotten it," I grumbled, knowing full well I'd been moving too slow.

"No you wouldn't have. But I think now I know why."

Gwendolyn snapped her fingers and I looked around, thinking she was calling a servant or something. But instead of someone appearing with a tray of drinks, Gwendolyn's plush chair moved itself from under the tree to in front of my face. My esteemed host took her time getting comfortable, and it didn't escape my notice that a cozy chair was not offered for me as well.

Refusing to let the immature snide get to me, I made myself at home on the feathery grass and leaned back on my hands.

"Do tell," I prompted, honestly hoping that she had an idea of how to fix this.

She ignored my attitude and crossed her ankles. "Your power is not your own, but an extension of mine. Because of that, I get an impression each time you use it and have been monitoring your progress. You've done well for learning as you go, but you should have come to me sooner."

There was no point in arguing with her. She knew why I hadn't come the first time she called, and I wasn't about to explain it again. The fact that this power wasn't mine kind of pissed me off, though.

"What do you mean an extension of yours? Can't you just hand it over already?"

It seemed unfair to me that I should have to fight so hard to control a power that Gwendolyn obviously wanted me to have. The damn thing almost killed me multiple times and was a risk each time I used it.

"I can't just *give* it to you. The next Healer gains her powers either when she matures or the current one dies."

"But witches don't mature until eighteen!" I cried. "You expect me to deal with this for another year and a half?"

I couldn't believe what I was hearing. The Dean needed to be dealt with now, not when I turned eighteen. A year and a half couldn't go by with him still in control, I wouldn't let it. But the Dean knew about my power, how it worked, its weaknesses. Unless I learned to control it, this power would make me into the worst kind of liability.

"Stop with the sad puppy dog eyes. This isn't a death sentence. I can help you to control your power until it is well and truly *yours*."

Gwendolyn stared me down, silently asking if I was willing to put in the work to succeed. I nodded at her unspoken question. I would do whatever it took to master this. There was no other option.

"Very well," she acquiesced. And we began.

"Major injuries might still pose a problem, but there is no reason for you to become a human popsicle at the slightest cut." Gwendolyn slid a knife across the skin of her arm as she spoke.

As I watched the blood well up in a thin line of ruby droplets, the tangy scent of copper tickled the back of my throat just as my fingers froze with the oncoming frost. Dammit.

"What do you feel?" she asked.

"It's like a cold current inside my body. It comes from the center of me before branching out." Even now I could feel my limbs locking into place.

One by one, I lost control of portions of my body until I was completely trapped under the spell of the blood before me. Gwendolyn's head tilted to the side.

"You said it feels cold?"

I nodded. "Yeah. Like ice."

I tried to lift my arm, but it hung like dead weight at my side. I was out of practice, but knew that I was capable of controlling this wayward power. I concentrated, forcing all my energy toward my fingers, refusing to let up until they obeyed my commands.

"Hmm. Why the center?" Gwendolyn's voice interrupted my thoughts, and I lost control.

My raised hand once again fell to my side. "I put it there. When we tried to control this before, I kind of forced the coldness into a ball in the center of my chest, and I've been pulling on it from there."

She made a small sound of surprise. "You have better control than I thought. The hard part is already done. Your problem is that the ball is too big, and it's overwhelming you from the inside. Make it smaller, tighter."

I did as she asked. I turned my thoughts inside until I could see the source of my power in my mind's eye. There, right in the center, swirled a massive crystal blue ball of raw energy. I strained to grasp it, to get a tight enough hold on it. It took all of my determination and will, but I forced it to condense.

I watched it grow smaller and tighter until all that remained was a silver-blue ball no bigger than a fig. A stray strand of power extended out from the back of it, leading down, down, down to the darkest depths of me. I knew what resided there. I double checked that its cage was locked up tight and made my way back to the surface.

When I opened my eyes again the sunlight had faded and fireflies danced around my fallen body. Gwendolyn still sat in her chair, a small cup of what smelled like herbal tea in her hand. She held it out to me, and I eagerly drank its contents.

My limbs shook and my stomach rolled. It took all my energy just to swallow, but I had done it. Proud and a little rejuvenated from what was in the cup, I handed it back to Gwendolyn.

"What's your power like?" I asked her, curious.

"It's similar to yours. Mine appears to me as a ball of flame, brighter and hotter than a thousand suns combined. Like you, I pull strands from it as needed."

Her words refused to settle in my mind. Was it because of my wayward control over frost that I was different? Or did that control change how my Healer's power portrayed itself? And what about the beast—how did it fit into all this?

"Why does mine appear as ice while yours is fire?" I asked her, silently begging that she would answer me this time. "And it's not just my healing power. I have control over frost as a physical thing as well. It's leashed to this … this beast inside me. Maybe I'm going crazy, but I hoped you could help me. Why is my healing different than yours?"

Gwendolyn was silent for what felt like an eternity. A desolate and desperate part of my brain cried out that she was going to ignore us once again. But she didn't.

"These are not questions that you need to be asking me." My heart sank. She *was* going to brush me off. "There are things you need to learn about yourself before I can help you further. Come with me."

She stood and walked past me, her footsteps glowing faintly in the grass. After a moment's hesitation, I followed. Through the silent hallways we moved like wraiths, invisible to everyone around us. The house was quiet on this side, an eerie silence that screamed abandonment. Not many people dared to travel here.

Gwendolyn stopped at a random door and pushed. I was hit with the scents of aged paper and ink and knew we were in a library before my eyes even saw the first book. What I didn't expect was the person sitting behind the mahogany desk, looking for all the world as if she belonged there.

Her bleached white hair stood out in contrast to the warm colors around her. She looked no different than the last time she stood before me, when she helped me and my friends to escape.

"Snow," I whispered. "What are you doing here?"

Chapter 36

Only the soft crackling of the fireplace punctured the aged silence of the room. Moth-eaten hardcovers and first-edition novels lined the shelves from floor to ceiling, helping to muffle the uninterested sounds Snow made from the desk.

I watched her from the corner of my eye as I took a seat in one of the overly fluffed chairs across from her. *Let her try to ignore me now,* I thought. Except so far, she was doing a good job of it. Her ivory hair hung straight past her shoulders and she firmly brushed the small strands aside that fell into her eyes when she leaned over.

She looked exactly the same, and the sight of her brought back unwelcome feelings I thought I'd buried. Anger boiled within me, familiar in its burn. The last time I saw Snow my world had fallen apart. I had been tortured and forced to flee from my home, forced to run from a power hungry Shifter with no regard for those that stood in his way.

After years of humiliation at the hands of this woman I once knew as my teacher, Snow flipped a switch that night and helped me to escape. But she hadn't let me wait for Eli, and the result of that was something I tried hard to not think about.

"I see you're still just as stubborn as you always were. Good to see your time on the run hasn't changed you much."

Snow's comments caught me by surprise, and I jumped. Bringing my focus back to the present, I met her gaze and held it. I felt her eyes wander over me, scrutinizing. Part of me wanted to hide from her calculated look. Could she seem them? Were my scars as obvious to her as they felt to me?

For a moment, I worried about what she thought of me, of who I'd turned into. A small voice inside me raised its head and screamed its outrage. Why should I care about what this woman thought? I had been through hell since the last time I sat in her classroom. There had been multiple people vying for my head, and one man even tried his best to break me.

I may be different now because of it, but I was damn proud to have survived. I refused to let her belittle that. The moment I accepted myself, broken pieces and all, Snow nodded, pleased with what she saw.

"Why are you here?" I asked. Seeing her here was the last thing I expected when Gwendolyn opened those doors.

"I knew you'd find your way here eventually and so ... I waited."

"But *how* did you know?"

Snow put down the pen she was writing with and leaned back in her chair. A thin pair of wire-framed glasses were perched on the tip of her nose and she removed them, setting them off to the side.

"I've been watching you, Casey, since long before you were born. I foresaw your coming and knew exactly who you were that night Eli brought you to my classroom."

A small shiver worked its way up my spine as I listened to her speak. Her voice resonated, the words filled with power as her pale eyes began to glow.

"I am the Seer, a Witch once a generation who is gifted with the Sight. I was chosen to document and record the history of our people."

Silence was a heavy blanket over the room, even the fire refused to break the stillness that surrounded us. Snow's revelation came as a shock, but was buffered by the fact that I already knew there was a Seer. I just hadn't known that she had been my teacher for the last ten years.

"So you knew I was going to be the next Healer?" I asked in a small voice, still trying to focus my thoughts.

She nodded. "And so much more. I knew you wouldn't be able to pick one of the elements presented to you because you already had an affinity for one that wasn't provided."

"And why wasn't it provided?"

Snow didn't answer. She only looked at me, patiently waiting for me to figure it out for myself. When I didn't reach a conclusion fast enough, she offered more help.

"What are the four elements that Witches have a connection with?" she asked.

I rolled my eyes. "Seriously?"

Snow raised an eyebrow, impatient now.

I sighed. "Water, Fire, Earth, and Air." *Der*, I mentally added.

"And anything outside those four?" she prompted.

Was she testing to see if I'd paid attention in her class? It sounded like something she would do.

"Only Vampires control anything different," I scoffed.

Rather than acknowledge that I was right, Snow only relaxed into her chair with her arms folded across her chest. Her selective silence was getting on my nerves.

"Can't you just tell me?" I growled.

"Why tell you what you already know?" she countered.

I growled again. She wanted me to figure it out for myself, I got that, but it was frustrating as hell.

"How is it, do you think, that you are able to distinguish a Vampire from the other races?" she asked, going completely off topic. I didn't even bother asking how she knew.

"I don't know. I assumed it was—"

"And you can control ice, a power that you know to be affiliated with them," she continued.

"Wait—" She was going too fast. Her words were leading to a conclusion I'd fought so hard to keep from being true.

"The facts have been gathering before you for some time now," she all but whispered, waiting for me to accept what she was saying.

I shook my head, like the action would keep her words from being heard.

"Stop. You don't know what you're talking about."

She lifted a brow. "Don't I?" Resting her palms flat on the desk, she stood. Her gaze was penetrating, like she was looking straight through me. "Enough hiding, Casey. The time has come to accept who you are."

My eyes widened and met hers, begging for her to change her mind and tell me that I was wrong.

"There's no way. You can't honestly believe that I'm a-a *Vampire*!" I practically screamed the word. "It's not possible. I don't drink blood. Look, I have no fangs!"

I was standing in front of the desk, pulling my lips back to reveal normal teeth. I was half lost to hysterics, split between demanding that she tell me the truth and swearing that what she thought was wrong. Snow waited for me to calm down, not moving to speak until I was once again seated in the chair with a hollow glaze to my eye.

"You are *half* Vampire," Snow stated, her tone leaving no room for argument. "Your Witch genes took precedence, but there are a few attributes that you inherited from your sire. The control over frost being one of them."

I didn't bother arguing this time. The fight was all drained out of me. The longer I sat there the more I knew she was right.

"Can you think of nothing else that you share in similarity?" she asked.

I started to shake my head, but then stopped. Inside myself sat the small silver-blue ball that was the center of my power. The reason it was cold instead of warm as Gwendolyn had described was now suddenly clear to me. How had I not made the connection before?

I checked out the small sphere of power from all angles as if I was seeing it for the first time. A thin strand led from the back to a darker place further inside me. It led to the beast. Unwittingly, I thought back to the night Orin and his men let their own beasts loose to help us escape the Imperials.

"There's a thing inside me—it's linked to my power. When I get scared or overwhelmed, or lose control and give into it ..." I shuddered. "It's paralyzing in its power."

Snow nodded, "It's part of the curse that all Vampires bear and it seems you will be no different. You are fortunate that your sire is around to teach you how to control it."

I gasped, the sound unusually loud in our quiet room. My fingers dug into the armrests of my chair as I leaned forward. "You know my sire?"

She inclined her head. "As do you."

I slumped back in my chair, my teeth worrying my lip in confusion. Details and their inevitable conclusions lined up in my mind, clicking into place. From my time at the training camp, I had come to know many Vampires, but only one had a known relationship with my mother. The same Vampire who also had control over ice. I wondered at how long Snow knew the truth. Had she known the night Eli brought me home that my father was still alive? Why didn't she expose me?

"Orin. He's my father." Snow nodded, only confirming my assumption. "You knew I was half ... Vampire the minute I arrived. Why protect me? You've never liked me, so why not kill me?" I asked.

For the first time that night, Snow's expression softened. "I'm sorry for what you had to endure growing up and for my part in it, but I needed you to be overlooked. I knew what you would mean to our world if you succeeded. I foresaw you as the fulfiller of the prophecy, and it only became more clear the older you grew."

And so we had come full circle. My safe world had ended with my knowledge of the prophecy and here it was again, still bringing death and torment with it. The only difference between then and now was that I was finally beginning to accept the role I had been destined to play.

"Upon the sixteenth year it shall begin,
She who calls to Fire but is born of Ice
From two separate worlds she will unite.
Born at the peak of the midnight hour,
A Daughter of the elements and wielder of power.
Through her sacrifice the fighting shall cease,
The Healer of races and bringer of peace."

Snow recited the prophecy from memory, her eyes taking on that weird glow again as she did so. When she finished we sat in silence. I thought about the words, finding multiple similarities between them and my life the longer I considered them.

"Your power revealed itself upon your sixteenth birthday, did it not? And at what hour were you born?" Snow asked.

"Midnight," I whispered. I knew where Snow was going with her line of questioning, but I didn't fight her.

"You are the daughter of the elements but forged from two separate worlds—that would be both the Vampires and Witches. I think that part is quite obvious to you now, yes? So let's see … you are born of ice, but call to fire." She tapped her finger against her chin absentmindedly. "I know Gwendolyn thinks Cedric is your Protector, so that might be the answer."

It was all starting to make sense now. The deeper we delved into the details the more I saw my life in those words.

"But what sacrifice? Surely I've sacrificed enough already?"

Snow sadly shook her head. "This I cannot see yet, child. It is tightly woven with your fate, and there are still many paths you could yet take. It's possible that you could have already met with the sacrifice required, but with your main adversary still unchallenged, it's highly unlikely."

Great. What more could the universe throw at me?

"It's best to not think on the words too literally. One never knows how they will come to pass," Snow advised. "Instead, focus on growing with your power. There is another that must be taken care of before you can truly fulfill the prophecy."

I knew who she meant: the Dean. He was still in control, still the leader of our Council with unlimited power and reach. A majority of the Imperials were loyal to him, and no one would listen to what I had to say until he was dealt with. That was all beside the fact that he was corrupted and needed to be put down.

"Can you see what will happen, you know, with the Dean?" I asked her, hoping for some good news for once.

But her answer was as vague as ever. "There are still many outcomes possible at this time."

She put her glasses back on, wiggling them until they aligned perfectly. Then, without a word of dismissal, she went back to her work. I knew she was finished with me for the time being, and I quietly let myself out.

I leaned against the wall outside the library doors. The coolness of the stone helped to clear my head, but it wouldn't silence my thoughts. I was half-Vampire and *Orin* was my father. I wasn't sure how I felt about it. I had spent my entire life being told that Vampires were evil, so naturally my first reaction was to still think that way. But after months of living, learning, and working alongside them, I now knew differently.

There was definitely a dark side to them, their inner beast was something to fear. But it seemed like I had one of those as well, so how could I argue with that? And Orin ... he was a good man, even if he pissed me off.

I had grown close with him on our journey to the camp, and despite how I left things, I missed him. Could I see him as my father? I wasn't sure. Eli had filled that role for me for as long as I could remember. He was the one who raised me, bandaged my wounds, and cared about my well-being. I wasn't sure what to think.

My head throbbed with a fresh headache, and all I wanted to do was lie down and turn my mind off. I glanced left and then right, seeing a nondescript hallway that looked exactly like every other one in this place.

"How the hell do I get back?" I murmured.

Like a blessing from the universe, Leif appeared at my side. For once, he had no smart comment to give me about my appearance or lack of following directions. Instead, he seemed to understand that I would not be up to my usual par of verbal banter.

"Follow me," he said, grabbing the hem of my sock and pulling me along.

I allowed him to lead, mindlessly turning when the tug on my foot pulled me in that direction. I took no notice of the rooms we passed or of the people inside them. We must have passed open windows, this place had a ton of them, but I couldn't tell you what the weather was like outside. There could have been a twister on the front lawn or Falon could have been petting a dragon, I didn't care.

The pull on my sock ceased, but it took me a while to notice. When I finally looked up, Leif was gone and I was standing in front of the door to my room. A soft push was all it took for the chunk of aged wood to swing inward. The window on the far side of the room was open, allowing a gentle breeze to caress the gauzy curtains until they billowed outward, bringing with them the scents of spring and earth.

I sat on the end of my bed, sinking into the plush mattress as I stared at the blank wall across from me. My life had taken another unexpected turn, and I wasn't sure how I felt about this change in direction. How did one wrap their head around something like this? I wasn't debating its realism; I knew that what Snow said was true. It was something I felt deep inside, something that couldn't be denied. *I* could deal with my newfound heritage ... but could everyone else?

What would Orin think about having a daughter? About *me* being his daughter? And my friends, they've grown up in the same world I did, a world that saw Vampires as the enemy. Sure, maybe history got a few things wrong, but I couldn't be one hundred percent sure that they would accept me. I didn't even want to think about my fellow Witches.

Was I going to have to hide from my own kind? Maybe going back to defeat the Dean wasn't such a good idea. Once word got out about me, I would be on every major hit list. I fell back until my head rested against the cream colored duvet. The ceiling above me was an obscure pattern of wooden beams and missed cobwebs.

I allowed my mind to shut down, to wander and think of trivial things instead of the shit show my life had turned into. Maybe, if I lie here long enough, people would just forget about me and I could live out the rest of my life in peace. It was wishful thinking.

Chapter 37

I was unsure of how much time had passed since my talk with Snow in the library. The moon now shone through my window in all its glory, the playful wind still dancing with my curtains. Falon had yet to return to our room, and no annoying bells demanded that I appear at dinner.

I *was* hungry. My stomach growled to remind me of that fact every fifteen minutes or so, but I didn't feel like interacting with anyone. I knew I would eventually have to, but I hoped to at least avoid it until tomorrow.

Highly unlikely. A hollow thud against the stone wall was the only warning I received before Cedric barged in; an expression of pure eagerness and pride plastered across his handsome face.

"You will never believe what Warin taught me today!" he started.

He sat on Falon's bed for a couple seconds before standing and pacing the floor next to me. There was no containing him, the excitement was wound too tight. He didn't even notice that I hadn't moved from my starfish position across the bed.

"—and he says that I'm a natural, and that you'll be lucky to have me as your Protector. He really is an awesome guy, Casey. I hope you have time soon to talk with him more. Hey, are you even listening?"

He pushed on my shoulder to try and get me to turn over. My head was buried under my pillow, but the small bundle of feathers did nothing to keep him out.

"You didn't show up for dinner tonight, is everything— Shit."

The bed sunk in beside me as Cedric's knees pushed down on the mattress. He pulled the pillow off my head, and with a small grunt, he rolled me over onto my back. I watched him through the tangled strands of hair over my face. His eyes went from concerned, to understanding, to confused almost simultaneously.

"I'm so sorry, Casey. I would have come sooner but Warin taught me how to turn off whatever it is that allows me to feel you, and I forgot to

277

tune back in. But that's no excuse; I should have paid closer attention." His brows creased with worry. "Luthos, what happened?"

His massive frame loomed over me as he looked down on my pathetic form. My heart thudded in unwarranted fear before my brain took over. This was Cedric, he wasn't trying to hurt me. It took a moment to cycle through all the crap my initial instincts started, but Cedric sat patiently at my side through all of it, not moving until I got my emotions under control.

When I opened my arms to him, he didn't hesitate. Scooting in closer beside me, he slid his arm beneath my side and pulled me against him. Using his other hand, he gently brushed my tousled hair from my face and gave me a small smile.

"Talk to me," he said.

And so I did. Once I opened my mouth it all came pouring out—every word discussed between me and Snow, every thought that had been running through my head since this afternoon, my fears and anxieties over what was to come. I had opened the floodgates, and soon I was even bombarding him with my suppressed feelings from my time with Kael.

Cedric sat silent through it all, taking in everything I threw at him. He nodded when it was expected and wiped my tears when they made my hair stick to my cheeks. I found myself snuggling in closer to him, unafraid of how I felt in his arms. By talking with him and finally opening myself to the pain, I was able to separate my feelings.

I could see the obvious difference in how Kael touched me to how Cedric held me now. I didn't understand how I could have confused it with something this real, and I was slightly ashamed that I had allowed myself to hide those feelings for so long. When I was finished and all my words had been spent, the first thing Cedric did was kiss me.

His lips were as soft as the butterflies that fluttered in my stomach. He was in no rush, taking his time to make sure I was comfortable before pressing his mouth harder against mine. His tongue brazenly asked for entrance as it gently stroked along my bottom lip. When my mouth opened beneath his and his breath mixed with mine, I tasted cinnamon. My heart skipped a beat, or two, then continued on in a rushed cadence.

His hand that cupped my cheek slowly traveled down my side, lingering in the curve of my hip, before gliding back up to my neck. Goosebumps broke out across my skin as I threw myself deeper into the kiss. I missed this connection between us. I'd avoided it for too long, and now I wanted more.

I slipped my hand along his cheek to behind his head and pulled him closer, trying to change the pace. He was treating me like I was breakable, but in that moment I felt stronger and more daring than ever before. I nipped at his lower lip, prompting him to act. Our breaths came in pants and our lips moved faster, clashing over and over until I became lost in it.

My hand clutched at his hair, tugging and pulling to match our frantic pace. Cedric tenderly gripped my wrist and pulled my fingers away. Before I noticed what he was doing, he had my hand held tightly against the small of my back.

He then pushed us back until my arm was successfully pinned behind me. I growled in frustration when he slowed our pace. With a resigned sigh, Cedric pulled back until his lips rested just inches away.

"Why'd you stop?" I whispered, my voice hoarse and confused.

Cedric rested his forehead against mine. "I only meant to talk to you, to reassure you. But when you leaned into me … with you so close, I just had to kiss you."

He placed another quick peck on my lips before letting out a groan and rolling away. We lay next to each other, close but not touching as we allowed our racing hearts to settle. After a few minutes of silence, Cedric reached over and threaded his fingers between mine. Looking over at me, he smiled before tugging me forward.

"Let's go," he said, bringing us to our feet.

I almost fell over, but his grip on my hand kept my face from eating the floor.

"Where are we going?" I asked, a bit disoriented.

He wrapped his arms around my waist to help settle my balance. His touch brought with it no fear, only comfort and a stirring of excitement. A smile tugged at my cheeks. It felt normal, felt right, to have him hold me like this. I hated how Kael made me feel about myself, and I wasn't sure if it was something I would ever get over.

But standing here with Cedric, I knew there was hope for us.

"Come on." Cedric started walking toward the bedroom door, towing me along behind him.

His grin was mischievous when he glanced back at me, holding a finger to his lips. I fought back a giggle—memories of the two of us sneaking around the Academy after hours fresh in my mind. He peeked out into the hall, checking that the coast was clear, before leading the way at a slight trot.

We snuck down the empty hallways like two ghosts. Our muted footsteps were the only sounds as Cedric lead me around darkened corners and across open doorways. I hesitated at a flight of stone steps that ended in a patch of pitch-black darkness, but Cedric called a flame to his palm and winked at me before descending. Attached at the hand, I had no choice but to follow.

We walked down only two flights before a warm glow outshined the one burning in Cedric's palm. The bottom step opened up into an antiquated kitchen complete with a working hearth. The walls and floor were made of solid stone while the ceiling above us was held aloft by thick wooden beams. A massive oak table sat in the middle of the room with various materials spread across it.

Cedric reached for the hand-woven basket in the center. Soft bread, still steaming, sat nestled inside the cloth and a plate of cheese enticed me from next to the fresh rolls.

"How did you …" I trailed off, my mind obviously putting together how he knew that I was hungry.

"Don't worry, this stuff is safe for us mortals," Cedric teased, before taking a bite out of a roll.

I could have kissed him again. My stomach clenched with pain as the scent of the warm bread reached me. Taking a seat at one of the stools along the table, I grabbed a slice of cheese and nibbled at it while reaching for a roll.

We ate in comfortable silence until nothing but crumbs were left. With my stomach no longer screaming with hunger, I was able to think more clearly.

By the way Cedric kissed me earlier, it was safe to assume that he didn't have a problem with my being half vampire. Having his support meant more to me than I think he knew, but that still didn't solve my problem.

Others of our race would not be as understanding. I risked persecution, imprisonment, and even death if my true heritage was revealed. On the other hand, the Dean *needed* to be defeated. I refused to let him get away with all that he's done both to me and my mother. My life could have been exponentially different if he had just left her alone.

"Here you are." Falon came skipping down the steps, her blonde hair floating after her. "I haven't seen you all day, Casey. Where have you been?"

I spared a glance at Cedric, silently asking what I should do. He frowned at me and nodded to the bottom step where Falon still stood. I sighed, understanding his hint. Falon was one of my best friends, and she had a right to know what was going on with me. We vowed to be honest with each other, and I wasn't upholding my end of that promise.

"Sorry, Fal, it's been a long day." I gestured for her to sit in the empty stool next to me. "I've learned some things today that you should know too."

"Somber much?" she joked, but I could see the concern pulling at the corners of her grin.

I didn't return her smile. I focused on making sure my teeth didn't bite through my bottom lip as I gathered my courage. Cedric delivered a not-so-subtle kick to my shin beneath the table.

"Ouch, Ced. That *hurt.*" I glared at him and tried to kick back, but he had already moved his legs.

"Get on with it, Casey. You're only making it harder," he replied.

I knew he was right. It didn't make the words come any faster though. I looked back at Falon whose expression was now more annoyed than worried.

"*I'mhalfvampire,*" I rushed out and not-so-patiently waited for her to react.

"So let me get this straight." Falon held up her fingers, ticking them off one at a time. "Orin is your father, making you half Vampire, half Witch—because of this you can control frost. On top of that, you now know for sure that the prophecy is centered around you, and as such, it is your job to defeat some Big Bad through an unknown sacrifice. Did I miss anything?"

I shook my head. "That about covers it."

"I can see how that would freak you out," she replied.

Cedric snorted. "That would be an understatement."

My foot managed to make contact with his shin this time, and his resulting wince caused me to smile. Cedric's indignation faded into a responding laugh, and soon the three of us couldn't stop chuckling. The cracks in my heart closed a little more as I basked in the acceptance of my friends. No matter what awaited me back home, I knew I could rely on their support.

We sat in the kitchen far longer than intended, discussing what was to come in the near future. We were unsure of how long we would be here, seeing as our departure was at Gwendolyn's discretion. There was plenty more to learn about my power, and I knew Cedric had an endless amount of questions for Warin.

Falon, the only one of our group without a current mentor, passed her time among the different Faerie classes. She continued to work on her fighting techniques with the few willing to teach her and had learned many useful skills in the days we'd been here—her knife throwing had improved and one of the brownies taught her how to pick a lock.

"What are we going to do when it's time to go back?" I asked them during one of our hushed pauses.

They looked back at me confused, unsure of what I was asking.

"What is there to figure out?" Cedric asked. "We go back, kick the Dean's ass, then life goes back to normal. Simple."

If only it were. I had still much to learn before I was ready to become a guardian, but I didn't know how I was going to be able to return to my old life. Algebra, curfews, and high school drama seemed dim in comparison to all that had happened and all that was yet to come.

"Okay, so we somehow manage to defeat the Dean, then what? What happens when knowledge of my heritage gets out? Once they hear the word Vampire, the Council isn't going to care that I was raised a Witch."

The expressions on their faces told me that I was right. If the truth of who I really was got out, I would never be allowed to return to my old life. And what about Orin and his men? The others from the camp? They all deserved a home that wasn't buried under mud half the year. They deserved acceptance just as much as I did.

"But ... what if we could change their minds?" I wondered aloud.

"Change whose minds?" Falon asked.

Excitement had me clutched in its over eager claws. "Everyone! We can change the minds of everyone at that school."

Now that I thought about it, it seemed so obvious. I was half Vampire and half Witch—what if I was meant to be the bridge between the races? I'd lived in both worlds, and I knew the truth behind the rumors and lies. If I could get my classmates and teachers to accept me, the real me, then it wouldn't be much of a stretch for them to accept Orin and others like him.

I knew Eli would be on my side, and we had Snow as well—a Seer's word was almost law.

"Once we've won over *our* school, we can move on to the others. With enough support behind us, the Council would have to listen." I was smiling now, a full on cheeky grin that I couldn't contain.

"I don't know, Casey. That's a risky plan. What if it doesn't work? You'll be imprisoned ... or worse." Falon whispered, unsure.

I knew it was a stretch. There were too many variables of this plan that could go wrong. My classmates could just use this as a new excuse to hate me, my teachers might not listen to what I had to say, hell, the Council could just say "screw this" and imprison me anyway. But I had to try.

I didn't want to live the rest of my life cocooned within a perilous secret. I would never be able to settle, would never stop looking over my shoulder and wondering when the truth would be exposed.

"What other option is there? Would you be okay with living the rest of your life like this? Running from our laws, hiding wherever I can, never staying in once place or feeling safe? Because that's what my life will be like if I don't do *something*."

I could tell that Cedric was going to need more convincing, but now was not the time to push it. I was exhausted. The warm food filled my belly and pulled at my eyelids. All I wanted to do was find my bed and sleep until noon.

Cedric's flame lit the way as we traversed the many hallways and found our way back to our respective rooms. The sheets on my bed were still rumbled and twisted from when Cedric and I were last here. The memories of that moment brought a crimson burn to my cheeks as I unconsciously brought my fingers to my lips.

"We've still got time to figure it out." Falon's voice carried over from her bed.

The window had been closed and the curtains drawn, the only light came from small glowing algae in the room's far corners. Still, I could make out her shape and heard the rustling of her sheets.

"And you know that whatever you decide, we'll stand by you." She finished with a yawn.

I smiled in the darkness, my heart glowing with a love so bright it could rival the full moon. I really did have the best friends in the world. I fell asleep like that, with a smile on my face and a heart full of hope.

Chapter 38

A loud crash, like the clanging of a gong, disturbed our tranquil sleep. The ringing rebounded inside my head more frantic than a bouncy ball in a small room. I jerked up in bed, the sheets sliding around my waist as I covered my ears. Not *again.*

I looked left to where Falon lay and watched her react in much the same way I just had. It didn't feel like much time had passed since we returned from our midnight excursion to the kitchen, but my mouth was dry and my eyes burned as I tried to keep them open. Sunlight shone through the window, muted by the sheer curtains, but offensive to our eyes either way. The alarm continued to blare while Falon and I danced around one-footed, trying to put on our pants with the grace of a half dead ballerina.

"What the hell is she calling us for?" I shouted to Falon.

Having acclimated ourselves to the set meal times, the alarm bells hadn't been used since our first day here. We knew the general layout of the home, at least to the areas we most frequented, and the dining room was one of those. So why the bells?

"My eyelids feel like sandpaper," Falon whined as we ran for the door, foregoing shoes in favor of escaping the deafening tolls.

In the hall, Cedric waited for us with his hands pushing on each side of his head.

"Do either of you know what this is about?" he yelled, fighting to be heard.

We shook our heads. We didn't even know where we were supposed to go. Hoping that the bells would lead us like last time, we started off at a fast walk down the hall. Thankfully, it *was* just like before. When we noticed the obnoxious chimes beginning to fade, we turned around and went the other way.

I paid no attention to where we were going. I didn't stop to identify landmarks and I didn't try to suggest a direction, I focused solely on following the damn bells. The faster we got to where they led, the faster they would shut up. When the alarm ceased its tolls and the clamor faded, it was a shock to all of us when we found ourselves at the archway leading to Gwendolyn's greeting hall.

Our elusive host already stood off to the side speaking to whoever had just arrived. Warin stood guard behind her right shoulder, a picture perfect Protector. The guest in front of them was dressed in finely crafted armor. The metal was thin, resembling a normal tunic when he moved, but was as sleek and glossy as a full suit of battle mail. A genuine, straight from medieval times sword hung at his side.

Carved into the front of the warrior's breastplate was a delicate engraving of a fiery sun. From behind it a massive tree sprouted strong and full, its branches heavy with thick leaves and flowers in full bloom.

"He's from the Summer Court," Falon whispered. "That's my mother's crest."

Her face was leeched of all color as she watched the warrior give a short, respectful bow to Gwendolyn before approaching the archway where we stood. Falon attempted to scoot behind us, but realized that the warrior already knew she was there. Rather than lose respect by hiding, she instead chose to stand beside me, back straight and hands clasped behind her to hide her trembling.

The Fae stranger approached and stopped three feet in front of Falon. He bowed at the waist, his head coming level to her chest with his fist over his heart.

"Princess, forgive the unannounced visit, but I have received orders to check on your wellbeing. I have traveled far to gain proof of your health and condition."

It was clear who the orders were from, and the confirmation that the queen knew Falon's whereabouts was enough to have her break her stance and grab my hand. The queen's messenger remained in his bow until Falon gave her acknowledgment. When she didn't move, I elbowed her in the side.

Clearing her throat, she finally spoke. "Thank you, knight. The fidelity of your person has been noted. Please return with the message that all is well and the concern is appreciated."

At her dismissive response, the Fae rose from his bow and placed a hand on the hilt of his sword. Cedric and I stepped closer, both of us flanking Falon at his movement. His weapon remained sheathed, but the air became charged with unspoken intent.

"I apologize; my message must not have been clear. I am to bring back *proof* of this wellbeing. You must return with me to show in person the truth of your words."

His face was that of chiseled marble: impassive, not revealing a single hint as to how he felt about his orders. There was no empathy in his eyes for Falon. He remained disinterested and uncaring. I wasn't sure if that was to distance himself from his task or because he honestly wasn't bothered.

Beside me, Falon stiffened. The ends of her hair frayed and rose an inch into the air. She pulsed with a low hum, like a current of electricity was running through her. Within my hand that she held, I sensed a growing warmth, and when I looked down I watched as her power swirled around our fingers.

It was a peculiar feeling, but not dissimilar to the parallel situations I've gotten into with Cedric. The hall and all its occupants lingered frozen where they stood as they waited for the spell to break. Small rustlings and uncomfortable coughs were unusually loud in the vaulted chamber as the spectators mentally took bets on who would act first.

Falon's anxiety grew by the second. The small amulet around her neck pulsed in time to the flickering mirage around her hand and her eyes took on a backlight glow. I recognized the attitude she was accumulating, like donning a specific costume to get the job done. Her back straightened as if a rod of steel rain through her spine. Her chin lifted and cocked to the side in that stubborn look I knew all too well. She was in full "princess mode" as I called it. Falon tended to take on this persona when the advantages and influence of her title were needed. The visitor, however, still looked unaffected.

"I don't suffer orders from the likes of you, *knight*." Falon released my hand and took a step forward. "Take your leave before I make you."

Lightning struck down against the stones between them. The fallout threw me back into Cedric, the two of us landing in a heap. More charged bolts danced around Falon's hands like mesmerizing blue sparks and her hair whipped around her from an unseen wind. When the dust and smoke from the demolished stone cleared, the warrior remained in front of her, his sword now fully drawn.

"However cute you think your tricks might be, this is no game, princess. The queen demands your return." His voice was deep with controlled anger, and I watched as his hand shook around the hilt of his blade.

His restraint was impressive, but I knew he couldn't hold onto it for much longer. As Falon geared up for another strike, a loud explosion shook the hall and threw us all to our knees. Between the two warring Fae stood Gwendolyn, her perfect hair not a strand out of place.

"Was it absolutely necessary to destroy the floor? It's nearly a thousand years old." Gwendolyn looked entirely forlorn as she stared down at the rubble beneath her boots.

Having impeccable timing, Leif materialized out of thin air with a small *pop!* Standing just to the side of Falon, he gestured for her to follow him.

"I'd suggest finding a good hiding place until the Mistress calms down," he whispered.

But when Falon moved to stand, the knight took a step forward.

"She has been *ordered* to return! I will tear down this entire castle if I must to see my task completed," he bellowed with a tempered rage.

Warin moved to intercept him when he stepped too close to Gwendolyn. His strong hand gripped the knight on his shoulder, creating creases in his armor in the shape of a very large handprint. When the knight spun to attack, Warin easily dodged the strike and knocked the heavy sword to the ground.

We took advantage of the knight's momentary distraction and followed Leif's advice. Running from the hall, my bare feet slapping on the stone, we were out of breath by the time we made it back to our rooms. The three of us locked ourselves inside and barricaded the door with the wardrobe.

"Do you think Gwendolyn will let him take me?" Falon asked, fear written in every crease on her face.

I wasn't sure what Gwendolyn would do. I didn't think she had to answer to the queen, but I wasn't familiar with Faerie politics. I did know that I would fight until my last breath to keep Falon here. And if Gwendolyn really thought I was so important, then she wouldn't let it come to that.

"You're not going anywhere, Fal. We won't let you." I shared a look with Cedric and knew we were on the same page.

The Queen of the Summer Court may be used to getting her way any other time, but she hadn't met me.

"You need to move faster. Focus!" Gwendolyn shouted at me from her cushioned chair in the shade of the tree.

The sun shone down against my bare shoulders as I crouched over the bleeding Imp. Her tail lashed back and forth as I slowly healed the gouge in her arm. I tugged on the string of power I held inside me and forced the last bit of it to close her skin with a seamless finish.

My ass landed in the dirt as I fell back, exhausted. That was the fifth time I had healed this Imp within a two-hour period. Gwendolyn said that I needed to build up my endurance, that way I didn't faint or pass out after the simplest of healings.

So far, it looked like her plan was to have me heal the poor Imp repeatedly until I lost consciousness.

"Again," she called to me.

The Imp used her razor sharp nails to create a cut in her leg this time, over a major artery. The blood in her wound called to me, and I immediately felt the stirring of my power again, even when I thought there was nothing left to pull from.

Unlike times in the past, the chill of my power didn't extend into the rest of my body. I held on tight and kept the majority of it within the ball I had created, only using small pieces as needed. This meant I no longer had a problem with movement. I could run a lap around this entire courtyard without difficulty.

Maybe not *now,* after healing so many damn times in a row. But the point remains the same.

"You need to work faster. Having the power to heal won't mean shit if you can't stop an arterial bleed," Gwendolyn criticized.

I knew she was right, but I didn't have much left in me. I was able to patch the hole in the artery, but small leaks continued to break through. My power wasn't strong enough to stick.

"You have to *want* it, Casey."

I did want it, dammit. But it just wasn't working. I yelled in frustration while thrusting as much power as I could into the wound. Slowly but surely, it began to hold. The Imp scolded me in her own language, obviously not pleased with my work.

I ignored her and sealed the laceration with the last of my will. When the Imp moved from beneath my hands, I threw up. There was nothing left in my stomach by the time I was finished, and I had just enough energy to move my body away from the vomit pile before my arms gave out.

"That was better," Gwendolyn said, but I detected faint sarcasm layered beneath the words. "You still need more practice, however. Let's break for lunch and then we can pick up where we left off."

I watched her stiletto heels crunch across the grass from my viewpoint in the dirt. There was no way I was going to make it to lunch, not unless the rocks in front of me were suddenly edible. My limbs felt like Jell-O as I pushed off the ground. The world around me swayed but a hand on my elbow kept me from falling.

"I thought maybe we could eat out here for a change?" Cedric asked, holding an overflowing basket in his other hand.

Falon stood beside him with her arms wrapped around a folded blanket.

"Just maybe as far as we can get from *that*." She gave my vomit pile a sidelong glance before leading us across the courtyard to a shady grove near the small pool.

It was a beautiful day, made even better by a picnic with my friends. The past week had been uneventful for us and the lack of drama allowed for a healing atmosphere. I hadn't noticed how exhausted I truly was until I finally had a safe place to rest my head.

From the moment the Dean took an interest in me, I lost all sense of safety, predictability, and knowledge of who I really was. I had been through a lot while on the run, and it wasn't until now that I saw how much it had taken a toll on my body and spirit.

For the first time, we were safe. This castle, with its stone walls and bizarre inhabitants, was the safest place I could be. Gwendolyn owned these lands and owed no fealty to either the Summer or Winter Courts. She's governed these lands since before a time of kings and queens; she was too powerful to challenge, a ruler in her own right.

When that knight arrived and tried to force Falon to return to the Summer Court against her will, Gwendolyn kicked his ass and sent him packing. She feared no repercussions from the reigning monarchs and told us that we were safe on these lands—as far as outsiders were concerned.

"Stop eating everything! Leave something for Casey." Falon smacked the strawberry out of Cedric's hand and watched as it fell back into the bowl.

Cedric shot me a sheepish grin when he caught me watching. The deep maroon blanket beneath us was already covered in crumbs and varied plates of foods. There was a half-eaten bowl of strawberries, some warm bread in a covered basket, sliced cheeses, and more KFC fried chicken. A lunch of champions.

"It's okay, Ced. I don't see myself eating that much anyway." I nibbled on a roll and watched him dig in.

Falon rolled her eyes, but she knew there was no controlling his appetite. After a few experimental bites, I figured my stomach could handle a little more, and I reached for a drumstick. My headache lessened and I begin feeling more like myself as the warm food filled my belly.

I stretched out along the edge of the blanket and allowed the warm sun and cool breeze to lull me into a contented nap. But it didn't last long. Cold drops of water sprinkled over my face, slowly at first, but ever growing until all of a sudden I was hit with a torrential downpour.

My clothes stuck to me like a second skin as the water continued to fall. Above me, a small storm cloud floated, angry and swollen. I rolled to get out from under it while weeds and ripped grass stuck to my legs like papier mâché. The cloud followed me, dropping fat drops of ice cold water all over me.

"I know you weren't taking a nap in the middle of your endurance training. That would mean starting all over." Gwendolyn cooed as she walked up to me.

She let the storm continue a little longer before waving her hand and the cloud shredded into nothingness. The sun returned, its rays warm against my now chilled flesh. My teeth clacked together as shivers racked my body. I glared at Gwendolyn, promising a gruesome death if she stepped any closer to me.

With another wave of her hand, my clothes were dry and the shivering stopped.

"Don't think that will cause me to forgive you," I called to her, brushing the now dry grass from my legs. "With every day that passes I only think of more ways to kill you."

Gwendolyn snorted at my threat, knowing full well I couldn't actually do anything to harm her. When I stood in front of her, grass-free and more wired than if I'd drank a cup of coffee, she looked over her shoulder and gestured to whoever stood waiting.

Out of the darkened doorway walked Warin, his arm around Cedric's neck and a knife pointed at his ribs. A stunned gasp escaped before I even realized I'd reacted, and Gwendolyn looked at me with a shrewd smirk.

"I think I've found the perfect motivation for you." She nodded to Warin, and before I could take a step forward, he stabbed the knife into Cedric's side. "Let's see how fast you can heal now."

Chapter 39

I lunged, my knees scraping against small rocks as I slid across the grass to reach him. Cedric wavered on his feet for a moment, but fell after Warin yanked out the knife.

"No!" I screamed, not reaching him in time before his body met the ground.

Blood already leeched into the dirt beneath him, the garnet liquid standing out in stark contrast against the velvet green backdrop he lay upon. My hands moved without me needing to command them and placed themselves over the wound in his side. I pushed on it, using pressure to naturally staunch the blood flow.

Internally, I called upon my power. It stirred in the presence of so much blood, but hadn't had the proper time to replenish itself. I called to it, begging for just one small strand to heal the gash I felt in Cedric's lung, but nothing answered.

I reached inside myself and attempted to just take what was needed by force. I gripped the quivering ball of my power and vehemently began to separate strands from it, intent on saving the boy in front of me. Nothing was going to stop me.

Until the cramps started. Down in my calves my muscles clenched and tore, the pain radiated up my leg until the same thing happened in my thighs. Still, I ignored the pain and ripped more strands of my power.

As the cramps continued to reap havoc through my limbs, I fought to bring the strands of my power down my arm and into Cedric's side. It was slow moving, but it was working. I used every ounce of focus I had to keep the open line of power flowing. The nick in Cedric's lung closed, but now I was tasked with clearing all the escaped air out of his chest cavity.

Pulling upon more power, I began to cough as my lungs tightened in my own chest. It was hard to bring in oxygen and too soon I was wheezing with the effort. I pushed the pain to the back of my mind and ignored my body's screams for air. Cedric couldn't breathe properly either. If he could hold on, then so could I.

As I cleared the free air from his chest cavity, the hole in his lung slowly started to reopen, tearing right along the seam I'd originally healed it on.

"No, no, no. Come *on*." A series of coughs wracked my body as my lungs fought to fill themselves.

Black spots swarmed across my dimmed vision and my head swam. Sights and sounds felt so far away, like I was on one side of a darkened tunnel and they were on the other. I struggled to get back to them, but the darkness only crept closer.

"Stop. Now." Gwendolyn's command was muted and warped, as if I were hearing her from underwater.

I still clenched strands of my power, and they fought my hold, slowly escaping my grasp with every shallow breath I took.

"If she doesn't release it now, she will drain her life force." I heard Gwendolyn's voice, but was too far gone to understand the meaning behind her words.

Light shone at the end of the dark tunnel, bright and strong, inching closer to me. My lungs hurt and felt weak, but were able to take in clear breaths as the light obscured my vision. The dancing spots were gone and in their place was the palest of blue skies.

The cramps in my legs faded and were exchanged for a warmth that moved through me, healing the aches and damages done. The moment my brain began thinking for itself again, I snapped to attention, scrambling to get to my knees.

A comforting hand pressed against my shoulder to keep me down. My eyes followed the hand, up past the strong forearm of tanned skin, to a broad shoulder connected to a corded neck. Cedric's worried gaze took in everything. I could feel him checking me over, trying to spot any lingering malignancies.

I wanted to cry with relief as my hand wandered over his side and felt only smooth skin. His chest rose and fell with regulated breaths, and no blood stuck to my hand as I brought it between us to cup his cheek.

"*This* is why we train instead of nap!" Gwendolyn was yelling from somewhere nearby, but I was too busy staring into Cedric's eyes to pay attention.

The connection between us sang, a feeling of pure joy dancing across it as my mind came to terms with what was presented to it. Cedric was safe. He was *alive.* Had I done it? Did my power finally give in and obey my command?

I opened my mouth to ask, but it was swiftly covered. When Cedric's lips met mine, any words that had been trying to escape were muffled and silenced. Our tongues danced against one another and our breaths came hurried but easily.

All other sounds and thoughts melted away as I lost myself within the feelings of this kiss. Cedric's hands roamed my body, both checking for further injury while also moving purely for pleasure.

A rude cough interrupted the mood, bringing both of us back to the present. We were sprawled on the ground, lying in a drying pool of Cedric's blood. Gwendolyn and Warin stood above us, awkward spectators to our lost moment of passion.

I blushed crimson and hid my face in Cedric's shoulder while he laughed. His shoulders moved up and down with his chuckles, bouncing me as I held onto him. I smiled, relieved that I hadn't lost this. I don't think I could have gone on if anything had happened to him.

When the flashes of *how* he had been injured reemerged, the heat moving under my skin switched from embarrassed to furious. Betrayal stung sharp in my chest. I slowly detangled myself from Cedric's arms and stood in front of him. Warin, sensing the change in me, put himself between me and Gwendolyn.

"Calm down. Think about the reasoning behind this," he ordered.

But I was done playing nice. I was so tired of Gwendolyn's meddling and of her acting without thought of anyone's wants or safety.

"Move," I growled, my eyes never leaving from the redhead behind him.

"You know I can't do that." Warin shook his head, both his palms open toward me.

My healing power might be on empty, but there was another force of nature swirling inside me. The only problem was, I didn't know how to let it out without releasing the beast. I tested the lock on his cage, wondering if I could leash him in some way so that we could both get what we wanted.

"Don't even think about it," Cedric whispered in my ear.

Both his arms wrapped around me from behind, caging me in. I stiffened for a moment before relaxing into his hold. Any accumulation of frost inside me melted at his touch.

Resting his chin on the top of my head, he spoke to the two Fae in front of us. "She needs to calm down before something happens that we can't fix." Cedric took a few steps back, slowly putting distance between me and the object of my ire. "We can pick up this conversation later tonight."

Snippets of words carried on the breeze as Gwendolyn spoke to Warin. When he nodded in agreement, Cedric lifted my feet from the ground and carried me back inside. It took a few moments for my eyes to adjust to the dim hallway we entered, and Cedric took advantage of my impairment to throw me over his shoulder.

"Hey! Put me down." I hit my fists against his back, but they went unnoticed.

I continued to struggle as we went, kicking and wriggling to get down. Finally, when he thought we were far enough away, Cedric set me on my feet. He held me close, the front of my body sliding down the front of his—not an inch of space between us.

With his hands on my hips, he controlled my descent, and it took a lot longer than it should have for my feet to reach the stone tiles. By the time he released me, my cheeks were hot and my breaths uneven.

He smiled his signature smirk and pushed on the wooden door to his right. My bedroom door swung inward to reveal an empty room and the lure of comfortable sheets.

I felt relaxed and calm, rejuvenated from my nap. My arm was a little numb from how I slept on it, and as I wiggled my fingers, they hurt with the sharp pin pricks of the returned blood flow. I had passed out the moment my head hit the pillow. Cedric knew exactly what I needed when he brought me back here.

Having rested, I could now sense my healing power thrumming within my chest. The sphere pulsed and answered when I reached for it. Somehow it felt stronger now, similar to how a muscle hardens as it's worked over time. I guess Gwendolyn had a point to her training after all.

But I was still beyond pissed that she allowed Cedric to be harmed. I didn't care that she stepped in and saved him. What could be so important that she had to put his life at risk in the first place? Nothing, in my opinion.

"About time you woke up," Cedric called as he pushed open the door. "I thought you were going to sleep through the night."

I looked out the window. The sun was just beginning to set; it couldn't have been later than five.

"It's not even dark out yet," I replied.

He shrugged. "You were out cold before I could even tuck you in. I figured you would need more than a few hours to get your strength back."

I would have thought so too. I felt completely drained by the end of that session, more so than ever before. The guard's leg back at the school was the only time I could think of where I had felt worse, and that was probably due to my lack of control at the time.

"You think you could stomach some food?" Cedric asked. "It's almost time for dinner."

He could feel my hunger pains probably as clear as I could. He wasn't asking because he was questioning my ability to eat. He was subtly checking to see if I could handle being around the people attending dinner: Gwendolyn and Warin.

There were definitely a few choice words that I needed to say to both of them, but I was past the point of losing my cool.

"I'll be fine," I answered as I pushed off the covers and followed his retreating form out into the hall.

The walk to the dining room was now a familiar one. This was the part of the house that I could find my way to and from without a problem, so I knew we were right around the corner as soon as I saw the framed painting of the Wild Hunt.

I steeled myself against the anger that bubbled under the surface. I hadn't lied to Cedric; I wasn't going to outright stab anyone, but I was far from okay with what happened. Cedric walked in ahead of me and sat at his usual chair to the left of Warin. Falon was already in her spot, leaving the seat between her and Gwendolyn wide open for the taking.

I walked past it and instead sat on the other side of Falon, as far from the redheaded bitch as I could get without moving to the opposite end of the table.

"I can see someone still has a temper." Gwendolyn casually declared before taking a sip from her cup.

My grip tightened around my fork as I stabbed at whatever meat we were having tonight. It looked like sweet and sour chicken, but I wasn't sure. I continued to serve myself from the platters in the middle of the table, ignoring the glances from the others and the pointed attempts at conversation from Gwendolyn.

"I think now would be the perfect time for us to discuss what happened earlier today." Gwendolyn tried again.

One scoop of white rice moved from its bowl to my plate. There was also a box of eggrolls that I hadn't seen on my first inspection. With my plate sufficiently full, I started to eat.

"You are under *my* rule as long as you are here. If you want to leave anytime soon, I suggest you get over your petty attitude and act like a grown up." Gwendolyn's anger finally reared its ugly head. But my temper was worse.

"You want to talk about being a grown up? Try not stabbing my boyfriend just to get the results you want." My words echoed off the walls in the small room until I heard them three or four more times.

The chicken went dry in my mouth as the anger inside me bubbled over. She didn't even seem apologetic about it. Did she really think she did nothing wrong?

"I refuse to apologize for doing what I thought was necessary to get you ready. I will do whatever I must to ensure your survival, even if it means temporarily causing pain to another," she argued.

I could tell she was speaking the truth; it was in her eyes, but that didn't make what she did okay. When I looked to Cedric, he was shaking his head, trying to tell me to let it go. If the person who was actually stabbed wasn't upset about it, did I have the right to be?

I regarded Warin, watched as his expression remained calm through all this, and decided then and there that damn straight I had a right to be mad, but I couldn't act on my anger if even the victim of the incident refused to. He of all people had more of a right to retribution than I did.

"Why did you do it?" I finally asked, my voice shaking.

"Ah," Gwendolyn placed her goblet on the table and faced me fully. "There was one important lesson I wanted you to take from that … incident, and instead you learned two. Can you think of what they are?"

"I need more practice?" The sarcasm flew from my mouth uninhibited.

I knew before she shook her head that that was the wrong answer. But really, finding a lesson in all that was the least of my worries at the time.

"The first lesson was that in order for your power to work, you have to *want* to heal. That want has to override everything else; it needs to be stronger than whatever you are thinking or feeling at that time. Your power can only do so much without your will behind it."

I nodded with understanding. It was similar with a Witch's elemental power. I'd heard Snow lecture about the will behind the means multiple times in class. That was easy enough to fix; it just took practice in blocking out distractions.

"So what was the surprise lesson?" I asked.

Gwendolyn frowned, looking noticeably worried as she went to answer. "The second lesson was one I had hoped to only have to tell you about. I never wanted you to have to experience it."

Warin grabbed her hand in a show of support when she paused. The fact that she cared so much had my anger going back down to a simmer.

"We've been working to build your endurance these past few days in the hopes that when you leave here, you will have a decent reserve for the battles to come. Each healer has their own threshold, one that can grow and change with age and experience. You reached yours today."

She didn't have to remind me. My vomit was still out in the courtyard as proof.

"But what you didn't know," she continued, "is that going past your threshold will kill you. At that point, you begin to draw on your own life force to heal, and if the wound is too big, you will die. That's why I stepped in today. You were pulling on your own life force to save Cedric, paying no mind to what was happening within your own body."

I recalled the cramping in my legs, the pain, and difficulty breathing. But I chalked that all up to being exhausted. I didn't know it was actually killing me. Cedric and Falon shared looks of alarm. None of us knew that my power could be so dangerous. When Cedric used up his reserves, it was just gone, there was nothing left until he rested.

It was unfair that my power could do such good and be so limited. But I was used to fate giving me the short straw—this was no different. I was just going to have to be more careful in the future, and my training was going to have a whole new focus from now on.

I excused myself from the table halfway through dinner. Cedric and Falon were far from done, but I didn't have much of an appetite anymore. I felt Gwendolyn's eyes tracking my every step until I cleared the doorway and was met with an empty hall. I leaned against the wall and took in a deep breath, trying to clear the jumbled thoughts that bounced around my head.

"Casey." Gwendolyn's voice was gentle, but it still echoed off the stone walls. "We need to talk."

I snorted. "I think we covered all that needed to be said back there."

I didn't want to hear any more about how my power was yet another thing trying to kill me. Would there be no peace for me? Not even just five minutes of silence in an empty hallway? I looked over at Gwendolyn—well, it *used* to be empty.

"What I have to tell you won't take long, and I assumed it wasn't something you wanted discussed in front of the others," she said, leaning against the wall beside me. "It's about the relationship between you and Cedric, and don't bother lying, I've seen the two of you together."

I rolled my eyes, already annoyed with the conversation. "A for effort, but that's not something we were trying to hide." The sarcasm dripped from my tongue, its use as natural to me as breathing.

"Be that as it may," Gwendolyn pushed on, "you might want to curb any more public displays of affection. Among my kind, and among others who remember the old ways, a relationship between a Healer and her Protector is taboo."

I didn't understand how my relationship with Cedric could be interesting to anyone other than ourselves, and the belief that we shouldn't be together was archaic and stupid.

"I don't care what other people think about my relationship," I countered, letting the anger in my tone be heard.

"Believe me," Gwendolyn chuckled. "I never thought you would see it any differently. I'm not here to warn you for the benefit of others, but for yourself." She held my gaze. "You and your Protector already share such a close bond, one that is just beginning to develop. As you grow together the bond will only become more intricate. If you encourage this relationship, you will have a connection with that boy unlike any you have ever had with another."

"And that's a bad thing, how?" I asked.

Something shifted in her eyes, bringing forth a deep sadness that she normally kept hidden.

"Because our Protectors are not fated to have long and healthy lives."

Chapter 40

O ur last week spent in Gwendolyn's home was uneventful. We followed the same routine we'd found ourselves bound to since our arrival. My mornings were spent training with Gwendolyn and whatever creature she brought along for me to heal that day. I continued to work on my endurance with a hard focus on my *will* to heal.

Gwendolyn provided a multitude of distractions, from spraying me with cold water while I healed, to having me dodge flying debris. So far, I found ducking from airborne rocks to be the most difficult. Moving wasn't the problem; it was easy enough to avoid something you knew was aiming for your face. What I had trouble with was getting back into the healing.

Once my hand broke contact with my patient, the connection between us fizzled out. Some of my power remained for a time, but too long apart and the body would start reversing all the work I'd done. When I placed my hand back on the wound, it was hard to pick up where I left off, prolonging the process. In a time when I was trying to complete a healing as quickly as possible, this was extremely frustrating.

Thankfully, Gwendolyn stuck with these tactics and respected my demand of not experimenting on those important to me—she hadn't bothered Cedric or Falon since I'd warned her away the other night. And she spoke no more on the topic of my relationship with Cedric—something I was thankful for.

I finished mending the Brownie's broken arm and moved aside so he could scamper away. I had a slight headache beginning at the base of my skull and my stomach growled with hunger, but there was no dizziness or nausea.

"You've improved since the last time." Gwendolyn seemed surprised. "It won't hurt to continue the exercises I've given you, but the hard work is mostly finished. All that's left is experience."

Gwendolyn was right, I *was* stronger. I'd healed more than a handful of Fae, ranging from all types and sizes, in less than three hours. I was more confident in my power, and it showed. I didn't shy away from injuries that I knew I could heal, I didn't pass out from exhaustion after mending broken bones, and for the first time I was doing good.

I could do good.

A huge weight was lifted off my shoulders when I realized that this gift would no longer be a handicap. The Dean was used to me being weak, was used to taking advantage of my lack of control. I'd like to see him try that now. He wouldn't recognize the three of us when we came for him.

Cedric has been working hard with Warin, both expanding on his training as a Protector and furthering his offensive techniques. His job requires more than just his ability to sense my feelings; ultimately, he was my bodyguard of sorts.

I wasn't sure how I felt about that. I appreciated help in sticky situations, don't get me wrong, but I wasn't okay with my friends throwing themselves in the line of fire for me. The three of us, we were a team. We took care of one another and worked well together. We all did our part. Our dynamic wouldn't work if one of us were not allowed to be fully involved.

I only hoped that Cedric knew this and wouldn't overstep the boundaries of our relationship to fulfill whatever duties he thought he owed to me. Even Falon could pull her own weight now after all that she's learned these past months. Her training started back at the camp in Florida, but the Fae here have expanded upon it while she's been in residence.

I watched her practice with throwing knives last night, and she hit the bullseye eight times out of ten. Eight! We had all grown in our time here, and I felt more than ready to return home and finish this. We walked side by side as Gwendolyn brushed her hands against the budding flowers planted along the path. They grew and sprouted, boldly reaching and blooming into her touch.

"It's time for you and your friends to leave," she declared. "There is nothing more I can teach you that experience won't reveal in time."

I came to a dead stop. "You want us to leave … right now?" I asked, completely caught off guard.

"You will leave in the early morning hours, allowing you to travel through the doorway undetected and unseen. Have you thought of where you will go?" She ignored the flowers and turned to face me. "What do you plan to do with the information that you've learned here?"

Cedric, Falon, and I had argued this very topic since the night my heritage was revealed. It took a lot of convincing, explaining my thoughts, and some serious brainstorming sessions, but we'd finally all agreed.

"We will return to the Academy and confront the Dean," I replied. "Others in our community need to know what he's done."

I didn't care what happened to me, but the Dean could not remain in the power seat. I would do whatever it took to remove him. That was the main source of tension between me and Cedric lately. He agreed with what we were doing, but didn't like the recklessness I added to it.

"And you expect life to then go back to normal? To sit through your remedial classes and eventually graduate like a normal girl?" Gwendolyn mocked. "What happens days, maybe years in the future when who you really are is revealed?"

"For your information, I've already got a plan," I snarked.

She raised her eyebrows. "Do tell."

Like any other time I'd spent more than five minutes with her, Gwendolyn's attitude was getting on my nerves. Was it too much of a stretch to think that I might have thought things through?

"I'm going to tell everyone the truth, the whole truth. I'll reveal what the Dean did to my mother, how that led to her meeting my father, which resulted in me. I will show them the prophecy and demonstrate with my power if I must for proof."

"Exposing yourself and your friends to a community sworn to fight Vampires is risky, don't you think? How do you know they will listen?"

There was no scorn in her tone this time, only honest curiosity.

"I don't." That was the main dilemma. I couldn't control the outcome if we took this risk. "People will have to judge for themselves based on the character of me and my friends. I know I can count on Eli to back me up, plus the word of a Seer, but ultimately I don't know what will happen."

Gwendolyn resumed walking, turning down the branch of the path that led to the east wing. She spoke no more on the subject, and I didn't try to make her. When she disappeared through the doorway, I stayed behind and kept to the path until a bend appeared that led to the west wing.

There wasn't much time before we were to leave and a lot needed to be done. Supplies needed to be gathered, my friends informed, last minute planning checked off, and hopefully a nap. My nerves began to build, and I pushed them aside. There would be time enough later to worry about what was to come. For now, I needed to focus on being prepared.

Fireflies blinked in and out along the edges of the path as we made our trek to another doorway. Gwendolyn said that she had multiple portals in her realm, and the one we were in route to took us through unfamiliar parts of her territory. Not that we were familiar with much outside those stone walls to begin with.

The half-moon kept itself hidden behind thick clouds, its light occasionally breaking through to lighten the path beneath our feet. That was both good and bad. The lack of efficient light made our travel treacherous at times, but also allowed for anonymity.

One never knew who was watching. The reward for news of our whereabouts was a staggering number—high enough to tempt even those who usually kept to themselves. It was best to remain unseen. We soon left the path in favor of a narrow game trail that wound deeper into the dense forest. Even the strongest gleams from the moon where blocked out in here.

The darkness felt bottomless. I couldn't make out the shapes of the trees let alone the shape of my own two feet. Cedric dared a handful of flame if only to keep us from bumping into one another. Up ahead Gwendolyn took the lead. Warin was at her side, Cedric close behind him, with me and Falon clutching at his shirt.

The redheaded Fae had many mysteries, and how she managed to navigate unkempt woods with no visibility was just another to add to the list.

"Are we close?" I whispered to Falon. The sound of my voice felt too loud in this oppressing gloom.

The scuffs of our shoes through the leaves were intensified, as were the sounds of our breaths. No birds chirped an early morning tune, small critters couldn't be heard foraging in the underbrush; it was dead silent. The hairs on the back of my neck itched as they rose, the uncanny feeling of being watched was something I was familiar with by now.

The small flame before Cedric was enough to allow us to be seen but served as a double sword; it kept us from seeing what was further around us. I almost told him to put it out, but without the small light we wouldn't walk three feet before running into something.

I was forced to push the uneasy feeling aside.

"Well?" I asked again, narrowly avoiding a branch at head level. Maybe she hadn't heard me the first time.

"We're close—but I can't tell by how much."

Great. We were close enough that Falon could feel the low frequency pulse of the portal, but not close enough that she could give us a time frame. I scrunched my shoulders and tried to make myself smaller. I didn't know how much more of this darkness I could take. I wasn't a fan.

Too many bad things could happen outside of the light; things I was still fighting to forget. I had been safe for the last few weeks and now, walking through this unlit trail, completely vulnerable, felt like tempting fate.

"Luthos!" Falon shouted, her voice exceedingly loud.

Cedric and I whipped around, going back to back as I pulled a knife from my pocket. My eyes burned as I pushed them to see through the endless black around us. I was ready to react at the slightest movement.

Falon gently put her hand on my forearm, and I jumped. "We're here."

It took a moment for the blood rushing through my head to quiet and another minute before I took in the meaning of her words.

"What?" I asked, turning around.

Sure enough, before me stood a cave. Its wide mouth hung low, and I could see a line of torches disappearing inside. The warm glow of the torchlight was a welcoming sight, and anything was better than staying out here, no matter how ominous it looked. I charged ahead, leaving my friends to struggle to keep up with me.

Bats hung suspended above us, peacefully sleeping even in the places the light reached them. I tried to keep my steps quiet so as not to disturb them. Having them panic and fly at me was the last thing I wanted right now.

The cave curved to the right, and we followed, mimicking the footsteps left in the dirt. When Gwendolyn and Warin finally reappeared, they were standing before a shallow pool of water in the rear cavern.

Ten torches were staked into the dirt surrounding the pool; its water so clear I could see straight through to the bottom. Nothing moved inside, enabling the surface to seem as smooth as glass.

"And so we have arrived." Gwendolyn's voice carried within the high cavern. "When I first sent my power out into the universe to find the next healer, I knew that eventually this day would come. When you step through this portal, Casey, your true journey will begin. There is no turning back once you've started, and fate will find a way to finish things whether you want it to or not. Be completely sure that this is the path you wish to take."

I felt everyone's eyes on me as they waited to hear my decision. And I'm not going to lie, a part of me wanted to tell her I'd changed my mind and have her return us to the castle. It was hard to intentionally move away from the security I'd felt within those walls, to the company and comfort that could be found there, but I knew what I had to do. I was never one to run when danger or misfortune came calling. I'd always met it head on. This was no different.

"How do we go through?" I asked.

I wasn't exactly sure where the portal was; there was no shimmering light like the last time. Gwendolyn lowered her arm and gestured to the water below. It was in the pool? With a snap of her fingers, the edge of the water began to flicker and move. Slowly, the water's surface changed from crystal clear to a blurred streak of colors.

The hazy smudge grew and expanded until it spread from the edges of the pool to the very center. With each breath I took, the image became more clear until reflecting back at me was a calm tree line at the edge of a familiar hemlock forest.

"When you're ready, just step into the water until you come out the other side," Gwendolyn advised.

Sure. Cause that made sense.

"I'll go first, to make sure it's safe," Cedric offered.

He waded into the water until it reached his waist and then with a quick glance back at us, he ducked beneath the surface. The water shone a brilliant white that nearly blinded me before dimming back down to the visual of the trees.

Falon was next. Rather than slowly wade in like Cedric had, she gave me a playful grin before charging at the pool with a warrior's battle cry. Leaping into the air, she did a cannonball right into the center. I couldn't hold back my laugh. That girl was ridiculous.

"And then there was one," Gwendolyn said from beside me. I hadn't even heard her move. She followed me to the edge of the pool and placed a hand on my shoulder, stopping me. "I wish you luck, young healer. Should you find yourself in need of another voice, you only have to call and we will be there."

She released my shoulder and took a step back. I glanced down at the water and still saw trees reflecting back at me. Self-doubt chose that moment to sneak up and kick me in my ass. Was I making the right choice? What if I'd just led my friends to a slaughter? I couldn't honestly be the most qualified person to make these decisions. There had to be a capable adult somewhere, right?

I let out a breath, trying to release all my negative thoughts with it. I could do this. I was meant to do this. There was no one else. *All right then.* Squaring my shoulders against an unknown future, I dove into the water.

Chapter 41

The first thing I noticed when I came through the portal was that my clothes weren't wet. And thank Luthos for that because it was chilly as hell. My denim shorts were no match for the harsh wind that tore across the street where I stood.

The asphalt was split into halves by two solid yellow lines, just like any other road in the country. But I had been on this one before. On the corner stood a shitty little gas station with the same broken lamp post I'd noticed the last time I was here.

The sleepy one-light town was as simplistic and barren as I remembered. It was dark here too, which was a blessing. It would have been hard to explain to the locals why a teenage girl was out here in shorts and a tank top when the weather obviously called for jeans and a hoodie.

"Casey!" Cedric called to me from behind a parked truck, waving me over to where they hid.

It was then that I noticed where I stood, smack dab in the middle of the road, beneath the swaying traffic light. Running over to where they were, I crouched down behind the side of the truck and crossed my arms in front of me.

"It's effing cold," I cried, already beginning to shiver.

Cedric ran his warm hands up and down my arms, from shoulder to elbow. It helped, but didn't last for long. He had to keep switching back and forth between me and Falon. We couldn't keep this up. We needed to find shelter and some fire; somewhere where we could hunker down and plan our next moves.

I looked over Cedric's shoulder at the silent trees on the top of the small hill. I could almost feel the presence of the slaughtered Imperials that Orin and his men destroyed in those woods. It was the first time I'd seen that notorious side of a Vampire, a beast so monstrous that it almost couldn't be controlled.

Although, I remembered Orin had a better hold on his than the others. Hopefully it wasn't due to his age and it was something I could learn as well. That would be one of the many things I needed to talk to him about one day, if I ever saw him again.

The three of us took off from behind the truck, heading for the trees up the hill. When we were safely out of sight, we took a hard left and made for north, where we knew the school to be. The running helped to warm me, and it was exponentially easier than the last time we came through here.

Without the thigh high snow, we were covering more ground in half the time. I could see the sun beginning to rise through the trees, and I grew excited for the extra warmth it would bring.

"Do we need to worry about being seen?" Falon asked as she pulled alongside me.

I briskly shook my head. "I don't think they expect us to be back here. We should be fine. It's closer to campus that we have to worry about."

We stopped for a rest at the half way mark, by that time the sun was high in the sky. I stood under a small patch of sunlight to soak in its warmth and catch my breath. The sweat was starting to cool on my skin, and I knew that we couldn't stay still for much longer. Hypothermia was still very possible in this weather, sunshine or not.

"So what's the plan?" Falon asked between gasps. "We can't just run up to the school and not expect to be caught. And Luthos, I can't promise that I won't pass out once we get there. How much farther is it?"

Strings of hair stuck to her face and neck. She was more in shape than the last time she ran through these woods, but that didn't make sprinting a mile any easier. Even I was breathless. And she had a point. We couldn't just walk up to the front door, unless … what if someone let us in? If we could find Eli, I was sure he could hide us somewhere until we were ready to strike.

Unfortunately, there was no guarantee that he wouldn't be in the Dean's dungeon, preventing us from having any support on the inside. I kicked the ground in frustration. We needed to come up with something before the sun set; the nighttime temperatures would be too much for us to bear without shelter.

"I'm open to suggestions," I told them.

"You can start with being properly dressed for the weather." The voice came from behind us.

We whirled around, a lot slower than I would have liked, and scanned the trees for whoever spoke. His blond hair had grown longer since the last time I saw him and there was a new scar across his cheek that still had a tender redness to it, but I recognized the stranger as my old trainer Sacha.

I blinked a few times to make sure that my mind wasn't playing tricks on me. He seemed so out of place here in the mountains. How did he get here?

"Sacha?" I called, still at a loss for words.

He walked toward us with a few others I vaguely recognized flanking his sides. They were all from the camp. Relief flooded through me as I realized that there were survivors. Kael hadn't managed to kill them all. I looked around, hoping to see Orin or any of his men. My hand moved to cover my heart as it tried to race from my chest.

"They're okay," Sacha told me when he got close enough to not have to yell. He knew who I was looking for and his words were a desperately needed comfort. "We've been waiting for you."

"How did you know we'd be here?" Cedric asked.

Sacha clapped him on the shoulder as he walked by. "I'm not the one to answer your questions. Come on, we're not far."

Far from where? We fell in line behind him while the others from camp closed ranks around us. Like a personal escort, they kept sentry on the surrounding area as we moved. It felt nice to give my eyes and other senses a break for a moment, to not have to be so hyperaware of everything.

Sacha guided us at a brisk walk, enough to keep us warm but without straining our already exhausted legs. We kept to the patches of sunlight, soaking up as much of it as we could.

"There should be plenty of spare clothes back at the cave for you to change into," he told us.

It was a relief to hear. I'd had permanent goosebumps since coming through the portal. I couldn't wait to finally feel warm again. After spending so much time down south in the Everglades and Louisiana swamps, it was hard for my body to acclimate back to the chilled temperature.

Thankfully, the cave he spoke of wasn't too far from where he found us. It was still early afternoon by the time it came into view. The welcoming shelter had some residual damage to the front from when we were ambushed by the Imperials. Hefty boulders broken from the upper ridge of the cave still laid scattered around the entrance.

Rather than inhibit our travel, it provided a type of shield that camouflaged the activity deeper inside. I smiled when I saw Leo and Mahon arguing out front. They fought over a midsized bowie knife, their voices carrying as their quarrel became more intense. Asa shook his head as he passed them, his shoulder bag filled with flowers and leaves from his foraging.

I stood off to the side and took in the sight, letting the others pass by me. The familiarity of the scene below tugged at my heart. I missed this, missed them. Leo's snarky jokes and teasing banter could always be counted on for an easy laugh. And how could I not feel safe around Mahon? The guy was a giant.

Even Asa's wise advice was welcome. Life didn't turn out as planned when we left the camp, and not a day went by that I didn't wonder at how they were all doing. They'd become my family, and it felt great to see them healthy and safe.

"My money's on Mahon," I shouted, making my way over to the disputing pair.

Their heads swiveled, eyes locking in on me with a predator's speed. Huge grins broke out across their faces when they saw me emerging from the trees. They immediately dropped the knife and ran for me, turning that activity into a competition as well.

Mahon pushed Leo into a boulder, gaining the lead in their ridiculous race to reach me first. I laughed when he swooped me up in his arms and squeezed. I returned his hug with all the strength I had. I barely had time to recover before Leo snatched me up as well.

"I missed you guys too." I chuckled.

"You have got a lot of explaining to do." Mahon tried to lecture, but his smile told me he wasn't actually mad.

Even so, we did have a lot to discuss. Our playful antics caught the attention of others around us, and I returned a few waves to those that I recognized. There were obvious losses to our numbers, but I was glad to see that a majority of the camp had made it. Their tents and handmade shelters spread around the cave, extending father than I could see.

The harder I looked, the more tents I saw. We had a mini army situated just outside the campus boundaries. My mind spun with the possibilities. This could change how we reached the Dean—I needed to talk it over with Cedric. Raised voices gave way to a small commotion at the front of the cave. Mahon and Leo turned to look, moving aside just enough for me to lock eyes with Orin.

My father. All thoughts of the Dean left me as my mind went blank. The shock on Orin's face matched mine, but quickly morphed into relief as he barreled through the crowd to get to me. His men stepped aside when he approached until he stood across from me, a mere arm's length away, and didn't speak.

We looked our fill, each checking the other for obvious injury. A few superficial wounds adorned his arms and neck, but altogether he looked to be in one piece. My time in Faerie allowed for my body to heal from all the wounds I had accumulated throughout our journey, so I knew my appearance shouldn't be too shocking.

But Orin still looked like he'd seen a ghost.

"Where have you been?" he yelled, his voice thick with emotion. He reached forward and pulled me to him. His gentle grip at odds with the anger in his voice. "I thought you were dead."

My face was pressed against his chest, so it was hard to answer him with a mouthful of jacket. When I finally got him to loosen his hold, I tilted my head back.

"I truly am sorry, Orin. There wasn't much we could do ... we had to run. I know a few weeks is a long time to go without calling, but—"

"A few weeks?" The veins in Orin's throat bulged. "Casey, you've been missing for *five months*."

"There must be some mistake." My high-pitched voice disturbed the colony of bats hanging from the ceiling of the cave.

After dropping that bombshell on me, Orin hustled me inside for further discussions. The fire crackled high in the back, warming me until a pair of clothes my size could be found. I wore a hoodie, borrowed from another member of camp, but my legs were still vulnerable to the slowly declining temperatures.

I bent my knees and tucked them inside the hoodie, and immediately wrapped my arms around them; it was both for warmth and for comfort—I needed something to hold on to. I couldn't have been gone for five months, we were in Faerie for three weeks at the most. It was April when we were forced flee from camp, but Orin told me we were now in September. I felt like a failure. I had meant to save Eli long before and this drastic change of the timeline meant he had been the Dean's prisoner for almost a year now.

"I'm afraid not," Orin answered.

I could hear the pity in his voice. More understanding of the situation, he was no longer cross with me for disappearing. He thought we ran because we had to, because Kael had attacked the camp. I didn't correct him. He didn't know that we were planning on escaping that night anyway.

My reasons for being angry at Orin had long since been deemed unimportant. It was in the past. Maybe if I'd listened to him, everything that happened with Kael could have been avoided. Then again, the likelihood of me finally finding my way to Gwendolyn's would have been slim to none. It was too late either way.

"But we left the camp a month ago, max." I just couldn't wrap my head around that much missing time.

"Well, you said you were in Faerie. Time moves differently there; this isn't as uncommon as you would think." He was trying to be reasonable—sensible—but I was still struggling.

"I know that, but *five months*? I thought a few days, weeks maybe. I've lost almost half a year." My seventeenth birthday had come and gone.

There was nothing he could say that would make this better. It was just something I was going to have to deal with on my own time. A gentle cough brought our attention to Asa, who was standing a respectable distance off to the side. In his hand he held a folded pair of denim jeans.

"They might be a little loose, but they should otherwise fit," he told me as he handed them over.

I smiled at him before giving him a hug in thanks. He returned the embrace before patting my shoulder and moving back to his corner. His work area was overflowing with all types of different plants; there were many hours of work ahead of him. Turning around, I moved deeper into the cave and changed into the borrowed jeans behind a man-made screen in the back.

With the thick material covering my legs, my body finally started to retain the warmth. I sighed in relief and moved back to sit by the fire. Orin remained where I left him, and I had a feeling he wasn't going to leave me anytime soon. Cedric and Falon were busy catching up with friends or trying to keep themselves busy. Orin and I were alone in the cave, aside from Asa silently working out of ear shot.

"So, how did you know we'd be here?" I asked him.

I was pretty sure I already knew the answer, but it didn't hurt to ask. I needed all the facts if I was going to fill in the blanks of this missing time.

"I knew you were chomping at the bit to get out and prove yourself. Those last few days at the camp were tense because I refused to let you go." I was glad to see he understood where my anger stemmed from. "When we ran off the last of the Imperials and checked for wounded, there was no sign of you or your friends. I figured you took advantage of the opportunity and were headed back here to face the Dean. I couldn't let you take him on alone."

I was humbled by his response. He had forbidden me to leave, and even knowing that I ignored his order, his first thought was still to protect me. What had I done to deserve that kind of loyalty? It couldn't just be because of the prophecy. Orin needed me to defeat his father, yes, but he could have tied me up and kept me close if he wanted to.

Instead, he treated me as a warrior and trained me until I was one he could respect. In honor of that respect, I had to be honest with him.

"We *were* planning on leaving that night, but we ran into Kael along the south end of the island. He did a lot of horrible things—terrible things. H-he killed Zora, right in front of me."

Orin nodded, the corners of his mouth turned down. "We found her body early that next morning. I'm sorry you had to witness it."

I think out of all the things Kael had done to me, killing Zora was what I hated him for the most. She was a kind, selfless, and honorable woman. She didn't deserve to die the way she did. Definitely not at the hands of a coward like Kael.

"We ran after that and made our way to New Orleans. I knew Kael followed, but hoped we could find our way to Faerie before he caught up. He captured us and took a ... *particular* interest in me."

I told Orin all the details, leaving nothing out. It was easier to talk about it the second time around, and Orin reacted much as I thought he would. He was outraged at what had happened to me, guilty over the fact that he wasn't there to stop it, and proud that I killed my tormentor.

I continued on to describe our time in Faerie with Gwendolyn. Orin didn't seem shocked at all when I told him Cedric was my Protector, that our connection was actually fated. And he was extremely impressed when I told him how controlled my power was now. The fact that I managed to achieve it in such a short amount of time was something I was proud of as well.

"The Seer was there. She told me a few things that were hard to believe at first." Orin made a small sound of interest, curious as to what a Seer could have to say to me. He didn't know that I had a history with her.

"Go on," He urged.

"Well," I took a deep breath. How did I tell him? Should I come right out and say it? "You see, a lot of confusing things were happening to me whenever I found myself in extreme danger. Things I couldn't explain until she gave me the missing puzzle piece. Now it all makes sense."

Orin patiently waited for me to work my way to the point. He never rushed me or tried to influence how fast I told my tale. I was thankful for that. I took another deep breath, prepared to just let it out.

"She said ..." I looked away from the fire and held his gaze. "She said that you're my father."

The only sound to be heard was the pops and sizzles of the fire. I waited for him to reply, growing more anxious with every passing minute of silence.

"Did you hear me?" I asked timidly, almost afraid to question him.

He was still looking at me, taking in my features as if for the first time. He tentatively reached out until he held a lock of my hair between his fingers. I got my hair from my mother, that much I knew based off memories of what she looked like. Orin released the strands to stroke my cheek with the back of his knuckle.

Where his skin touched mine, a cool burst spread through my skin. I could feel a thin layer of frost coating my skin where we touched. Orin jerked his hand back and stared at me in horror.

"Casey, I'm so sorry. I don't know what to say. My power's never gotten out of control like that before."

I giggled at his unnecessary panic.

"It's okay. I'm pretty sure that was me—or both of us." I waved it off. "Either way it didn't hurt."

Now he just looked confused. Poor guy. I held out my hand, palm up, and looked within myself to focus on the thin thread that extended from the back of my center of power. I knew the frost was connected with the beast, but didn't yet know how to access it without letting him loose. I did a test thrum along the line, smiling when I felt a small surge of ice in my fingers.

"I'm still learning, but I want to try something. Watch."

I hoped this worked. I thrummed along that line again, harder this time. The beast growled inside his cage, but I ignored it. I urged the ice to appear in my palm and almost squealed when I felt cool crystals forming against my skin.

At Orin's sharp intake I knew the crystals were large enough for him to see. I opened my eyes to take a quick peek and lost my hold on the line. My progress rapidly melted.

"You can control ice?" Orin marveled.

"Well, frost. I haven't tried to do anything larger yet," I admitted. "And I wouldn't use the word control. It's more like accidental spurts."

He stared at me with a mixture of pride and awe. Without warning, he reached over and pulled me into another hug. My skin tingled wherever it touched his, but it only made him smile.

"My daughter," he said, still stunned by the realization. He pulled back to look at me, utter happiness and pride filling his gaze. "You are so like your mother, in more ways than I can count. Asa and I argued many a time over this, of the probability that you could be mine. But I never thought it possible."

"So you're not mad?" I wondered, silently praying that he wasn't.

He shook his head, hugging me to him again. "I am the luckiest man on this earth."

Chapter 42

Cedric, Falon, and I made our beds in the rear of the cave. The warmth from the fire lulled me to sleep each night after spending hours talking with Orin. It had become a nightly routine of ours. I pestered him with questions of my mother, a topic Eli never liked to speak about. And in return, Orin asked to hear stories of my childhood.

A missing part of me, one I never knew I had, was suddenly filled. I had a father; I wasn't an orphan anymore. It was a sobering thought. I grew up thinking my family was dead. Sure, I loved Eli like a parent, but there was just something different about knowing that there was someone alive who shared your blood.

It was a special kind of bond as I was slowly learning.

"I could ask you to stay here tomorrow," Orin started, and I gave him a look. "But, I know it wouldn't stop you. So just promise me you'll be careful."

I nodded that I would. "Thank you. And I'll be all right. My friends will be with me."

I glanced over to where they slept and grinned. The both of them were snoring. Thankfully that was something I'd learned long ago how to sleep through. I should be next to them, resting up for tomorrow, but I couldn't sleep.

Tomorrow would be the conclusion of almost an entire year's worth of work. The girl that escaped the Academy that wintry night would have failed in her attempt to assassinate the Dean. She was too scared and too weak to overcome her fear and do what needed to be done.

But I wasn't that girl anymore. Far worse things have happened to me that made the Dean look like a cheap bully. Which was exactly what he was, a cheap bully with power. And I was about to take it all away from him.

"What do you plan to do once the Dean is taken care of?" Orin asked me.

"Address the school," I replied without hesitation. "I will need to get ahead of the rumors and panic that are bound to come with your arrival."

We came up with the original plan together. The entire camp would converge on the Academy en masse. There were still large groups of Imperials patrolling the campus, but far less than there were originally. Probably because a majority of them were still out searching for me.

After we took control of the school and the Dean was eliminated, the bulk of our numbers would stay to control the guards and maintain order. The rest, mostly the Vampires, would return here to the cave and await the all clear.

My plan was to reveal the truth about Vampires, using Orin and my own heritage as proof of the humanity in them. I knew it wasn't going to be easy, and certainly not something everyone would accept overnight, but I had hope that my people could change.

If not, we were all doomed. From what Orin's told me, Sebastian has only grown stronger in his exile. If my people couldn't learn to change, then we were all fated to perish.

"If things don't go as planned, you remember what you promised." Orin's voice had become firm, the tone of a leader giving orders.

This was one that I planned on following, however. If things got bad, either we couldn't gain control of the school or if the student body refused to listen, then I was to grab my friends and return to this cave as fast as my feet could carry me.

"I promised, didn't I?"

I couldn't blame him for not fully trusting my word. We probably wouldn't be in this mess had I not disobeyed his orders in the first place. A hard yawn forced its way out, popping my jaw with its strength. My mind was still teeming with hundreds of possibilities for tomorrow, but my body had had enough.

It was time for bed. I bid goodnight to Orin and crawled over to my sleeping bag. Sandwiched between Cedric and Falon I was protected on both sides. I could see the sentries at their posts near the entrance to the cave and beyond. Imperials wouldn't be able to ambush us this time.

We were so close to what we had been working toward. I had cried and bled all over the southern states so that I could be right here. Tomorrow, I was going to kill the Dean.

Five of us remained in the cave: Orin, Asa, Cedric, Falon, and myself. Our mini army moved out sometime around dawn, and the silence we were left with was driving me crazy. The first phase of our plan was underway and there was nothing to do but wait. Leo and Mahon, as well as my old trainer Sacha, each commanded their own unit.

They were tasked with disabling the security around the school, and after, Leo was to return with the news of their success. Phase two would then commence. This stage of the plan was supposed to be the easiest. The Imperials had no idea we were coming, and there should be little casualties if any at all.

But we had yet to hear any word.

"This is ridiculous. Someone should go out there." I had half a mind to go myself, but I knew Orin wouldn't let me get two feet outside the cave.

My patience was wearing thin. At first, I thought it was because of nerves, since I was so close to ending all this. But when hours passed without any updates, my imagination went into overdrive, and I worried that everything was falling apart.

"Relax, Casey." Orin had repeated those words back to me every five minutes it seemed. "This isn't something that can be rushed."

I groaned. He was right, but I couldn't help myself. If anything went wrong, we risked serious losses. There were enough Imperials down there to turn the tides if given the chance to organize. Subtlety was key.

I tried to distract myself by concentrating on what my role was for when we eventually joined the others. When the Imperials were tied up, the front doors would be open for the rest of us to move right in. I knew exactly where the Dean could be found: in his office or in his dungeon. I planned to head straight there, with Cedric and Falon as back up for the sadistic twins that I knew never left the Dean's side.

I wasn't naïve. I knew the dean wasn't going to surrender. There was only one way to end what he began. The Dean needed to be put down, and I would be the one to do it. It wasn't easy to take a life, no matter the circumstances. Nightmares from killing Kael still woke me, haunted memories of what it felt like to slide the knife between his ribs caused my hands to shake.

During those times, the beast within me felt closer than ever to breaking out of its cage, and it took hours for me to calm down enough to fall back to sleep. I usually never did. But I would do what needed to be done if there was no other way.

"Look, out past the birch tree—to the left." Asa's warning had all of us grabbing for our weapons.

My hand toyed with the hilt of my knife, the very one I'd stolen from Kael. A lone shadow ran toward us, dodging the trees in a beeline for the cave. If it was an Imperial, then something must have gone horribly wrong. I let out a sigh of relief when I saw that it was only Leo.

He slowed to a jog around the fallen boulders, but didn't stop until he was safely inside. His panting could be heard echoing off the cave walls, but he otherwise looked unharmed.

"Did everything go smoothly? What's happening out there?" I peppered him with questions, unable to hold off my impatience.

Leo was bent at the waist, his hands on his knees as he tried to catch his breath. He held up a hand, telling me to give him a minute. Sweat dotted his brow and dripped down the side of his face, and when his breaths were more under control, he slowly stood to his full height.

Orin put a hand on my shoulder and gently moved me to the side. With Orin now in front of him, Leo gave his report.

"There were three casualties, only one of them on our side. The other Imperials have been dragged further back into the woods and securely tied to the trees as agreed upon." Leo looked at me when he said that. It was my idea to tie them up. How could we gain the trust of the community if we killed all their warriors? Leo winked at me and continued his report. "The Shifters have volunteered to stand guard while the Witches and Fae await your arrival."

"And the Dean?" I asked. "Have you seen him?"

Leo shook his head. "He's either not there or he's hiding deeper inside the school."

I'll bet he was. The Dean was a coward. He wouldn't risk a fight that he knew he couldn't win. It didn't matter, I planned on going in to get him anyway.

"All other personnel and students are being kept inside," Leo finished.

That meant both the Dean and Eli were in there somewhere. As much as I wanted to check on him and assure myself that he was okay, finding Eli was going to have to wait. I couldn't give the Dean a chance to escape or call for help.

The six of us left the cave at a trot. The school wasn't far from where we were—less than a mile— and it didn't take long for the wooden rooftop of the main building to appear. My breath caught when the campus came into full view. The trees around the school were colossal and still heavy with leaves.

Fall colors had come early and the normally green landscape was already dotted with orange and red. I was used to seeing students wandering the grounds at this time of year, taking advantage of the sunshine and good weather before winter locked them all inside, but there wasn't a soul to be found. Leo said all the students and faculty were told to remain in their rooms until further notice. Mahon oversaw the group in charge of guarding the dorms. He made sure that the students were kept inside and away from any dangerous areas of conflict.

The front doors of the main building flew open, disturbing the fallen leaves on the ground before them. Orin and Cedric both moved to cover me, acting as living shields for whatever was about to emerge from inside.

"Holy shit," Falon's whispered exclamation had me straining to see over Cedric's shoulder.

I caught glimpses of a man— tall, with a stringy build and pale blond hair. He wore the all black uniform of a trained guardian and kept his hair in a long ponytail down his back. The beating of my heart slowed, until I almost couldn't feel it, before kicking into a full on gallop.

"Eli!" I screamed as I ran to him.

Cedric reached for me, but wasn't fast enough, his fingertips barely skimmed my hoodie. Orin, however, was quicker. He wrapped a strong arm around my waist and pulled me back, holding me against him as I struggled to get loose.

"Let me go, Orin. That's Eli." I fought his hold, about to lose my mind.

Eli was alive. Why wasn't I allowed to go to him? Orin refused to release me, and Eli stopped walking only a yard away from the front doors.

He looked nothing like the man who raised me, taught me, and protected me. He was thinner, much thinner than I even thought possible for a man of his frame. His shoulders were wide but sharp, as if all the muscle and padding had melted from his bones. His chest and waist tapered in tight until he resembled a wiry teenager playing dress up with football padding.

His skin was pale and sickly looking, even from here I could see the blue veins resting beneath the surface. His blond hair was limp and greasy, the color matching that of the unkempt beard on his face. He was nothing but skin and bones.

Bruises beneath his eyes had taken up permanent residence and his clothes were rumpled and stained. Who was this man?

"What happened to him?" Cedric questioned, in shock at what stood in front of us.

I knew exactly what had happened, or more like who: the Dean. There were obvious signs of torture on Eli's body. If you looked past the starvation, muscle loss, and the empty gaze, you would see the raw marks around his wrists from being shackled. The slight hunch in his back was from being made to crouch for days on end.

E.M. Rinaldi

If we were to look closer, I knew we would find other wounds and markings associated with different forms of torture.

"Why don't you ask Orin?" I told Cedric, anger darkening my voice. "He looked like that once, worse even. I'm sure he could tell you all the gruesome happenings from the Dean's dungeon." I tilted my head to look at Orin. "You know exactly what he's been through. Why keep me from him?"

Orin clenched his jaw, unappreciative of my tone but unable to argue with my facts.

"Fine." He relented, freeing me from his hold. "But until we know what is going on, you do not leave my side, even to see him."

Orin looked back at Eli, his distrust of him obvious. I could understand why. Eli was held and tortured by the Dean for nearly a year. That was way longer than it usually took to break most men. Orin didn't trust that this wasn't a trap. I knew he was being smart, but my heart was overriding my brain in this situation.

I gave a firm nod, agreeing to his terms, then walked forward. The closer I got to Eli the worse he looked, and smelled. But he looked so relieved to see me. There was a slight wobble to my smile as I tried to fight back tears. And even though I knew it would piss Orin off, I lunged forward and threw my arms around Eli's battered frame.

I would deal with the repercussions later. I held my breath as I hugged him. The stench that rolled off him was enough to make my eyes water, but I didn't care. Eli held me tight, his arms thinner and weaker than what I remembered. With my ear against his chest, I could hear a viscous rattle each time he inhaled.

I opened my power to him and took stock of his injuries: two broken fingers, five fractured ribs, malnutrition, dehydration, fluid in his lungs, bruised wrists, an offset shoulder, and more open wounds on his back than I could count. Infection had long ago set in, but thankfully it had yet to reach his blood. Small mercies.

I pulled strands of power and sent them down my arms in waves. I moved my hands until they rested on the bare skin of his lower back, beneath his shredded shirt. I fought off the infection first, blasting it from his body and sealing up all the wounds that fed to it. His bruises and broken fingers were next; I could hear the bones popping as they moved back into place and regained the proper strength.

I couldn't fix the malnutrition or dehydration, those were things that rest and a proper diet would take care of. Instead, I healed the overextended muscles around his shoulder and cleared the fluid from his lungs. What would have once taken me all day and a majority of my

318

strength, now only took ten minutes and I was still standing upright, if not a little winded.

"Thank you," Eli breathed and he held me tighter.

Cedric stood off to the side, a small smile on his face as he felt the fluctuation in my energy. He knew what caused it, but didn't say anything.

I pulled away from Eli, reluctant to let him go but needing to breathe some fresh air.

"You're alive." Eli's voice was rough from lack of use. "And traveling with strange company."

His fixed his glare on Orin as he stepped up behind me. I had a plan for introducing Eli to the idea of friendly Vampires, but it was a gradual process. And right now I was out of time.

"Eli, this is Orin and Leo." I pointed to the blond Vamp next to Falon. "They are my friends."

No need to share the newfound familial ties quite yet. All that could come later. For now, we just needed to get the introductions over with, get Eli to safety, and find the Dean. My body jerked forward as Eli yanked on my arm. He tried to pull me behind him, but Orin reached out and tugged on my other arm.

Stuck between the two men, I felt like the centerpiece in a tug-of-war game.

"I don't know what they've told you, Casey. But that man is a Vampire." He pulled on my arm, strong, but rapidly weakening. "Let her go, beast!"

Of course, Orin refused. My shoulders began to hurt from the misuse, and I silently begged Cedric to do something. I didn't want either of them to get hurt, and Eli's gifted strength was already beginning to deteriorate.

As Cedric got to work on Orin, I turned my head to the damaged man beside me.

"Trust me, Eli. They're friends."

"Vampires are not friends, Casey. Have they brainwashed you?"

He pulled on my arm again and this time my body came with it. Orin was held back by Cedric as my body softly collided with Eli's. He turned to run, intending on dragging me along with him, but I dug my feet in.

"Stop! You don't know the whole truth, okay? And I promise that I will explain it all to you very soon, but I have to take care of a few things first."

Eli stopped trying to drag me once he realized that I was stronger than him. He couldn't make me go if I didn't want to. His shoulders slumped with exhaustion and his body swayed to the right. Leo appeared out of nowhere and caught him before he fell. I mouthed a quick thank you as Leo began to carry Eli back inside.

"Wait. I need to ask him something first," I called out, jogging a few steps to catch up. I gave Eli's cheek a light pat until his eyes opened. "Eli. Eli, I know you're tired but I need you to answer one question. Where is the Dean?"

His eyes fought to stay open, but I could see them losing the battle. I gave his cheek another pat and his lids pulled back to reveal just a bit of eye.

"Eli, please," I begged.

"He's not here." The words were so soft that I almost didn't hear them. "Tell them he fled."

I could tell the moment he lost consciousness and quickly shooed Leo away to drop him off at the infirmary. I spun around and stared at my friends and Orin.

"What does he mean, the Dean fled?"

Chapter 43

Unbelievable. Falon and I stood in the open doorway to our old room and gawked at the absolute destruction that we found inside. The colored rugs had been ripped up and tossed around, knickknacks and personal belongings from our desks were strewn across the floor, even our dresser drawers were unhinged and hanging.

Someone had come through here looking for something, and I bet I knew just who. The Dean probably thought there would be clues here as to where we had run off to. He even ripped open my mattress to see if there was something hidden inside; fluff still hung from a broken spring as it reached for the floor.

The shelves on my bookcase had fallen, some of them even broke in half, and my precious books were ripped and torn. It was like being violated all over again. This place had been my sanctuary for as long as I could remember and now it was ruined. I could practically see the Dean's invisible grubby handprints all over my things.

"It's just stuff, Casey. Possessions can be mended and rebought; at least we're still okay." Falon wrapped her arm around my shoulders in a comforting hug.

A few of her things were damaged, but not as bad as mine. I knew she meant well, but it still hurt to see my entire life just scattered across my bedroom floor like trash. They weren't just meaningless possessions, this room held my memories from up until a year ago. With a heavy sigh I bent to pick up my fallen books, needing to start somewhere.

We made piles as we moved through the room, one for the trash and another for things that were salvageable. Within a few hours we had straightened what we could, and I had to admit that it wasn't as bad as I'd originally thought. We left the pile of trash in the middle of the floor, a problem for another day, and crawled into our respective beds.

I was thankful that my mattress was still usable, it only needed to be flipped over and it was good as new.

"I can't believe he isn't here. After all that …" I spoke into the darkened room, giving a voice to the turbulent feelings inside me.

Orin and a few of his men had done an entire sweep of the school, even the Dean's office and his dungeon. Nothing. There was no sign of him or his twin bodyguards anywhere. Eli was right.

"We'll find him. I doubt he'd stay away for long; he's basically obsessed with you." Falon was trying to be reassuring, but her words were anything but.

I didn't like the thought of the Dean being out there, watching and waiting to make his move. How did he know we were coming? Did we make a mistake and accidentally tip him off, or was he just out of town for another reason?

I would hopefully know soon. Presently, Cedric was across the path at the boy's dorm, speaking with his previous roommate and some old friends about what life was like in the year we were gone. It was his idea, but I encouraged it. He was once very popular here, and I needed him to rekindle those old relationships in preparation for the announcements I planned to make tomorrow. I still wasn't sure how to broach the topic of "good Vampires."

If I were in their shoes and this was taking place a few years ago, I would have thought someone was pranking me. It wasn't going to be easy to erase generations of brainwashing. I just prayed a majority of them would be open-minded.

The slight creak of footsteps on the back staircase had Falon and me moving like lightning until we were crouching at the ends of our beds. The moonlight coming through the large window glinted off the knives we held in our hands as the door slowly pushed inward, revealing only the shadow of a person.

"I've had a long night, and if you could try *not* to stab me, that would be great." Cedric's face peered around the edge of the door a few seconds after he spoke.

I had already put the knife back under my pillow by the time he'd locked the door and tucked his shoes under the bed. I waited until he had climbed in and got himself settled before asking my questions.

"So what did they say?" I rolled onto my side and threw an arm over his stomach, curling into him and resting my head on his shoulder.

"It's not a happy story," he started. "And it's pretty much as we expected. The entire campus has been living in fear since the night we left. The Imperials were given more power almost instantly, and it was apparently common practice for one of them to grab a random student and disappear with them into the Dean's office. My friends said those that went in came out different."

"Different how?" Falon asked.

I felt Cedric shrug. "Just different. Slower to smile, jumping at shadows, that type of thing."

Sounded to me like the Dean had gotten more liberal with his tortures. It was like he didn't even care anymore that he could have been caught. His desperation turned him into a madman.

"They said it was like a prison here. Students went to class or meals and then directly back to their dorms. There was no more laughter or games in the halls, not even quiet whispers at meals. They lived in fear that they would be the next one picked by the Imperials and taken to the Dean." I could feel the pity in his words, and I was right there with him.

Luthos, it sounded horrible. I felt a little guilty that the student body had to suffer because of my disappearance. Not that I could have done anything to change what happened, but still, these students were innocent casualties.

"It continued that way up until earlier today. When our camp swarmed the grounds, some of the Imperials gave the Dean notice and he ran, with his two minions, abandoning the school," Cedric finished.

"I always said he was a coward." I growled, both pissed at what he had done to my classmates and at the fact that he managed to escape.

The only upside to any of this was that the students and facility might be a little more willing to hear what I had to say. The enemy of my enemy is my friend, right? We were all against the Dean at this point, so what did they have to lose?

I threaded my fingers between Cedric's and gave his hand a light squeeze. It couldn't have been easy to see his friends after all this time or to question them about the horrors they'd witnessed. And I was sure they had dozens of questions for him in return, most of them he probably couldn't answer. Hearing what the other students went through was hard enough, but to know that some of those hurt were once your friends, friends we had abandoned in our run ... well, that wasn't an easy thing to swallow.

I lent him all the support I could and wished that tomorrow would dawn a brighter day.

I went to visit Eli in the infirmary the following morning. I planned to address the school after breakfast, but I needed to speak with him first. He was more alert today than when I first saw him. In fact, I caught him fiddling with the wires behind the television when I arrived.

I crossed my arms and leaned against the doorway.

"I'm pretty sure the doctor ordered bed rest for you. This is the exact opposite." My voice caught him by surprise and he jumped, nearly toppling the chair he stood on.

He carefully stepped down and looked at me with exasperation. "Not you too. I told that damned doctor that I felt fine." Despite his grumbling, he went back to his bed.

I covertly checked him over as he situated himself. The marks and bruises I'd already healed and no amount of food or water could cure his body's damage overnight. But he really did seem to have a good amount of energy. The purple rings beneath his eyes were still there, but faded and not as sunken in. He had a long road ahead of him before he was back to his original strength and he was well on his way.

"I'm surprised to see you. I thought those Vampires would have killed you, now that they control the school." He was scowling as he spoke, his face scrunched up like he had a bad taste in his mouth.

I rolled my eyes. "It's not just Vampires out there you know; Witches, Fae, and Shifters are part of this group too."

Wonder flashed in his eyes before he hid it with a grunt. "Well, I wouldn't be surprised if those beasts killed them off after they've served their purpose. Would serve them right too for betraying their kind."

"Eli!" I scolded. "I get that you've lived an entire lifetime with Vampires being the enemy. Hell, you fought in the war against them. I freakin' get it. But what I'm trying to do here isn't going to work if you keep being a closeminded ass."

At my outburst, Eli just sat there with his mouth hanging open. I'd never spoken to him like that, ever. But my frustration had gotten the best of me. His attitude was exactly what I feared would happen, and whether he knew it or not, I was included in those he thought were betraying our kind.

At least, that was how everyone was going to look at it unless I could change their minds. Starting with Eli.

"Look, all I'm asking is that you listen, *really listen*, to what I have to say. Okay?"

He slowly nodded, watching me with an odd look that I couldn't place, like he didn't know the girl that was standing in front of him.

"You've changed," he told me.

He was right, I had. In a lot of ways. You couldn't go through the things I had gone through and come out the same.

"I have." I gentled my voice to an almost pleading level. "And if you'll let me tell you what's happened to me in the last year, you will understand why."

I took his silence as a consent to start. I pulled the chair up to the side of his bed and made myself comfortable. This was going to be a long tale.

"You know that the Dean tortured me deep down in the catacombs of his office. What you don't know is the *reason* he tortured me. There was another prisoner, shackled to the walls for I don't know how long. His body was broken, oozing sores covered his emaciated body, so bad that I thought he was already dead at first."

I purposefully went into detail of how Orin looked when I first met him. I watched Eli's reactions as I did and knew that he had inside knowledge of how it felt to be that prisoner. I hated to make Eli uncomfortable, but I needed him to see the correlation, to understand that Orin was no different than him. They were both victims.

"Instead of killing him, like I'd been ordered, I took the nightly beatings and used whatever energy I had left to heal the prisoner. Maybe it was my gift or maybe it was because he we so close to death already, but I was able to see inside that man, Eli. I could sense the goodness in him, and it only strengthened my resolve to save him. So the night we planned to escape, I went back down there and brought him with us."

Eli nodded, like he knew I wouldn't have made any other choice. I steeled myself for the next part of the story; his reaction would decide how the rest of this played out. I rushed through what was left, describing how it felt to get lost in that blizzard, to watch your friends freeze and give in. I told him how I was saved by a bunch of strangers who I later learned were honorable men, serving under the very prisoner we had saved. I eventually realized that those men were all Vampires, ostracized from their kind as they traveled around and thwarted the plans of those that truly were our enemies.

"But why did you stay?" Eli asked, still not understanding how my training could have failed me.

"Because he knew my mother."

I fully expected Eli to freak out like I had at the thought of my mother befriending a Vampire, but he took the news in silence. He was never one to show his feelings about her—he always suffered them internally. A fact that drove me insane growing up.

After giving him a moment to absorb the news, I continued. And this was going to be the hardest part. I described the meeting between Orin and my mother and how their friendship grew into something more.

"That's how I know that not all Vampires are the monsters we've been told they are. Because that would mean that I'm a monster too."

Eli's face drained of all color, and he shook his head in denial.

"No, no, Casey. They're lying to you. Can't you see?" He reached for my hands, squeezing them so tight I thought he would crush my fingers.

I tried to pull away, wincing as my knuckles rubbed against one another. His grip was unbreakable and his large hands completely engulfed mine.

"Eli, stop. You're hurting me."

But he wasn't listening. "They lied to you, using your feelings for your mother against you. They just wanted the girl of the prophecy for themselves."

The girl of the prophecy? Eli never put much stalk in the Dean's ramblings about that. I knew *now* that all of it was true, but he didn't. I stared hard into his eyes, and what I saw there broke my heart. The Dean's torture had taken its toll, and now he was lost within his own ravaged mind. It wasn't an uncommon reaction to the trauma he'd been through, sometimes a single word could set off the reactions, but I'd hoped he would have been spared this long road of recovery.

I needed to give him some time to calm down and come back to himself, but he still wouldn't let me go. Out of pure instinct, I plucked that frozen strand inside me and allowed the frost to erupt from my hands.

Eli released me with a yelp of pain. He looked down at the crystals on his palms and then back at me with an accusing glare.

"I'm sorry, Eli, but I have to go." I began to back away, my heart crumbling with every confused emotion that crossed his face.

With one last look back, I left the infirmary and headed to the dining hall. It wasn't too long of a walk, and before I knew it, I was letting myself in the back door of the kitchen. The startled staff nearly dropped their dishes when they saw me, and I gave a small smile in apology.

Seated at a worktable in the back corner were my friends. Cedric was finishing off a plate of eggs, while Falon and Asa fought hard to not look at one another. Leo, Mahon, and Orin had their heads bent in a quiet discussion that was halted when they noticed my arrival.

"How is he?" Orin asked, more out of concern for me than for Eli.

I shook my head. "Physically he will be okay, but it will take time to heal what the Dean did to his mind."

A somber quiet overcame the table, but I didn't allow myself to get lost in it. There were things still to do.

"Are we about ready?" I asked Orin, and he nodded.

"The kids are just finishing breakfast. Now would be a good time to address them before more rumors can spread."

I braced myself for an all-out mutiny and headed to the door of the cafeteria. I could hear the roar of multiple whispers before I even stepped foot on the small platform in front of the gathered crowd. Before me was the entire school, all the students that I'd grown up with and the entire staff responsible for caring for them.

And all of them were staring at me. An awkward moment passed where I just looked out at them, the words frozen in my throat. For a brief moment I was overwhelmed with panic as I realized what I was about to do. I was going to try and convince people who had hated me for nearly my entire life that they could trust me.

I was going to literally reveal my deepest, darkest secret to kids who didn't give two shits about what happened to me. What the hell was I thinking?

A warm hand grasped mine, and I looked over into the encouraging green eyes of my boyfriend. On my other side, Falon also stood, her arms crossed as she gave a subtle challenge to everyone before us.

I took a deep breath. "So, I guess you're all wondering what the hell is going on?" Murmurs and slight nods answered me and I relaxed slightly. I could do this. "A year ago I was just like you, going to class, hanging with my friends, and dreaming of graduation. But that all changed when the Dean took an interest in me."

Not a single person spoke. I could feel the weight of their eyes on me; I had their full attention.

"He had it in his mind that I was the bringer of this prophecy, and he wanted me to help him create a better world for our people. To him, that included killing innocents that he saw as threats. When I refused to do his dirty work, he tortured me."

I saw a few heads duck at the word torture, and I grew angry on their behalf.

"I never told anyone what was happening to me, but my friends knew something was wrong. When the truth eventually came out, we made a plan to run. In all the chaos of that night I met someone who would forever change how I looked at our world."

I held out a hand, signaling for Orin to come out of the shadows. More whispers rose as he took his place beside Cedric, but they quickly died down.

327

"Many of you have seen this man and his men around campus. Some of you probably watched them remove the domineering Imperials from our grounds. They have liberated us and even now continue to protect us from the grave abuse of power that the leaders of this campus forced upon you. I know of the injustice that has been done here, not only to me, but to many of those sitting next to you. I know the pain you feel, the fear, the anger at being wronged. This man," I pointed again at Orin, "is here as a promise to you that we will *never* let that happen again."

Shouts of approval and a few scattered pockets of applause answered my declaration. I waved off the praise and prepared myself for what came next.

"I recently found out that this man is my father, and today, I couldn't be more proud to share that. But to many, this is cause for alarm. We've been groomed and raised to hate his kind, to see them as the ultimate evil. I am living proof of that contradiction."

I paused, letting my words sink in.

"It was Vampires that saved us yesterday. Vampires working together with the other races for the benefit of all."

I raised my voice, making it stronger and deeper so that it could be heard over the growing clamor.

"We have been lied to, our minds have been clouded, and it's time for us all to learn the real truth."

Chapter 44

The outrage was expected, and so I let it run its course. Orin and Cedric remained vigilant, their hands kept within reach of their weapons just in case. Neither of them wanted to hurt anyone, and it wouldn't help our cause if they had to, but we didn't know yet how this would play out.

Students and teachers alike were on their feet, shouting and pushing one another as they argued. There were an obvious few that reasoned on our behalf, and their numbers were higher than what I could have hoped for. I could also tell who was reacting off years of trained instinct. Much like Eli, their first reaction was to see us as enemies. Most of the student body and even the teachers were just confused.

"How do we know you're telling the truth?" One voice carried high above the others and drew the attention of those around him.

Standing dead in the center of the growing chaos was a very familiar face. Tony stood on a chair as a couple of his friends secured it so he wouldn't be knocked over. The last time I saw him, he was bleeding out on the training room floor and I had just healed him. He had stopped bullying me after that, but a year could have wiped his memory of my act of kindness.

The crowd calmed down and went quiet amidst widespread shushes. With their attention on him, Tony spoke to me again.

"What she says about that man saving us is true. He unshackled me from the Dean's wall himself." Tony's glare dared those around him to say anything. Admittedly he had gained some respect from me; it wasn't easy to admit your vulnerability, especially for a guy like Tony. "But I want proof that he's a Vampire."

As one, a sea of heads turned to us, waiting for the proof he demanded. I looked to Orin and shrugged. If confirmation was what they wanted and it would keep them calm, then why deny them? Orin raised his hands in the air and the students closest to him backed up. I held in a laugh. With his eyes closed, Orin pulled at the moisture in the air and morphed it at his will.

The atmosphere was like a vacuum around him as the pressure within the room changed. No one else seemed to notice the difference except me. Inside, the frozen strand of my power began to hum in reaction to whatever Orin was doing.

I looked over at him and found him watching me, as if he too could feel the connection. Seconds later, big fluffy snowflakes fell from above. Varied sounds of awe rolled over the crowd as many reached out to touch the flurries. Orin paid no attention to the positive reactions, he was still watching me.

I could feel the coldness within me reacting to his power. Chilled waves moved down my arm and settled in my palm, making it tingle. Warily, I gave an internal flick to the root of where the ice resided. The beast in his cage didn't seem to like it, but I felt my hand grow colder.

I looked back at Orin, who nodded for me to try again. Raising my hand like he had, I closed my eyes and yanked. The gasps from the other students had my eyelids fluttering open. Over my hand swirled the smallest of snowflakes, their little bodies glittering like crystals as they began to dance around my fingers.

I wasn't sure how I was doing this, or if it even all stemmed from me, but the proof was now out, there for all of them to see. My show of power, however, didn't have the same reaction that Orin's had.

"So she's been a Vampire this whole time?" one student shouted.

"No wonder she claimed not to have a power, she was just using us to infiltrate our society!" another exclaimed.

Other students picked up the cries as the overall mood of the crowd began to turn against me.

"You're all idiots." Tony's voice once again cut through the disorder. "She's a Cross, they're one of the strongest Witch lines of all time. So she's half vampire," Tony lifted a shoulder like it was no big deal.

I think my mouth dropped wide enough that my molars could be seen. Never in my wildest dreams did I expect to see Tony defending me against a crowd of our peers. As the richest kid in school, he held the most power and sway over who was considered popular. How he treated me had always been the structure for how the other students viewed me. His support could make all the difference in convincing them to aid us.

"Why are you helping me?" I asked Tony. I probably should have kept my mouth shut, but I had to know.

He looked me in the eye and for once I didn't see hatred staring back at me.

"You saved my life," he simply said. "From the day I met you, I have gone out of my way to tell you that you didn't belong and I have no excuse for why. I have beaten you, taunted you, and turned almost every other person here against you at one time or another. But despite all that, you saved my life. You didn't have to; you could have protected your secret—but you didn't. And I will never understand what I did to deserve that."

The grating of wood against tile had us all turning to the giant double doors in the back of the room. With obvious effort, Eli shoved his way through the crowd and made his way up to me. He had changed out of the ragged clothes I'd last seen him in and traded them for a more respectable uniform.

He had showered, shaved, and once again resembled the Academy's training master. His limp was prominent and he still had a lot of recovering to do, but this was the first time I could see a little of the old Eli inside, fighting to remain in control.

Cedric helped him up onto the platform and supported him as he made his way to my side. Eli smiled at me, and he looked so much like his old self that I wanted to cry. He brushed his hand down my cheek before turning to face the student body.

"I know the past year has been a trying one. We've all been betrayed by the one person who was supposed to put our wellbeing above all else." His voice rang out strong and clear. "Let's take a step toward preventing this misfortune from ever repeating itself. Trust Casey, trust her friends, and we might just make it through this."

If Tony's words hadn't already swayed the crowd, then Eli's sure would. Relief flooded through me so strong that it was almost impossible to breathe. I beamed at Eli, so happy to have him back, but he wasn't looking at me. I followed his line of sight over my shoulder to Orin, who returned Eli's glare with one of his own.

Days passed in an uncomfortable truce. The students were once again allowed to roam freely, and it felt great to see the joy on their faces as they enjoyed their long overdue freedom. The Academy was slowly returning to the home I once knew. Classes had resumed and the daily schedule helped to dissipate any leftover apprehension people felt over the roaming Vampires.

A few of Orin's most trusted men remained back at the cave. They were tasked with sorting through the captured Imperials to see who was truly loyal to the Dean and who was only trying to survive. It was a lengthy process, but we could only benefit from the added support it would bring.

On a more personal note, I had been spending most of my days with Eli. The more time I hung around him, the more he came back to himself. Today we were walking through the charred ruins of his gym. He'd set it on fire as a distraction that night that I'd escaped. What I didn't know at the time was that an Imperial had caught him starting it and that was how the Dean knew Eli was privy to my plans.

He spent the next year in the Dean's dungeon as answers were forcibly pried from him.

"We have a real opportunity here to piece the school back together and to rebuild it in the way it was always meant to run." Eli inhaled the cool mountain air and looked around his ruined gym, seeing only untapped potential.

I kicked over a singed wooden board with the tip of my shoe.

"I completely agree," I told him. "But there is so much more that needs to be done in order for that to happen. Our way of life has been warped into the idealism of one man's thinking. Did anyone even question the Dean when he and the Council declared all Vampires the enemy? No, they just went along with it."

"We didn't just go along with it," Eli sputtered. "I was there, Casey. I saw what the Vampires can do. There are pictures of entire towns, whole families, mutilated by them."

Indeed, there were. I had seen the pictures myself many times. I had grown up on stories Eli used to tell me from the war. My generation had been trained since birth to view Vampires as the number one enemy. And that was my point.

"Not *all* Vampires are evil. Just look at Orin and the others from our camp." Eli snorted in disbelief, but I chose to ignore it. He just needed time. "Orin's camp was founded by people from all the races, including Vampires, who wanted peace. Sebastian and his loyal followers are the true monsters, but their classification doesn't extend to their entire race. Just like the Dean's cruelty and madness doesn't describe the Shifters as a whole."

I tried to impress upon him the flaws in what he's been told. He needed to know where the real danger was coming from. Sebastian was still looking for his son, his followers were still roaming around and murdering in his name. Just look at poor Jenna, the Witch they killed here last year.

"You didn't see what they're capable of, I did. There is no humanity in their eyes when they hunt." Eli shuddered with the memory.

"Actually, I've seen it. I know all about the beasts that hunger inside them—but it can be controlled." I thought back to that night in the woods when Orin and his men voluntarily gave into their beasts to save us. I knew exactly what they were capable of.

Eli scoffed. "If they fed you that line to gain your trust then I'm sorry you couldn't see through it. There is no controlling that thing inside them."

It hurt that Eli was fighting so hard against accepting the Vamps. I'd watched him glare at them, mumble as they passed, dispute every idea they had at our daily meetings. I know how hard it can be to change. It means letting go of everything you thought you knew, and to many that was a scary thing. For Eli, a man who already had so much taken away from him, it was downright terrifying and I knew that.

"I fight every day to control the beast inside me, and I can tell you, not only is it possible, but it's damn hard."

He had the decency to look contrite. "Casey, I'm sorry. I …"

His unsaid words hung in the air between us. I pushed around more debris with my foot and let the moment pass. I tried to enjoy the rest of my time with Eli and vowed to steer our future conversations away from any potential triggers for argument. That was going to be easier said than done.

It was hard to talk with Eli without wanting to share all that I had planned for our future. But since that included Vampires, we always ended up here, in the awkward silence that followed a disagreement.

I tried to get Eli to spend more time with Orin, so that he could get to know him. If he saw for himself the kind of man he was then maybe that would help to change his mind, but Eli would have nothing to do with him. In fact, he had been trying his best to keep me as far from Orin as he could.

At meals, during meetings, any chance he had to pull me away, he did. I know he's just being overprotective because he doesn't trust him, but that didn't make it any less aggravating.

"Come on. Let's get this over with," Eli called to me, already walking out of the burnt rubble and toward the school.

Every afternoon Orin held a meeting, those invited were only the people he trusted—and Eli. Only because I forced Orin to include him. At these meetings we went over plans for the next day, issues that needed to be resolved in order to move forward, and just overall ideas of how we could make things better.

Eli usually wasn't much help at these meetings; he only ever sparked debates that increased unneeded tensions. Surprisingly, he was the one who offered the secure location for today's get-together. Further into the school he went, with me close on his heels. Too busy lost in my thoughts, it took a while for me to notice where we were going.

When I did, I almost tripped over my own feet.

"The Dean's office? *That* was your idea of a good location?"

He pushed open the door to reveal the darkened room behind it. I could make out the shape of the desk as soon as I walked in and my gaze was automatically drawn to the bookcases to my left. Eli walked around the desk to turn on the lamp and I blinked against the sudden glare.

I hadn't been in this room since the night we freed Orin. It looked like nothing had changed—it even had the same dank smell. I walked over to the window and opened it, gulping down fresh air like it was my lifeline. Eli and I were the first ones here, but I hoped that the others would arrive soon. I couldn't stand this place for much longer, the memories were already too strong.

"What in the world made you choose this room of all places?" I asked Eli, focusing on a swaying tree outside the window instead of the damp halls that I knew hid only feet away.

It made no sense that he would suggest having the meeting here. Maybe it was an attempt at a subtle dig for Orin? He might have thought that being this close to the dungeon would set him on edge. But that didn't make sense. Eli spent more time in that dungeon than either I or Orin ever had.

The Eli I used to know would have sealed this office shut and buried the key somewhere in the far reaches of the grounds. I didn't understand.

"Come, have a seat." Eli offered me the chair across from the desk. "I'll go see what's taking the others so long."

I accepted his offer only because he made it seem like it was no big deal. He really looked like he was putting in the effort to try and make this work. I didn't want to worry him, or even insult him, by freaking out about something as stupid as a chair.

Telling me he would be back in a minute, Eli stepped outside and lightly closed the door behind him. Alone now, there was no holding back the swarm of uninvited memories from my times in this office. At the forefront was my first visit. I had sat in this very chair, isolated, with guards on the other side of the door, and the Dean's secret passage in front of me. Although, at the time I didn't know what it contained.

I shuddered and gave the bookcase a wary glance, expecting it to swing open at any moment. Deciding that I would rather wait out in the hall, I stood and headed for the door. Just as my hand wrapped around the doorknob, a voice from my nightmares spoke out from behind me.

It was a voice I hoped to never have to hear again. For all my assurances to both myself and others that I could do this, one look at the Dean had me near wetting myself.

"Hello, Casey," he crooned as a hidden slit in the wall finished sliding open.

He stood behind his desk, his favorite set of twins grinning maliciously at his side. His appearance was immaculate and well-kept, his purple robes draping across his powerful shoulders. How had he gotten past the sentries? Orin's men had these grounds locked down.

I frantically pulled on the doorknob, but the door wouldn't open. Daric used air to hold it shut with an evil smirk. At least there was no water around for Deon to use against me, but in the back of my mind a small voice told me that they didn't need their elements to hurt me.

The twins moved around the desk, inching ever closer. When they got near enough, I lashed out with a kick to the knee. They kept enough distance for me to miss and patiently waited just out of reach. Daric moved his hands, controlling the air. My attacks against them grew weaker as the cool air forced its way past my lips and down my throat. It hurt, each small movement only enhancing the painful swelling of my lungs.

With me disabled they began to beat me, letting up on the air only because they enjoyed hearing me scream. I knew that screaming wouldn't help, that no one was around to hear me. But I screamed anyway out of fear, out of hate, and out of despair.

Chapter 45

Deon had just finished breaking a second finger when the doors blew open. Eli's boots came to a stop right in front of my bruised face as he looked down upon the scene before him. My heart began to race with the faith that he would get me out of this.

But rather than get angry as he once had long ago, he deflated with defeat.

"You said you wouldn't hurt her," he all but whispered.

His words took a minute to register. Maybe it was from the beating, maybe it was fear that twisted the words, because I couldn't believe that Eli—*Eli*—was working with the Dean. It was inconceivable that he would have betrayed me like this and just handed me over. Not the man who loved my mother and had raised her daughter as his own.

Not the man who taught me how to protect myself, who gave me my self-confidence; the man who was quick to laugh at my temper and slow to punish me for it. It couldn't have been Eli. But as the twins gripped my arms and began to drag me after the Dean, after Eli who *followed* him down yet another hidden tunnel, I realized that the man in front of me was not Eli. He was his broken shell.

The Eli I knew and loved was no longer inside. Betrayal flooded my veins, mixed with a deep sadness. I had failed him; this was all my fault. If I had gone back for him, if I had saved him from the Dean as I'd promised myself I would, then he wouldn't have become this wraith of his former self.

I tried to remember if there were any signs that could have prepared me for this. And when I remembered his emotional outburst at the hospital, his refusal to listen to me or trust me, I knew I'd made a grave mistake. Eli was the one who had originally told us that the Dean had fled, it was his word that we went off of as we built our cocoons of safety. Eli had been the Dean's puppet all along.

The Dean's mysterious door led us through a long tunnel, dark, but with spaced lanterns hung on the wall. All too similar to the tunnel that connected to his dungeon if you asked me. The walls themselves were made of dirt, solid soil with ancient roots that wound through it like worms. It felt like we were moving deeper into the earth, but I was unsure. There was no incline or descent, and we didn't turn right or left, only veered to the side occasionally.

I didn't know when exactly I'd lost feeling in my legs, but they were numb from the knees down. The tingling sensations shooting through my calves told me as much. I wiggled my toes, a feeble attempt at bringing feeling back to them; only sharp needle pricks answered. Ahead, a faint light appeared and grew bolder and brighter the closer we got to it, and the tunnel emptied out into the woods, far from campus grounds.

The twins continued to carry me, dragging me across the forest floor as my legs hit every stone and wayward branch. I winced as the larger stones cut clear through my jeans to the tender skin beneath. I couldn't feel the cuts now, but I knew my legs could be a map of bruises by the end of this. Eli walked just ahead of me, utterly defeated. Every so often, he would glance back to check on me, but the man inside was dead. I could see it in his pale and dreary eyes; he had given up long ago.

Far off shouts could be heard from the direction of campus. The Dean and his minions paid them no mind until the earth around us exploded in waves of fire. The Dean held up a hand for us to stop moving as he lifted his nose and sniffed.

With a growl, he spun around just in time to see his favorite twins knocked on their asses. My body didn't even have time to hit the ground before I was enveloped in a familiar warmth. A strong arm wrapped around my waist while the other cradled my back. The smell of cinnamon and spice overwhelmed me and I clung hard to Cedric's neck.

Cedric carried me a safe distance from the scuffle and tenderly set my feet on solid earth. Mahon and Leo held the twins to the ground, the both of them fighting with a ferocity that rivaled a wild tiger, and Daric broke at least one arm trying to free himself from his hold. Were these guys machines? Did they feel nothing at all, not even their own pain?

From behind me, Orin approached with a steady and confident gate, ignoring the nearby scuffle to instead focus on the enemy before him.

"You must be the Dean I've heard so much about." Malice dripped from each syllable. "Too bad we were never formally introduced. You chose to let your minions do your work for you instead."

Eli took a step back, fear and distrust causing him to spit on the ground at Orin's feet. Orin stopped just beside me and Cedric, his face as solid as stone, his lips a thin line beneath a stern brow. He was pissed, but calm. Deadly. I watched as the Dean assessed the new threat before him, picking up on every detail.

The jagged crystals within Orin's palms grew to fine points until sharpened sickles glinted off the dying sunlight. The curved blades were perfect for beheading.

"Vampire." The Dean spat out, as if the very word left a foul taste in his mouth. "You and your men have no place in this matter, let alone on these grounds. Take your leave now and I will spare your lives."

I knew a bluff when I heard one. The Dean would never grant his enemy mercy. If Orin did as ordered, he would be slaughtered the moment he turned his back. Not that the Dean had any power to negotiate; his treasured pets were disarmed and disabled. That didn't make him any less dangerous, though, and Orin moved with caution as he stepped closer.

"Your paranoia-fueled quest for vengeance against my kind has forever altered the lives of those I hold most dear. I could have ignored you, spared your pathetic excuse of a life if it weren't for the atrocious acts committed upon two of the most beloved women in my life."

Orin's fingers clenched around the frozen weapon on his hand a moment before he let it fly. Like a boomerang, it sailed through the air, a dead aim for the Dean's neck. The Dean dodged the flying weapon as his eyes narrowed and flashed, the pupils thinning to the fine slits of a feline. The two lethal predators circled one another in a rigid dance, sizing up their opponent, looking for any weaknesses or chinks in their defenses.

"The tortures and agony you inflicted upon Carina were enough to run her off, and that's where our paths crossed," Orin continued. The Dean seemed surprised at the mention of my mother, but didn't react. Instead, he kept just out of reach. "She made me a better man, taming the feral beast inside me—but that control was obliterated the moment you laid a hand on our daughter."

Orin's eyes flicked to me for a brief second, but it was long enough that the Dean caught onto his meaning.

"That's impossible," he whispered as his face morphed into a mask of disgust and outrage. "She's an abomination!" he shouted as he launched at me, insanity tearing at his composure.

Caught off guard, I could only lift my arm in front of my face. With his hand morphed into that of a massive panther paw, the Dean reared back for his first strike, and I squeezed my eyes shut. There was a hiss of pain, but it didn't come from me. Orin had stepped between us and the Dean swiped his nails down the side of Orin's chest.

Blood welled and ran, its coppery scent calling to me even as my adrenaline overwhelmed even the strongest of my senses. I gripped the sphere of power inside me with all my strength and kept it from spinning out of control. When I became accustomed to the smell, the urge to heal wore off.

Orin was once again completely centered on destroying the Dean, the atmosphere growing heavy as he drew water from the air. Knowing that the growing moisture could be used against us, I shouted a warning.

"Mahon, watch out. Deon controls water!" I cried.

Before Deon could even move to react, Mahon snapped his neck. Daric screamed beside him, raging at the loss of his brother. Leo struggled to contain him, Daric's fury giving him an uneven advantage of power. The smell of burnt flesh clogged my nose as Leo used acid to subdue him—he refused to quit.

"A little help over here!" Leo called, and Mahon joined him in pressing Daric to the earth.

His cauterized flesh smoked where the acid touched him and Leo's hands sunk deeper into his body the longer he struggled. It wasn't until Daric's body was completely severed in half that he stopped moving.

Intestines and blood spilled freely onto the ground around him. Vomit burned the back of my throat and I fought to keep it down. Across from me and behind the twin's dead bodies stood Eli, revulsion the strongest emotion on his face.

Orin and the Dean were locked in battle, blood splattered across the both of them. The Dean was half shifted, swinging his claws like deadly swords. Orin used his ice to slow the Dean down while simultaneously dodging his blows, but he couldn't keep that up forever.

Then, with one mistake in Orin's footing, the Dean sliced a deep gash across his stomach. Orin fell to his knees, pressing his hands to his wound to keep everything inside.

"No!" I left the safety of Cedric's arms and ran forward, Cedric and the others close behind.

I heard them as they tried to call me back, but I was focused solely on getting to Orin. So focused, in fact, that I didn't notice Eli until my arms were pulled tight behind me. Eli held onto my wrists as he walked me forward, the movement pulling on my already overstretched shoulders.

Straight to the Dean he led me, ignoring all my pleas. Arms outstretched, the Dean gestured for Eli to hand me over, which he did without argument.

"Let her go!" Cedric ordered as he charged at the Dean.

An arm as wide as a tree branch wrapped around his chest and held him back. Looking over Cedric's head, Mahon held fast. There was worry in the Vamp's eyes as he surveyed the man who now had a hold of me.

"I would put a leash on that boy were I you," the Dean called as he drew a knife from his robes and held its cool edge against my neck. "One more move and her head will roll."

Cedric ceased his struggles, but his chin held strong with defiance.

"Go help Leo," Mahon ordered, gesturing to where said Vamp was hard at work keeping pressure on Orin's wound. When Cedric didn't listen, Mahon grabbed him by the collar and threw him in the right direction.

The Dean laughed as he watched my father bleed out. "Fate always favors the rightful winner of any battle."

I thrashed against the Dean's one handed hold, trying in vain to break free. Annoyed with my attempts, he used the hand that held the knife to backhand me before tossing me to the ground. Whether intentional or not, the knife's tip ripped a gash across my cheek, sending a sheet of blood coasting down the side of my face.

Eli reached for me, a glimmer of concern in his eyes, but I must have imagined it because he retracted his hand and stood at attention the moment the Dean looked at him.

"Eli," he droned, walking toward him with an over-exaggerated swagger. "You have served me well these past few months, but I'm afraid I no longer have a need for you."

The knife in his hand suddenly found itself buried in Eli's heart. His body fell in slow motion, clutching at the protruding chunk of metal as his life's blood spilled out from around it. His eyes were wide with shock, as if he didn't see this betrayal coming. I crawled across the ground the short distance to where Eli now lay on his back. I cupped my hand under his neck and lifted his head.

Already his lips and teeth were stained red. His body shuddered beneath me as his heart fought to get blood to the other parts of him, not yet realizing that all of it had pooled in the dirt below.

"I'm so, so sorry, Eli. I should have been there to save you. I was a coward and selfish, lost in my own fears that kept me from coming back for you."

Blood from the cut on my cheek dripped off my chin and onto his chest, it was there that I noticed the hand that reached up to grasp the knife.

"Use it," he told me as he pulled the steel from his heart and placed it in my open palm.

Behind us, the Dean grew impatient.

Close enough to swipe me with one of his claws, he growled. "That's enough stalling. Unless you want the same to happen to each of your little friends, I suggest you not keep me waiting."

I could feel his gaze on my back, burning through me with a hatred that matched my own. I gradually turned to face him, concealing the knife within the sleeve of my jacket. The look in my eyes was no less than hostile. I didn't care that Eli had betrayed me, for sixteen years that man had loved me. It was the barbarous asshole before me that had morphed him into something else, but in the end he couldn't completely eradicate Eli's love for me. I now held the weapon meant to destroy him, and he didn't even know it.

"Come on, girl. I haven't got all day," the Dean barked, his patience gone.

I walked over to him, trying to keep a relaxed grip on the hilt of the knife, less he notice I was holding something. He took one last hard look at me before smirking. He reached into his robes and the unmistakable rattling of metal gave away what he had in store for me. The iron shackles were dirty and crusted over with dried blood. My upper lip curled at the memory of how they dug into my skin.

"Remember these? I thought you might like to have them back. Arms," he commanded.

I peered back over my shoulder at where my friends stood around Orin's body, close enough to see but too far to reach me before the Dean's claws.

"Don't get any ideas," he warned. "They know better than to try anything. I could slice you open from hip to throat faster than it would take for them to take two steps. Now, come here."

I took a step and leaned forward, but then faked a stumble and threw my hands out in front of me. Now within striking range, I slashed behind his knee with my knife and severed the tendon nestled there.

The Dean's right leg gave out, dropping him to knees. The shackles hit the dirt with a thump and laid there forgotten. Even kneeling, the top of the Dean's head still came up to my shoulders. The entire front of my body was vulnerable to his sharp claws, and I knew I only had seconds to act.

Gripping his hair, I pulled his head back to reveal his throat and with a steady slice I drew the knife across it. The strength of my cut was enough to send the blade halfway deep into his neck causing the blood to spurt out like a fountain in pulsing jets, coating the entire front of my jacket. I stood there and watched him gasp to only choke on the blood welling up just beneath his jaw.

I grinned, slow and menacing as the color dimmed in his eyes.

"Casey, hurry!" Cedric's panic broke through my trance.

He was huddled over Orin's body, his hands pressed against his stomach to help stop the bleeding. A large pool of blood spread out on either side of the fallen Vampire, and I knew he didn't have much left in him.

I stood between Eli and Orin. The two men were the only family that I had left, and I knew I couldn't save the both of them. Both had lost too much blood, the thickening pools grew steadily beneath them as the seconds passed. I didn't know what to do.

My hands shook as my mind and heart went to war over who to save. I had known Eli practically my entire life, but he had betrayed me in the worst possible way. Orin was my real father, had fought by my side multiple times, and was gravely injured due to his sacrifice for me. Eli had ultimately come through for me in the end, but was it too little too late?

I looked over at the shell of the man who raised me as he took his final breaths. His head fell to the side and our eyes met. His were bloodshot and guilt-stricken, the stare of a man who knew he was meeting death head on with guilt in his heart. I walked over to him and knelt by his side. Taking his larger hand in my own, I kept a tight hold on my power and watched as the light slowly left Eli's eyes.

"I'm sorry," I whispered.

There was no sobbing, no whimpering—nothing but silence and a growing hole in my chest. I let his hand gently rest back on the ground and stood there for a time, looking down on his corpse as the last bit of his blood leeched into the earth.

"Casey!" Cedric's panicked call reached through to me, and I turned around.

Orin's life force was like a flickering candle in the middle of a hurricane. One minute it was vibrant and sturdy, then the next it sputtered down to a single spark. I ran to him and fell to my knees, sliding through the sticky fluid to replace Cedric's hands with my own.

Silently thanking Gwendolyn for her speed training, I threw myself into the wound, searching high and low for any signs of major damage. Orin had been lucky; the Dean's claws hadn't perforated any intestines. He was only suffering from major blood loss due to the gaping hole in his abdomen. That was the first thing I healed. I stuck around a little longer to make sure no bacteria transferred from the claws into Orin's bloodstream.

Within minutes the wound was sealed and his body was busy regenerating its own cells. It would be a while before he woke because of the amount of blood he'd lost, but Orin was going to be just fine. I wish I could have said the same for Eli.

Leo and Mahon each gave me a nod of respect, twisting their hands over their hearts, before lifting Orin and running him off to the infirmary. Cedric stayed behind with me, both of us walking over to stand next to Eli's body.

Gently, I used the tips of my fingers to lower his eyelids. Despite his gruesome death, his face looked at peace. I honestly hoped that he was. Inside I was more twisted than I had ever been before. Everything was upside down, and I didn't know how to make it right again.

I tried to release tears for his death, but nothing would come. My eyes were now as dry as a riverbed in the Sahara. What was wrong with me? I knelt there, surrounded by dead bodies and I couldn't feel a thing. Not pity, not remorse, not even anger. It had all fled out of me when I pulled that knife across the Dean's throat.

Footsteps thudded around us as the backup finally arrived, too little and too late. Cedric gathered me into his arms and led me back to my room where Falon was waiting. She took one look at me and shooed him away. Inside our bathroom, steam billowed out from the shower running at full heat.

Falon ushered me inside and gently helped me out of my ruined clothes. The material was stiff with dried blood and in some places it stuck to my skin. We tossed everything into a heap on the floor as I stepped under the hot water. Instantly, red rivulets melted off of me and swirled around the drain. I couldn't tell whose blood it was; it could have been mine, Eli's, or the Dean's. Probably a combination of all three.

I tilted my head and watched as the water at my feet grew in color.

"I wish I could have warned you," Falon murmured as she helped to get the sticky blood out of my hair. "I've had this gnawing feeling deep in my gut that something wasn't right. The longer we stayed here the worse it got. If I wasn't such a lousy Fae, I would have known what it meant."

I didn't blame Falon for not telling me. She couldn't have known the depth of Eli's betrayal or that he would lose his life because of it, but I didn't have the energy or even the mental capacity right now to tell her that it was okay. I only stared at the bloody water, lost in my hollow trance of desolation.

When all traces of blood had been removed from my body, Falon wrapped me in a warm towel and left me to dry myself. She returned with a large t-shirt and a clean pair of underwear that she helped me get into before running a brush through my tangled hair. We didn't speak for the rest of the night, not even when Cedric came back and joined me in the bed.

Even his warmth couldn't melt the growing cold inside me.

The next morning dawned dreary and gray. Eli's funeral was today and the entire school dressed out for the occasion. Witches wore green to funerals, to represent the return of the body to the earth; coincidently, green was how I felt. I thought I was going to throw up before I even made it to the cremation site.

Eli's body was placed high on a pyre in the center of an open field and far from any trees. As his family, I was the one who would ignite the highly flammable mixture that rested beneath his body. Cedric stood by my side for support as we waited for the sun to rise to its peak. Per tradition, the school encircled the pyre, all facing east—a direction associated with the rising sun, the dawn of a new day, rebirth, and the shining of light into places where darkness once dwelled.

No words were said, relating back to an ancient lore that spoken memories would draw the spirit to you and keep it from passing on. Besides, I'd already said my goodbyes. My hand trembled around the torch, and I feared I would drop it. I knew he was already gone, but I just couldn't bring myself to light the pyre.

"Cedric, I ..."

"It's okay," he whispered, and kissed the side of my head.

With a flourished wave of his hand, he ignited the dead grasses and other materials beneath the platform that held Eli's body. The wood caught within seconds, Cedric's power urging the fire to move quickly. As I watched the flames dance along his skin and the black smoke rise up into a black cloud above us, the ice within me finally cracked.

My eyes filled with tears until they overflowed, leaving tracks down my cheeks. My wails could be heard over the roar of the growing fire as I let go of all my anguish and released it into the sky. I fell to my knees with Cedric's arms around me, feeling clearer headed and warmer than before.

Cedric helped me down the steps next to the platform and walked us over to where Orin waited. There was no love lost between him and Eli, but he knew what he had meant to me and so was here out of respect for that. I took my place at his side and watched as the flames engulfed the entire platform. Hours from now, when even the embers had cooled, those with affinity for air would help to spread Eli's ashes so that the earth could recollect what was hers. With those ashes I would release my sorrow and free myself to truly heal once and for all.

The mourning atmosphere was ripped asunder as a flood of Vampires descended from the trees. Like a rolling wave of bodies, they fled down the hill as if the very hand of death were upon them. Voices rose around us as the crowd reacted to the thick scent of fear in the air.

Orin stepped forward, his hand held high as he commanded his men to halt. They stopped feet from him, their eyes wild as they gazed around, looking for whatever it was that caused them to run in the first place.

The longer I watched them, the more injuries I noticed. Blood dripped down faces and out of open wounds. People were limping and holding on to one another, looking all the worse that they had left a battle zone. My first thought was that the Imperials had rebelled and were now on the loose.

My heart rate increased as I scanned the trees around me.

"What happened?" Orin asked, his voice unruffled and steady.

His lack of panic served to calm the others and gradually one of the men in front began to speak.

"They're all dead, sir. Every last one of them."

Curses and cries of alarm escaped from the crowd behind me as Eli's body continued to burn not feet away. The Vampires before me looked as terrified as I had ever seen them. These men and women were battle worn warriors, having fought for their lives more than once. They were survivors of the purge Kael tried to force upon them back at the camp, and I knew it would take more than an assault on their lives to make them tremble as they did.

Turning to address the student body behind me, Orin ordered the funeral to continue.

"The three of you, stick close to me until we figure out what's happening," Orin spoke to me and my friends.

He held my gaze until I nodded. I knew he wouldn't pull me from Eli's funeral unless it was absolutely necessary. Ever since the showdown with the Dean, he had kept me near, afraid to let me out of his sight. Being that close to losing me had really shaken him.

With a final glance over my shoulder, I watched the fiery blaze that consumed what remained of Eli and next followed along after Orin, Cedric holding tight to my hand. The first Vampire that spoke was the one to lead us into the trees.

By the direction we were taking, I knew he was leading us to the cave. My overactive imagination ran wild with possible ideas for what could have happened out here. Being that less than half the men stationed at the cave had returned, I knew it had to have been something horrible.

The cave wasn't even in sight when I smelt the overwhelming scent of blood. It saturated the air and mixed with the putrid odor of death—the kind of death only seen on the field of battle or at the site of a massacre. It wasn't just the smell of blood, but the spilled juices from open intestines and the rancid stench of warriors that had soiled themselves in death that marked the difference.

Fifteen yards away from the cave's entrance is where we found the first body. A young man, with a mask of horror on his face, was ripped in half, the lower part of his body ten feet from the upper. I tried not to look at him as we continued on, but his face I knew would be forever burned into my memory. More bodies appeared until there wasn't a direction I could look without seeing one. There were split throats and decapitated heads, intestines protruding from abdomens and severed limbs spread so far and wide that I wasn't sure if we'd be able to match them with their proper owners.

The blood on the ground was so thick that I could hear it squelch under the soles of my boots. The earth was painted red, and small rivers of the gore ran down rocks and the trunks of trees.

"What kind of animal could do damage this severe?" I asked aloud as we stepped over even more unrecognizable bodies to enter the cave.

No one answered my question, and I thought it was because no one knew the answer. But when I stepped around Orin's rigid frame, I realized it was because the answer was right in front of me. On the cave wall, written in streaks of blood, was a warning.

A traitor's crimes are paid for with death. Such punishment awaits for all who refuse to kneel before the king.

A sigil was crudely drawn beneath the words, a tribal sun with two inverted triangles beneath it, like fangs.

"He's found us," Orin whispered in disbelief, his words falling like heavy stones on my heart. "Sebastian has found us."

THE END

Acknowledgements

To my family,

As always, you stand behind me with full support. Thank you for believing in me and being my biggest fans. Even if my written words fall into obscurity, I know that your eyes will have read them and that there are others out there who love my characters as much as I do.

To my fairy godparents,

You both have helped me make it through another year. Your support, words of encouragement, and love have pushed me through some of my toughest times. Your kindness and selflessness are a light in this world, and I'm so grateful that you let it shine on me.

P.S. Still saying hi, Marky!

To my betas,

Miss Jennifer, Baby, Abby, Cheree, Lynn, Rachel, and many others who have read the small bits of wording I shoved before you, thank you! Your honest opinions and squeals of excitement helped me through those rough patches. You all are what keep me going from day to day and this book would not be here without you.

To my peeps in the biz,

Stacey, Elizabeth, Amber, Regina, and all the others who worked to give me this opportunity, a giant and heartfelt thank you. Your combined efforts have helped bring this book into the world and it's all the better for it I think ;)

To my readers,

As always, you are the heart and soul of my writing spirit. I love getting lost in a story filled with adventure, romance, and a little magic. It makes me so happy to share this experience with likeminded book nerds!

About the Author

E.M. Rinaldi lives in Charlotte, North Carolina with her fiancé, Milz, and their slightly psychotic pup, Boone. She works as a Registered Radiologic Technologist, taking pictures of mangled bones for hours on end- then she writes about all the bizarre situations her characters get themselves into while she was away. She is a Second Degree Blackbelt and can't write a story without at least one fight scene in it.

When she's not writing or trapped at work, E.M. likes to read (obsessively), clear her DVR, and have all night Buffy marathons with her friends, complete with cookies and cinnamon rolls.

Her love for writing stems from an early age where she would create stories on an old computer program and force anyone within grabbing distance to read them. Not much has changed; be warned: stay out of grabbing distance.

42873415R00198

Made in the USA
Middletown, DE
24 April 2017